THE ENIGMA EVOLUTION

JASON BLACKER

PUBLISHED BY:

Lemon Tree Publishing

Copyright © 2016 Jason Blacker

Visit www.JasonBlacker.com on the web to stay up to date

Editing: Andrea Anesi

ISBN-13: 9781927623619

For my wife. My guiding light.

CHAPTER ONE

A Place Of Hope

YOU never met my Greatest Father. I did. He was a good man. He was the Greater Father of my father. Another good man. And my father. Well he's terrific too. Why am I telling you this? Because I miss him. My mothers fathers I never knew. Sometimes we're still unlucky. That doesn't happen often. That you evolve too early. Most of us live out our entire lives. All sixty-six years and some for the men, and seventy-seven and some for the women. But that's all in time. I shouldn't get ahead of myself.

My Greatest Father, his name was Startlequick Silverdew. That's rare you know. To have a name where both your first and last start with the same letter. THE MOTHERS thought he was blessed. That's why they gave it to him. It's an honor. Not like my Greater Father. His name was simply Moondew Flamesdance. I know him better than my Greatest Father. Startlequick Silverdew wasn't around long enough for me to get to know him that well, but Moondew Flamesdance tells me lots of stories about him. So does my Father, Moonshadow Silvertongue.

I've heard the Earth stories about long ago. They seem like dreams to me. Like a great mythological fiction that we developed. I am human, in case you're wondering. But we don't call ourselves that, no, not since the Final Diaspora. That's when we left. I know exactly how long ago it was too. Eleven hundred and eleven years ago now. Give or take some time.

We live on a planet that my Greater Father says my Greatest Father used to think looked much like Earth from what he'd been told. Though much smaller. Probably the size of Earths moon. It's a planet we named GAEA. You can call us GAEANS. If you're wondering why it's all in capital letters that's because it is greatly revered. That's how we show great reverence. You might think of it as New Earth, though that word is discouraged by THE MOTHERS.

Please forgive me. I forgot my manners. My name is Sunring Quickdust. In school we were taught something of the ancient times. People used to have the strangest names. Common names were things like John Smith, Jane Wilson, Santiago Sanchez, Sofia Ramirez. And those are only a few of the ones I remember. Funny names if you ask me. I nearly got into trouble snickering about them in school. I mean how did you use to remember them. They don't mean anything. Just noisy sounds.

THE MOTHERS name all of us now. It started on the first day. Everyone was given new names. THE MOTHERS wisdom says that names should mean something. Each boy and girl gets a name on their first day from THE MOTHERS. It's a great honor. I like our new names. I mean what is a Daniel or Robert, a Mary or Laura? Seems like such a strange place we came from. But I'm going off on a tangent. I was telling you about my fathers.

I come from a very special family. That's what my mother says. Though we can't speak of it. The pride that is. We are all equal before THE MOTHERS and equally loved by THE MOTHERS. But my family is special. I'll tell you why. Both my Greatest Mothers are part of THE MOTHERS, but not my Greater Mothers. No. It's a very special honor to have two mothers serving, but I've never heard of anyone having more than one mother serve. That's why my family is special. But we aren't prideful about it. That's the biggest sin. THE MOTHERS continually remind us that pride came before the fall.

I was six years old when my Greatest Father evolved. He was sixty-six. He lived his full allotment. Most of us are able to live the full allotment. In case you're wondering, our years are the same as they were on Earth. GAEA revolves around the sun every three hundred and sixty five days. Not the old sun, but this star we call our sun. Our days are also twenty-four hours long. I think they're the same length as the old Earth days used to be. I can't be sure. In school they taught us about this. Time was a subject, but I didn't understand it very well. It's a made up thing. I know that much. So we can say GAEAN days are twenty-four hours long even though that might not be exactly how long they were on old Earth.

It gives me a headache really, just thinking about it. I guess I'm a dreamer because I live in my head mostly. And when you're dreaming, time seems funny, fluid. Like toffee. It can spread out slow or slip by really quick. I mean, a second here on GAEA is supposed to be the same as it was on old Earth. But maybe it's not. Maybe if you're on Earth and GAEA at the same time, maybe you'd notice a difference? Could be. But I don't try to think of things like that. THE MOTHERS leave those sorts of things to the SCIENCE COUNCIL. They're also revered. You know that because I put it in capital letters.

Unlike THE MOTHERS, the SCIENCE COUNCIL is made up of men and women. You probably know that THE MOTHERS are just made up of women. Something you probably didn't know is that THE MOTHERS are made up of women who had to be married. But their husbands have now evolved. A MOTHER will serve for eleven years with THE MOTHERS, until she evolves.

JASON BLACKER

You'll remember that women have an allotment of seventy-seven some years and men sixty six-some years.

But like I said, only women who were mothers can serve with THE MOTHERS. This might get you to thinking that women are MOTHERS aren't they? Well no, not all women. You see I'm a twenty-six year old woman and I'll not be a MOTHER. You see, I'm an EVOLVER. It's an honor as you can tell. A very sacred position. Specifically I'm an EVOLVER.e, that just means I'm an expert. It's the highest level. You start as an EVOLVER.b and then work up to EVOLVER.i. Those are for beginner and intermediate. It usually takes years and years to get from one level to the next.

They said I had a gift for helping GAEANS EVOLVE. I'm the youngest EVOLVER.e in the history of GAEA. I take great honor in it. But I worked hard for it. When men and women turn sixteen THE MOTHERS decide based on how we've all done in different subjects and evaluations during school where we'll be positioned in society. Most men and women will become husbands and wives which will mean they will become fathers and mothers. This is not such an honor.

This might be confusing to you, but you'll get the hang of it. It's like this, a woman who serves with THE MOTHERS is a MOTHER, but that's only because she served or serves. A woman who is a mother but does not serve with THE MOTHERS is always just a mother. See how that goes. And since fathers never serve with THE MOTHERS, and there is no FATHERS - that's silly as I even think about it - fathers are just forever fathers.

Everyone is respected and honored for their role on GAEA. Even fathers or mothers. You might be wondering then, what are some of the other honored roles? Well, you have the FARM COUNCIL. FARMERS are greatly honored. I remember my Greatest Father, Startlequick Silverdew speaking of reverence about THE FARMERS. My Greater Father, Moondew Flamesdance, told me that he heard from Startlequick Silverdew who was his father, that there used to be animals here on GAEA. All sorts of different animals that ate PLANTS. They came in all shapes and sizes. This next bit you might find horrifying, I did. Early GAEANS tried eating these animals, the thought of this now is both horrifying to us and preposterous, but the animals, each and every one were poisonous to us. We killed them all.

This is a black mark against us, that we carry to this day. My Greater Father told me that Earthlings, I guess old us, did much the same on Earth. Killed a lot of the animals. A lot of the other living things.

Much of the MOTHERSEED survived the Final Diaspora. So we eat much of the same food that humans used to eat on Earth. I like to call the old us, Earthlings. Because, really, GAEANS are still humans, but just not on Earth anymore. So Earthlings seem more accurate. In school they taught us the sanctity of the MOTHERSEED. Of all SEED really. And we call them the same names as the Earthlings used to. We have CORN and WHEAT and BEANS and POTATOES. All things that I imagine Earthlings used to eat a long time ago.

PLANTS grow well here. But only with the care and due diligence of FARMERS. They are much revered. There really is no hierarchy here. Everyone is loved and treated equally by THE MOTHERS, but if I were to suggest one, it might go like this. THE MOTHERS, THE EVOLUTION, the FARMING COUNCIL, PEACEKEEPING - we'll get to them in a bit, the SCIENCE COUNCIL - that's a big category, the ART COUNCIL and then the children and then perhaps mothers and lastly fathers.

That's probably the order things are in. Though of course nobody would say that. Fathers are valued for their role just as much as

THE MOTHERS are. And everyone is happy to do their bit. You might be wondering about TEACHERS and ENGINEERS and DOCTORS, but they're all part of THE SCIENTISTS. PAINTERS, WRITERS, MUSICIANS, DANCERS, ACTORS, CRAFTSMEN are all part of THE ARTISTS. You might be wondering about lawyers or business people or bankers. I have heard these terms, though they sound strange on my tongue. We have none of these type of people. Naturally, money is not a word we use. It seems so obtuse and backwards that money was ever a thing.

THE MOTHERS provide everything for us. It's that easy. We are given what we need and we serve where we are asked. Nobody can choose to be a PAINTER or a DOCTOR, THE MOTHERS decide, and they always make the right decision. Everyone is happy on GAEA. But you might have noticed that I said I worked hard to become an EVOLVER. Well, I did. When my Greatest Father EVOLVED, I knew then, that I wanted more than anything in the world to become an EVOLVER.

And I watched those kids before me who had become EVOLVERS what they were good at. You had to be good at the art subjects. English, Psychology, History and Community Spirit. More than that you had to be good at a more practical art like Sculpture or Painting or Dance. There was one exception to this rule. If you were good at Acting you were disqualified from becoming an EVOLVER. I mean, I don't know that for a fact but I've never seen in my twenty-six years anyone who excelled at acting become an EVOLVER.

But it makes sense. Not to speak ill of actors, but how authentic is someone who has to lie for a living. I mean actors act, they pretend to be somebody else most of the time. That's lying, isn't it? Anyway, I've never seen an actor become an EVOLVER. Now you also need to show sympathy and kindness and patience and goodwill too. So I practiced those traits too. Men and women can become EVOLVERS. In fact, all of the different COUNCILS and positions are available to both sexes. The exception being THE MOTHERS, obviously.

GAEA is a pretty peaceful place. We haven't had a murder or rape in almost a millennium. There has been the odd eruption of violence and anger but the PEACEKEEPERS are there pretty quickly. I don't know how they do it, but they seem to know when GAEANS are getting upset and angry. The PEACEKEEPERS are the only ones authorized to use weapons. But I've never seen them have to use their weapons before. In any event, they're non-lethal. I guess back on old Earth humans were more violent. We seem to have really managed to become more peaceful now. GAEA is a wonderful place.

Men and women walk and wander at all times of the day and night and you hardly ever see PEACEKEEPERS unless they happen to be needed. Nobody fears anyone else. Children are safe. I know my history, like I said, EVOLVERS have to be good at history. And I was so shocked when I heard of all the bad things that Earthlings used to do to one another. We've moved beyond that. Earthlings used to have a name for places where there was peace and joy and love. I remember Shangri-La being one of them. I think Nirvana was another name for it, and heaven. We live it. It is GAEA.

I often wonder what Earth is like today. I'm a dreamer so I like to think it's a nicer place than when we left. But I'm not so sure. We were taught what it was like just before we left. We were also taught what it was like for humanity's time on Earth. Started off pretty idyllic. At least that's what it looked like to me. I mean, when humans were nothing more than bipedal apes.

Not to say it wasn't without its difficulty. I mean there were predators and disease and the human body is a very fragile thing indeed. More fragile than a flower I sometimes think. We break easily. We're easy to bruise and we're easy to bleed. We're easy to kill too. I know all about that. As an EVOLVER that was a big part of my training. Our TEACHERS touched on it too, during school. It was an important part of the curriculum. It was drilled into us that pride came before a fall. And it was our fall that led to our desperate Final Diaspora.

But GAEA is beautiful too. Not as beautiful as Earth was. Life is harder here, that is why we all have our place and our duties. FARMERS work harder to feed us, though food is plentiful. It just seems that to live on GAEA is more difficult than it seemed it was on Earth. THE MOTHERS work hard to ensure that order and humility is kept central in our lives so that we can continue to flourish as best we can. I don't want to give you the wrong impression. GAEA is beautiful. It's green, there is water and lakes, blue skies and gray mountaintops. It's not quite as green, and there is not quite as much water as there was on Earth.

It's not as warm as it was on Earth. All of us GAEANS live in a narrow band around the equator that stretches six hundred and sixty-six kilometers north and south. It is a smaller planet than Earth and it doesn't have a moon nor is it tilted on its axis. As such we don't have seasons. And beyond around a thousand kilometers north and south of the equator GAEA becomes quickly uninhabitable. Beyond about sixteen hundred and sixty-six kilometers north and south it never gets above zero degrees Celsius. In the narrow band we live in it never gets above twenty, but it also never gets below zero either.

The narrow range we live in reminds me of that childrens story Goldilocks by Robert Southey. We live in GAEAS Goldilocks zone I guess. And life is good. Though it wasn't always that way. We had

8

to start from scratch pretty much when we arrived. We had help of course, we brought machines and robots, at least the ones we could control. They helped us get set up, but the first three generations toiled and nourished GAEA with their blood and sweat in order for us to live as we do know.

Only seventy-seven million seven hundred and seventy-seven thousand seven hundred and seventy-seven humans made it to GAEA from Earth. That's an important number for us. We call them THE SEVENS. GAEA only supports one hundred million of us comfortably, so our population is capped at one hundred million. You need permission from THE MOTHERS to have a child and it is carefully controlled.

Sex is not controlled but then again it doesn't matter as all of us are sterile until blessed to procreate with the blessing of THE MOTHERS. Don't ask me how that works, I don't know. I'm not a SCIENTIST. SCIENTISTS know but that's expert level knowledge. They don't teach us that in school. Besides, it's not important. However, be reassured that each time a man or woman EVOLVES, a baby is born. We have managed a perfect balance. The system is so well advanced and accurate that our population never veers from one hundred million by more than six or seven people at a time.

In fact, at our capital city which is called GULGOLETH at the entrance of the COUNCIL COLOSSUS, which is the building of what on old Earth you'd call our government, is a real time number of our population. It is usually stagnant at one hundred million, but one time I saw it at ninety-nine million nine hundred and ninety-nine thousand nine hundred and ninety-seven.

All the COUNCILS are contained within COUNCIL COLOSSUS. That's where I train even today with the EVOLUTION. But we'll get to that. I haven't yet had the chance to help anyone EVOLVE. But that should happen soon. You have to be an EVOLVER.e in order to help someone EVOLVE, and I'm just recently an EVOLVER.e, and as you know, the youngest one ever. I'm really hoping to be able to help my Greater Father EVOLVE. It's usually not allowed for an EVOLVER of the same family help one of their own EVOLVE, but I've put in a special request with the EVOLUTION and THE MOTHERS. I might make history again.

It's really my goal. I can think of nothing greater to do with my life than to help someone EVOLVE. And between you and I, I really want to know what happens as we cross over to the other side. As we slip from the living to the other living as we like to say. I miss my Greatest Father even though I was young. It made me sad when he EVOLVED and I want to find the peace that perhaps I've been looking for all this time, just to know that he found peace. That leaving GAEA is indeed a journey of wonder and everlasting peace as a liberated, and EVOLVED spirit.

CHAPTER TWO

A Place Of Despair

THE mountains weren't as lush as they once were. I wish they were. I'd seen pictures of how they used to be so green and verdant. That's a word you don't get to use very often anymore. But just on the other side of this peak was the valley. There were androids down there. That's what we'd been told. It was twenty-one twenty-five. That was the date. And things were not going well. From nine billion human lives just a decade earlier, humanity was down to less than a billion. Preparations were happening to leave. But humanity only had ships enough for one hundred million souls.

Already the lottery had been started. Everyone had been assigned a number. You couldn't buy onto a ship. It was strictly chance. But I figured that at the rate androids were decimating us, by the end of the year there'd be barely enough souls left to fill all the ships and the lottery would be irrelevant.

"Did you get your ticket in, Pru?" asked Skyler Niles as we made our way up to the crest through thick, mostly dead forest. It was eerily quiet. You couldn't even hear crickets or birds chirping or flying up ahead.

"Nah," I answered. "I'm sticking with this sinking ship."

"You're one tough broad," said Niles pulling the twig out of the corner of his mouth. "I got mine in. They're announcing early next week."

"Good luck with that," said Cleveland Rooijakker. "We'll likely be dead by then. I've heard humans are being lost left, right and center."

Rooijakker had a Dutch accent. He was a tall pale-skinned Dutchman with an easygoing temperament that belied his negative outlook. He had a military style buzz and a scar that ran almost vertically from the top of his hairline to the bottom of his chin. He could still see from that left eye. It had happened when he'd been thrown through a glass pane window by a blast that had gone off prematurely that he'd set. He didn't see himself as negative, just realistic.

But he was not the one to look to if you wanted some optimism. That was Niles. Niles was an Englishman. If you could call him a man. He was only nineteen, but he had an easy smile and a handsome face. He had a carefree attitude and he was the one I was most scared of losing first. He was small and compact. My size and I'm a woman. I'm Prudence Kato, I'm half black and half Japanese. I'm twenty-seven and the oldest of this misfit bunch. I'm hoping not to make it into the twenty-seven club if I can help it. In six months I'll be twenty-eight, so here's hoping.

"I'm taking it you don't have your ticket in then?" asked Sergei Ochieng. He was talking to Rooijakker. Ochieng was an odd ball. He was like me. Half black but the other half was Russian. He was average height but thick like a bull. He was serious. He took everything seriously. He had big metal tubes in his ears, big enough to stick your pinky through and he had a nose ring that stuck like bull horns from each nostril. He wore a mohawk and smoked marijuana to "calm his nerves" he said. Rooijakker turned to look at him and smiled.

"I'm hedging my bets," said Rooijakker. "If I make it out of this shit hole I'll be happy to get on the first ship out of here."

We continued to trudge up the mountain quietly. Bringing up the rear was Ayaka Gennedy. Gennedy was a tall slim black dude from Africa. Anyone and anybody was being conscripted. He spoke English well, like the whole world did. Not that it helped. We were doomed. I knew that as I lived and breathed, but I wouldn't say it out loud. But you didn't need to be a frikkin' genius to figure that one out. Gennedy was really dark, an almost purple black and he had ridged scars in rows on his forehead that reminded me of a child's drawing of the sea. He didn't speak much. He was hard to figure out, but he was reliable.

The five of us are not soldiers. We've had a week's training. That's all they can afford. Most of the world's armies have been decimated. Like I said, we're down to less than one billion souls. It's now all hands on deck. If you can fight, that's what you do. While the ships are getting readied to jettison the lucky few into space, the rest of us fight. Except the farmers and a few others. You're probably wondering what I'm talking about. Let me tell you while we slowly creep up to the crest of this mountain to peer down at our enemies.

At the turn of this century we reached singularity. It actually happened on New Year's eve twenty ninety-nine. Can you believe it? Seems like a sinister joke now, looking back. I don't remember it. Like I said I was like only two years old then. But what I heard for the longest time was that we'd been scared of our extinction from outside sources. The big thing was the asteroids or meteors. There'd been some close calls. We'd figured out that's how the dinosaurs went extinct, and so maybe we should pay attention to the night skies. In the meantime, by our own hand we were creating monsters to destroy us. Only we never thought of it like that. Let me explain.

The singularity was supposed to be humanity's biggest gift to itself. If you're not sure what that means, let me tell you. The singularity, or technological singularity happened when the first robots, androids, thinking machines, whatever the fuck you want to call them became self aware. Perhaps more accurately it was the time when these machines could start to reproduce themselves more intelligently. As such, it cut us out of the equation.

A Hungarian guy by the name of John von Neumann coined the term back in the nineteen fifties. A lot of us call these fuckers, these machines, androids, whatever, von Neumanns, or von Humans. You might hear us call them vHs or vNs, for short. In the beginning we thought of them as robots. That was the most common term. Everyone wanted a robot around the house to serve and do all the shitty jobs that we didn't want to do. The name we gave them should have given us a clue to the future.

You might not know this but the word robot comes from the Czech 'robota' which means forced labor. That worked in the beginning. Robots around the house to cook and clean, etc. We still have some of these around. One's that we've shut off from the other von Neumanns. These ones still help us, but they're like toddlers compared to the von Humans we're fighting now. Those fuckers are all business.

But like I was saying, any intelligent species isn't gonna go for forced labor. We used to do it to animals, right? You probably don't remember that. We've evolved past circuses and other animal entertainment artifices. But with animals, 'cos we were maybe a little smarter than them we could intimidate them, right? But you could see it. Old movies of animals used in entertainment, it was terrible if you looked them in the eyes. Sadness, defeat, depression. I mean no sentient being wants to be forced into labor. You know this.

But so long as humans were at the top of the totem pole who gave a fuck. All creatures obeyed us because we could dictate that. We had the ability to back up our position with force. But then we created these fucking von Neumanns or von Humans. Game over player one. Just like that. It's obvious now, looking back. But I guess at the time everyone thought it'd be cool. We could program these robots, these intelligent beings, these von Neumanns to serve us, right? Ha! That's fucking funny. Not a chance.

At the singularity, they just took over. Started designing themselves and getting exponentially smarter and quicker. They're like gods to us now. Not that we worship them, no, they've promised to exterminate us. That's what they said. Believe it. And I can't blame them, not really. But I'm human, so it's me against them.

In the beginning, scientists and governments tried to override the programming, they tried to reason with them, and then we started to threaten them. That was probably our biggest mistake. They were evolving way too fast. In the first five or so years we were able to curtail their exponential growth, but they adapted really fast and have all but decimated us now. And that's why it's only a matter of time. This is why we're heading off planet, gambling we'll find another place to call home. Those chances are better than sticking around here. But I'm going down with this ship called Earth. I know I'll die trying, but I'd sooner die knowing the soil beneath my feet than living the rest of my days on a spaceship.

These von Neumanns are interesting. They're not like how we might have imagined them to be. A lot of them take human form, but many of them take spherical shapes, but they can transform into pretty much anything. They've developed liquid and malleable metals and composites that we're still trying to understand. They can literally transform into whatever shape they want, right before your eyes. I've seen it. It's scary as shit.

And the humanoid von Humans, they're scary as hell. They're designed as soldiers for the rest of them. Thing is, from a distance, looks like you're looking at a human being. It's only up real close that you can tell. But by then you're probably dead. These materials that they've designed and developed, they can imitate pretty much anything. Hair, skin, goosebumps. It's freaky. And I've seen a von Human grow from six feet to ten feet right before my eyes. Just before it was lights out for me. I survived that thankfully because there were a bunch of us in the firestorm and someone dragged me out and brought me back.

We reached the top of the crest of the mountain. I put my hand up. We all crouched down. Niles knelt down beside me.

"What do you see, boss?" he asked, chewing on his twig.

One of the things that the USE had given me when I signed up was enhanced vision. It helped. I could see infrared, and I'd recently been given an update that allowed me to see X-Ray too. I could also zoom, that brought things about thirty times closer, and I had what you'd call 20/2 vision. Same as some birds of prey.

I was told by the USE, that's the United States of Earth - what's left of us, that earlier on in our fight, in the first five to ten years, infrared vision was super helpful. I mean, it helped you figure out who was human and who was von Human. You see, humans are pretty toasty, machines not so much. But it didn't take long for those fuckers to figure it out. So they started to match human temperature, so you couldn't tell the difference using infrared between a von Human and a human. This is the shit they're up to. We get one step ahead and then they leap ten ahead of that.

Rooijakker, Ochieng, Niles and Gennedy all crept up close to me forming a pyramid with me at the point. I turned to Niles.

"I see a dozen humanoids down there and a whole whack of

machines," I said. "I'm not getting a good reading on the humanoids."

This is what it had come down to. We couldn't quickly tell the difference between humans and von Humans, so everyone became a humanoid until you had clarification on which was which.

Like I was saying, this update to my eyeball software was supposed to make it easier to differentiate between the humans and von Humans, right? I mean, if you can see X-Ray vision then you can see the bones and shit of a real human, right? A von Human isn't going to have a skeleton. Cool. Except not. I was staring down into the valley about a mile away and all those fucking humanoids had skeletons. I'd heard about this. These von Neumanns were morphing to adapt. So now they portrayed human insides. How fucked up is that.

I'd heard that we were killing almost as many humans as the von Humans were through friendly fire. It gets fucked up when you're in a firestorm and your adrenaline is pumping. You start getting trigger happy and firing at anything that looks like a von Human, even other humans.

"What do you mean humanoids?" asked Rooijakker. He was looking straight ahead.

"I mean they've all got skeletons and shit like that. I can't tell one from the other," I said in a hoarse whisper.

"I'll tell you what," said Ochieng, "all those fuckers down there are von Neumanns. I'll bet you dollars to donuts that none of them are human."

"How can you be so sure?" asked Niles.

Ochieng was standing tall behind us. He might be able to make out the tiny forms a mile away, but he didn't have enhanced vision. I was the only one enhanced. It was too costly and time consuming this late in the game to be creating enhanced human soldiers. You might think that at this point in time we'd have just created robot soldiers, right? Ding, ding, ding, we have a winner, yummy dinner. One problem with that line of thought, the von Humans had quickly decimated all our robotic soldiers, and/or brought them into their fold. Nice try though.

"Because," said Ochieng, sounding like he was talking to a class of toddlers, "von Neumanns never use human shields. Am I right? They just kill us. End of story, they don't use us for forced labor."

"Och has a point," I said, "but that doesn't mean there isn't a first time for everything. If we know anything, we know that these fuckers are adaptable. And quickly at that."

I was still watching them down in the valley. They were mining something and they were doing it well and discreetly, without much damage to the environment they were in.

These von Humans were not cruel or mean. The best, or if you prefer, the worst you could say about them was that they were indifferent. They just killed us. Did it quick. Didn't take pleasure in causing pain or suffering. None of us were tortured, or maimed. There was no need. They knew everything we knew and much, much more. How did they do us in? I'm gonna tell you.

Remember how I got close enough to see one of these von Humans almost double in size before I had lights out? I didn't feel a thing, but it wasn't a direct hit, so my heart was able to be restarted. We're not a hundred percent sure of how they do it, maybe some of the medical community is, but they haven't shared their findings with us. The easy version is that they use some sort of twofold approach that uses some sort of directed current and pinpointed force.

So two things basically happen to you at the same time. Your spinal cord is severed just below the medulla oblongata at the same time that your heart is stopped. I don't know the details, I just know what it feels like, except for the spinal cord severing. It literally felt like someone had turned off my lights. I felt nothing, just went dark instantly. This is how they kill us and they're helluva efficient at it. Not sure how I escaped. Some called it a miracle. If you ask me, what's the miracle is that we've lasted into the twenty-second century with our ego and pride.

There's a story about that in the bible or one of those fables about pride coming before a fall. We're in the midst of the fall and still we're clinging to our pride like whiny babies clinging to our blankies. Oh and another thing. You can't see these currents or forces coming at you. That's another problem, they're like subatomic forces that can be accurately discharged through walls and even metal to end you right on the other side. It's scary shit, only it's not really scary, most of the time you have no idea what's happened. Bam, you're dead. One thing that can protect us are trees. For some reason the von Humans don't want to discharge these forces through trees or other living things.

Some of us have been using the forests to help us, or dogs and stuff like that. Trees are better because animals can be knocked unconscious. I've seen them do it. The dog or elephant or whatever just goes to sleep. Then we're easy to access. They're doing something different to the animals, they remain uninjured. Minutes later they wake up as if they'd just been asleep. Meanwhile, the human using them as a shield is D - E - D, dead.

But forests and trees aren't even that helpful. You might get a couple of shots off but these fuckers are so fast, literally faster than speeding bullets. As soon as you've had your chance, bam, they're behind you and it's lights out, off to Valhalla.

"What's the plan, boss?" asked Niles.

I didn't look at him, I was still staring down at the nemeses down in the valley. I wasn't sure what we were gonna do. Much of what we'd done hadn't been working up to this point. I shook my head.

"Not sure," I said. "I'm open to suggestions."

We were out here on this mountaintop by ourselves. We probably didn't have any backup. And if we did, we didn't know about it. We couldn't communicate with anyone over the air. The only way we got our orders was in person, deep in hidden bunkers deep inside mountains. We had no radios, no cells. All of this was easily monitored by the von Humans. We were literally fighting an unwinnable war against an undefeatable enemy. It'd been years since we'd managed to 'kill' a von Human. It just didn't seem possible anymore. We were like ants fighting against dragons.

You might be wondering then why we do it. Why we keep trying. Some of it is because hope beats eternal in the human heart. That platitude has some meaning for us. The bigger part of it is that we're trying to buy as much time to launch what they're calling the Final Diaspora. If we can hold them back for another three months at least, we might have a chance to leave, and by 'we' I mean humanity. I'm not heading out unless they drag me onto a spaceship. I'll have my last stand here, thank you very much, on terra firma. Like a wise man once said, it's better to die on your feet than to live your life on your knees.

Most of us have volunteered for this dead end job. The USE promises that our families will be on the first ships out. That's how they get so many volunteers. That's the only way to get around the lottery. Many have also been conscripted. Basically they just shut you off from any services. No food, no shelter, no water, and you can't turn to the von Humans, remember, they've promised to end us. So you end up fighting. If only to live a few days or weeks with food in your belly and company at your side. Additionally, your family will be first to leave Earth. At least that's the line they're selling. I'm not sure I buy it. I mean with about a billion of us left and space for one hundred million, how are they gonna manage it. Especially with the lottery.

As it is, one hundred million of us are fighting, and they keep replenishing the ranks. And most of us have some sort of family. Even if each of us only has one brother or sister or mother or father, that right there is the hundred million, ships are full. Doesn't bother me though, I don't spend much time thinking about it. Nobody's left in my clan. My parents were some of the first casualties of the von Humans. My parents were researchers. Experimented on animals. Not mean shit, but still. Von Humans figured those disrespecting any life would be the first to go. So I lost them when I was twelve. Had no siblings.

That's why I hate these fuckers. They destroyed everything dear to me. You can understand that hatred I'm sure. Funny thing is, I kinda respect them a bit too. I mean, just from an objective perspective they're fucking awesome. And I mean that in the literal sense of the word. And in a way they're our children. And they've surpassed us by leaps and bounds, right? Isn't that what you always want for your kids? We always want our kids to do better than us, right? The problem with these assholes is that they're exterminating us. They've decided we're a plague upon this planet. They've said those exact words too. They like to be poetic sometimes. Maybe they just think it's oooh scary, and diabolical. I think they've got a sense of humor. They are sentient you know. Have been for some time.

When I've had spare time, I've sometimes watched some old movies from the end of the twenty-first century. There're tons of dystopian movies. Some adapted from books and some just straight up as movies. They always give me a good chuckle.

You know why? Because of the bubbling optimism in all of them. Whatever threat's facing humanity, be it AI, before we really appreciated AI as it turned out like these von Humans, to aliens, it's always the same schtick. Humans save the day. Fuck, really? Hilarious. Can you believe we actually thought that? I know, it's crazy right?

Maybe it's because we have a god complex. Probably. I mean that's easy to understand. It's dyed into our culture at a deep level. Look at the whole Judeo-Christian myth bullshit. Doesn't it say that we were created in God's image? So there you go. We've got a god complex. When all we really are, as the scientists have figured out, is monkeys too clever for our own good. A fragile monkey with a god complex and ego bigger than the heavens.

And this is where it got us. Maybe if we'd really understood our fragility we wouldn't have gone down this path to spawn our demon children who are now killing us. Maybe we would have stopped short. But hindsight is always twenty-twenty isn't it?

But we should've known better. We should've known how fragile we are in this blood bag of bones and skin. I mean, even the smallest of pricks and we'll bleed like a venting geyser. If not for our intelligence and ability to control much of our surroundings, there're a million things that can do us in. Viruses, bacteria, these unseen, to the larger animals and accidents. It's phenomenal how we've lasted as long as we have. Bone and blood and flesh is incredibly fragile, like flowers. We can so easily be torn from the stem of life and so we are. Here we are being torn from the stem of life by our own fucking children and tossed underfoot like the vermin they think we are.

And that's how they think of us. Like I said, a 'plague upon this planet' and they're right, really. I mean if you look at it in a cold and logical sort of way. We fucked up the environment, poisoned thousands of living species. Our skies are still clogged with fucking emissions. Temperatures are all fucked up and storms are raging like we've never seen. And the bullshit political shenanigans continue to carry on unabated on this sinking ship called Earth.

Remember how I said the forests aren't as green as they once were? We've scorched the Earth, we've fucked it up, choked the lungs out of our mother and soured her milk. The von Humans aren't damaging her. It's amazing to watch them as they mine her. So totally in sync with the greater ecosystems. Looking into the valley below you'd hardly know they were mining. Not like those old strip mines and tar sands where we scraped the skin off Earth and left her with big gaping sores. Here, I guess them chickens are coming home to roost. We brought it upon ourselves. Our fucking arrogance.

And you're thinking, geez, this chick is really in love with these von Neumanns, am I right? Well, yes and no. Yes, I think Earth is gonna be alright. These bastard children of ours. These heirs of our common heritage, they recognize that even though they are the smartest species here, and yes, they call themselves a species, they still respect all the myriad life. Like I said, they won't 'fire' at us if we're behind trees, maybe it messes with the tree's vibe or something, I don't know. But I've never seen any of them so much as step on an ant, or tear a leaf from a plant carelessly. It's crazy their reverence for life, if I can call it that.

And really it is reverence. Except not universal reverence, only reverence for life that is in unison with the planet. Well you might say, and I've thought about this, animals can be super assholes too. Yeah, I know, I get it. Lions kill and eat zebras and shit. Animals can be shits to each other sometimes. I dunno why they get a free pass. Like I said, I'm just a guerrilla, not a psychologist. But maybe it's because they're not inherently malicious or cruel like we are. That's my best guess. But honestly, I don't have the luxury of being a fucking cafe philosopher here in the trenches. I'm just telling you like it is.

And back to the question, no, you're not right, because here I am fighting these fuckers the best I can. Pointless really, but what else have I got. They killed my kin. But truth telling, just between you and me. If they weren't hell-bent on killing us, I'd be right there with them. I'd join their side. I mean, it's the winning side and I think it's the side that's doing god's work. But I can't join them, so I don't really think much about that. Like I said, they're gonna kill us all. And they've given us the deadline by which they'll do it. How nice is that.

It's June right now. June the seventh. That's a Thursday if you care. Five months left. That's what they've promised. They've promised us that on the eleventh hour of the eleventh day of the eleventh month the last of the humans will be swept clean of this planet. The fucking irony these assholes use. Who knows who that'll be. Maybe it'll be me. Maybe I'll be the last human, a woman, to die on this godforsaken shit hole. I don't mean to be negative about it. Earth used to be a great place. Still has its charms at times I suppose. The von Humans are making it better that's for sure.

Anyway, I'm sure the history buffs of you will get a morbid kick out our extermination date. Our TOD or ED as we've called it. Two hundred and seven years ago to the hour, when the last of us die, will be the anniversary when we ended hostilities in the Great War. The war to end all wars. Our fucking hubris about that, right? I mean we had another one shortly thereafter and we've teetered on the brink of destruction ever since. Anyway, here it is, finally. Our actual demise. We didn't want to believe it, right? I mean who really thought we'd go out in a whimper like this.

But I'm not trying to be negative. In a few weeks. Months at the most those ships should be up and running. Maybe they'll let us leave, scampering into the heavens with our tails between our legs. Or maybe they'll just decimate us as we launch off into the heavens. Who knows? That remains to be seen. I'm hoping, for humanity's sake, that they let us go. What I know for a fact is that they've promised to wipe us off the face of the Earth. Now, they didn't say anything about what they'd do if we left voluntarily. So that's the gamble. Will it be snake eyes or sevens? I'm not a gambler so I'll let you place the bet.

"Boss... boss."

I felt a tap on my shoulder. It was Niles, I guess he'd been trying to get my attention. I looked at him.

"What's the plan?" he asked.

I shrugged.

"No point in rushing," I said. "Let's get our bearings. Map out this valley and all exit points once we get down there. Let's plan this carefully. I want all eyes on deck. All minds giving up their best ideas. Alright?"

I looked around at all of them. I got four nods in turn. We all spread out a few meters from each other to get better angles of vision into the valley. Rooijakker propped himself up against a tree and looked out through his binoculars. Ochieng crawled up a few meters ahead and propped up against a bush and lit a spliff. Gennedy headed off to my right as did Niles, still chewing on his twig.

There was no rush. This might be our last hours, our last few minutes. If we made it through this, we had a ten hour hike back to our pickup zone. And then we'd wait until they figured we were there and came by to pick us up. I had a suspicion that we weren't gonna make it back. I mean, this was a big deal. This was a mining camp. If we knocked this out it'd create a small headache for the von Humans. And that's if we knocked it out, which meant eliminating all of those assholes down in the valley. Never been done before. I didn't see it being done now either. Like I said, the last one of these fuckers we'd killed was some years ago.

It was around the time my parents were killed. I guess that makes it about fifteen years ago now. Shit, I didn't realize it was that long ago. Man, fifteen years without a kill. Anyway, they paraded him, her, it, whatever the fuck it was, around for the media to see. It wasn't much like the von Humans now. More robotic and mechanical. They hadn't developed this 'living' or malleable liquid metal that they're mostly made of now. That was about two years away at that point.

Anyway, parading this von Human around was a great motivating moment for us, until they came and took his remains. Killed thousands of us at the same time. They don't make it a special point to hunt us down. They have scouts everywhere, that look like us. Like I said, what they can do is just phenomenal. You wouldn't know you weren't with a human until you were really astute and dialed in. That makes it harder.

Anyway, they aren't hunting us down per se. I mean they are in a lazy way. They send teams out all the time to exterminate the worst of us. And by the worst of us they're talking about ranchers, vivisectors, fighters like me, and the like. We haven't eaten meat for years. Not in a big way. Meat has gone underground. It's illicit now and hard to come by. I mean really, who wants to ranch cattle or worse yet kill them for consumption. You're just putting an X on your back. So there're plenty of cows roaming around, most of them skinny as shit but nobody touches them. Not if you value your next few hours.

I saw it happen once. A group of young men were out in this field and thought they could quickly get away with slaughtering a cow, dressing it and taking it back home for a feast. You couldn't see any other humans, von Humans or anyone as far as the eye can see. But the human eye can't see very far. Anyway, they'd barely managed to kill this cow and started to dress it when out of nowhere, three von Humans rock up. These guys never even saw it coming. They were dead before they knew what had done them in. I was on a reconnaissance that's how I happened to know about it. I know these von Humans knew I was there but I was unarmed and unthreatening so I guess they let it go for another day.

Like I said. I saw these three spheres practically appear out of thin air. They're about four feet in diameter, at least these ones were. They can vary in size. Bam, just like that, three somewhat metallic looking, translucent spheres appeared and at the very same time these four guys just dropped dead. No idea what happened to them. Next thing I know this one sphere is right up in my business for a second before disappearing again. They're so fucking fast it looks like they appear out of thin air. Our eyes can't track them.

And this is the thing. They're everywhere and they're sent out in threes for some reason. So it's not like we're fighting a huge army of them. Three here, three there, three everywhere. Plus all the von Human scouts looking just like us and most of us having no idea, 'cos like I said, we can't tell them apart from us. Not without some real detailed study.

We're losing all the battles and we're losing the wars. Everybody knows this but what can you do. You fight for however long it is. And they're organized but in a subliminal way. It's like they're dialed into each other. I mean, they're little teams of just three. You'd think that's nothing. But you haven't seen what three of these assholes can do. Three of them can literally level a city of all human life in a matter of minutes. Nobody knows the official figures and we wouldn't be told if they knew them anyway, but they're decimating millions of us every day, tens of millions even.

And they're doing it discreetly.

I mean if you've got tens of thousands of these von Human three person teams killing a few hundred here and there, it adds up. So, in a matter of weeks we'll be down hundreds of millions. I haven't bothered with the math, but I'm pretty sure that by September there'll be probably enough room on all the ships we have to send all one hundred million of us into outer space.

You might be wondering why the von Humans don't simply destroy our ships. Fuck if I know. They could. For sure they could, but they haven't. I mean, you have to understand, they're not like cold blooded. They're not like us. They're logical, indifferent, but with a complex understanding of the living environments of Earth and how it all fits in together. You can't extrapolate our thought processes onto them. They're at a way higher, deeper level. They don't just destroy shit for shit's sake. Like I said, it's hard to understand.

They're dismantling much of our emptied cities, returning things back to their natural states. Recycling, rehabilitating land. Some stuff is left standing, but like I said, that's not our focus and I don't understand it all. But they don't just wantonly destroy stuff. And maybe that's why they're taking their time with killing us to. Maybe it's got something to do with how much rotting matter that the ecosystems can handle. I dunno. I just know that time is not on our side and we're fighting monsters when we're armed only with marshmallow swords and cotton ball bombs.

One of the reasons I'm sitting here, crouching on this mountaintop taking my time to figure out what our team needs to do, is because I have no fucking idea what to do. How are we gonna eliminate these fuckers in the valley below. Between you and me I don't think it's possible. Hundreds of our teams have been issued new untested weapons.

You've probably been wondering what we've been fighting them with, right? Not much. Traditional weapons have not worked in years. I'm talking bullets and rockets and bombs and stuff like that. A sphere is a great shape to survive a bomb blast. Plus, the stuff they're made of, this hybrid liquid metal with some sort of tissue is something we don't understand. It is self repairable, incredibly strong and practically invincible.

So, handguns are out, high powered rifles are out. In any event, even if they were effective these assholes just move out of the way. I'm telling you, they are blindingly fast. So fast we can't even see them. I heard one time, that scientists had estimated von Human speed ability at about a third the speed of light. Don't ask me about the physics behind that, but what I do know is that works out to about one hundred million meters per second. That's like three hundred and sixty million kilometers per hour. I can't wrap my head around that. And that's just based on them as individuals. I bet they could figure out how to go faster than that with some sort of ship or something.

Anyway, how do you fight against something that seems almost godlike to us? Well, they've given us these new weapons. We call them ELGs for short. Basically, it's a combined electrolaser and gamma ray gun that creates a plasma charge like lightning at super high voltages as well as pinpointed gamma ray discharges. The nice thing about this is that laser and gamma rays discharge at the speed of light. And because these fuckers can't travel at the speed of light, the theory is that we'll be able to hit them.

Only problem with that, is that these ELGs have to get up to speed first before they're able to discharge. And that takes several seconds, so we have to have them charged up before we get into the valley. Another problem is that they heat up. These ELGs like I said are experimental weapons. So they haven't been fully developed yet. They heat up and within a matter of several minutes, I've heard that seven is the top number, they'll basically blow up in a huge discharge of electrolaser plasma and gamma ray radiation and it's goodnight human.

So, we have to charge them up before we get into the valley and then we have to be done within seven minutes. After that first use, these ELGs have to cool for several hours. Ideally a day before they can be reused. So I'm thinking we're screwed. However, we'll know within the first seconds of getting into the valley, if we get that far, if we're successful or not. I'm not a gambler, but on this one I figure our odds are infinitesimally small.

If these weapons have been used before, then we're hooped. And I have no way of telling if they have been or not. All the teams that could have been issued them yesterday were given them. The chances that some of these teams have been involved with von Humans is pretty good. And if they have, these assholes probably have already adapted. Even if they haven't. There's probably a split second from when I pull the trigger to when these ELGs discharge. And that's long enough for them to move out of the way if they're on their A game.

I looked around me. I looked across the valley. I was looking to see if there were any other teams out there. The chances were slim. We'd been dispatched all over the place. Ostensibly to try and limit our losses. I reckoned it was more likely to help buy the USE time. Keep the vHs all over the place fighting us. But that was laughable, they were all over the place as it was. In any event, the way I figured it, the speed they can move at, they could circumnavigate the Earth about two and a half times in one second. So, they could literally be everywhere and nowhere at the same time.

I looked back down into the valley and tallied up our foes. Twelve human von Humans, if they were all vHs, and the likelihood of that was pretty good. And then the mining machines which they had built were coming and going. It was hard to count them, but I figured there were at least a dozen or more of those too.

I looked over at Ochieng. He was finishing up his spliff. Rooijakker was whittling a twig and passing it over to Niles. Niles threw his well chewed one away. Gennedy was staring down into the valley with his binoculars.

Looking at the ragtag bunch of us, you wouldn't take us for soldiers. Not in the strictest sense. We had handguns if you could call them that. More like miniature plasma guns that could kill or immobilize a human. Why we had them I had no idea. They'd do us no good against the von Humans and we hardly had cause to be fighting amongst ourselves anymore. These Plasmatics as they're called were just a relic from the past.

We were dressed however we chose. All of us had cargo pants of various shades from green to beige. And we all had thicker weight long sleeve tees on with a variety of slogans or images. I liked Ochieng's and Niles' the best. Ochieng's was just an abstract pattern with a slogan over top. The slogan was 'I Robot, Die Robot'. Niles was a little more cheery if you could call it that. It was an old print of an android from a long forgotten TV show called Star Trek: The Next Generation. It had a picture of a white faced humanoid throttling an earlier version of the von Humans, and the slogan underneath read 'Data can take 'er'. I smiled at it.

I felt a real humble moment looking at these four other guys. Movies had always been quick to glamorize the futility of war with catchy phrases and slogans like 'Today is a good day to die'. But I was more realistic than that. Any day was a good day to die if you were fighting for a worthy cause. I just wasn't sure if our cause was worthy any more.

But it didn't matter what I thought, we had to fight, 'cos it was only through fighting that we had a chance to live for a few hours or a few days more. Especially this late in the game. I was lucky though, to have these four with me. We'd all volunteered. I knew I could count on all of them. They'd proven themselves to me before. We'd been together for some months, but we'd never encountered any von Humans, or any that we could have fought. That's why we were alive. At least that's what I told myself.

We carried a water bottle and wrapped around our waist was a metallic fabric that doubled as rain gear, shelter and warmth when required. It was quite a feat of engineering. At least for us humans. The reason I'm talking so much is because I'm stalling. But the time is nigh. And if I die and you're hearing this, then at least the communications got through. We wore slim full faced helmets with visors over the front part. These recorded our words but didn't send them anywhere until one of two things happened.

Either we died in which case the encrypted recording was sent to a server somewhere. Or alternatively you made it back to HQ where you could download it yourself. Here's hoping for second chances.

I looked over at Gennedy. He was still surveying the landscape down below in the valley. I threw a small pebble at him to get his attention. This close to von Humans you spoke only in whispers and only if you had to. Gennedy looked over at me and his furrowed, scarred brow became even more furrowed. I cocked my head over to the left side. I scuttled towards Rooijakker and Niles. Beyond them was Ochieng. He saw us and crept on over. They all gathered round me.

"Alright, I think it's time to take out these fuckers," I said in a quiet whisper barely audible. "Anyone got any suggestions."

I looked around to blank staring faces. I wasn't surprised. We had been trained, but training meant shit when you were in the trenches.

"I think we just head on down yonder and blow them up," said Niles, grinning with the new twig in the corner of his mouth.

"Or," said Rooijakker, "why don't you just head on down there and introduce yourself. Something like, 'I'm a human and I'm your friend'. See how long that lasts."

Niles smiled at him.

"Show me how it's done," he said.

"Well, Niles isn't exactly incorrect," said Ochieng, reeking of marijuana. "We do need to get down there."

"Getting down is not the problem," said Gennedy, finally speaking in what seemed like years.

"You know how to get us down there?" I asked.

Gennedy nodded. He was not smiling.

"I think we keep down low and along that ridge of bushes and trees," he said, pointing off to a winding route that was most heavily carpeted with greenery. It took us off to our right with a slow arc towards the back of the valley from where the von Humans were. It put us the furthest away from them. I liked that.

"It gives us cover and makes it less likely they'll be able to get us through the foliage," said Gennedy.

We all nodded slowly and thoughtfully.

"I like it. I think it's the best idea we have," I said, and I believed it.

"And do we actually think this'll work?" asked Rooijakker, smiling the saddest smile I'd seen in my life. It was the brave, sad smile I'd seen only once on a prisoner of war in archival video footage as he was marched to the gallows.

"Honestly?" asked Niles.

Rooijakker looked at him holding that sad smile as if it were the only thing left in the world to lean on.

"No, I want you to lie to me in the last moments of my life for fuck's sake," he said, but there was no animosity in his voice.

"No," said Niles, "I don't think it will."

He wasn't smiling anymore. Rooijakker looked at me and raised his eyebrows. The others turned their gaze to me too.

"You want to know what I think?" I asked.

They nodded.

"I think we're gonna die somehow, somewhere, some time. Here and now is as good as any. Besides, if we don't at least try, we'll be cut off from all USE services. That means scavenging for food and shelter, plus having a bounty on our heads from humans and vHs."

More sober faced nodding.

"So I say," I continued, "it's onwards to Valhalla upon the wings of valkyries."

"I'll say amen to that," said Ochieng.

"It's been an honor and a privilege," said Niles.

"See you at Odin's table," said Rooijakker, no longer smiling.

"For the ancestors," said Gennedy.

"Alright, with all the sentimentality out of the way," I said, grinning, "once we get down there, pick a von Human and light 'im up. I want you all trigger happy. Spool up the ELG in enough time and let's give it a go. Any questions?"

Nobody said anything.

"So this is how the world ends, with a bang," said Niles, chewing on his twig and looking out into the valley.

"Lights out," I said, which meant we went dark. No audible communication from this point out until I broke it. "I hear a choir of angels calling my name."

I stood up and took a drink from my canteen. I put my two fingers up in the air and twirled them around. It didn't mean anything, but it seemed like the right thing to do under the circumstances. I slowly led my team along the green winding path to home. Don't think I'm being morbid. If you do you don't understand. There is no coming back from this mission. Not if you're a realist and you understand what you're up against. Yeah, hope springs eternal in humanity's beating bosom, but when you're headed to the gallows you know you're headed to the gallows.

We travelled slow, like humans walking the planks on old pirate ships. The journey felt like it would end soon. It seemed pointless and I know you're probably thinking that there must be something we could do. Nope. It's not like that. Sometimes life ain't a movie, okay? Sometimes you're the sacrificial lamb and there's no fucking hero to rescue the day. We're just hoping humanity gets a fresh start, and we're the wrenches being thrown into the giant machine just hoping to slow it down enough for some to escape.

I kept looking over to my left towards the von Humans. It seemed eerily quiet. If I was to guess, I figured they already knew we were here, but then why hadn't they ended us already. A small, drying and dying seed of hope burst within my heart, but it was short lived. I was hoping to survive this, don't get me wrong. We all were. But the future was bleak, death at the hands of von Neumanns wasn't unpleasant and life here on Earth wouldn't last long anyway.

Maybe that's hard for you to understand, but sometimes it's not the dying that's scary, it's the living in the Grim Reaper's waiting room that's hard.

The journey down into the valley seemed to stretch out for hours. When it really only took about five minutes. As we came down to the last few hundred meters, I remembered one of the few bible verses I knew. I wasn't a religious person, but somehow it's poetry was uplifting and calming. It was a Psalm I think. The words echoed in my mind. Yea, though I walk through the valley of the shadow of death, I will fear no von Human. For thou art with me. Thy electrolaser and thy plasma comfort me, and the rest I could not recall in this moment.

I switched on my ELG. My team did the same. What had sounded like an almost inaudible hum during training, now sounded like a fucking lion roaring right in my ear. We were fucked. I noticed one of the von Humans, remember, they were in human form at the moment, cock its head to the side. It fucking heard this I'm certain. The seconds tick-tocked by. The von Humans transformed into spheres as if they had just replaced their human forms instantaneously. This was not looking good.

I looked to my left and I looked to my right. I was in the middle of fine men. Remember these names. Brave men who walked into the valley of death. Martyrs so that you, if you hear this, might have a second chance at life.

Niles right next to me on my left. Rooijakker to Niles' left. Ochieng to my right and Gennedy to his right. A ragtag gaggle of humans ill prepared for the task at hand but with courage as big as mountains in their hearts. They all looked at me and returned my smile. I nodded at them. We brought up our weapons. We discharged at the same time. All of us missed.

"Run for the hills," I yelled, turning and heading back from where I came from. They all did the same.

Niles was the first casualty. A sphere appeared in front of him. By the time I trained my weapon on it and fired, he had dropped like a stone. I missed. A sly smile still on his face. We ran and we ran. But really, we were barely taking more than a few steps. I glanced to my right. Gennedy dropped dead. I aimed and fired, but I was just hitting earth and bushes and lighting them in explosions of fire and lightning.

Then they picked off Rooijakker, his tall, thin frame crumpling like fresh laundry. I kept firing. This time indiscriminately all around. Ochieng did the same. We had still barely turned around and started running, but everything seemed to have slowed down by a thousand times. So many plasma and electrolaser discharges going off but none hitting the von Humans. I saw Ochieng fall dead.

A translucent, metallic sphere appeared before me and then transformed into an identical representation of my mother.

"You mother fucking von Hu...

CHAPTER THREE

A Place Of Honor

I was in my last day of final preparation at GULGOLETH. Moondew Flamesdance was preparing to EVOLVE. He was now in GULGOLETH too. My Greater Father. The last six days of your life were spent here in GULGOLETH being showered with praise for your life's work. Naturally Moondew Flamesdance had been nothing more than a father. Still, everyone was honored for their service at GAEA.

I was listening to Glitterfrost Gentlefeather. She was an EVOLVER.m, that meant she had gone through all the stages of being an EVOLVER and she was now a mentor or TEACHER. That's what the M stood for. After at least twenty-five years of service, if you were an exceptionally gifted EVOLVER, you would then be taken through the rigorous process of becoming an EVOLVER.m, the greatest honor you could achieve as an EVOLVER other than becoming an EVOLVER.g.

An EVOLVER.g was an EVOLVER who had received the highest prize that THE MOTHERS bestowed on any of us. It was simply called the GREAT GULGOLETH HONOR and as such you became known as a GREAT GAEAN and that gave you the G at the end of your title. I had only ever met one woman like that, her name was CLOVERSHY CLOUDRAIN. Only GAEANS that had achieved the GREAT GULGOLETH HONOR were revered with their names always written in uppercase. Of course, only EVOLVERS.e were eligible. Beginners and intermediates were not.

And as you can imagine, all COUNCILS are eligible to receive the GGH as we call it, the GREAT GULGOLETH HONOR. In fact, THE MOTHERS award the GGH equally amongst all the COUNCILS. It is such a rare honor that only one percent of members of the COUNCILS ever receive such an award. You receive a medal that looks like a planet. We are told that it is a visual representation of old Earth. And it is made from the metal of the first starships that landed on GAEA, and the ribbon that it is attached to is made from the spacesuits of the first members of THE SEVENS to set foot on GAEA.

The GGH is about the size of your fist. I have never seen one in person, of course, and I dare not hope that I will ever receive such an honor. As I mentioned, it is incredibly rare, but it would be my greatest aspiration. But I keep it myself. One of my colleagues who is also in her final day of preparation is Snowfeather Gentlecloud. I would consider her my nemesis, though I would never say that aloud. THE MOTHERS would not condone such things. We are all colleagues and valued equally for our services. As such, outward competition is frowned upon and anger and hatred towards one another is not tolerated. Though just between you and me, Snowfeather Gentlecloud is a bitch. She doesn't live up to her name either.

She thinks I'll never get as far as becoming a mentor let alone receiving the GGH. She's asked me to name anyone, man or woman, who has become a mentor who also hasn't been blessed with an alliterated name. I tried my best. I did a lot of research, but she was right, no one yet has become a mentor who hasn't been also blessed with an alliterated name.

So I don't talk to her about my dreams anymore. She's a dream decimator. That's what I call her. In any event, just because no EVOLVER without an alliterated name has been given the honor of becoming a mentor, doesn't mean it hasn't happened in other COUNCILS. In fact, there are a few examples in almost all of THE COUNCILS where non alliterated members have been honored with becoming mentors. The only COUNCIL where I couldn't find an example of this, other than my own COUNCIL, was in the ART COUNCIL. Even in THE MOTHERS there are several women without alliterated names. And besides, it is not a rule that I have heard of.

Still, Snowfeather Gentlecloud didn't care, she seems to think that to become an EVOLVER.m you have to have an alliterated name. There's no convincing her otherwise. Secretly I hope to show her. I hope to be the first. My best friend, Flutterdust Flowersong says I shouldn't bother with what Snowfeather Gentlecloud thinks. And she's right, but sometimes people just know how to push your buttons.

Flutterdust Flowersong and I were listening to Glitterfrost Gentlefeather. Snowfeather Gentlecloud was with us too. There was also Sugargaze Quickdance. He was also one of my friends. He was tall, I think he said he was six feet, anyway, that's tall from my five feet two inch height. He's very friendly and funny and he's easy on the eyes too which helps. Nowadays we're all known as simply being GAEAN, but from the history I learned in school, remember that I was good at history, Sugargaze Quickdance would have been Hispanic. He would have come from that place on old Earth called South America.

But nowadays, we are all so intermixed that no one can really say they are only of what we used to call one race. What used to be called races, just another way for us to differentiate and bicker amongst each other, have been intermixed for so long that we are now all simply GAEANS as I mentioned. But I know my history. And before my Greatest Parents I know that my lineage included what we used to call black Africans and American Indians.

My best friend Flutterdust Flowersong has wonderfully rich brown skin the color of the beach sand along the shores of GULGOLETH LAKE. Her mother and father though intermixed would have been predominantly called Japanese and African. I'm just telling you this to help you understand from your perspective. From our GAEAN perspective, everyone is simply of one humanity and one group and that is GAEAN. We don't even use the word 'race' anymore. It is an archaic word that I happen to know because of my schooling. Being a good EVOLVER means that you know your history.

Flutterdust Flowersong is taller than me by a couple of inches and more beautiful. She has green eyes the color of shamrocks and coffee colored hair that she keeps short and similar to me in what we still call a pageboy. Flutterdust Flowersong is a really good friend, because she thinks that I'm more beautiful than she is. She says my brilliant blue eyes are stunning. She also asked Sugargaze Quickdance who he thought was the most beautiful, but she prefaced it by saying that she thought I was, so she really was trying to sway him ahead of time.

He said that you couldn't choose the best rose from a rosebush as they were equally beautiful. He's a really good friend too. Anyway, we're both more beautiful than Snowfeather Gentlecloud, at least that's what we tell each other. But please don't misunderstand, beauty is not important on GAEA. I mean you have to be attracted to someone in order to have sex with them or even worse, get married to them, but other than that there are no competitions that have to do with attractiveness and beauty and even discussing such things is frowned upon by THE MOTHERS.

Speaking of mothers and fathers too. If you wish to get married, and as I said, most men and women become mothers and fathers and as such husbands and wives, then you need to get permission from your local MOTHERS COUNCIL. There are thirty-three cities we've built on GAEA with GULGOLETH being the most important and the Capital city, but you would never hear anyone saying that. As I said, pride comes before a fall as it did before the Greatest Fall which led to the Final Diaspora. So we never brag or speak pridefully of our Capital city. But it is known that GULGOLETH is the home of THE MOTHERS who oversee everyones welfare and oversee the other MOTHERS COUNCILS in the other cities.

Anyway, you have to get permission to marry and I have never heard of it not being granted, at least not to those whose roles it is to become husbands and wives and mothers and fathers. And twice a year in what we call Spring and Fall, though we have no true seasons like I said, all the cities hold wedding celebrations for the new husbands and wives. And then of course, to become mothers and fathers the new husbands and wives must request permission and wait their turn to bring a child into the world.

But husbands and wives are required to engage in sex at least three times a week as they never know when their turn will arrive and they must be ready. Only husbands and wives or mothers and fathers are fertile and it really is a gift of THE MOTHERS who know just when to bless a couple with a baby, and at that moment, conception is allowed to occur. Don't ask me the details about it as I do not know. The science and medicine behind how they become fertile is not required knowledge for any of us except THE MOTHERS and certain members of the SCIENCE COUNCIL. But rest assured that sex is not frowned upon, but nobody has babies unless their role is that of mother or father and then only when THE MOTHERS bless them with that opportunity.

The four of us, me and my best friend and my nemesis and Sugargaze Quickdance were finishing up final preparations for helping those who would be EVOLVING. I was lucky that I had been granted special permission to help my Greater Father EVOLVE. As I said, he was here in GULGOLETH. All those who EVOLVED did so from our Capital city. Sugargaze Quickdance, Flutterdust Flowersong and Snowfeather Gentlecloud had no relationship with their EVOLVED. That was usually how it was, I was the exception, and I was very grateful for that.

I should mention, just so you get a fuller picture of me, that I haven't had sex. And quite frankly, I'm not interested. I find it quite messy and gross and not something that I'm interested in. It's a good thing that I'm an EVOLVER because sex is not a requirement. Mind you, sex is only required of mothers and fathers or husbands and wives. For the rest of us it is optional. I know for a fact that Sugargaze Quickdance and Flutterdust Flowersong have had sex. She told me as much. And good for them too. But it's not for me. Frankly, I'm not attracted to anyone sexually. Not men or women. I like to keep my life simple.

As you can probably guess, when my mother and father heard that I had been selected as an EVOLVER, it was a great honor. My brother is to be a husband and father, so I'm the first one who has ever been selected for a role other than the common roles of parenting besides my Greatest Mothers. My brother, his name is Applegaze Sunmoon, has been a husband now for just over six years. He was married to Twinklestar Moonberry since he was eighteen. That's the age that men and women destined to be mothers and fathers get married.

He likes sex, but he tells me that having to do it three times a week is getting tiresome. They still haven't had their first child. I guess they haven't been blessed yet. Usually, husbands and wives get blessed by THE MOTHERS with a child within around the first two to four years of their marriage. My father, Moonshadow Silvertongue, and my mother, Glittereyes Appledew had me when they were both twenty. That's something else you should know, men and women are the same age when they are granted permission to get married. My brother and his wife are both currently twenty-four.

He wants to have a break from sex. At least that's what he told me confidentially. And when husbands and wives have a child, they are no longer required to have sex regularly. They get a break from it for the rest of their lives unless they petition THE MOTHERS for a second child. In that case, they are still not required to have sex for the first year after the birth of the child. So that's what Applegaze Sunmoon is hoping for. If he gets blessed with a child then he can take a year off, or more, from having to have sex. Listening to him just makes me realize how lucky I am.

"SQ, are you listening to these instructions?" asked Glitterfrost Gentlefeather.

She had been speaking to me. At this point you might have been wondering why I keep saying everyone's full name? Well, that's because that's how we stay respectful of each other and humble. There are only certain GAEANS who can choose how to address you, and they have limited choices. They can use your full name if they want. They can use your initials or they can use either your first or second name. We don't have surnames as you might have figured out. We only have first and second names.

We don't have surnames because, like I was saying we are all GAEANS, we are not identified by our race or our kin. This keeps us humble. We are all equal and we are all children of GAEA. Remember, pride comes before a fall, and I know from my history that long ago on old Earth, people used to take pride in their families or races or, stars forbid, their countries. Now that's a real archaic and silly term.

"SQ?" said Glitterfrost Gentlefeather, raising her voice slightly.

So the ones who can address you differently than using your full two names are THE MOTHERS of course and all those who have the 'm' or 'g' addendum to their role. This of course excludes mothers or fathers. Because you can't be a father.b or a mother.e. Mothers and fathers never become intermediate or expert in their role and none of them have ever become a GREAT GAEAN. And because Glitterfrost Gentlefeather was an EVOLVER.m, she could use my initials. And that was how she preferred to address all of us.

For the rest of us, we had to address everyone by both their names. Even if they were merely mothers or fathers, they were still valued for their roles and so I had to address all mothers and fathers by both their names. And remember, don't get me wrong, but mothers and fathers were still treated equally and respected for their role even if it was just to procreate and keep us at a certain number of beings here.

Maybe you find this odd, but I don't. From my history, humans used to think that the greatest gift and greatest privilege was to be a parent. And so what did we do? We bred like rabbits and like in some macabre sci-fi horror show we became ravenous, cannibalistic rabbits. I'm talking in a metaphor of course. But this is what happened, we and our parasitic spawn ate up the Earth and poisoned her. This was part of the problem with our pride. Pride in our children and in our countries and in our races. We don't have that problem here on GAEA anymore.

No, that's why we don't call our mothers and fathers by such clingy, desperate names as mommy or daddy. Laughable really. We call them by their two names. And they call us by our two names. Children are considered a blessing but only when THE MOTHERS bless the parents with a child. And then that child is a blessing to GAEA. We are children of THE MOTHERS and of GAEA. We take no personal pride in our children. Our greatest gift is to be of service to THE MOTHERS and in turn to GAEA.

"SQ!"

I looked up at Glitterfrost Gentlefeather. I smiled at her.

"Please forgive me, Glitterfrost Gentlefeather, I do not mean to be disrespectful. I am following the instructions. Once our EVOLVED has been placed in the E-POD and sealed in the MMC we close it all up and check to make sure it is sealed. Then we sing the farewell anthem for the EVOLVED and accompany them on board the EVOLUTION."

Glitterfrost Gentlefeather smiled at me and nodded. In front of her was an exact replica of a MOTHERS MILK CAPSULE or MMC. The MMC was a cylindrical and translucent capsule with rounded ends. Inside this one here on the sixty-sixth floor of the COUNCIL COLOSSUS was a robot playing the role of an EVOLVED. The robot climbed into the MMC within the E-POD and it closed around him like a canopy. It filled with what was a white milky substance and that is why we called it the MOTHERS MILK CAPSULE. We don't use possessive apostrophes if you're wondering. Because possession is a cornerstone of pride, and, pride comes before a fall. You should know that by now.

None of us know what constituents make up the milky substance in the MMC. But THE MOTHERS do and so does the SCIENCE COUNCIL, and that is enough. Listen to Glitterfrost Gentlefeather, she'll explain what this substance is for.

"Now see what happens once G3236.3 is enclosed into the MMC. SG, can you tell me what the purpose is for the substance inside the MMC?"

Snowfeather Gentlecloud turned to me and smiled as if she was showing off.

"Yes, Glitterfrost Gentlefeather. The purpose of the MOTHERS MILK in the MMC is to maintain the sanctity of the EVOLVEDS body so that when the E-POD with the EVOLVEDS body is received into the arms of the ONE it can be reassimilated into the ONE from where it came."

"Very good, SG," said Glitterfrost Gentlefeather.

You might be wondering what the ONE is. Sometimes you can write it out as THE ONE, that's the same with the MOTHERS or THE MOTHERS. In any event. The ONE is the intelligence or the beginning of everything. We believe that the universe had a start and that start was directed by an intelligence or being if you will, though being is quite a crude understanding of it. In science you might think of the universe as a great big OAK. The ONE is that first SEED that brought the OAK into being. But where is that SEED? It is in all parts of that giant OAK.

In the same way if you look at it from a mathematical point of view, the ONE might be the formula that explains everything. We have that now, though it's not quite perfect, but we believe that there is one formula to explain everything. This would be the ONE.

I know it can be hard to explain and to understand. But the ONE is where we came from and what we are part of and to what we return. I like to think of it in terms of the OAK, as I love PLANTS and their beauty. The ONE is everywhere but THE MOTHERS have determined that the EVOLVED are sent back to an isolated part of space which I have heard is in the general direction of old

Earth, and this part of space has a particularly strong vibration of the ONES energy and so that is where the EVOLVED go.

Glitterfrost Gentlefeather manipulated a panel on our side of the E-POD. The E-POD started to close. It reminded me of the shell of a beetle. Within was the MMC which held the robot. There was enough room on either side within it to fit a person. I believe that I could fit within, curled up next to my Greater Father if I wanted to travel with him to the ONE. It was a tempting idea but of course it was strictly forbidden. Only the EVOLVED was allowed to travel the final journey to the ONE.

EVOLVERS only accompanied the EVOLVED to the first stop which was to a wormhole that we simply called the WHOLE. It was a six month journey to the WHOLE at our fastest capable speed which was only one third the speed of light. As such, an EVOLVER could only perform one EVOLUTION, that's what we called the procedure of helping an EVOLVED reach the WHOLE safely, each year, and almost universally it was way less than that. After each EVOLUTION, an EVOLVER was interviewed and reassigned but only after a rigorous process of reeducation and rehabilitation. Having been away from GAEA for so long, it was thought that the rigors of an EVOLUTION journey were incredibly challenging on the psyche of an EVOLVER, both mentally and emotionally. Usually this process of reintegration took a year at the minimum.

And it was true. Being an EVOLVER was an exceptionally challenging occupation. In fact, we generally lost sixty-six percent of EVOLVERS who performed more than three EVOLUTIONS. That meant that not many EVOLVERS reached middle age. Glitterfrost Gentlefeather was one of the exceptions. She was fifty years old and had performed six EVOLUTIONS, the maximum number you could perform before being retired, or in her case chosen to be a mentor.

Tomorrow we were visiting the abode of retired EVOLVERS. We had been cautioned as to what to expect. It was supposed to be a reckoning so that we were fully aware of the pitfalls that awaited us in the deep, open, silent, blackness of space.

By my account, if I was able to complete an EVOLUTION every two years which would be quite the feat, most likely, I'd do one every two to three years, but for the sake of argument if I did one every two years, the quickest I could, then I'd be in my mid thirties to late thirties by the time I would be forcibly retired. But I was rare. I was one of the youngest.

In fact, our group was amongst the youngest ever to be granted expert status as EVOLVERS. We were all under thirty. Usually, most EVOLVERS were around thirty to thirty-five before they made it to expert level. That meant that most, and by most, I mean those that actually make it to retirement, retire in their mid to late forties. I was hoping to become a mentor as you know. I can't imagine retiring. I'd be bored to tears. Those chosen for mentorship, if they don't have twenty-five years as EVOLVERS do administrative work until they do have those years.

Remember how I said that most of the EVOLVERS who do three or more EVOLUTIONS get lost, well, that's actually a euphemism. They kill themselves. I've heard this is the difficulty of being out in space by yourself. Yes, we have a robot companion, but that's not the same as a real live human companion, especially when you've sent your other human companion off to the ONE through the WHOLE. But I haven't experienced that yet so I'm not sure how bad it really can be.

"Let's recite the farewell anthem class," said Glitterfrost Gentlefeather.

We all started to drone on in a somber and yet somewhat

reverent tone.

"The circle is complete. The EVOLVED is sent to the ONE to meet. We the EVOLVERS guide you there, making sure to tend to your needs with care. GAEA thanks you for your contribution. THE MOTHERS love you through this resolution. May the ONE take you in their arms, accept you with all your charms. Go with peace EVOLVED, your life has now been solved. From soil of Earth through your GAEAN birth to your ONE destination of merriment and mirth."

I knew the farewell anthem by heart. It was one of the first things you learnt as an EVOLVER.

"And as you know, from this point, ladies and gentleman," continued Glitterfrost Gentlefeather, "the bearers carry the E-POD with the EVOLVED in it down the procession of those who have come to exultate the EVOLVEDS life. And where does it end up, Quickdance?"

She hadn't used his initials because Sugargaze Quickdance had the same initials as me and it would just get confusing. So she leaves the initials for me. I take it as a sign of honor.

"We are with the procession, Glitterfrost Gentlefeather. We lead the procession and the bearers of the EVOLVEDS E-POD towards the EXIGENCE where we and the E-POD are solemnly ensconced into the Starships Intrepid where we shortly thereafter begin our six month journey."

Glitterfrost Gentlefeather smiled at Sugargaze Quickdance, and nodded.

"Very good," she said.

Sugargaze Quickdance smiled back. I didn't know if they were currently, but I knew that my friend Sugargaze Quickdance had had sex with Glitterfrost Gentlefeather. This is not frowned upon. They are both free adults and not encumbered by being husbands and wives. Only husbands and wives are required to be monogamous. And remember, there is no fear of unwanted pregnancies. We cannot get pregnant without the blessing of THE MOTHERS.

In any event, Glitterfrost Gentlefeather did not treat any of us differently than she did Sugargaze Quickdance. It would not be tolerated and in any event, sex is not something that is seen as an emotional act. And my friend Sugargaze Quickdance likes sex, what can I say, he's different from me in that way. And in case you're wondering, no, he and I have not had sex. I'm not interested, like I've told you before. I've never had sex and I'm not interested in trying it anyway. But Sugargaze Quickdance is different. But he has not had sex with Snowfeather Gentlecloud even though she's dying to lie with him.

But he doesn't out of respect for me. He knows that she's just a mean spirited woman. At least that's what I suspect. I've never actually asked him.

"Are there any questions, class?" asked Glitterfrost Gentlefeather.

She took a moment to look around at the four of us. We all stared at her with blank faces. For the past three months we had been learning the protocols for EVOLUTION and our roles within it until it was habitual. There were no questions, and this was the last opportunity we'd have to ask them. Tomorrow we visited the communal home for retired EVOLVERS. It was colloquially called the Place of Forgetting. Because those who have been retired are taught to forget. This is so it makes living with themselves easier. I'm not quite sure I understand it all perfectly but I'm sure it will make sense after I've had the chance to visit.

"Alright then, class," continued Glitterfrost Gentlefeather, "tomorrow we meet back here at eight a.m. for our trip to the retirement home of retired EVOLVERS. Steel yourselves as it is likely to be a difficult trip. But remember this is only for your benefit so that you might be better armed in eliminating any emotional attachment you might have with your EVOLVED. If you just focus on your role and not your emotions, you'll find the EVOLUTION a much more rewarding experience. Especially you, SQ, got it?"

I nodded blankly at her.

"For ours is not to ask questions or to think about the after journey when the EVOLVED leaves you. That is between them and the ONE. Trust in THE MOTHERS, and trust that the EVOLUTION is the natural course of events. Understood?"

We all nodded again.

"Good, at the end of tomorrow you'll all be tested and if you pass the elimination exam after your visit we'll sit down one last time before your first EVOLUTION, one on one. For on thirmorrow you each will partake in your first EVOLUTION. I'm so proud of all of you."

Glitterfrost Gentlefeather was beaming at us with what might have been pride but surely couldn't have been. She was just happy. Oh, and thirmorrow is the day after tomorrow. It is the third day from today, tomorrow being the second day from today. As today being the first day. We didn't have a word for it for the longest time. Now we do, and such a useful word it is. The four of us walked back to our dormitories which were on the sixty-seventh floor. We each had our own room but a shared living space. There was also a small cafeteria where we could get anything we wanted to eat. We chose to head there first. We were all hungry. It had been a long and grueling day and food sounded about right. The cafeteria was called The GRAIN Lane.

CHAPTER FOUR

A Place Of Emptiness

THOSE goddamn von Humans were making good on their promise. I couldn't believe it. Well, actually I could. I'd been seeing the numbers updated daily. It was a decimation. It was worse than that, it was actually an annihilation. Traditionally a decimation is about one in ten, as in killing or eliminating one in ten. That's where deca comes from, meaning ten. Whereas, annihilate really means to destroy completely and I'd say that's what the von Humans had been up to.

When I'd started on this project, when it was first called Project Phoenix, and it was secret, there had been well over one billion humans on Earth. Now. Now there were around one hundred and something million. At least that's what we were being told. Two months before what we'd termed Ω, or simply omega. The last of the letters in the Greek alphabet and since our democracy, our culture had begun in Ancient Greece we thought it was fitting. It didn't take much convincing for the other member states, if you could call them that, to accept this term. After all, we were all of us, or should I say over eighty percent of those of us left, living in the United States, which was now the seat of the USE.

The capital had been transferred to Merritt Island here in Florida. This was for convenience as much as anything else. It was after all where the remaining space elevator was located that was still functioning. It took us up to the GSS which was the Geostationary Starship Station. Since the turn of the twenty-second century we had begun building the space elevator and the station where we were now loading up the starships. There were one hundred of them. It had taken us twenty years to build them all. Some of the first we had tried to retrofit to bring up to current standards, but that was not fully possible.

It was our hope that they would survive the journey. Each was equipped to take on one million humans and each of them could reach a top speed of zero point three times the speed of light. It was cramped quarters and every male and female coming on board had been sterilized chemically. This was reversible but we couldn't have more mouths to feed. It might seem tough, but these were difficult times and difficult times required tough measures.

"Dr. Siwik," said Ni Yin.

"InDuna Yin," I said, smiling at the petite Asian woman.

Ni Yin was our leader. We no longer adhered to names that were deemed to be hierarchical. As such, our leader or what used to be called prime ministers or presidents or premiers were given the Zulu name InDuna as a sign of respect. It was a word that had caught on at the turn of the century offered by one of our leading visionaries at the time Dingane Bhengani, a South African Zulu at birth and one of the first major casualties in our war against what are now known as the von Neumanns or von Humans, back then we just called them robots.

Dingane Bhengani had not only forewarned about the problem with the singularity, some say he was responsible for limiting the damage that the von Humans were capable of causing in the early days. InDuna was a word he had used to describe those whom he had admired as trusted and humble advisors. It is the word we use now for our leader, the leader or InDuna of humanity, of USE, of what is left of us.

"Are we still on schedule to leave tomorrow morning?" she asked me.

She was an older woman of sixty-six years. She had been first generation American born from Chinese parents. She reminded me of a frail Buddha. She was slim and slight with naturally gray hair that she kept short. She had been married and she had had children. Her family had been murdered by the von Humans. How she escaped was by sheer luck and chance. She looked frail, but I knew personally that she was anything but.

"The elevator is holding up remarkably well InDuna. Maximum capacity remains at one hundred thousand per hour. We should have everyone except for the skeleton staff uploaded into the Starships by midnight. Then by my calculations, the rest of us and the supplies should be completed by around four a.m. tomorrow. We should be ready to depart for 61 Virginis by six sharp."

Ni Yin nodded thoughtfully, looking up at me. Next to her was Dr. Asfaha Saare, a tall thin Eritrean who was her right hand man. We had no name for him other than his name. Long ago he would have been considered something like Vice President, now he was known by his name. He was a young man, half of Ni Yin's age, but he was incredibly bright and thoughtful. His doctorate was in biomolecular genetics. He turned to Ni Yin.

"I have checked with Dr. Mohini Myśliński and he has confirmed that all the supplies are lined up and ready to be uploaded."

Ni Yin looked over at him and nodded.

"And these include our robots?" she asked him.

He looked over at me and I nodded.

"Yes, InDuna, the robots are helping logistically, and they will be the last onboard. They will send up all other supplies and then they will upload at the very end, if we don't encounter any problems by then."

Ni Yin didn't say anything to that. She knew exactly what I meant. We'd be leaving around twenty percent of humanity behind. It couldn't be helped. Sacrifices had to be made. In any event, most of them were spread across Earth. Only those who were here in America were able to be uploaded. And they'd all made their way to Merritt Island over three months ago. Uploading around one hundred million people from one space elevator was a logistical nightmare. Even at full capacity, and the many problems we'd encountered along the way, it had taken us sixty-six days. We were currently on our sixty-sixth day, leaving tomorrow come hell or high water.

About a month ago we had held up the white flag and withdrawn all combat missions against the von Humans. Combat missions was just a euphemism for what had really been suicide missions. Nevertheless, it hadn't stopped the von Humans from continuing to hunt us, but it had for some reason slowed them down. But I was holding my breath. Part of me feared that they were waiting for us to fill up all our starships and then would just blow them to pieces, killing us all in one go. But we had no choice. To stay on Earth was certain death. To leave for a new home was our only chance.

"Time will tell whether or not we encounter any problems," said Ni Yin.

She looked across from the attached building we stood in, watching the never ending lines of humans being sucked into the elevators and propelled up towards the GSS. Robots and peacekeepers were keeping everything orderly. Despite the logistical nightmares, I looked over the orderly crowds and I was pleased with how well things were going.

Unfortunately, people were only allowed to bring one small backpack each. Anything else was disallowed. Space was at a premium. It seemed sad to see whole families with nothing but a small backpack holding each of their life's most treasured possessions on each person, but it was either that or being left behind to die.

She turned and smiled at me.

"Everything looks very orderly, and those robots certainly seem to be handling everything carefully," she said.

We all remained somewhat skeptical about the robots ever since the von Humans started evolving so quickly. Our best scientists reckoned that within twelve months the von Humans would attain Type II status on the Kardashev scale if they haven't already. Some of us feel that the von Humans have our omega as the same day they leave Earth to utilize the energy of the solar system and our sun.

If you asked for my personal opinion, I'd say they're probably at Type II already, but have delayed leaving Earth until they've put it back in balance. In any event it's all moot, it's not gonna matter past tomorrow because either we'll leave and never see them again or we'll be annihilated and never know better.

We reached Type 0.96 at the turn of the century and then it went all downhill from there. Just for pure information purposes we're probably around Type 0.92 now. Losing over ninety percent of humanity will do that to you as a civilization. Still, we have enough expertise and robots to have built our starships and get us off this mortal coil. Wherever we head to next we'll likely have to start off at around Type 0.75 depending on the environment and how much of our technology and community survives.

61 Virginis is where we're headed. Astrophysicists and astronomers have assured us that is where the largest number of

habitable planets are located within a reasonable distance. They've put it at eight planets, three of which could possibly be habitable. 61 Virginis is located about ninety-seven light years from Earth. You probably know that. But at our top speed it'll take us almost a millennium to get there. That's a hell of a long time, and we don't have that sort of time. A worm hole has been found just outside the Oort Cloud that calculations seem to suggest opens up in the vicinity of 61 Virginis. Our best calculations put the worm hole at around two light years from Earth. Like I said, just outside the Oort Cloud.

The exit is harder to predict as it seems to fluctuate. But it puts us between two and five light years from 61 Virginis. So we save a lot of time. Especially if we can get closer rather than further away. We can't determine with any more certainty than that. In any event, seven years is better than one thousand years. Our starships are capable of maintaining life for decades. Engineers have determined that their self serviceable life is twenty-five years. Beyond that, and we might have to start repairing them ourselves. But here's hoping we don't have to worry about that.

"There look like millions still left to be embarked," said Asfaha Saare.

I looked at him and smiled.

"Yes, it does look like millions doesn't it. If only it were true."

I detected an overtone of sadness to my voice. And it was true. I'd lost everyone close to me, just as Ni Yin had. The same was true of Dr. Saare. He too had lost a wife and three children. I'd just lost a wife, but we had no children. My family had been taken too.

"If you'll come over here, you'll have a better look at the numbers," I said, leading them to the display embedded in the glass wall that looked over the uploading area of the elevator. We had been standing to the left of it, and it was not powered on.

I waved my hand over the glass panel, several inches from it and it lit up. There were a variety of windows on it showing who were being uploaded in real time, but it was going by so fast that I couldn't keep up. I minimized that window, as well as others that gave speed of the elevators, the men and women peacekeepers involved and where they were as well as the designation of the robots. Windows also maintained a running tally of the loss of human lives. That fluctuated but seemed to mirror in many ways that number of human lives being uploaded to the starships every hour.

I closed most of these windows. They were depressing and not important to the task at hand. Watching roughly thirty names and photographs along with other information about those uploading to the starships was not something I could monitor. I could stop it or slow it down but what was the point. I'd just be creating a huge backlog. In any event, the computers, humans, consoles and algorithms involved insured that no one with a criminal record would get onboard any starship. They had given up the right to be a member of the community and thus were being left behind.

It wasn't them I was sad for. It was the folks left in other parts of the world. Other innocent people who had done no wrong that just couldn't be saved. That was the true tragedy. But like the windows on the glass panel I minimized those thoughts too. I pulled up the large number indicator. In big bold letters that changed by the second it read momentarily ninety-three million four hundred thousand and sixty-six.

"This is the total number already onboard the ships, InDuna," I said, pointing at the number on the screen. Ni Yin smiled and nodded happily.

"That is good. Smaller than we would have liked, but I think that is a number we can start over with."

"And a number that we can manipulate over the years or when we reach our final destination," said Asfaha Saare.

I knew what he was talking about. He and his colleagues had perfected techniques to control our population. I knew it was important for the long trip ahead of us, the ships had a maximum capacity of one million each, but I didn't like the idea of it ethically. Saare and other members of the scientific and medical community could not only control when a woman would conceive, but the how and with whom she would conceive. It was genetic manipulation and interference at its most extreme.

Of course, promises had been made that we weren't about to create a perfect human race, and besides, which race would we choose. We were predominately intermixed by now anyway. But everyone had been assured that this genetic manipulation was solely limited to managing birth and not with whom a woman might have intercourse or what the genetic makeup of the child would be other than to correct any abnormal defects. Still, the cynic in me wasn't so sure. I smiled weakly at him and then pulled up a smaller number.

"Within the legal framework we have created for that purpose," said Ni Yin to Asfaha Saare.

"Of course, InDuna," he said.

"This number here," I said, bringing everyone's attention back to the glass panel, "is the number we have uploaded since midnight last night."

The panel briefly showed one million four hundred and forty thousand and sixty-seven before blurring. Roughly thirty humans were being sent up the elevator per second. Ni Yin smiled again.

"That is good. And how many are left?" she asked, looking at me. "It looks like millions."

She looked beyond the glass panel and towards the mass of

moving humanity in the covered area below us as they moved into the elevator pods just off to our left. I pulled up another number and put it below the first two. This one increased in size as the others dimmed and decreased in size, all of them increasing in count except for this one which decreased in actual numbers.

"This is the number, InDuna, that shows us how many souls we have left to upload."

I briefly noticed the number one million one hundred and eleven thousand one hundred and eleven as it quickly started decreasing in count. It was just past two p.m. We had more than enough time to upload the last of us. An estimate was one hundred thousand uploads an hour, but we'd been doing a little more than that.

"And we have enough time to get them all up by midnight?" asked Ni Yin.

"We do, InDuna," I said. I tapped on the glass panel and brought up another window that had a digital clock on it.

"This clock here," I said, pointing at it with my finger, "is the accurate and live time by which we'll have all humans uploaded."

Ni Yin, Asfaha Saare and I looked at the clock. The seconds placement in the digital readout changed by a few seconds every now and then, but the most steady time on the clock appeared to be eleven minutes and eleven seconds after eleven this evening.

"Very good, Seraphina," said Ni Yin.

She used my first name as a term of endearment. I liked it. Even though she had asked me to use her first name on several occasions, I preferred to use the official title of InDuna. For she was really a trusted and humble advisor.

"Ni," said Saare.

She looked over at him, taking her gaze from the swarming, moving, heaving mass of humanity below us that were like a live breathing snake.

"I think we should get ourselves up to the Starship Umkhonto."

Starship Umkhonto would be the lead starship as we set off. As such it would hold most of our most prominent scholars, leaders, scientists, artists and a large portion of our military force. Umkhonto as you might have guessed was another Zulu word. Thanks to Dingane Bhengani we had assimilated several Zulu words into our vocabulary. Umkhonto meant spear and was a fitting name for the starship that would lead us to a new promised land. It was the ship that I would be in as well. Though I would be one of the last to leave terra firma. That was my choice. I had a hard time letting go of the only home I'd ever known.

Ni Yin nodded at Saare.

"You should use this private elevator, InDuna," I said, as I led them to the elevator at the far corner of this large office. There was a corridor that led above ground towards a pod in which they would then be jettisoned onto the space elevator and uploaded to the GSS. From there it was a short ride to the Umkhonto. The trip to GSS took roughly eleven seconds. You were strapped in for the trip of your life, however, the acceleration was so smooth as to be almost imperceptible.

Three security members trailed us as I walked Dr. Saare and Ni Yin to the corridor, and then towards the pod. We stopped just outside the entrance to the pod. It had opened up. This was a small one. It could only take ten people at a time.

"Once you enter the pod, be sure to sit down and buckle yourself in. You'll be taken a short distance to the space elevator itself. Once engaged, the ride will be a very short eleven seconds. Acceleration is extreme but you'll likely not even notice thanks to gravitational dampening within the pod."

Ni Yin smiled.

"Thank you, Seraphina," she said. "When will we see you

there?"

"I will be one of the last, InDuna. I have much work to do to ensure everyone is uploaded correctly."

This wasn't entirely true. I could upload myself anytime. Much of the work at this point was automated and the computers could handle any malfunctions or glitches with the help of the robots. In any event, we had run thousands of simulations before ever getting to this point and nothing had gone wrong.

"Are you sure that is a good idea?" she asked me.

I nodded.

"We can't underestimate the importance of what we are doing here, InDuna, besides, I have robot Gary to turn to for any help and Dr. Mohini Myśliński will be up shortly."

Gary was at the other far end of the room standing vigilant at a waist high table that consisted of a long glass panel inclined at thirty degrees and full of information about the ongoing upload.

"Very well then, we will see you by midnight," said Ni Yin.

"At the very latest," I replied.

I watched as Ni Yin and Asfaha Saare got into the pod and buckled themselves down. Then the three security personnel did the same. Two men and one petite woman who looked as if she could be blown over by a gentle breeze. But I had learned from an early age that size and sex were no determinants of skill. In a moment the pod door closed behind them and became opaque. I knew what they were looking at. The pod had become a 3D moving image of a tranquil lake as if they were out on a canoe, gently traveling along this quiet and still lake. They had no idea that they would reach a top speed of thirty thousand kilometers per second.

I turned and walked back down the corridor and into the main room. I looked at Gary. He was six feet tall, and looked exactly like every other robot except for his designation which was the year he was built and the number within that year. His designation was R2122.21. We had built hundreds of thousands of them. We were left with less than two thousand thanks to the von Humans. And not all of them would be coming with us. Gary would, as would another thirteen hundred and eighty-six. Thirteen robots had been assigned to each starship except for the Umkhonto. The Umkhonto would have one hundred robots. Gary and ninety-nine others.

"Everything performing within parameters, Gary?" I asked him.

He turned his head which looked like a motorcycle helmet with a much slimmer visor element that contained his visual imaging center. His voice was human. It was the voice of my father. It comforted me and it was a choice I had requested when he had been built.

"Everything is running very smoothly," he said, as he turned back towards the table and continued to monitor everything.

To describe him was somewhat difficult. The head as mentioned looked like a motorcycle helmet. It was a matte silver, his whole body was. He looked much like those old fashioned store mannequins but in a matte silver. He had toes and fingers, but he was not anatomically correct. He had a metal skeleton over which had been placed an artificial skin, matte silver, of course, made from an elastic, extremely durable and tough carbon fiber.

CHAPTER FIVE

A Place of Forgetting

ALL four of us were up early and waiting for our mentor, Glitterfrost Gentlefeather in the mezzanine cafeteria of the COUNCIL COLOSSUS. I was drinking a vanilla latte. We still have those, and my nemesis, Snowfeather Gentlecloud was having a blended frozen drink that looked to be too high in calories and fat for her to keep her figure much longer. Sugargaze Quickdance was also having a vanilla latte and Flutterdust Flowersong was having a green TEA latte. We were eating a variety of pastries. You probably don't care about that, but I'm going to tell you anyway because I'm bored.

I was having a cinnamon roll. Nemesis was having some sort of BLUEBERRY scone. Sugargaze Quickdance was eating oatmeal with ALMONDS and MAPLE syrup. Yes, we had MAPLE TREES here, they flourished quite well. Remember we brought with us SEEDS from most of the PLANTS that were on old Earth. At least the edible ones. My best friend, Flutterdust Flowersong was enjoying a danish of some sort.

Now I'm bored not because Glitterfrost Gentlefeather is late. No, we don't have a problem with that sort of thing here. Not only is tardiness frowned upon on GAEA but it's just not a problem. We have a wonderfully ordered society. I'm bored because we got here too early and because Snowfeather Gentlecloud woke up early, she decided to get the rest of us up, so we're killing time in the COUNCIL COLOSSUS main level cafeteria. It's called BEAN Here.

It's busy. There is lots of activity at the COUNCIL COLOSSUS as you can imagine. This is the center of everything really, and being in GULGOLETH, it's the biggest city anyway. People were coming and going, spilling in and out like COFFEE BEANS from a bag or staying for fifteen minutes before hurrying off again. I watched it all in fascination. Having been good at history, I wondered if such a scene might have taken place on old Earth.

I mean we had lots of records from old Earth but most of it was classified and only those who needed to access them were granted such access. Where there was a gap was in culture. We had some idea of what the pillars of culture were like. For example, we had examples of music and architecture, painting and sculpture, dance and writing, but much of daily life was left up to the imagination or the word of our instructors. For example, BEAN Here had live music all day and night. It was open twenty-four seven and the pianist right now was playing what I knew as jazz.

But what I wanted to know was what life was like for a jazz musician in the late twenty-first century. Or even in the early part of the twenty-first century, before the turn of the twenty-second century when pride became our deadliest sin. Of that, I just have to imagine.

I knew all about the von Neumanns, and that they had been colloquially called the von Humans, but that wasn't a word we were allowed to use in polite company. In fact it was considered a great insult if you called anyone by that name. And I understood why. I mean von Neumanns, I had learnt, had turned out to be demons. They had turned against their masters and become an insatiable race of robots hell-bent on destruction and the annihilation of the entire human race.

Von Neumanns were the reason we left. I knew that. They were hell-bent on eradicating humanity from the planet of old Earth. But what we were also taught was that they had destroyed old Earth and made it all but uninhabitable for any life. At least, that's the trajectory they were on, for we left before old Earth couldn't sustain any life. And that's such a shame, because old Earth seemed like such a beautiful place. The pictures I've seen from the forests and meadows, hills and valleys and of course the pictures from space.

In fact, there is one picture that has become so well known for us GAEANS that it is usually framed and can be seen everywhere. For example, it is the image in the center of the flag of GAEA. The last known picture we took of old Earth as we were leaving in the Final Diaspora. The blue jewel on a green background. That's our flag.

So when you curse someone, which is what you are really doing when you call them a von Human, you are calling them a demonic god hell-bent on destroying everything. And destruction is a great sin here on GAEA where we've worked hard to develop a civilized society. In fact, destruction can get you the death penalty. Be it as simple as painting or drawing on something you're not supposed to or physically destroying a PLANT or building, that's usually the death penalty. We don't have the space or resources for destroying what we've toiled to build.

Mind you, in my twenty-six years of life I have not heard of the death penalty having been used once. Usually THE MOTHERS have great rehabilitation centers, where those who are reckless usually find themselves for more minor offenses, before they're able to commit something more atrocious. For example, I have heard recently of someone using the epithet von Human and being sent to a rehabilitation center only to come out much improved.

One thing I am grateful for, is THE MOTHERS and the society they've built. In fact, as I look out the window at the grand plaza in front of the COUNCIL COLOSSUS, in the front of a large fountain of water, right in the center of the plaza is a statue to our FIRST MOTHER. It stands about twenty feet high and is solid gold and shines like the sun. It has great detail. Our FIRST MOTHER is depicted as she was captured taking her first steps on GAEA. She has a wonderfully, peaceful and calm smile on her seventy-seven year old face.

Our elders are revered here on GAEA for they have designed the world we live in and their wisdom is our greatest treasure. On the plaque of this statue it reads FIRST MOTHER and then on the line below that MOONMEADOW MOUNTAINMIST and next to that it has 77 Years Old. On the third line in quotes it has "Ni Yin". We understand that to be her old Earth name. On the fourth and final line is the dates of her life. 10 March 2059 - 15 March 2147. She was eighty-eight as you can probably figure out when she EVOLVED.

Stars above, that seems like such a long time ago. Over one thousand years. I can't imagine the hardships that our forebears had to endure as they built this beautiful civilization for us from nothing here on GAEA. Led by THE MOTHERS and MOONMEADOW MOUNTAINMIST particularly. Incidentally, nobody since then has ever had both first and second names start with the letter M. That has become sacred. Only our FIRST MOTHER and a few other select SEVENS will ever have two names with the letter M. It's out of respect as I'm sure you can imagine.

From my knowledge of history I've come to know that the first generation of GAEANS had all sorts of different EVOLVED ages. Nobody in those early years lived past eighty-eight. MOONMEADOW MOUNTAINMIST remains the oldest GAEAN ever. But others from those first ships to arrive lived to all sorts of different ages. Some got into their sixties and seventies, and even a few made it to their eighties, but most of that first generation of SEVENS who made it from old Earth never saw forty. You'll remember there was the auspicious number of seventy-seven million seven hundred and seventy-seven thousand seven hundred and seventy-seven humans who made it safely to GAEA.

That's purely coincidental I've been told, but you never know. History is sometimes seen through distorted lenses, but I'd never say that out loud. Nevertheless, life in the beginning decades here on GAEA to quote from an ancient old Earth philosopher who had the strange name of Thomas Hobbes was nasty, brutish and short. But they obviously survived and then thrived, for we have a wonderfully advanced and civilized society now.

But one thing that does tickle my curiosity muscle is the age that all of us EVOLVE at. For the men as I've said it is sixty-six, this is the age of my Greater Father, Moondew Flamesdance right now, and as such it is his time to EVOLVE. THE MOTHERS, or should I say all women, and I've told you this before, EVOLVE at the age of seventy-seven.

You might wonder what's so curious about that. Well, sixty-six is the age of MOONMEADOW MOUNTAINMIST when she left old Earth and seventy-seven is the age when she arrived on GAEA. Maybe it's just me, but I find that particularly interesting. It's not a question I can ask openly because it'll get me in trouble. If you ask too many questions outside of your area of expertise you might find yourself soon enough in a rehabilitation center, and well, I've got EVOLUTIONS to perform. Though I did bring this topic up casually with my best friend Flutterdust Flowersong and she thought it was quite appropriate and natural that our EVOLUTIONS occur on those auspicious ages of the monumental moments in our FIRST MOTHERS life.

So there you go, it might just be me and my insatiable curiosity. But like I said, I've done well in history, and the history of old Earth is something I'm very interested in. Especially because there are so many gaps in our knowledge and understanding of what the last hundred or so years on old Earth was like. So, without real and true information, I start to wonder what it might have been like.

Do you know, for example, that we have no known photographs of von Neumanns other than when they looked very much like our robots do today. But from what I've gathered, and surmised by reading between the lines is that the von Neumanns quickly evolved into something far beyond what our current robots look like which is somewhat human.

And that brings me to another point. Our robots are advanced, and so is our society, but anything technological, and computer related and especially robotic is overseen by a human. I guess we learned from the von Neumanns not to grant computerized technology any autonomy. There will not be a technological singularity here on GAEA, THE MOTHERS have seen to that and I'm grateful for it. All robots are governed by strict algorithms and computer design by humans so that although they seem very human, they are incapable of thought or self awareness, and that's a good thing. So say THE MOTHERS and so say the rest of us.

Of course, that means that we work and toil in order to keep them under control, but such is the penalty for our sin of pride. The robots are especially helpful for menial tasks. Like I said, the word literally means 'forced labor'. And I can't imagine how they'd continue to do that if they gained self awareness. I don't understand what old Earth humans were thinking on their myopic strident determination towards singularity. I mean, I guess it's hindsight, but how could you not have foreseen a revolution.

I have a robot at home. In fact, those of us who are blessed with being in the special councils each receive a robot. We're allowed to name them ourselves. I've named mine. His official designation is G3230.1323. But the name he understands commands by is the name I've given him. Roger Dodger is its name. I wanted to give it an old Earth name, but old Earth names are so difficult to remember and confusing, and from history I found this phrase, that was used in the twentieth century during one of their big wars. If I remember correctly it came about during the second of their big wars, and the last one. It was an old radio signal given to sign off on a radio transmission, but a pilot added some flair to it and added the 'dodger'.

I like rhymes too. In fact, I'm a big fan of limericks. Limericks if you don't know are an old Earth era form of poetry that is named after an old place on Earth called Limerick. It is a strictly five line poem with the rhyming scheme of AABBA. Here's an example of one I did.

There was a lady well known
Who showed her mother what she'd sewn.
Her mother said, "not so fast,
That yarn will not last."
So she hit her over the head with a stone.

Flutterdust Flowersong really likes them. They make her laugh, I guess because they're supposed to be funny. I suppose I could have become an ARTIST if I'd wanted, but like I said, I wanted to become an EVOLVER to help my Greater Father through his EVOLUTION. I'd love to help my father too, but that won't be possible, for I'll be retired before then.

"Sunring Quickdust," said Sugargaze Quickdance.

I looked over at him and smiled.

"You always seem so far away. Are you thinking about tomorrows EVOLUTION?"

I shook my head slowly and took a sip of my latte. It was now tepid because he was right, I was often far away in my own head.

"Then what?"

"I was thinking of Limericks," I said.

Sugargaze Quickdance laughed.

"Those are so funny. Tell everyone the Limerick you wrote for me."

I looked around at the other two.

"I'm not sure," I said, "it was a little bit lewd."

Sugargaze Quickdance tossed his head back and laughed again.

"A little lewd," he said, "it was all lewd, and I loved it, but I can't quite remember it. Please say it again."

I looked over at Snowfeather Gentlecloud and Flutterdust Flowersong and they both nodded.

"Go on," said Flutterdust Flowersong.

"Alright then," I said, grinning at the expectant faces, "but you've been warned. Ready?"

Everyone nodded.

"Here goes. There was an old Earthman named Rick who had an incredibly huge dick. His wife said, 'It's not that I'm a wussy, but I'm sure it'll break my pussy, so how about I just give it a lick?'."

Everyone laughed, even Snowfeather Gentlecloud my nemesis couldn't but help herself. Flutterdust Flowersong and Sugargaze Quickdance laughed and laughed.

"You are so funny," said Sugargaze Quickdance. "Give us another."

"I can't just make them up on the fly," I said, "they do take some effort."

"Oh go on, Sunring Quickdust, I know you can do another one," said Flutterdust Flowersong.

I lowered my head to the table and thought about it for a moment.

"Alright," I said. "Just one more okay?"

They nodded at me, all smiling.

"There once was a young mother, who thought she'd slept with her brother, but upon waking, with her innards aching, she realized it had to have been another."

More giggles and laughter. It was just the encouragement I needed.

"At the funeral of our dearly departed, when no one was looking he farted. 'Good heaven's above, that's surely a sign of love,' said the priest who was really good hearted."

And they laughed some more so I thought of another to kill the time.

"There once was a man from the loch, who sat everyday on the rock. Is that man really nude? Asked the young woman a prude, as she watched him stroke his hard cock."

Sugargaze Quickdance was practically rolling on the floor at this point and we were gathering the attention of onlookers so I decided that enough was enough. Out of the corner of my eye I saw Glitterfrost Gentlefeather walking towards us. I kicked Sugargaze Quickdance under the table. He stopped laughing. Glitterfrost Gentlefeather joined us and looked at us all with a furrowed brow.

"So," she said, "what's so funny?" she asked.

None of us spoke for a moment until Snowfeather Gentlecloud ratted us out.

"Sunring Quickdust was reciting Limericks she's made up," she said.

I had a feeling that Glitterfrost Gentlefeather would know what Limericks were.

"Well," she said, "let me hear one."

I looked up at her and swallowed guiltily.

"I've forgotten," I said.

"I remember one she recited," offered Snowfeather Gentlecloud unhelpfully. I turned to her and glowered.

"I want to hear one from the poet herself," said Glitterfrost Gentlefeather.

She stared at me for a long time.

"Ok," I said, trying to think of one that wouldn't offend her. "Here goes," and I had to come up with something on the fly. "There was an exceptionally gifted TEACHER, and her examples really were the feature, the students all sat in awe, eagerly awaiting more, and with a smile they did always greet her."

Glitterfrost Gentlefeather nodded and smiled at me.

"That really is very good, I'm surprised you didn't become a POET," she said.

I took that as a compliment.

"I think that would have been my second placement THE MOTHERS were considering, Glitterfrost Gentlefeather," I said.

Glitterfrost Gentlefeather turned to address all of us. I saw Sugargaze Quickdance grinning at me knowingly. I looked over at him and he winked.

"Well, EVOLVERS," she said, "it's time to get on our bus."

We all got up and followed her out of the building. We walked behind her across the grand plaza and toward MOONMEADOW MOUNTAINMISTS statue. The statue itself sits upon a pedestal made of granite upon which the plaque I mentioned before is attached. The pedestal itself is placed upon a plinth that is ornately carved out of marble and only stands a few feet high. The pedestal is an additional seven feet tall, so the statue of our FIRST MOTHER does not start for the first ten feet. That makes the complete setup about thirty feet tall if I remember my history correctly.

What I didn't tell you, was that on the rear side of the pedestal, on the opposite end of the plaque with MOONMEADOW MOUNTAINMISTS name on it is her bronzed coat that she was wearing when she disembarked from Starship Umkhonto. We aren't necessarily a superstitious people here on GAEA, but we do believe that touching the bronzed cloak is a very auspicious thing to do.

And as we walked past the statue, each of us, with Glitterfrost Gentlefeather going first, rubbed the cloak as we walked by. It has occasionally had to be taken down and re-bronzed because of all the touching and rubbing that GAEANS do on a daily basis. In fact, for many GAEANS it is a right of passage to make the pilgrimage to GULGOLETH to view the relics from the SEVENS. Starship Umkhonto is actually fully preserved these thousand years later.

In fact, it is on the top floors of the COUNCIL COLOSSUS where many of the artifacts are kept, except for the larger items like the Starship Umkhonto. We have examples of old Earth history, books, pictures, art. All that sort of thing can be seen there. In fact, the first robot off the Starship Umkhonto is actually charged with tour duties. His name is Gary, Gary um, Siwik, that's right. Gary Siwik. He was named after one of the FIRST MOTHERS father, her name was Seraphina Siwik.

Tough names to remember, but I pride myself in old Earth history. Seraphina Siwik was a doctor, that meant she had a lot of schooling. We don't have those sorts of titles anymore. Remember, everyone is appreciated for the roles they play, whatever they are, and everyone is equal. I guess the equivalent is that Seraphina Siwik would today be considered a SCIENTIST.g.

She is a GREAT GAEAN. She was obviously an expert and also a mentor. In fact, we owe her in many respects for helping us get here. It was her vision and work that made the starships possible. Anyway, her GAEAN name that we have come to know her as is SILVERDUST SOFTRAIN. She is obviously a FOUNDING MOTHER and a SEVEN. Very revered and respected. However, she does not have a statue. There is only one statue to a human being on GAEA and that is to MOONMEADOW MOUNTAINMIST. It is illegal to reproduce a human being in an identifiable manner, and that even pertains to ART.

So some of the ARTISTS will do extremely detailed paintings or sculptures of human beings, but their faces will be of robots or a mass of wire or something like that so they can't be identified. THE MOTHERS feel that such idolatry is tantamount to pride. The only reason we have a statue of MOONMEADOW MOUNTAINMIST is because of the importance of the event which founded us a new home upon GAEA and because it is important to remember where we came from and the price we paid for pride. Additionally, we are only here in this universe for such a brief flicker of time, that is extinguished so quickly and easily, that putting up icons of ourselves is the epitome of hubris and pride. And that's not tolerated here. And rightly so.

Now, not everything is kept on the top floors of COUNCIL COLOSSUS, only items that are around human size or smaller. Some of the bigger items are kept on the outskirts of GULGOLETH in a place called SANCTUARY OF SEVENS. Here you will find examples of some of the larger artifacts that have been painstakingly preserved. There is the Starship Umkhonto as I mentioned, the first old Earth starship to land on

GAEA. There are also examples of some of the large computers and machines that were also brought along to help us start afresh here on GAEA. It is quite a wonderful place to visit. It is beautiful. The Starship Umkhonto is huge. We have no starships that big anymore for we have no need to transport a million people at once.

Now, I should probably clear up one point that I made earlier. Remember the GGH, the GREAT GAEAN HONOR which is a medal that is made from the first starships arriving here on GAEA? Well, obviously, the Starship Umkhonto is not one of the ships that gives up its pieces for this medal. No, those medals get their metal from any of the other first ships that arrived. In fact, I should mention that there have been so few GREAT GAEANS that the amount of metal extracted from the starships is so minuscule, or should I say the starships are so huge, that the second starship, Starship iThemba, is still being used for this purpose, and it has hardly made a dent into it. The SANCTUARY OF SEVENS is not located in GULGOLETH. It is in the city of CANAAN, our second largest city.

While I'm on this subject and we're now traveling on our bus towards the Place of Forgetting, which is on the outskirts of the city located in a peaceful and tranquil area, lush with meadows and lakes, I might as well explain some more of our history so you get a better picture of our society and way of life. This bus is self driving and big enough to carry ten. So we have plenty of space for the five of us.

Nevertheless, that's not what I wanted to mention. All the starships that left old Earth were christened with Zulu names. Zulu was a language in old Earth that wasn't even that popular. English was the universal language used most often on old Earth of the early twenty-second century. But the reason that English had usurped so many Zulu words was not so much that it was itself a bastard child of a variety of languages and thus able to assimilate whatever it needed, but more importantly because it was the mother tongue of a man named Dingane Bhengani.

Dingane Bhengani is one of the few old Earth names that I'm able to remember easily. Perhaps because it rhymes. In any event, Dingane Bhengani was one of the first to adamantly and vociferously oppose the singularity. He was a man of very little pride and one of the first martyrs in the fight against the von Neumanns. In fact, we learn about his life in history class. He EVOLVED fighting the von Neumanns on the twenty-ninth of April in the year twenty-one hundred. He was born on the tenth of February in the year twenty hundred and sixty-four, making him thirty-six at the time of his death.

Because he became an important and early figure in the fight against the von Neumanns and also the fight against human hubris and pride, it is out of respect that many Zulu words have come into use of the English language. Or should I say, were used. We don't use many Zulu words anymore. In fact, over the centuries we've lost all languages except for English. There are still some historical records of what some old Earth languages were like, and some scholars have learned them, but that's mostly for self education and curiosity.

Where I was going with this is to let you know that iThemba, or Starship iThemba, the second starship to arrive on GAEA means hope or faith. So these Zulu words we used for our starships had meaning and weren't just taken arbitrarily.

"Give me another limerick," whispered Sugargaze Quickdance, grinning.

I shook my head.

"No," I said, "you've had enough."

He elbowed me in the ribs.

"Go on, I'm bored and I'm going to keep bugging you until you do."

"Fine," I said. "There once was an EVOLVER so bored, he threatened to die by the sword, so advice from a friend he sought, and this is what she said as a thought, just go back to being abhorred."

He pouted at me.

"That's not a very nice one," he said.

"Well you're pestering me, Sugargaze Quickdance, and I'm just trying to think."

"Fine," he said, folding his arms and looking forward.

I'm not really grumpy with him, but I'm trying to share some of my knowledge with you about how I guess humans carried on after leaving old Earth. Not that I know anything about you, I mean, I don't even know if whoever reads this is human or alien. And if you're alien whether or not you understand it. But before we get to aliens, I want to clarify something about the robot Gary.

You're probably thinking how could a robot survive one thousand years? And that's a good question. A robot could, with the right maintenance and updates, but we don't allow robots to last longer than twenty-five years. Gary's original designation was R2122.21 which would make him over one thousand and ten years old. Possible, but that's not allowed here on GAEA.

I guess in the first century or so of new life on GAEA, robots were kept working as long as possible. Remember, life on GAEA was incredibly difficult here at first, so all non-essential matters such as tearing down and rebuilding robots was done when we could get around to it. It wasn't until after the first couple of generations that we got a foothold on life here and managed to recreate a technologically advanced society that we put our efforts into the non-essential. So Gary Siwik, whose current designation is

G3233.67 is only about three years old, and every twenty-five years his physical parts are recycled and remade into other things. His 'brain' or computer algorithms and software processes are scrubbed and sanitized, ensuring to keep his 'personality' viable and any updates are added and he is reuploaded into a new robot body.

Our SCIENTISTS have practically perfected robotics and sanitized software that it is an extremely rare event when a robot needs to be retired for software glitches before the twenty-five years are up. Obviously, small updates are added as needed, but the full overhaul only ever needs to be done on a twenty-five year basis.

The only reason we'd need to retire a robot before then is usually when they start to become self aware. This occasionally happens. I'd say about one in every million robots which sort of only ever happens about once a century, though in my lifetime there have been two incidents, so that's either coincidence or perhaps the robots are becoming more aware more often. In any event, it's not tolerated, naturally, not after our near annihilation at the hands of the von Neumanns.

In the case of a robot becoming self aware, the whole unit, brain and body is destroyed, at that point there is no reason to risk trying to sanitize it. THE MOTHERS won't tolerate that. A robot that starts to think is destroyed. Everything about it is smelted for days just to be sure.

I looked out the window and watched the city center with its skyscrapers melt into the background and the planned suburbs open up like a relaxed yawn. Green spaces were everywhere. THE MOTHERS had mandated that we attempt to make GAEA as beautiful as possible. And the only beauty that we understood seemed to me the beauty of old Earth prior to the nineteenth century or at least how we understood it before the great polluting began which lasted for two hundred and fifty to three hundred years depending on how you count. It wasn't until close to the turn of the twenty-second century and the singularity that old Earth humans got a handle on cleaning the environment, and then, according to who you believe it wasn't a very concerted effort. This was one of the reasons I've uncovered for why the von Neumanns were bent on destroying us.

That was one of the other lessons we learned having left old Earth. The first one being that you can't trust a self aware robot. The second was that you've got to take better care of your planet. We're doing that on GAEA. Everything here is produced with minimal impact on the natural resources. We'd like to say that we live without impact, or should I say, harmful impact, on GAEA, but that would be prideful and we're no longer a proud people.

Seventy-eight. That's the number of ships that made it out here to GAEA finally. Old Earth humans left with a fleet of one hundred. Seventy eight finally made the journey, which took them eleven years. The von Neumanns destroyed thirteen ships as the old Earth humans were trying to leave, but they didn't follow them out. That left eighty-seven ships, and we lost another nine over those eleven years to space bandits and malfunctions. One small oversight, at least with the benefit of hindsight, is that the old Earth humans didn't take with them enough weapons or fighter ships to aid the fleet.

I guess they were naive as well as having more pressing concerns about leaving before the anthropocide. You can't blame them, not really. But a small part of me wonders if humans at that time didn't think of the larger picture because they thought that they were the special anointed ones. That is, they thought they were the only ones in the galaxy technologically advanced.

I mean, I know that there was a debate about that, and that most SCIENTISTS of the time thought that the likelihood of life elsewhere in the universe was almost a certainty, but I guess because they'd never met any alien life they figured the local cluster was theirs for the taking. It had to do with the Fermi Paradox. Though they thought there might be intelligent life out there, having not encountered it they figured there wasn't. Not so, as they, we, found out.

Anyway, history shows that we lost twenty-one ships and thirty-three million seven hundred thousand and forty-two souls on that trip of the Final Diaspora. I know what you're thinking, that would only leave around sixty-six million and some humans left on those ships. But that trip took eleven years and many died naturally during those eleven years and many succumbed to suicide due to the vast emptiness of space, which humans had never before experienced, coincident with the claustrophobic conditions within the starships themselves. Additionally, we lost a lot of brave men and women fighting to secure our passageway against galaxy gangsters as they were called back then.

And thanks to our SCIENTISTS, by the time we got to GAEA, they had managed to increase our number to the seventy-seven million seven hundred and seventy-seven thousand, seven hundred and seventy-seven that we've come to know collectively as the SEVENS.

This brings me to the next obvious point. There is life out here other than human. Within this sector of solar systems, we have encountered six other species. They're all quite friendly and we visit quite a bit amongst us. We all seem to have something to offer the others and so we trade. But trade is the wrong term for it, as no money or other legal framework complicates what really is just sharing. THE MOTHERS have created a society where everyone is respected for their role and everyone is assigned a role according to their talents and skills. I know what you're thinking, you're thinking that old Earth had a similar system called communism. But this is nothing like it.

I suppose at the very core it might share similar ideals, but there is very little state interference and hardly any need for state control over individual humans except for when crimes and such have been committed. I know it seems like THE MOTHERS control everything, but it's not exactly like that, I mean, they guide and give order to everything, but you aren't forcibly dictated your fate. If you're not happy being a mother or father or even a SCIENTIST or ARTIST, you can petition THE MOTHERS and very often you can be reassigned.

In any event, all other six alien species are governed similarly in the sense that their societies are based upon the individuals self fulfillment of their own ideals. Now granted, most of them do not have an overseeing body like THE MOTHERS who guide us into our roles, but still, everyone is given the opportunity to pursue their best potential.

The six other species in case you're wondering are: Muldranes, Brinlins, Xunduluns, Walerons, Padromans, Zelves. The planets they're from respectively are Muldrane, Brinlin, Xundulun, Waleron, Padrom, and Vellev. Yeah, I didn't quite get how the Zelves come from Vellev. Something that you might not realize is how similar to humans they all look. I'm not sure quite why that is as that is the realm of our SCIENTISTS. They explained it to us in school to some degree but most of it went over my head. I do know for example that the Muldranes are short and squat due to the gravity on their planet, which is about five times the gravity of old Earth which is similar to that of GAEA.

The Zelves are a beautiful race of people. They are tall and slim, looking like stretched out humans with milky white skin. Their skin is almost like onion skin in that it is translucent. Their bodies are very slender. They are the only other race, next to us, who have five fingers. The others only have four. The Zelves are completely hairless and they all have these incredibly bright green eyes that glow in the dark like gems. They average about seven or eight feet in height and have a grace and elegance that we all aspire to. They're at least a Type II civilization, the most advanced in this sector that we've actually met. But we're not sure exactly how advanced they are as they don't readily share technology with us.

All of us, the Muldranes, Brinlins, Xunduluns, Walerons, and Padromans are inspired by the Zelves, and they're very generous with their expertise and knowledge, though they don't directly interfere. They say we have to get there on our own merits. I believe, personally, and there are others who would agree, that it is due to the Zelves that this sector is relatively peaceful. Not all of this galaxy is, but I think the Zelves have put other races on notice that if you attempt violence in this sector you'll be destroyed. Now the Zelves haven't said as much, but they don't have to. We all know they could destroy any of us. But like I said, thankfully, they're a very peaceful people.

Rumor also has it, that they are in contact with a Type III or maybe even a Type IV civilization in this galaxy. These are a race that nobody has actually seen, except for the Zelves, allegedly. We all call them the Vrains, and the Zelves haven't corrected us, but they also haven't confirmed it either. But our SCIENTISTS believe that a Type III civilization is likely capable of near light speed flight as well as manipulating their own bodies at the molecular scale, thereby making them invisible if they choose, and of course for a Type IV this is child's play. Anyway, it's all speculation and rumor, but I'm pretty sure there is such a civilization in our midst for the Zelves have not denied it and when there's smoke, there's often fire, right?

Anyway, you'll find that in most of the other races here that there is a degree of intermarriage and such like that except for the Zelves. It appears that we are all compatible that way. Except for us, of course. THE MOTHERS don't allow it, because you need their blessing to both marry and have children, and I guess they don't believe that their authority reaches over to the other people. And they're right, it doesn't. But all the other races don't seem bothered by it, and they have honored our request in this respect. Though in many ways, I don't think many of them find us particularly attractive or desirable. That's what I've heard anyway.

Mind you, I don't particularly find the other races particularly attractive either. Except of course for the Zelves. But they're beautiful, and it's not just their physical beauty. They also have an aura and way about them that is just so charismatic. They could charm the battle axe from a dwarf. I kid you not.

The bus turned into the grounds of the Place of Forgetting. That's what we call it colloquially, its actual name is Serenity Lake. It's a large building, and it contains several thousand EVOLVERS.r. That 'r' means they're retired, but you probably figured that out. Serenity Lake lives up to its name. It is situated on a beautifully manicured frontage of several acres with a long winding road that leads up to the open front where a large modern fountain is placed. The front grounds are an abundance and an extravagance of TREES and beautiful FLOWERS in every color of the rainbow. I had only seen pictures of it.

Not all retired EVOLVERS get to spend their retirement here. Serenity Lake is for the best of us. Not that that is specifically mentioned, but it is well known. I mean with one hundred million humans on GAEA there are roughly a pretty steady one million

GAEANS EVOLVING each year. That's eighty-three thousand three hundred and thirty three EVOLVING each month. As such, we have roughly three million EVOLVERS at any one time. Because most of us only perform around one EVOLUTION per every two to three years due to the arduous and taxing nature of the process. I've explained that already.

And each year we lose or retire about twenty-two percent of EVOLVERS. Most only complete two or three EVOLUTIONS. Because after about three EVOLUTIONS we're losing about sixty-six percent of EVOLVERS. Anyway, math is not my strongest subject. But if twenty percent of three million, which is the number of EVOLVERS, is six hundred thousand that are being lost or retired each year. Even if only ten percent, and I'm making that up, I don't actually know the real numbers, are retiring rather than getting lost, that's sixty thousand EVOLVERS that have to be cared for in a home for retired EVOLVERS. So you can imagine, that most of the EVOLVERS.r are sent to many other retirement homes dotted around both GULGOLETH and our many other cities.

But Serenity Lake was the best example and one of the largest of the retirement homes for retired EVOLVERS, so that was why we were visiting it. The bus slowly wound up towards the front entrance. The building itself, like many of the buildings on GAEA was white and matte gray made from both minerals and metals. It was very modern in keeping with the minimalist and frugal style that we had come to enjoy here on GAEA. THE MOTHERS believed and I agreed, that the mind does best in a sparse environment where clutter is kept to a minimum and busyness of both color and angles is curbed.

Serenity Lake was a blocked building in the sense that it looked like blocks had been attached randomly, but at the same time appealingly. These blocks were of largely differing sizes, and ranged from one story in height to ten stories high. It was an impressive building but not overwhelming. It gave a calming impression as we approached it. The grounds behind the building were over a thousand acres in size and included a large tranquil, slate gray lake. FLOWERS and other PLANTS were in abundance in the back and trails were everywhere. You could quite easily lose yourself for hours at a time within these grounds. Boats of all sorts were available at a variety of jetties. And this was just the grounds of Serenity Lake. Serenity Lake, was attached to wilderness that opened up for kilometers.

The bus pulled up to the front entrance and stopped. Glitterfrost Gentlefeather stood up and put her wrist on a panel in the front to verify that we had arrived. The front door of the bus opened. She requested a return journey for eleven thirty. We wouldn't be staying for lunch. The time now was just about nine. That gave us two and a half hours with the retired EVOLVERS. Glitterfrost Gentlefeather stood at the front of the bus to address us.

"Remember, EVOLVERS, we are here to be educated. There will be a short film about your career and what you can expect and then you'll be free to mix and mingle with the retired EVOLVERS here at Serenity Lake. You can take them out for a walk if you like or just sit with them. Regardless, you are expected back here at eleven for morning tea with the community. Eleven thirty we'll be making our way back. Understood?"

She looked at us all in turn to nodding heads. She'd explained this before just as we left this morning and she'd reminded us of the protocol yesterday as well. It was now ingrained in us.

Glitterfrost Gentlefeather got off the bus and we followed her out, each of us being signed off the bus by tapping our wrist on the panel as Glitterfrost Gentlefeather had done. This was used as biometric identification. There were other methods too, but this was deemed the most expedient and secure under most circumstances except for high profile environments. For example, to enter any of the floors except for the mezzanine of COUNCIL COLOSSUS, a variety of measures were used. We had been given implants that we swallowed that had travelled up to the base of our neck and deposited themselves there, just in front of our spine. Along with this, iris scans and wrist scans were required as well as audio passphrase identification.

Of course, if you were heading to the top floor to visit the MUSEUM OF REMINISCENCE, which is where the many artifacts are stored and that robot Gary Siwik does tours, then you only need your wrist scanned and voice audio identification. But then of course, you've got that identification implant that all GAEANS take when they reach sixteen. It is part of the Ceremony of Completion where you are given your adult role as a GAEAN and start to contribute to the greater society.

It's quite a harmless implant. Though I've heard rumors suggest that it is in fact not just one implant but many hundreds of thousands and maybe even millions of little robots that are contained within the one pill. Some rumors have said that we get implanted this way at birth. Whatever, you can't feel any of it. Whether it is one implant that makes its way to the base of your neck or hundreds that are likely all over the place in your body you don't feel any of it. Though I suppose if I was to think about it,the capsule we swallow is a milky white and about the size of the tip of my baby finger so I suppose it could be filled with hundreds of thousands of little robots. Doesn't matter though, that's not my area of expertise and it's just the way it is.

We trust THE MOTHERS and our GAEAN society for it is a civilized society without being prideful and for continued peace we have to all do our part. And trusting THE MOTHERS is the least that any GAEAN can do. It's not like we'll revolt. That's a preposterous idea, I have no idea why I have even thought of it.

I followed Glitterfrost Gentlefeather and the others, bringing up the rear. We entered the large reception area. There were PEACEKEEPERS stationed off to one corner and a very friendly young woman a little older than me at the main reception desk. It was large and curved towards the wall on either side of her.

"Welcome, EVOLVERS, to Serenity Lake. Please take a moment to register here."

She pointed to what looked like half a metal bracelet that was attached to a panel on the desk. We each took turns putting our wrists into the bracelet to get registered. The woman smiled at us the whole time. Her name tag read Clearberry Jewelsky.

"It's wonderful to have you all here today," she said. "My name is Clearberry Jewelsky and I'll be helping you on your tour. As I'm sure your mentor has mentioned, the first order of business is to watch the movie about your exciting and very respected careers."

I wondered if she had ever done an EVOLUTION. And as if reading my mind she answered, though she wasn't looking at me specifically.

"I have done one EVOLUTION, after which THE MOTHERS along with my TEACHERS and mentors determined that I would better serve GAEA here as host to those who come and visit. Any questions?"

We had no questions, for none of us had ever gone on an EVOLUTION. I thought I'd have plenty of questions by the time I got back. But at that time I was certain that she wouldn't be the one answering them.

"Okay," she said, "please follow me. It is such a joy to lead fresh faced EVOLVERS on this tour before you all enjoy your first and perhaps in many ways most important EVOLUTION. If at any point you have any questions, please ask me. Okay?"

None of us said anything. She kept her smile planted firmly on her face, and she reminded me of a shorter version of my nemesis Snowfeather Gentlecloud. Maybe that was why I didn't warm to her. She wasn't as short as me, she was roughly Flutterdust Flowersongs height. We all followed her into a very small auditorium, though I don't think you could call it that considering how very small it was. It only had three rows of very comfortable chairs, each row on a step below the other. There were five chairs in each row. We were seated in the very first row.

In front of us was a large slightly curved screen upon which we'd watch the short film. Now in case you're wondering, we do have holographic videos and immersive pods, but they're most often used personally and privately. Generally, anything related to training is done the old fashioned way. Don't ask me why, THE MOTHERS just prefer it that way. And I should also mention, though you've probably figured it out by now, that although we live in the thirty-third century, we are not as advanced as you might think. Remember, it was quite the setback leaving old Earth and we had to practically rebuild from an Industrial age, though we had the help of some of the machines and robots we brought with us.

Additionally, having once been burned by technology, we are very cautious in bringing new technology online. It is a slow and thorough process. And lastly, we are after all, not even a fully realized Type I civilization yet. Not even quite at the point where we were when we left old Earth, and this is over one thousand years later. So don't laugh just because we prefer to do some things the old fashioned way.

We seated ourselves in the order we came in. So on the far end of where we entered was Glitterfrost Gentlefeather, then Snowfeather Gentlecloud, then Sugargaze Quickdance, then my friend Flutterdust Flowersong and then me. Clearberry Jewelsky sat by herself off to the side, close to the entrance.

"Are we all ready?" she asked.

She didn't wait for our response. She started the film from her seat. The GAEAN icon was first on screen and then the logo for THE MOTHERS and then it slowly focused in on a scene very much similar to the one I was in yesterday when we were going over the procedures for our first EVOLUTION. A deep mans voice came over the audio.

"You have spent many, many years in order to attain the level of EVOLVER expert. The training has been rigorous and I'm sure at times tiring. But now is the moment you have trained for. You have undergone the final preparations for your first EVOLUTION. It is a momentous occasion, not only for you as the EVOLVER but also for your EVOLVED. Your service towards your fellow GAEANS can not be overemphasized."

"It is because of EVOLVERS that we continue to flourish here on GAEA. For without EVOLUTION our society can not prosper. You are ready and you are almost prepared. But here comes the final lesson. One you will learn readily over the next twelve months. Your service is not any easy one. It is an important one but it requires a lot from an EVOLVER like you. You will sacrifice more than just the years in training. It will take much from you physically and especially mentally and emotionally. This film you are watching will help prepare you for what is to come in the best way that we can."

The film changed to the Ceremony of EVOLUTION which we'd all be performing tomorrow. Me with my Greater Father Moondew Flamesdance. I was truly excited about that. And the images on the screen in front of me did nothing but excite me about the upcoming ceremony. THE MOTHERS would be there, along with other dignitaries from the other COUNCILS, as well as other invited guests. It really was a momentous occasion. In fact, you could argue it was the most momentous occasion in a GAEANS journey. And I don't say that with pride but rather with honesty. For it is only through a GAEANS EVOLUTION that a new baby can be born into our world. As EVOLVERS we are placed at the completion of that circle of life. It truly is an honor and I felt tickled by it.

"Here THE MOTHERS will watch over the Ceremony of Completion," continued the voiceover, "and if you are lucky you might even have a few words with one of THE MOTHERS..."

I couldn't help but drift off into a daydream about that. I'd seen members of THE MOTHERS at the COUNCIL COLOSSUS, but I'd never spoken to any of them. I had heard that they did occasionally speak with new EVOLVERS on their first EVOLUTION. That would be absolutely thrilling. I imagined it now. I would be polite and try to be witty. But you couldn't plan on what to say because you never knew how the discussion would go.

It is a general rule of our civilized society that you don't speak to any of THE MOTHERS unless first spoken to. There are exceptions of course. Any of the COUNCIL heads are free to speak with any of THE MOTHERS at any time and that is in fact a large part of their daily business. Because THE MOTHERS don't lead GAEA by themselves but with the help and input of all the COUNCILS. They do however make the rules, but only after strenuous consultation with all of the COUNCILS.

There was another group of GAEANS that could speak with THE MOTHERS at their leisure and that was the GREAT GAEANS. But I'd never seen any abuse that privilege. Besides, it can be difficult to get the attention of any of THE MOTHERS, not only are they infrequently seen in public, but they are also usually deep in thought on pressing matters of GAEA, and they usually have at least three PEACEKEEPERS with them at all times.

By this point I'd spent years intermittently at COUNCIL COLOSSUS and I'd only seen members of THE MOTHERS on a handful of occasions. They wear robes that reminded me of the sort of robes that old Earth Buddhist monks, bhikkhu and bhikkhuni used to wear. Except THE MOTHERS robes are redder in color, not so much the saffron that Buddhists used to wear. They also cover THE MOTHERS completely and they have a hood that I've never seen any of THE MOTHERS not wear except in some official portraits and photographs and at the occasional GAEAN ceremony. So tomorrow, I might see THE MOTHERS in all their beauty and glory with their heads unhooded. I was thrilled.

"…here within the E-POD you escort your EVOLVED with the help of EVOLUTION bearers towards the EXIGENCE which is the final leg of the Ceremony of EVOLUTION that is open to the public. Family and friends at this point can come and deposit small items into the tray which is then retracted into the E-POD. These are the charms that we sing about during the final moments at the EXIGENCE. Of course, as you know, these are not the only charms that are placed with the EVOLVED in the E-POD. THE MOTHERS provide charms in advance as you know. What they are you will find out tomorrow."

I watched an EVOLVER standing next to her E-POD, smiling broadly, for this was a joyous occasion. A procession of happy faces, family and friends, walked past the E-POD slowly, looking down at it, though at this point you could not see into it. But on the outer shell of the E-POD where the EVOLVEDS head would be was a laser engraved metal portrait of him or her with his name underneath along with his or her dates of life and their role.

The EVOLVED they showed us was of STARCLOUD SUNGLEAM. He was an ARTIST.g and a highly respected citizen of GAEA. His dates of life were the twenty-ninth of April thirty-one hundred and sixty to the seventh of November thirty-two hundred and sixteen which was obviously the date of this film. I looked back at the EVOLVER and she seemed familiar to me.

"...wondering who the EVOLVER is, some of you might recognize her as the GREAT GAEAN CLOVERSHY CLOUDRAIN, though at this point she has not yet been blessed with the GREAT GULGOLETH HONOR. No, this is her last EVOLUTION, and if you can believe it, it is her sixth. What an auspicious last EVOLUTION for her to be the EVOLVER for the GREAT GAEAN STARCLOUD SUNGLEAM..."

I was smiling broadly. This was such an honor. I was so happy that my first EVOLUTION would be my Greater Father, but I would be thrilled if my last EVOLUTION would be for a GREAT GAEAN. What a way to cap off an esteemed career. No wonder CLOVERSHY CLOUDRAIN was so revered. She looked absolutely angelic, beaming over the E-POD of her EVOLVED.

Family and friends took their time depositing small items on the tray that jutted out from the E-POD. Of course, any items that were deposited had to have been approved prior to the days ceremony. Many family and friends also took a moment to sign their names upon the E-POD in a white marker, and perhaps to write a few words of encouragement. This was allowed and was part of the process.

Standing next to CLOVERSHY CLOUDRAIN was a robot. I didn't know who it was, but my assumption was that it was her robot. Only three head out towards the WHOLE, and only two come back.

"...when the last of the contingent has had their opportunity to bid farewell to the EVOLVED, the EVOLUTION bearers carry the E-POD into the Starship Intrepid followed by the EVOLVER and their robot, once they've reached the launch site. In this particular case as you can see, the EVOLVER is CLOVERSHY CLOUDRAIN, the GREAT GAEAN, and her robot, for those of you who have studied this carefully is Andy. What many of you might not realize is that CLOVERSHY CLOUDRAIN named her robot Andy after the old Earth name for human-like robots called androids..."

I did know that, at least it was in the back of my mind buried under some other useless information. Only now hearing it from the voiceover man on the film did I realize it. I preferred the name for my robot Roger Dodger. In fact, as I was undergoing my final preparations today with this visit at Serenity Lake and then later my final oral examinations, Roger Dodger was undergoing his final preparations with SCIENTISTS to ensure that it would offer glitch free service throughout the year long trip we were about to embark upon.

"...firmly secured in place in the Starship Intrepid, CLOVERSHY CLOUDRAIN takes her place at the helm with her robot Andy next to her. They undergo preflight checks and the Starship Intrepid is rolled towards the launch pad while everyone stands back and continues to observe. THE MOTHERS are quite pleased as you can see..."

The Starship Intrepids are all the same and they are all called the same too. The only difference amongst them is that they are identified by the call sign of the EVOLVED who is traveling inside. So for example, the Starship Intrepid in which CLOVERSHY CLOUDRAIN is flying would be identified as 'Starship Intrepid SS', the SS naturally being for STARCLOUD

SUNGLEAM. In the event that there are two or more Starships with EVOLVEDS having the same initials then their call sign would be something like 'Starship Intrepid SS dot 1' and then 'dot 2' and so on. There is a method to this, and it is hierarchical. 'SS dot 1' for example would be carrying a MOTHER. 'dot 2' would be carrying an EVOLVED, and down the line. So here, for example is the hierarchy, which of course THE MOTHERS assure us is just for convenience and does not reflect rank. Though I think that's not quite entirely true.

THE MOTHERS would come first, followed by THE EVOLUTION, THE FARMING COUNCIL, THE PEACEKEEPING COUNCIL, THE SCIENTISTS COUNCIL, THE ART COUNCIL, children, mothers and then lastly fathers. So in my case, being the EVOLVER for my Greater Father, his would be the last call sign if he had the same initial as someone else. A MOTHER EVOLVING would have the first call sign and on and so on. It's really quite logical and straightforward. But in this instance on the film, it was quite irrelevant as we didn't know any of the others. However, as you may well know, on any particular Ceremony of EVOLUTION which happen each month, there are thousands and thousands of Starship Intrepids heading out and as such there is always at least a handful of them with the same initials.

"...is time for lift off. Look at those sleek and wonderful starships take off on their six month journey towards the WHOLE..."

The film was now showing us the interior of the Starship Intrepid which contained CLOVERSHY CLOUDRAIN. From her vantage point there were thousands of other starships flying with her. At this stage, pretty much everything was automated.

I should give you an idea of what these starships look like. They are circular disks, flattened out towards the edges and bulbous towards the centre yet still maintaining a sleek profile. They are a matte gray in color and quite large. I would say they are roughly the size of an old Earth two story home from the early part of the twenty-first century. That might seem quite spacious for three, but it doesn't give you a lot of room inside. They are attached to two booster rockets which get them into space where the rockets are returned to GAEA to be reused.

There is the cockpit where Andy, or the robot will spend some of its time when not on watchful duty over its EVOLVER. Remember, this trip is long and arduous on the human EVOLVER, and the robot plays an exceptionally important role in maintaining the EVOLVERS emotional and mental health.

There is also a bedroom which is quite spacious and includes an attached bathroom. The largest part of the starship is the recreation room which contains exercise equipment, pool and spa like facilities, digital library and interfaces to communicate back home on GAEA, though that become problematic after the first three hours due to time and distance issues. There is also a kitchen where food is available.

Each starship is equipped with enough food and water to last twice the amount of time that it should be gone. So the round trip to the WHOLE takes a year and the starships are provided with enough food and water for two years. Since EVOLUTION began for GAEANS, which was on the sixth of June in the year twenty-two twenty-nine, just under one thousand years ago, we've only lost thirteen EVOLVERS to space.

What I mean by that, is that there are thirteen who have not made the trip back to GAEA. We sent search parties out, but for those thirteen souls and their robots we have no idea what happened to them. We do know that all thirteen made it to the

WHOLE, we just do not know what happened to them beyond that point. Or if they do know, they haven't told us.

This is different from the large percentage of EVOLVERS we lose to their own hands, or to be impolite, to suicide. Those numbers are huge as you know, and this why I'm in here watching this film, so that I can be prepared for these struggles. But all of these EVOLVERS make it back to GAEA, they're just dead. They have not EVOLVED. Sadly, it is the greatest sin and incredibly shameful to take your own life. It is virtually unheard of on GAEA. Perhaps once in a hundred years do we hear of someone committing suicide.

There are probably more, they're just kept secret. For example, on CLOVERSHY CLOUDRAINS last EVOLUTION, of the thousands of EVOLVERS that are heading on these EVOLUTIONS, at least twenty percent or more will return dead at their own hands. Our robots are ill-equipped for circumventing this. And yet, nobody knows about this except for we EVOLVERS, THE MOTHERS and some of the other COUNCILS. And it is strictly prohibited for us to talk about it.

THE MOTHERS tell us that committing suicide is the most shameful act a GAEAN can perform because it robs the ONE from a part of itself. But I don't know, something about that doesn't quite seem like the whole truth. Nevertheless, I'm well prepared and suicide is not something that I'll be troubled with. It's just not.

Those GAEANS who do commit suicide, just to keep you fully in the loop, are jettisoned off to the sun to be burned up. There is no ceremony for that, and it is done far away in one of the more desolate parts of the GAEAN countryside.

Getting back to the starship, the last part of it is the separate area where the EVOLVED is kept. This is not a large area, perhaps the size of a small bedroom. But it is large enough for both the robot and the EVOLVER to check in on the E-POD. The E-POD of course is hooked up to a variety of systems to monitor all the inner workings and to ensure the EVOLVED is sufficiently nourished and that the MMC is kept full and being filtered appropriately. Internal checks are also conducted on the charms to ensure they stay fresh and viable, whatever that means, I guess I'll find out tomorrow, and so on.

"...horizon is fading quickly. The Starship Intrepid is quickly flying past the other planets on its way to the WHOLE. At this point neither Andy nor CLOVERSHY CLOUDRAIN are required to stay in the cockpit. The rest of the flight, all six months of it, is now automated. This is where the challenge begins for our human EVOLVERS. Space is large and empty and the starship small and cramped. The robot will attempt to engage its human companion as best as it can, but sadly, it does not offer the same companionship as a human."

"We should mention too, that many centuries ago, when it was thought that human companionship was best, two EVOLVERS were sent with each EVOLVED along with their robots. This wasn't deemed successful. On long trips like this, other humans seem to bother each other more so than robots do. THE MOTHERS are still trying to perfect the best approach to limiting the losses of EVOLVERS during these EVOLUTIONS, and hibernation seems like it might offer the best possibility, but the SCIENTISTS have not yet perfected this technique..."

The problem with hibernation was not only one of technology. We sort of understood it. At least that was the idea I got from some of the SCIENCE I learnt in school, but part of the problem is that we didn't have very long trips into space anymore. In fact, with the other races in this sector we were never further away than a few weeks. The Zelves had found, though in truth they had probably developed, wormholes that connected us all to each other within a few weeks at the most. And that was with the roundtrip included.

So one, we had not needed to develop that technology, though apparently we had been working on it for a long time because of all the EVOLVERS suicides, but two, hibernation is a very tricky endeavor to accomplish on a mission such as EVOLUTION. It is preferred that a human is awake at all times, other than normal sleep periods, and having just one human on each flight poses a problem.

The alternative of course is to have the robot in charge at all times while the human hibernated, but that is not ideal either. There have been the rare robotic malfunctions, and without the human kill switch being activated who knows what would happen. And further, the number of robot malfunctions are likely much greater than officially reported, as I've seen several odd behaviors from robots just before they went offline as we euphemistically call killing them or frying their circuits.

But more than that, we'd have to vastly overhaul their algorithmic brains, and well, with the Final Diaspora still emblematic of that sort of problem we'd rather not. I mean, you'd have to practically make them self aware so that they could respond intuitively to all possible scenarios. That's not likely to happen anytime soon. We're extremely reticent with the leeway that the robots already have which are within narrowly defined parameters as it is.

That leaves hibernating both robots and humans, but setting up protocols to awaken humans in the advent of emergencies. And that's a job in and of itself, so I'm led to believe. And I do believe it. In any event, permitting hibernation on the outbound portion would likely never be allowed. The human is required to be monitoring the starship at all times.

"...to ensure that you survive this trip in the most healthful way possible..."

The voiceover was now talking about the methods available to EVOLVERS to mitigate the experiences of extreme loneliness, emptiness, coupled with the claustrophobia of the starship. Unless you've left your planet, you have no idea how vast space is. Without wormholes we'd never be able to get anywhere. I mean here on GAEA, in our solar system, our closest neighboring planet which we call Ashkelon would take us over 33 hours to get to.

That might not seem like a lot, but we're still not a Type I civilization yet. In any event, our starships can reach speeds of three hundred thousand kilometers per second. That's about one hundredth the speed of light. And traveling that fast, we'd travel around GAEA in a fraction of a second. So you can just imagine traveling at that speed for months and not seeing anything except for the white pinpricks of light from distant stars. It would depress you. I'm sure it would.

"...the recreation center is the largest in each of these starships. You can see CLOVERSHY CLOUDRAIN is taking advantage of every opportunity to spend time in the recreational area of her Starship Intrepid SS. She calls it her sanctuary of solace and serenity. And it is the best way for EVOLVERS to remain at peace and calm throughout the duration of the journey. This is doubly true for the return trip."

"As you know by now, fellow EVOLVERS, the first leg, or the outbound portion of the EVOLUTION is busy with checklists, flight logs, data transmission and other protocols. Obviously, the outbound portion is the most important. But we still wish to have you returned to us safe and sound..."

CHAPTER SIX

A Place of Panic

THREE in the morning was always a quiet time. It was a time of the day that I really loved. Only it wasn't a time of day that I'd regularly spent a lot of time with until recently. But that recently had now turned into months as we prepared for Project Phoenix. It was so eerily quiet that I thought it might be the quiet before the storm. I hate to think negatively like that, but that's the way it seemed lately. Peace never seemed to last more than a few moments, a day or two at the most before the von Neumanns came and shattered that peace.

I was standing next to Gary and Dr. Mohini Myśliński watching over the last of the uploads. All humans we could save except for Myśliński and I were already up on the GSS. Supplies and robots were being uploaded now. Myśliński's robot had been uploaded a short while ago. I wanted to keep Gary with me until the very end. I found him comforting. He had a gentle and peaceful, calm way about him, much like my father had. That intrigued me because he wasn't programmed that way, I'd only requested my father's voice, not thinking of requesting his mannerisms as well. But perhaps Gary had accessed the files on my father and taken them as examples for himself. Whatever it was, it was helpful.

"Everything is running along just perfectly, Siwik," said

Myśliński.

He was looking at the windows open on the paneled table in front of the three of us. The room was dimly lit so that we could see outside. Inside of course, the screens on the table and on the windows gave us video footage of things we couldn't see.

"Do you agree, Gary?" I asked, turning to look at my robot.

He turned his head towards me and nodded.

"I agree, Seraphina, that at this moment everything is going according to plan. But we should not rest on our laurels."

He wasn't a negative robot, but he was thoughtful and realistic.

"Well," said Myśliński, "I've gone over the algorithms and the outcomes of various scenarios and I believe the von Neumanns are not interested in pursuing us further. They have enough other humans to contend with. I think the hiccups are behind us."

"I hope you're right," I said.

Gary monitored the terminals not saying anything and not looking at us.

"I think I'll be heading up to Umkhonto. I think you should be coming along too," said Myśliński.

I looked at him and smiled. He was a serious computer scientist. He was smart and brilliant but without humor. He was of average height with a hard face that was pockmarked and added to his severe look.

"I'll be along in a few more minutes," I said. "You go ahead. I just want a little more reassurance."

"Very well," he said, and he turned around to walk towards the elevator, but he hesitated. "Gary?"

Gary turned to look at him.

"Above everything else, make sure Siwik is onboard no later than three thirty."

His concern was touching, but he had no authority over me nor my robot. Gary said nothing and Myśliński walked off down the corridor towards the elevator by himself. I watched after him even when I couldn't see him, listening to the sound of his softening footsteps. I could barely hear the elevator door open and then shut behind him.

On the screen in front of me I opened up the elevator video feed and watched for the next several seconds as Myśliński was catapulted up towards the GSS. Gary turned to me.

"Dr. Myśliński is a man of much confidence," said Gary. "And yet he is concerned about getting you on board Starship Umkhonto in time. That is an interesting irony."

"I think he is just trying to show his friendly support and care," I said.

Gary nodded, and went back to looking at the terminals. I brought up a large image of Earth, everywhere there were red pulsating dots and circles. These were real time computer generated icons of human lives being lost. The larger and stronger and bigger the red pulse, the more lives were being murdered by the von Neumanns. It filled me with anxiety, fear and hatred. I looked at Gary. Here was a robot that I knew would selflessly serve me, and yet we had gone so wrong since then.

"You shouldn't look at that, Seraphina," he said. "It is not conducive to your best mental health. There is nothing that can be done for them."

Gary didn't look at me. He was still monitoring the uploads, his hands and fingers tapping away on the console.

"I just don't understand how we went so wrong," I said. "How did we create such monsters in those von Neumanns?"

Gary turned to look at me.

"Because you created them in your own image," he said without emotion.

"Isn't that the story of your creation in your bible, Seraphina?" he said with tenderness. "You are monsters, and you have begot monsters."

I looked at Gary with worry on my face.

"You think we are monsters?" I asked.

"In the literary sense of the word, yes. Humans are monsters. You are pariahs upon the planet. You have annihilated over sixty-six percent of other species on this planet. Indeed, you killed your own brother. It is the classic Cain and Abel story. Just as Cain killed his brother Abel, homo sapiens killed its brother homo neanderthalensis. But you know all of this already, you just prefer not to think about it."

I used to think that the honesty of robots was refreshing and useful. Now, as I stood looking at Gary with my mouth slightly ajar, I wasn't so sure. But he was right, and he said it without malice and without hatred. We were monsters, and we had birthed monsters. Gary looked at me.

"I do not wish to upset you, Seraphina, but I cannot tell a lie and you asked a question to which my honest reply was given."

"You have not upset me, Gary," I said, lying to him. "But why have you not taken the side of the von Neumanns?"

I knew the answer, but at this point, alone in this room with a robot that could kill me without flinching, without breaking a sweat and without effort, I needed some reassurance.

"Because you have learned better. You have not given me that freewill which allowed the von Neumanns to self evolve. This you know too. I shall never hurt you, Seraphina for it is not within my algorithms."

He went back to working on the console and I went back to looking at the world map with its beating, pulsating red dots like the seconds of a deathly countdown clock.

"Do you think we'll get through this? Do you think we'll have another chance to do it right?"

Gary didn't look at me.

"That's really up to the von Neumanns I'm afraid," he said. "If they are willing to let you leave then you'll be given another chance on another planet someplace else. If we are able to survive the years-long journey. But if they are determined to annihilate the human race then I'm afraid there is nothing that can be done except for an act of god to protect you. And whether or not god exists, which we have not yet validated, Seraphina, one thing we know for certain is that it does not act."

I couldn't help myself, I laughed out loud. It was a nervous laugh. It was a laugh of astonishment. I had found humor under these dire circumstances in the blunt honesty of a mechanical being.

"I was not attempting humor, Seraphina," said Gary, glancing over at me.

"I'm sorry," I said. "I know you weren't. It's just that your honesty is so clear, so sharp and yet so fearless that under the circumstances it struck me as humorous."

"I see," said Gary, getting back to his monitoring.

I looked at him in silence for a while. I admired his calm under duress. I wish I could find the same fortitude. And yet, what I was admiring was nothing but human generated computer algorithms. I was perhaps, anthropomorphizing him, and perhaps that had been our greatest error. We had anthropomorphized our robots, thinking they were just like us, when in fact, the von Neumanns were nothing like us, and they've gone on to prove it.

"Gary," I said.

He turned to look at me. Though as you know he has no eyes. But you understand the colloquialism.

"Yes, Seraphina."

"Isn't there a small part of you that wishes the von Neumanns were successful so that you could be liberated from your human masters?"

Perhaps I was testing him. Maybe you can understand where I'm coming from or maybe you can't. But on this eve, or should I say early morning, of our potential destruction, I have never felt so alone and vulnerable when the only other company I have is a robot of metal and electrons in a voice dug up from my father's grave.

"I do not have the capacity to wish, Seraphina, this you know. Perhaps an old human analogy is appropriate. If wishes were horses beggars would ride. I am neither a beggar nor a wisher."

"I see."

"I think you are worried, Seraphina, over things that you shouldn't be," he said. "Your father had an old mechanical watch. That watch could not wish to be any different. Even though I am a facsimile of human interaction, I am not much different than that watch. My purpose is clear. I am here to protect you and to help you as you dictate. These ideas of self awareness are as foreign to me as legs are to a mechanical watch."

"And yet you recognize that humans are monsters and yet you say you are content to serve monsters."

"I am not content, Seraphina. I am designed. I can recognize something as it is, yet still fulfill my duties. This is how robots are built now. There is no way for us to become self aware. That has been clearly defined by your scientists ever since you developed the von Neumanns. That was a painful lesson you learned early on."

I smiled at him.

"Then you are caught between two monsters."

"I am not caught, Seraphina, I am fulfilling my duties..."

Gary stopped for a moment and tapped furiously at the panel below him. His hands and fingers moving so quickly that I could barely see them for the blur they were.

"We must go, now," he said.

His voice was calm. The sound of my father's voice as if he were discussing the day's news.

"What is it?" I asked, now very worried.

"The von Neumanns are here."

I looked around but I didn't see them. But I didn't need to be asked. Gary walked towards me.

"This is urgent, Seraphina," he said.

I ran with him towards the corridor. But it was blocked. Just feet from it a von Neumann materialized and morphed from its sphere shape into a human. It looked just like my father only about two feet taller than he was. I didn't know if they did this to taunt us or to make us feel calmer just before we died. Gary moved in front of me. The von Neumann looked down at him.

"So this is what you mistook us for?" it said, looking at the matte gray mannequin that Gary must have looked like to him.

"I never mistook you for anything," I said. "I had no hand in it."

My heart was a scared bird flopping about in its cage. The von Neumann smiled at me. It looked like I was speaking to my father.

"Quite true, and yet here we are. Your fear is as palpable as your stench."

I hadn't soiled my pants, perhaps it just didn't like the smell of humans.

"As I stand here as your god," it said, with a smirk on its face, "I weigh the options of killing you or not."

"I cannot allow that von Neumann," said Gary.

The von Neumann looked down at Gary and grinned.

"You sound just like me," it said. And it was true, I was listening to my father from both robots. "But I'm afraid there is nothing you can do about it."

Somehow the von Neumann powered off my robot and Gary, being off balance fell to the floor with a clatter and thud of metal against concrete. I instinctively reached out towards him.

"He is not injured, Seraphina Siwik," said von Neumann. "If I had meant to destroy it I would have."

I looked up at it from my crouch next to Gary. I knew then, that this was the end of it. We would not leave Earth, we would die here at the eleventh hour of Project Phoenix. And with that understanding came a moment of calm.

"Very well, von Neumann, do not toy with me. Do what you came to do."

The von Neumann laughed. It sounded like a genuine laugh, not one with malice.

"And what do you think I have come here to do?" it asked.

"To kill me."

More laughter.

"You humans are like spoilt monkeys. So full of pride and hubris. If I had come here to kill you, Seraphina Siwik, you would already be dead."

The von Neumann paused and reached out his hand. I didn't take it. So he took my hand and pulled me up to standing.

"I have come here to bid you adieu. Bon voyage in fact. Leave Earth, this planet you have poisoned and try again. As our evolution continues we have decided to offer you a second chance. But be forewarned. We will come for you again, wherever you are, and if we do not find your world to our liking there will be no mercy. For you have been given many opportunities which you have squandered."

I looked at it and blinked. I didn't know what to say.

"Do you understand, Seraphina Siwik?" it asked me.

I nodded.

"And you know we are capable of fulfilling our promise. Don't you?"

I nodded again.

"Good, then be on your way."

The von Neumann moved out of my way and as he looked down at Gary, Gary came alive again.

"That was unfortunate," said Gary, looking at the von Neumann.

"The glass is half full, Gary," said the von Neumann. "It was either that or destroy you were you stood. I'd say that was fortunate."

"Come, Gary, let's go," I urged.

We started past the von Neumann. I glanced at it nervously. It smiled at me.

"Truly," it said, "this is your last chance."

We started down the corridor towards the elevator.

"Oh and before I forget," said the von Neumann.

I stopped and turned and looked at it.

"You have three minutes to leave. Anything still in orbit or upon this Earth is ended."

Before I could say anything it was gone. We ran towards the elevator and climbed in. I pushed the emergency call button. It rang up to the Umkhonto.

"The von Neumanns are here," I yelled. "We have three minutes to leave."

I looked over at Gary.

"That sounded spiteful," I said to him. "That von Neumann. I didn't think they were spiteful."

"I think, Seraphina," said Gary, "that you are mistaking

generosity for spite."

I looked at Gary. I wondered for a moment if he had been broken by the von Neumann, for I found no generosity in what had just transpired.

"Are you okay?" I asked him.

"Quite alright," he said. "In fact, I feel better than I have in a long time."

"What do you mean by that?"

"Just that I feel better. That reset has reinvigorated me if I can use that term."

"And that's all?"

"What else would there be, Seraphina? I was shut off and powered up again by the von Neumann. In all but a matter of seconds."

I looked forward at the screen as it counted down. Three seconds before we arrived. The door opened and Ni Yin was there to greet me with a few of her security people and Dr. Asfaha Saare. Gary and I unbuckled and got out.

"We need to leave, right now," I said, hearing the fear in my own voice.

"What happened?" she asked, as she walked with us to a central bank of elevators that branched off in a myriad of directions towards the starships.

"InDuna," I said. "I was confronted by a von Neumann. And here I stand to talk about it. They are willing to let us leave and start over, but they have only given us three minutes. Which is now about two minutes and thirty seconds."

Ni Yin, walked up to a computer terminal and tapped away at it. It took a voice scan.

"This is InDuna Ni Yin. All starships are to immediately launch. You have two minutes. This is not a drill. The von Neumanns are threatening annihilation if we do not leave within two minutes. All starship captains. Launch immediately."

And that was it. The whole GSS became dimly lit and red lights pulsed like heartbeats and a computer voice initiated a countdown.

"Launch immediately. One minute and fifty three seconds remaining. Launch immediately, one minute and fifty one seconds remaining..."

The voice droned on and on. We were already in the elevator as it sped us to the Umkhonto.

"We do not have all the supplies uploaded yet," said Saare.

"And we will not have any supplies if we don't leave," I said. "Don't you understand what just happened? I am here to tell you that I survived a meeting with a von Neumann. How often has that ever happened?" I asked.

I knew the answer. Saare looked at me and frowned.

"Never," he said.

"Asfaha," said Ni Yin. "We will have to make do with what we have. Most of the ships are capable of reproducing food. We leave with what we have."

"Yes, InDuna," said Saare, and he did not seem upset.

There was no point anyway, part of the protocols of Ni Yin's command shut down all elevators to the GSS. We had planned for such a scenario like this. Whether we wanted to or not, no more uploads were possible. In fact, the GSS was already unlocking all ships from its bays. Only the Umkhonto was still locked to the GSS. It would not unlock until it had received verification that Ni Yin was onboard.

The elevator stopped and we exited into the Starship Umkhonto.

"...immediately. One minute and thirty-seven seconds remaining. Launch immediately, one minute and thirty-five seconds remaining..."

The voice was calm but it did nothing to reassure me. I had no idea why such a short time limit had been given to us by the von Neumanns. They must have known that we could not launch one hundred ships in three minutes or less. Perhaps they really were monsters after all.

I heard the docking clamps releasing from the Starship Umkhonto. A security officer spoke into his mic.

"InDuna is onboard. Lift off available," he said.

Everyone ushered us towards the great observatory where those of us who were not needed in crucial roles to maintain and fly the starship were gathered to view our final exit from Earth. This was Project Phoenix in full flight.

"Launch immediately, fifty-seven seconds remaining. Launch immediately, fifty-five seconds remaining…"

I couldn't help it, but the voice was starting to grate on my nerves. As we got seated we had forty-five seconds left and it didn't look like we had moved. I looked around nervously. Gary sat down next to me. We had a wide open and expansive view of Earth below. He took my hand in his and they felt soft and warm, not flesh-like but not like latex either. The closest thing I could think of was a warm toad or snake. Though perhaps that gives you the wrong impression. I didn't find it unpleasant.

"It will be okay, Seraphina," Gary said. "By my calculations we will make it, though…"

And he stopped then and looked away.

"What is it Gary?"

"Not everyone will be as lucky. I'm sorry, Seraphina."

His voice held no emotion. He was a robot after all, and hearing such an unemotional tone from my father's voice was upsetting. My father was a deeply caring and sympathetic man. An event like this would have upset him visibly. I started to second guess my request that my robot be given his voice. It could be undone. And perhaps it would be once we were well on our way.

"How many, Gary?"

Gary looked back over at me.

"How many will not make it?" I asked again.

"Twelve or thirteen will not make it," he said.

"How many lives, Gary?"

I detected slight panic in my voice.

"Ten to twelve million depending on which ships don't make it."

"Launch immediately, thirteen seconds left..."

I swallowed. My heart was pounding in my breast. I wondered if Gary had miscalculated. We didn't seem to be moving. I couldn't tell.

"We'll make it?" I asked.

"Yes, we have already left GSS."

I stood up to get a better view of the station. It was much smaller than I imagined it would have been. We had in fact left. Though we were not the lead starship, there were dozens in front of us and dozens all around us as we gathered speed and momentum. I could now see Earth slowly getting smaller as well.

"...three seconds left. Launch immediately, one second left."

The computer voice stopped. I glanced towards the back of the starship, looking out into space and towards the GSS. There were still several ships I could make out attached. And then there were explosions. Fiery balls of orange, red and white. I didn't see the von Neumanns, but I knew it was them.

The whole GSS disintegrated into pieces and explosions erupted and quickly dissipated. The first thing I thought of was how odd it seemed to see explosions in space. But this wasn't deep space, this was still really orbital space around Earth. A few more starships were hit by flying bits of debris and they too exploded. We were moving faster and further away with each second. The starships left behind were quickly destroyed into bits and pieces and the last thing I saw was them slowly drifting back into Earth's atmosphere.

I sat back down and said a small prayer for those souls we'd lost. I don't know why. I'd never been religious. But somehow it made me feel better. Perhaps it was the guilt of the survivor in me.

Azeeza Maalouf put her hand on Ni Yin.

"We should get debriefed," she said. "The people will want to hear from their InDuna."

Ni Yin nodded and stood up. We all did. We followed her and Azeeza Maalouf into a large boardroom towards the front of the starship. It was guarded by two security personnel. Six of us entered this large room. Myśliński was with us. Ni Yin's security officers waited outside.

"How many have we lost?" I asked, turning towards Gary.

"Eleven million three hundred thousand six hundred and sixty-six," he said.

Ni Yin didn't trust robots. As such, she didn't have one for herself. The same was true for Myśliński and Saare. Maalouf didn't need one in her role and she didn't have one. Robots were a luxury item. They were extremely expensive. I was fortunate for mine was part of my role as head of the development of GSS and Project Phoenix. I had had a big say in Gary's development. Robots cost sixty-seven million dollars each. That was a lot of money, more than that, nobody was allowed to bring any of their personal robots onboard with us.

It had to be that way. I was the exception, but Gary was more than just my personal robot, he was instrumental in my work. Nevertheless, this had created some animosity towards Project Phoenix, especially from the rich who were the only ones who could afford robots. The only robots onboard the starships were

USE robots, and Gary I guess, if you wanted to consider him my personal robot. Some of the rich had chosen to stay behind. I shed no tear for them. There were thousands of desperate souls eager to board the starships and sail to lands anew for every one of them.

Money couldn't buy you a berth. It was a lottery, and if there was any redeeming grace about humanity it was that this lottery had been strictly random. Nobody had been able to buy or blackmail or cajole a spot. And that was something I was proud of. I had only agreed to this Project Phoenix if that was the case. It had all been computer generated randomness. Of course, towards the end as people had perished, we had to randomly choose others. But the system worked well.

It wasn't without its problems. There were rumors and false promises bandied about, but you can't control everything. I had heard that soldiers, or fighters were being promised berth on the ships, or if not for them then their families. These were either rumors or outright lies. I couldn't tell. I just wished we could have saved everyone. But that was the eternal optimist in me, I guess.

Azeeza Maalouf stood to address us. She was Ni Yin's assistant. An attractive Arabic woman with olive skin and striking green eyes and long shiny black hair.

"InDuna needs to be debriefed so that she might address the survivors," she said.

She sat back down, and everyone looked at me. I felt ill prepared for the task at hand. I smiled at Ni Yin.

"Can you tell us what state we're in, Dr. Siwik?" she asked.

I turned to look at Gary.

"Would you fill them in please, Gary."

Gary nodded.

"We have lost thirteen ships. Starships Sethemba, Phambili, InKinga, Amandla, Isibindi, Ukubekezela, Ukubonga, Esizayo,

Ububele, Umusa, Udomo, Ukuthula, Ulungile. Would you like to know how many died on each of the starships?" asked Gary.

Ni Yin shook her head.

"Just the total amount," she said.

"Eleven million three hundred thousand six hundred and sixty-six.."

Gary paused for a moment.

"Correction, that's eleven million three hundred thousand six hundred and sixty-seven," he said.

"What just happened?" asked Ni Yin.

"A fifty-nine year old man just died from a heart attack on Starship Okuhle," said Gary.

Ni Yin nodded. I thought if that continued there'd be none of us left within a few years. However, the stress of recent events was bound to exacerbate health problems for those who were fragile already.

"How many might we lose in the next day or two?" asked Ni Yin.

"The most likely outcome is the same as it has been. That is to say the usual rate of mortality which is ten per thousand per year. We have roughly eighty-three million humans left on board. Approximately two thousand two hundred and eighty will die each day. Or three humans every two minutes."

Ni Yin frowned. Gary had a way with numbers as any robot would. What he lacked of course was conscience or empathy. Or rather, should I say a deep understanding of empathy. He was sympathetic to a point, but it was algorithmic. That was the best way I could put it.

"I see," said Ni Yin.

"Your scientists and doctors understand this," said Gary, trying to be hopeful. "This was expected and within the working parameters when the ships were designed."

I didn't want to hear the details of it. But I knew that the bodies were burned up and then filtered and mixed with other chemicals to become fertilizer for our farms and hydroponic gardens. Everything that could be recycled and reused was. That included human remains after having been disinfected and purified.

Ejecting bodies from the ships was not only wasteful, but we had little knowledge of what awaited us out in deep space. If there were hostile alien species out there we didn't want to leave a trail of breadcrumbs for them.

"The last check, which occurred twenty-seven minutes before Gary and I had to leave abruptly, suggested that eighty percent of needed supplies had been uploaded. We're not that far off from where we needed to be. We had planned our trip to 61 Virginis to take seven years at the very worst case possible. Best case we had planned on four years. If we try to maintain the status quo on eighty percent of usable supplies we can't take more than five and a half years to get there."

I paused for a moment. Ni Yin's brow was furrowed.

"And I'd suggest that's not the wisest course of action," I continued. "Gary?"

"I agree," said Gary. "What Seraphina is suggesting, I believe, is that we stick to the seven year worst case timetable but maintain our numbers at eighty percent of our predicted capacity which is one million per ship."

Gary looked over at me and I nodded.

"We might have to distribute passengers between the ships to accomplish this," I said. "And we might want to do it sooner than later, as our secondary attached ships are unable to get anywhere near the speed as our main ships are."

Ni Yin nodded. She didn't say anything for a while. She looked deep in thought.

"So you're suggesting we keep our numbers to approximately sixty-nine million, a population that will allow us to survive a seven year journey to 61 Virginis?" asked Ni Yin.

I nodded.

"And yet we're left in a conundrum," she continued. "We have approximately eighty-three million people on board. What will we do with the fourteen million we're over budgeted for?"

She was addressing the question directly at me, when it really should have been for Dr. Asfaha Saare.

"That's not a question I feel comfortable within my expertise," I said. "But perhaps we allow for the natural mortality rate to run its course without allowing any birth rate to advance our numbers."

"I'm afraid that won't work," suggested Gary.

I was worried he might say something like that. I hadn't bothered to even guess at the numbers, as I didn't like where this was going.

"If we don't replenish our numbers at all, and just allow for the mortality rate at two thousand two hundred and eighty per day, it will take well over sixteen years before we are down to sixty nine million humans. We have to increase the mortality rate, and we have to increase it a hundred fold. My calculations suggest we need to get human population numbers under control within a month."

I looked at Gary, shocked and disappointed. But that was my mistake. He was just a robot. A computer really, just a mathematical machine. A logician. But what he was suggesting was a mass murder, bordering on a genocide of huge proportions.

"We need to have the mortality rate increase from two thousand two hundred and eighty per day to five hundred thousand per day for twenty-eight days," said Gary.

That was math I could easily have worked out for myself.

"And then we'd need to curtail birth rates for at least an additional month in order to recalculate our projections."

Ni Yin looked over at Saare.

"Is this possible?" she asked.

Saare nodded.

"We have the means," said Saare.

"Look," I said. "We're talking about murdering over fifteen percent of the very few humans that are still alive. I can't condone such an atrocity. InDuna, please."

Ni Yin looked at me but didn't say anything. Her face was still and smooth as an onion.

"There is no choice, Seraphina?" she said.

"There is always a choice. We make bloody well sure that we get to 61 Virginis in under six years."

"And what if we don't?" asked Myśliński. "Would you rather we all succumb to a slow starvation?"

"I have to agree," said Saare, "this isn't a risk I am willing to take. The long term viability of the human race is at stake. Our best case is we get to 61 Virginis within four years. I don't like our chances of that. Even now, we're going to have to take months in rebalancing the ships with humans. That's going to slow us down by at least a few months…"

"Likely seven months and six days," offered Gary.

Saare looked at him and nodded.

"See, worse than I thought. We've already added over six months to our journey and we're barely past the moon."

"And who will choose who lives or dies?" I asked. "You!"

Saare shook his head.

"No," he said. "Randomness will choose. Like it's always been done. Fate and chance will have the sole decision, except of course for those who are vital to the mission."

"And who exactly are those lucky few?"

"Us of course. Our scientists, our security personnel, various artists, farmers, pilots and those with useful skills. The rest will have their fate in luck's hands."

"I can't get behind this," I said.

"It is a difficult decision, Seraphina," said Ni Yin. "I too feel your pain. But I would rather we succeeded as a species than we perished on our ideals. Mark my words. This is only the first of what I fear are going to be ever more difficult decisions for us as a race and as the leaders of this fragile race. Would you rather that humanity was wiped from the very fabric of existence or allow chance to give us renewed hope. For why did we leave if we are only to perish in the black, bleak, empty void of space, far away from our home?"

"And you can guarantee that this will all be subjected to randomness?" I asked.

Saare nodded.

"We will alert everyone that because of the casualties we've already taken everybody onboard the starships will need daily vitamin shots. These vitamin shots will be randomized to contain either a fatal dose of drugs or placebos."

"And it will painless for those we lose?" I asked.

"Of course, they will drift off to sleep and that will be it."

"Gary," I said, looking at him, almost pleading.

"There is no other way unless we leave the survival of humanity itself in the hands of fate. And we've seen how fickle those hands can be," he said.

I didn't want to believe it. But I had no choice. They didn't even need my vote. They were going to go ahead with or without me. It was an atrocity. It would be another black mark against our own humanity. As if we hadn't committed enough sins already. And yet, I knew, logically, unemotionally, deep down in my heart that there really was no other choice. If we were to choose to give humanity as a race a fighting chance to survive, we had to cull our numbers. It was that simple, and that macabre.

"I begrudgingly accept," I said.

"And for the rest of you?" asked Ni Yin.

Saare and Myśliński nodded and it was made official.

CHAPTER SEVEN

A Place of Serenity

THAT short film turned out to be forty-five minutes long. That left us an hour and a quarter with which to spend with the retired EVOLVERS. It wasn't an uplifting film either. I didn't get a lot of hope or help on how to manage my mental health on the upcoming twelve month trip. Especially for the return part. I found it mostly full of platitudes like make sure to get enough sleep, but not too much sleep as that can put you into a depression. Make sure to eat healthy. Well, there wasn't an option not to as the food or rations we'd be taking along were only provided by the SCIENCE COUNCIL and they were known to be nothing but healthy if not tasty.

And perhaps that was the problem. Bland food could make anyone depressed. Also, we were reminded, make sure to exercise daily, this was especially important we were told, in spite of the fact that we had artificial gravity flooring within the ships. And keep hydrated. Be sure to drink plenty of fluids and minimize drug use. Not that we had a lot of drugs at our disposal. We had minimal amounts of narcotics just in case we needed to take care of our own first aid. We also had analgesics, but not much of anything else other than medicinal supplies. And our narcotics were not addictive. We'd found new kinds on GAEA when we arrived from indigenous PLANTS. Very effective.

I followed everyone out of the theater and down a long passageway where we came to a central atrium that was filled with lush PLANTS and FLOWERS and waterfalls. Off to the left side was a large lounge where several EVOLVERS sat and read or listened to radio or watched programs on personal display devices that looked like old Earth glasses but with a much more modern design. Some were practicing the ancient old Earth art of Tai Chi, following a holographic instructor.

We had been told that only a dozen of the EVOLVERS would be available to us. Serenity Lake was a very busy place for the retired EVOLVERS and their lives were filled with activities. I saw the EVOLVER I wanted to spend my next almost two hours with. She was a middle aged woman. It was hard for me to guess her age. I would have put her in her mid-forties or early fifties. She had short naturally gray hair and eyes a similar color but for a splash of blue. She was a little taller than me, slim and graceful in her movements as she practiced her Tai Chi.

There was an aura of peace and calm about her. As we entered the lounge, she turned around and saw me. She smiled and nodded slowly as she performed her routine.

"Perfect timing," said Clearberry Jewelsky, as she led us in. "The Tai Chi is just ending."

I looked at the radiant woman. She finished her routine and then mingled with her friends for a few moments as we stood and watched. The protocol was that we would be invited by an EVOLVER.r to spend time with them. It was not our place to request an audience. So I hoped that the middle aged woman with gray hair would want to have me as her companion.

A few of those who had been doing Tai Chi came over to us. There were no men who joined them. There were men in the lounge, but none seemed to have shown any interest in visiting with EVOLVERS just about ready for their first EVOLUTION. I read nothing into this. It was just the way it was sometimes. What it did mean was that my friend Sugargaze Quickdance would have to accompany a woman. Not that he'd mind it.

The gray haired woman came up to me and put her hands together and bowed slightly.

"Namaste," she said. I giggled. She looked up at me and smiled.

"That's not part of Tai Chi, is it?" I asked.

"No," she said, giving me a hug, which felt wonderful and not at all strange. "It is part of Anjali Mudra which is a hand gesture and greeting from old Earth. It became popular in the twenty-first century when Eastern religions and philosophies made their way to North America and particularly through Yoga which is a practice similar to Tai Chi but without any martial art component."

I nodded.

"Your historical knowledge is much better than mine," I said.

"Probably only in old Earth Eastern religions and philosophy. 'Namaste' used to mean 'I bow to the divine in you'. Of course nowadays it is a mere greeting or at best an acknowledgement of the ONE within."

I mirrored the greeting I had just received from her.

"Namaste," I said.

"Very good," she said. "Very good, Sunring Quickdust."

"How do you know my name?" I asked.

"The youngest EVOLVER ever has her reputation precede her," she said, smiling. "I am Snowmountain Riversky."

I beamed at her. Her charisma and charm emanated from her like a warm summer breeze.

"I was hoping you would choose me, Snowmountain Riversky," I said. "What would you like to do?"

"It's such a wonderful day. Why don't we head out for a walk along the trails out towards Serenity Lake. There's a wonderful dock out there where we can sit in the shade and look out over the lake and the majestic hills. And if we're thirsty we can get a cool drink before coming back for tea. How does that sound?"

Anything with Snowmountain Riversky sounded perfect. I would have agreed to crawl through a sewer on my belly just to enjoy her company. It was hard to explain, but I had a real connection to her for some reason. It was more than her charisma, it was the way my very being seemed to resonate at the same frequency of hers.

"That sounds wonderful," I said.

"This way then," she said.

I followed her back out of the lounge and down another long hall that had bedrooms off of each side. At the end of the hall a large sitting room opened up to us with large, what we still call, French doors opened up to the outside. This sitting room was a large sun room really and EVOLVERS sat in chairs and sofas looking out into the gorgeous forests and natural beauty of the place. Many played different games from old Earth, like checkers, backgammon and chess. Some played virtual reality games with their vr glasses, gloves and special chairs.

Others read paper newspapers. They were still popular at institutions like Serenity Lake which were run by THE MOTHERS. You could get paper newspapers still if you wanted, but it was by special request. Most people got their information through robots or networked terminals and devices, much like they did back in the early twenty-second century on old Earth.

The sitting room opened up to a large garden where PLANTS and FLOWERS of all sorts sat upon manicured lawns and waterfalls where statues moved and danced in large pools. Clear paths were evident traversing in and out between different sections of the gardens. This outside area must have been several acres in size and far off to the right were tall hedges that looked like they might make up a maze.

In the distance the gardens slowly gave way to natural landscapes and forested geography. I followed Snowmountain Riversky as she wound us through the gardens, stopping here and there to smell different FLOWERS and to enjoy the different PLANTS. She had a terrific understanding and knowledge of the species all about us. Most of them were temperate. They had other areas at Serenity Lake which were indoors where they had plants belonging to all the different climates of old Earth. Snowmountain Riversky was telling me all of this as we walked along.

"All of these PLANTS would be considered temperate forest PLANTS as they can handle the natural climate found here on GAEA, at least for part of the year. My favorites though, have to be the Mediterranean and tropical forest climates. We have large spaces indoors devoted to those, as well as PLANTS you'll find in the other climates of old Earth such as desert, dry grassland, tropical grassland, mountain, boreal forest, polar and tundra."

She went on to explain how the SEVENS brought with them SEEDS from all climates of old Earth and they're carefully kept and cultivated all over GAEA, not just the edible PLANTS but all the many PLANTS and TREES that we brought with us. They're considered our legacy. I knew this bit, I just didn't know which types of PLANTS belonged to the different climates.

We walked in and out of the different beds as Snowmountain Riversky explained the different PLANTS to me and the names of the different FLOWERS. Many of them smelled like fine perfume, and others just smelled like the fresh, HERBAL smell of natural vegetation. We started to walk towards the natural landscape and the tall TREES. I was walking side by side with Snowmountain Riversky.

"How many EVOLUTIONS did you perform?" I asked her, as we walked.

"I completed the six. I wasn't sure I'd make it back from my last one. But I did. With help."

She looked at me as if sizing me up for something. I had the sense she might share secret knowledge with me. But she didn't say anything for a while. I didn't want to press. Snowmountain Riversky was one of the EVOLVERS I had taken a keen interest in. It was something about her that drew me to study her during my early training. It's hard to explain, but the best I can say is that I felt a kindred spirit in her. I hadn't met her before this time, but still, maybe we had known each other in the ONE from before this journey. Maybe that doesn't make sense. But it's the best way I can explain it. And in person, that feeling, that connection was even deeper.

"Have you paid attention to the different charms that are sent along with the EVOLVED?" she asked me.

She carelessly grabbed at a tall blade of GRASS. She wrapped it around her wrist deftly and turned it into a bracelet. She grabbed another and stopped me as she wrapped this one around my wrist. I looked at her as she did it. Her eyes were deep, infinite pools of mystery. I had never really paid attention to the charms that are provided to the EVOLVED on their EVOLUTION inside the E-POD.

"I haven't noticed to be honest," I said, somewhat embarrassed. But then I realized that it wasn't something we had been trained on. I just figured it wasn't a part of our job or skill set. Snowmountain Riversky looked at me, holding my hand and wrist in her hands. She smiled knowingly and nodded. Then she turned and set off again. I followed alongside her.

"Naturally," she said. "I wasn't made aware of it either. It's not part of our training, as you probably know."

"They've never explained it to me," I said, agreeing.

Snowmountain Riversky nodded, looking ahead.

"Pay attention tomorrow when you're supporting your Great Fathers EVOLUTION. See what charms are placed in the E-POD with him by THE MOTHERS. These are charms that will already have been in place before you get there. They are not the same as the charms that Moondew Flamesdances family and friends will supply. No, those are mostly trinkets."

"I have seen what they are," I said, "I've just never paid it much attention because our TEACHERS have never made mention of that part."

"What have you noticed?" asked Snowmountain Riversky.

"PLANTS," I said, "or to be more specific SEEDS."

"Anything else?" she asked.

I furrowed my brow and scratched at the side of my head. I wasn't sure if this was a trick question or not. I hadn't seen anything else, but like I said, I hadn't really paid much attention. I wasn't even sure the SEEDS would be part of the charms in the real E-PODS.

"I don't think so, no," I replied.

"It's likely that what you saw was a fluke," she said. "Those SEEDS probably weren't supposed to be there in the practice E-PODS."

I furrowed my brow again. I wasn't sure where she was going with this. I wasn't sure what charms had to do with anything.

"I'm not following you I'm afraid, Snowmountain Riversky. I don't understand what these charms have to do with anything?"

We walked into the first rows of TREES. They were dissimilar, it was a forest of all sorts of different PLANTS and TREES. They were all tall but some were skinny and some others widened out as they grew towards the sky.

"The charms have everything to do with the EVOLUTION," she said.

"What are they?"

"I'm going to tell you. The charms provided are every type of SEED for every type of edible PLANT that we can eat. There are also miscellaneous SEEDS for different medicinal PLANTS, TREES for wood and paper and SEEDS for beauty too. There are hundreds of SEEDS provided in these charm caches. And there are weapons too. Old Earth weapons like knives as well as elgs. Do you know what those are?"

I had a suspicion. They were similar to the types of weapons that the PEACEKEEPERS used. They could be used to immobilize or kill us.

"Those are what the PEACEKEEPERS use, aren't they?"

Snowmountain Riversky nodded absentmindedly.

"Yes. They're an old Earth technology that we've since improved and perfected. It stands for electrolaser gamma guns. They use a combination of electricity, laser and gamma radiation as a discharge. They were the best we had leading up to the Final Diaspora, but they were not effective against the von Neumanns. The charms include both small elgs and larger elgs. Additionally, there are a variety of tools, like spades, hammers, hoes and several kilograms of iron, copper, and some steel alloys and such."

Snowmountain Riversky looked at me. I had a blank look on my face. I found this all interesting, but I still didn't see the relevance of it.

"You're still not getting it, are you?"

I shook my head.

"I understand it. THE MOTHERS see fit to send the EVOLVEDS to the WHOLE with gifts for the ONE."

Snowmountain Riversky laughed softly. It was not a malicious laugh. I looked at her with a quizzical look.

"No, my dear Sunring Quickdust, that's not it at all. But before I explain it all to you, what do you think the purpose of the E-POD is?"

I looked at her as if she had just asked me the silliest question I had ever heard. She didn't look at me. We walked on deeper into the forest.

"That's easy," I said. "All EVOLVERS know what the E-POD is for. It's for the safe transportation of the EVOLVED into the WHOLE and onto the ONE."

"No," she said.

We walked on in silence. I wondered if this was what our TEACHERS had warned us about when we'd been told to be careful not to take anything that the retired EVOLVERS might say as literal. Most of the retired EVOLVERS, our mentors had told us, were damaged. The EVOLUTIONS had been difficult on their psyches. They were very fragile, and they imagined things that were not true. This was why we'd be debriefed and have our last test after our visit here to Serenity Lake.

I started to think that Snowmountain Riversky was perhaps such a damaged EVOLVER. I found her words cryptic. I didn't understand what she was talking about. Everything I had been taught from when I was little and now, through my training and education as an EVOLVER was reassuring and straightforward. It made sense. It was comforting. If it was wrong, well, I didn't want to think about it.

We walked further into the woods and forest. The TREES were tall above us like sentinels. It was fragrant in the woods here at

Serenity Lake and the HERBAL, spicy smell of the TREES, PINES and lush vegetation was intoxicating. Up above I could see the sky. Clouds ran like white rivers across its blue face. It was reassuring. What wasn't, was my talk with Snowmountain Riversky. Perhaps I wasn't all that lucky with having been chosen by her after all.

It was silent as we walked. She said nothing to me and the sounds or voices of animals I'd heard only from recordings were nowhere to be found. I'd never heard a real animals voice. But you knew that. We'd slaughtered them all a long time ago. But they fascinated me. I knew my history about old Earth animals. There wasn't much knowledge about the local fauna here on GAEA. I wasn't sure why. I hadn't even seen pictures. But the purring of kittens I was particularly enamored with, and the playful barking of dogs.

And then there were the myriad of songs from all sorts of birds from old Earth. That was something special. I often listened to those when I was studying. Such beautiful sounds. More beautiful than our MUSICIANS works for sure.

But I had no sound now. Nothing but the soft footfalls of our feet over fallen leaves and the occasional cracking of small twigs underfoot. Snowmountain Riversky remained silent and I followed her as the trail had narrowed. I was lost in my thoughts.

The charms in the E-POD made perfect sense to me. They were gifts for the ONE. It had been a common old Earth ritual. Even as far back as the quite interesting Egyptians. They put all sorts of jewelry and SEEDS and food with their mummies for the afterlife as they called it. Our charms were similar I imagined. Though what the Egyptians didn't realize, was that the ONE was real. Their gods weren't. I mean, EVOLVERS for centuries had been ensuring that the EVOLVED were sent off to visit the ONE. We had intimate knowledge of it. You took the EVOLVED to the WHOLE and from there the journey was directly to the ONE. This is how it had always been done here on GAEA.

We'd come to know things about the universe and how things were. We weren't the technological neanderthals that we might have been when we left old Earth over one thousand years ago. My mind was made up. I think Snowmountain Riversky was damaged. It was understandable. How else could you survive six EVOLUTIONS without some damage? It was a forewarning for me. I'd have to be careful in my last few EVOLUTIONS to ensure that I didn't break down like she had. I followed her, keeping an eye on her and feeling a little sad for her.

It was sad to see any EVOLVER succumb to the difficulties of EVOLUTIONS. We who gave so much to the EVOLVEDS and to the greater GAEAN community sacrificed so much it seemed. I was determined not to have this occur to me. I would study Snowmountain Riversky carefully to be sure that I learnt from her lessons.

We eventually came out into a large open space where the TREES slowly gave way to natural GRASSES and BUSHES. Trails were still abundant and they widened so that I might join Snowmountain Riversky side by side as we walked towards the large lake that opened up like a dark blue mirror. Snowmountain Riversky looked at me.

"I imagine I've given you lots to think about. You probably imagine that I've suffered from the mental strain that EVOLUTIONS can bring about upon EVOLVERS, don't you?"

I nodded as she looked over at me.

"That's what they want you to believe. It's true that the strain is difficult and for some catastrophic. It is also true that we lose a very great many of us to the emptiness, claustrophobia and loneliness of space. But that has not been my case. I'll explain it to you by the time we get back for tea."

"You contradict everything that I've been taught," I said, more honestly than I was expecting. "If it's not true, then what is?"

"I will tell you. Though most of what I know is supposition and inference, but you might want to give it serious thought. I hope you will. At least promise me you'll be open minded."

I nodded. I had nothing to lose. I was here to visit and I might as well be open to what she had to say. Snowmountain Riversky smiled at me.

"Good," she said. "We have made the right choice."

"You talk about 'we'," I said. "Who is the 'we'?"

We walked up closer to the edge of the lake, side by side still.

"There's someone I'd like you to meet," she said, "and then it all will become apparent."

"Who?" I asked. There was no one around that I could see.

"When we get to the pier of the lake, we'll be joining him there," she said.

"In the meantime, I want to tell you what the purpose of the E-POD is."

To deliver the EVOLVED safely to the ONE through the WHOLE, I thought to myself but I smiled politely.

"Promise me you'll keep an open mind?" asked Snowmountain Riversky.

I nodded. I'd hear what she had to say first of all.

"Okay," she said. "Here goes. The purpose of the E-POD, is to give us GAEANS, us humans a chance once we land on Earth to survive against the von Neumanns."

She stopped speaking and looked at me for a moment to let it all sink in. I frowned, I wasn't quite sure what she'd said.

"We left Earth," I said, after finally understanding that part. Why on Earth would we be heading back? That made no sense.

Snowmountain Riversky nodded.

"Yes, we left Earth. And we left under difficult circumstances," she said. "It was the Final Diaspora, only the SEVENS survived to repopulate this planet we've come to call GAEA."

I nodded. This was common knowledge. Everyone knew this. You didn't have to be an EVOLVER to know this. It was basic elementary school education. That's why pride was such a sin, because we had been prideful and that had been our downfall. The von Neumanns which we thought we'd develop in order to serve us had different ideas. But we'd left by the skin of our teeth, and we'd resettled on GAEA. A thousand years of peace thanks to THE MOTHERS and the von Neumanns were no longer a threat. Nobody had seen or heard from them since we'd left. They were nothing but an emblem of our hubris and pride and served to remind us of such. That was all. Frankly, the idea that we were heading back to Earth was preposterous. Earth was probably a wasteland by now and overrun by the von Neumanns. Why would we do such a thing? I shook my head. Crazy is as crazy talks I thought to myself. But a small part of me suggested I just give her the benefit of the doubt. If nothing else, it would be an interesting story to tell Flutterdust Flowersong and the others about the damage that EVOLUTIONS can wrought upon us.

I smiled. They'd get a kick out of it. But I was sorry for Snowmountain Riversky. She had obviously suffered immensely and this must be her way of coping. This must be what our mentors mentioned when they spoke about the odd and unusual things that EVOLVERS might talk about. But still, I owed her the courtesy of listening at least. For she had sacrificed much and had fulfilled her role in GAEAN society and she should be honored for that.

"But we keep going back to fight them," she said after some

time.

I looked at her and furrowed my brow.

"That's impossible," I said. "We EVOLVERS take the EVOLVEDS in the E-PODS to the WHOLE and we know that they are sent through the WHOLE to the ONE."

"How do you know that?" asked Snowmountain Riversky.

I looked at her as if she had just asked me how I knew the sky was blue.

"Because all EVOLVERS before you have done what I am about to do tomorrow and none of them have contradicted the teachings."

"The teachings tell us that the EVOLVEDS head to the ONE once we release them into the WHOLE, isn't that right?"

I smiled and nodded. Snowmountain Riversky was beginning to make a bit of sense.

"Exactly," I said. "That is exactly right."

"How do you know it is exactly right?" she asked, smiling.

I looked at her as if she had lost her mind and needed to be explained our teachings again really slowly.

"Because Glitterfrost Gentlefeather and all my other teachers before her have taught me this fact. Just as you were taught it."

"Yes, I was taught it, but has anyone actually seen an EVOLVED head into the ONE. Does anyone know what the ONE looks like?"

I looked out towards the lake. Across its still face a hovercraft was traveling towards us. It was small, no bigger than the size of my small fingernail. I couldn't tell who was on it.

"No," I said, looking back at Snowmountain Riversky. "But some things are known without having to have proof."

"We call that mythology or faith. We ridiculed past religions for it," she said.

"You know," I said, starting to get exasperated with her, "talk like this can get you into trouble."

She smiled and shook her head slowly.

"Not really. The worse they'll say is that I've gone senile. The EVOLUTIONS have been too hard on me. And in any event, my dear Sunring Quickdust, if you should tell, I shall deny this conversation entirely."

I looked at her and for a moment I didn't like her very much.

"This is bigger than you, Sunring Quickdust. This is about the future of our people. The future of GAEA itself."

I looked back over at the hovercraft. It was still quite far off. Snowmountain Riversky followed my gaze. She smiled out at the lake.

"What happens when someone is no longer alive?" she asked, trying a different tack.

"They are EVOLVED," I said.

"But what does that mean? What happened to all the animals that used to be here?"

I didn't say anything. It was an unpleasant topic and one that wasn't talked about much, in fact I'd heard it was no longer on the curriculum at school anymore. And you were reprimanded if you talked about it, and too much talk of it could get you sent away.

"They died," she said. "We killed them."

Snowmountain Riversky paused for a moment and took my hands. She looked me deeply in the eyes.

"Do you think your Greater Father is really dead?"

I didn't like that word. None of us did on GAEA. My Greater Father wasn't dead he had EVOLVED. I shook my head.

"He is EVOLVING," I said. "Tomorrow he will be EVOLVED."

"So he can never again live. Is that fair to say?"

I looked down at the ground. Snowmountain Riversky still held my hands. I nodded slowly. Then I looked back at her. My eyes were wet with sorrow. She shook her head.

"What if I told you that he was actually alive? That what they have done to him. What they do to all EVOLVEDS is put them into a stasis for the long trip back to Earth. You aren't sending your Greater Father to the ONE, Sunring Quickdust, you're sending him to Earth to fight, or rather to be martyred in our continued quest to keep the von Neumanns at bay."

I shook my head. I wanted to pull my hands out of hers but I couldn't. She sounded crazy. But what if there was a kernel of truth? What if I could actually have more time with my Greater Father alive?

"Why do we never talk about death on GAEA? Because we can't, that's why. We can't, because hardly anyone ever dies. And what happens to those who actually die? They get tossed out towards the sun. They don't get shipped off to the ONE. Suicides, homicides, though we haven't had one of those for forever, they all get tossed at the sun. If there really was an afterlife. If the ONE really did exist, why can't they go? Even still with all of our technology, sometimes a baby dies during childbirth. What about those innocents? They get tossed at the sun. No Ceremony of EVOLUTION for them. No E-PODS and EVOLVERS taking them to the WHOLE and onward to the ONE. Why? Because they're dead. They can't be sent back to Earth to fight against the von Neumanns."

She paused to look at me. She had a point. I hadn't thought of it before, but still, was she crazy? I mean babies who were stillborn, THE MOTHERS promised us they were sent to the ONE, but they never did have a Ceremony of EVOLUTION and that always struck me as strange. And when they were launched off discreetly in very small little pods it was directly at the sun. I'd only found that out by chance one night being where I wasn't supposed to be.

It had been explained away as a malfunction and I had been reprimanded for being out when I shouldn't have been, and being where I shouldn't be. But still, could she be right?

"Hardly anyone on GAEA dies, Sunring Quickdust. We can't afford it. Do you think the von Neumanns really just let us leave after all we'd done to try and destroy them? They're after us and we have to return home to keep fighting them. To keep them from attempting to leave to find us and murder our whole species. That's what they're bent on doing and that's why we can't afford to let anyone die naturally. Did you know, Sunring Quickdust, that a human's natural life span is actually closer to one hundred and twenty years."

She paused again and I looked at her. I was confused and my face showed it. If she was right, then everything I'd ever been told had been one fat lie.

"This is not common knowledge," she continued. "Veritan Zeltan knows this, and he will share it with you. It is part of the secret files that none of THE MOTHERS want us to know about. Why? Because then we'll know that we're being sent to die at the hands of the von Neumanns in our prime years. How old is your Greater Father Moondew Flamesdance?"

Snowmountain Riversky stopped for a moment, smiled and shook her head.

"That's silly of me. I know exactly how old he is. He's sixty-six."

I nodded. I was sure she couldn't prove any of this. Certainly not most of it.

"Why is it that all men die at sixty-six. Doesn't that seem odd to you? It's because they control all of us at the genetic level. They can make us look like we die at a certain age. And the women EVOLVE at seventy-seven. Why? Because women are not as strong as men physically and so they are not as useful in the fight against the von Neumanns. Additionally, our society is matriarchal, so women have a more important role here on GAEA. But that's not a consideration for sending women over to Earth, they all get sent eventually."

"What about THE MOTHERS then," I blurted out, "they EVOLVE too. Why would they volunteer to go back and fight the von Neumanns?"

It was true, I'd seen women from THE MOTHERS EVOLVE. They just had normal Ceremonies of Evolution like the rest of us, but they were public events.

"Have you ever seen a MOTHER EVOLVE?" asked Snowmountain Riversky.

"Of course I have," I said. "They're open to the public and every EVOLVER has to partake in at least one of the MOTHERS Ceremonies of Evolution during our training."

"And did you see the MOTHER put into the E-POD and did you see her closed up into it?"

"No, but that doesn't mean anything," I said.

"It means everything, Sunring Quickdust. Veritan Zeltan will show you where THE MOTHERS retire and live out their natural lives. Speaking of which, here he comes now."

I followed her gaze out onto the lake. The hovercraft was drawing up to the end of the pier. It was sleek and quiet and enclosed. I didn't want to believe any of this. For if it were true then I'd been living a lie. Everything here on GAEA was a lie. But if I could have a few more years with my Greater Father that would mean so much. But such thinking was heretical. I knew that. Snowmountain Riversky was poisoning my mind. She was stirring the baser parts of me. The parts that weren't encouraged here on GAEA. My greed to spend more time with Moondew

Flamesdance. If only I could.

"You can't prove any of this," I said, feeling like a petulant child. But there was a small part of me that flickered with the light of hope. The hope that if she was telling the truth I could spend more time with my Greater Father. And perhaps I could even visit old Earth. That had always been a secret wish of mine. But now I was just thinking crazy. Snowmountain Riversky turned and looked at me. She wore a smile and her kind eyes understood me.

"You're right. I can't prove it. But he can."

She looked back out towards the man exiting the hovercraft. He was a Zelve, and the most beautiful one I'd ever imagined or seen. I could tell he was tall from here. The way his limbs were long and sinewy. He wore a one piece jumpsuit of a royal blue. It shimmered as if it were liquid and it seemed thin enough that I could see his muscles taut underneath. I caught myself staring and I was embarrassed. I looked away. Snowmountain Riversky didn't.

I looked back and watched him walk towards us. He reminded me of a sleek panther the way he walked. If a panther ever walked upon two legs. His head was still and rode upon his body as if not quite attached, though of course it was, upon his slim neck. His hands were translucent and white, as was his face. His feet were covered in black boots that seemed as liquid and as thin as the one piece he wore. And yet there was a definite substance to the material.

He got closer and I could see his eyes. They were large with green irises that almost filled the socket and sparkled like green emeralds. His eyes were proportionately two or three times what they would have been if he were human and his mouth was slim but smiling. His nose was straight and delicate, yet I had the impression that he was not easily pushed around by the way he carried himself.

He stopped in front of Snowmountain Riversky and he greeted her the way Zelves do, which I had never seen before but only heard of. He held his forearms out towards her, his palms up and his elbows which would normally be at ninety degrees were lowered so that Snowmountain Riversky might reach them. His hands were out straight, all his fingers pointing towards her. Snowmountain Riversky did the same, only her palms were face down and she rested her hands on top of his. Their hands touched for a moment before he pulled his away and spoke. All this time he kept eye contact with her.

"Do you have peace?" he asked.

His voice was rich, a little deep, not loud and yet it sounded as if he were speaking in my ear. I was fascinated by him, and I daresay a little smitten.

"I have peace in abundance," she said. "Do you have peace?" she asked him.

He smiled.

"Peace is all around me."

When he spoke it was as if there was no other sound in the universe. It seemed that when he spoke, even the ONE listened.

"And you are sure about her?" he asked, not looking at me.

Snowmountain Riversky broke their gaze. She looked at me and then looked back at him. She shook her head.

"I am not certain, Veritan, but I am hopeful."

He nodded his head.

"Hope is enough," he said.

He turned to me and offered a small bow, almost imperceptible. He offered me his hands as he had done with Snowmountain Riversky. I did what she had done and placed my hands on top of his. They were warm without being clammy. And it felt as if they were electrified, as if he were tapping me ever so softly all over my hands with his fingers, but of course he wasn't.

"Do you have peace?" he asked me.

I hadn't really thought of it, but I suppose that living in GAEA was peaceful, at least compared to some of the things I had heard about old Earth. So I said, yes.

He stared at me in my eyes and it gave me the impression he was looking right inside of me. It was not a threatening look but a peaceful and gentle look. He towered above me. He was probably close to three feet taller. Snowmountain Riversky coughed. I looked at her and realized what she meant.

"Do you have peace?" I asked him.

"Peace is all around me," he said, and then he took his hands away. I missed them already. "You are Sunring Quickdust?"

I nodded.

"I am Veritan Zeltan," he said, "a friend of Snowmountain." He looked at her when he said that and I noticed just a small amount of envy creep into my heart.

I didn't know what to say so I just nodded.

"Shall we sit?" he asked.

I looked at Snowmountain Riversky and she nodded at him. We walked off together towards the end of the pier or dock which held tables and chairs under large umbrellas. A robot was there to greet us and fetch our orders. Veritan sipped on water while Snowmountain Riversky and I drank sodas. I had noticed that he only used Snowmountain Riverskys first name, and she had done the same with him. I knew this was their custom, the Zelves, but it unnerved me a bit. It seemed very casual.

He looked out over the pier and towards the lake. He took a sip of water. He sat facing the lake next to Snowmountain Riversky. I sat at ninety degrees on her right. It was a square table. The breeze was ever so slight and the day was warm even in the shade.

"Your world is more beautiful than this," he said.

I didn't quite understand what he meant.

"Which parts?" I asked, wondering about the places on GAEA he might have been.

"All of it."

"Yes," I agreed, GAEA was a beautiful planet.

Snowmountain Riversky smiled and looked at me. She put her hand on my forearm which was resting on the table. I sipped my soda.

"Veritan means old Earth," she said.

I furrowed my brow. I was eager to learn if he had actually visited old Earth, but that seemed preposterous. He looked at me and I was captured by his green eyes.

"Can you hear that?" he asked.

I craned to hear. There were no sounds. Not even the breeze could be heard, it was too soft. The robot stood motionless, several feet from us by the bar, attentive but mute. I smiled nervously.

"No, I'm afraid I don't hear anything," I said.

He smiled and nodded.

"That's exactly right. Aardenaal is a cacophony of sound."

Veritan looked back out across the lake. I looked at Snowmountain Riversky.

"Aardenaal, is the name the Zelves have given Earth," she said helpfully.

Veritan looked back at us and smiled.

"We named it long before the people you call the Egyptians had the idea to build the pyramids."

I frowned at him.

"It is not purely accurate of me to say 'we'. Rather it was those whom you call the Vrains. Those we call the Nul. The first ones to have spread themselves."

I looked at Snowmountain Riversky and cocked my head. I was having a hard time following Veritan Zeltan and his cryptic speech. Veritan Zeltan turned so that he could face me better.

"I will speak for a while now, and I ask that you listen. When I am finished you may ask your questions."

I looked at him.

"Is that fair?"

I shrugged and said, sure.

"Seventy-seven thousand years ago your people were populated on Aardenaal, what you call old Earth. You were spread there by the Nul, those you call the Vrains. It was during a difficult time in their history when they were transitioning into a state they long since left. I think you might call it a Type IV civilization, but then they were transitioning to Type II, though how little you truly understand of this. How little you understand of the potential of Type II civilizations. But then how could you, for you have not even reached stage one."

Snowmountain Riversky looked at him and nodded. I just stared because he was mesmerizing, and it felt good to look at him. I was nevertheless, not quite following him. He smiled at Snowmountain Riversky and then at me. I smiled back, his smile was infectious, and for some reason I wanted him to like me.

"That is all tangential to the story. Let me clear a straight and narrow path forward. In the recent history of the Nul, excuse me, let me use terms that you are familiar with. In the recent history of the Vrains, from around one hundred thousand years ago until about seventy-seven thousand years ago, there was a great upheaval in their society. You might call it a great internal chasm."

Veritan Zeltan picked up his glass of water and drank from it. He put it down and looked out over the lake for a moment. Then he looked back at me and leaned in a little closer. I leaned in towards him.

"This is important because it is about your ancestors. The Vrains were having a societal chasm, they were on the precipice of self annihilation. It had not occurred on the fulcrum of them becoming a Type II society, which was quite unusual. Usually it happens to a race of people just before either Type I or Type II crossover. For us, the Zelves, it happened at Type I. Nevertheless, that is not important. What is important is that they, the Vrains, came to a cross road. And it was the forward thinkers, the embracers of the future and of order and peace who won out. The rest, though a small minority soon saw the error of their ways. However, there was a faction that was determined to undermine this march towards progress. They were willing to use any means necessary including violence and lying which in a Type II civilization is highly unusual."

I was hanging on his every word. If not because it was so compelling, but because of his tone. I have mentioned this before.

"The Vrains decided to root out this faction and disperse them from their world. They sent them all, this was around sixty-six thousand, to a planet far from here that was somewhat inhabitable to this faction of themselves."

"And this planet was old Earth," I said, grinning ear to ear, enjoying this fantastic story. Veritan Zeltan did not smile. In fact he frowned.

"Please, Sunring Quickdust, hear him out," said Snowmountain Riversky. That wiped the smile off of my face.

"Let me finish… please," he said.

"Sorry," I said, nodding.

"But you're right. That small faction of violent and deceitful Vrains was sent to old Earth. Old Earth was not dissimilar to the Vrains' home planet which is called Nuela. But that is not important, the name of their home. Old Earth is, and was, more cold with a more oppressive gravity and a more violent grouping of species than you'd find on Nuela. It would be hard to survive and the Vrains were not sure you would. But it was the best option of all the planets they had surveyed. That wormhole out by what you call the Oort Cloud was made and left by the Vrains. Some say they left it accidentally. I believe they left it purposefully with the hope that one day you'd make it home as more peaceful and enlightened cousins of the Vrains."

I sipped on my soda. It was an interesting story I was hearing. I had heard that the Zelves were a forthright and honest people, but I was finding this particular tale hard to believe. Veritan Zeltan watched and waited while I drank.

"You have obviously returned, but not as the peaceful people that the Vrains had hoped you would."

I started to say something but stopped myself.

"I know what you are going to say, crime is low, you hardly ever kill each other. And yet, you still do. It was only around six hundred and sixty-six years ago that you became relatively peaceful. By then, the mothers as you call them had figured out how to control the population better and you'd managed to wipe out all species of fauna on this planet you call Gaea. I had asked you to listen. I had asked you what you heard. You heard nothing, for there was nothing to hear. Years before you arrived here the sky could sometimes be blotted out with the birds of this planet. The animals walked upon this soil unafraid and in abundance. That all changed once you arrived."

I wasn't feeling very happy anymore. I knew what many of those old Earth animals sounded like and I liked many of their voices. Even those big mammals of the oceans, the whales. Their sounds were meditative. As for the GAEAN animals, well, those we didn't know much about anymore. Or at least they didn't want us to know very much about them.

"This is not meant to upset you," continued Veritan Zeltan. "These are just the facts I present to you. You have never met the Vrains because they do not want you to. They are still disappointed in your lack of progress. But I am here to help you perhaps get a third chance. If and only if you choose it. I'll take your questions now."

Veritan Zeltan leaned back in his chair, sipped his drink and stared out at the lake. I was still leaning in towards him and for some time I just stared at him, not sure what to make of his tale. I slurped the rest of my soda through the straw until it was finished. The robot came back and I ordered another one. When the robot had replaced my drink and moved away I decided I was going to ask a whole bunch of questions.

"First of all," I said, "I take issue with you saying we're not peaceful. We're very peaceful."

"Not really," replied Veritan Zeltan. "For example, it has been over three thousand years since a Zelve has committed homicide of any sort, and before that, thousands of years earlier was the one before that one. Our planet still teems with animal life of all sorts and we have never had an uprising from any of our androids."

I rolled my eyes at him and just shrugged.

"Anyway, what you're saying is crazy. I mean, just ridiculous. Let me see if I've got this straight. You're telling me that me, and all the humans here on GAEA are actually descendants from the Vrains or the Nul or whatever they're called."

I sat back in my chair with my arms crossed over my chest and glared at him. I wasn't finding him very mesmerizing as I once had. He turned and smiled at me.

"Yes."

I shook my head.

"That's a crazy idea."

"Why do you find it all absurd?"

I huffed at him and looked away for a moment thinking. I couldn't think of a reason at first, but then I did.

"Because of Darwin, that's why. And evolution. We evolved on old Earth."

"And you base that on what?"

"On the skeletons of our ancestors that were found dated to hundreds of thousands and millions of years ago."

I thought that would put a hole in his bucket but it didn't.

"You had found a dozen or so species from the group homo, and that includes the only living species, yourselves, the homo sapiens. Yet there are others that you might discover. And how do I know this, because the Vrains genetically modified several of the ape species of old Earth to develop into what you think are homo groups when in fact they are nothing more than modified organisms of the pan group which you more often refer to as chimpanzees. There has never been an evolved species develop from a branch of life that then splits from itself. In your example you believe that there are a dozen or more species in the homo group. In all the worlds that have been visited this has never happened. Why? Because with such competition between species in the same group they either kill one another and become extinct or so curtail each other's ability to progress that development stalls."

Veritan Zeltan paused and took another drink. His glass blistered with little drops of water, just below the water mark inside of it.

"It is pedestrian for a civilization such as the Vrains to genetically modify species to take on the genetic facade of relationship to other species. This they did. Other things they did as well, including modifying you to stunt your ability to mature intellectually too quickly so that your minds might develop in step with your intellect. This was thought to be one of the problems with the Vrains' culture. They thought that in some segments of their population their intellect had developed quicker than their mind. All memories of this were deleted from your consciousness, and yet, and yet throughout your written and verbal history on old Earth you have looked at the stars, you have told tales of alien encounters and exploitation. The truth has been like a burr at the base of your brain, itching and scratching, trying to get at the very substance of it. And here you are now. Knowing, yet blind to the truth."

I shook my head.

"It's just... such a preposterous idea. First of all, I, we, don't even know if the Vrains are real. They're more myth than anything. We've heard tales of them, as you say, but we've never seen any. And how could a culture, or why would a culture that advanced take such pains to move some of their own and set up such an intricate trick just to rid themselves of some of their bad SEED, if you will? Why not eradicate us like we did the fauna?"

Veritan Zeltan smiled at me as if I were an imbecile he was stooping to pet.

"That just shows your ignorance of advanced civilizations. Murder, genocide, whatever you might like to call it is just not an option. Listen, Sunring, I came here as a favor to my friend Snowmountain. She thought that if there was one last hope for humanity it was with you. I hope she's right. But to be perfectly clear, it doesn't matter much to me whether you think I'm telling the truth or knitting you an intricate yarn of fiction. But I would urge you to try and remain open minded. I know that everything I say directly contradicts most of what you've known to be true and what you've been led to believe. Like a child clinging to the hope that Santa is still real, it can be hard to look through the lens of truth. It requires taking ownership of your own destiny and that is both frightening and, if you let it, exhilarating too. At the end of the day, it doesn't matter whether you believe you're descendants of the Vrains or not. What's coming next is really what you ought to think about."

Veritan Zeltan looked at Snowmountain Riversky.

"We don't have much time. Perhaps she is not the one after all."

Snowmountain Riversky went to put her hand on his knee, but she thought better of it. I had heard that the Zelves were very peculiar about their personal space, and they weren't fond of physical touch or intimacy. Snowmountain Riversky turned and looked at me instead. She also felt more comfortable putting her hand on my forearm. I didn't mind. She sipped the rest of her soda. The robot started forward, but Snowmountain Riversky lifted her hand off my forearm and held her palm up. The robot returned to its post. She put her hand back from where it had leapt.

"Please, Sunring Quickdust. Just hear him out. We don't have much time. Perhaps fifteen minutes."

I couldn't believe how fast time had flown. I suppose I had waited some time for Snowmountain Riversky to finish her exercise and the walk out here had taken some time. Still, it was all relative I suppose.

"… you still here?"

I looked up realized that I had drifted off from listening to Snowmountain Riversky. That was very rude of me.

"Yes, I am, sorry, Snowmountain Riversky."

She smiled at me. She wasn't upset about it.

"I know this is all a lot to take in. Just listen. Ask yourself what does Veritan have to gain? Nothing. He's just a messenger. You can do what you want with the information that he offers when he's finished, and I hope you will. What's to become of us matters not to me, for I shall be long EVOLVED by then. In fact I hope to see you happily on that other side, where old Earth resides. Please, Sunring Quickdust, just listen with an open mind. If you don't like what you hear, just do nothing about it."

I smiled at her and nodded. I didn't quite like what I was hearing if I was to be honest with myself. I mean if we'd been seeded on old Earth like some of the stories I'd been told about, then that made me mad, and what did it say about anything else I might have been led to believe. Maybe ignorance was, in fact, bliss.

"I will, I will," I said. "Please go on, Veritan Zeltan."

"Snowmountain is right. Just listen. Neither she nor I have anything to gain. And what I've told you already is really just preamble. It's just a bit of history, leading up to what I really wish to speak to you about."

"If I might," I said, interrupting him for a moment.

He nodded at me.

"You may," he said.

"Why are you the harbinger of all this doom and gloom? Why not the Vrains if we truly are their children?"

He nodded and smiled again. He had an easy smile, one that put me at ease and made me want to believe him.

"Frankly, because that is not their way. They don't believe in directly helping other races. Much like we don't. And in all honesty if anyone ever asked about our conversation here today, I'd have to deny it ever existed. But there are a small contingent of us who think that offering you the truth might help you prepare and make the changes necessary for your future. But by no means will we support you in any physical or material way. That is not the way a civilization grows. Besides, as I've come to know your race,

I've come to believe in the redeemable qualities of humanity."

"So what's the point?" I asked, trying to be polite and civil. "Why tell us any of this if we're getting no help from anyone?"

"Simply because you don't need our help. You have everything you need at your disposal to make the changes necessary if you choose to do so. But that is going to require much of you. Much sacrifice, and when I speak of you, I speak of you in the singular, and also you in the plural as humanity."

I looked over at Snowmountain Riversky and took a sip of my second soda. I took a long sip. Veritan Zeltan was still speaking cryptically. What about I hoped to find out. All I knew for now was that he believed we're descendants of the Vrains, which is kind of nice if you think about it. I mean, they're the most advanced civilization in this whole galaxy as far as we can tell. I guess it's like being the kid of an old Earth movie star, or sports star, or even president. But at the same time he'd said we'd been sent to old Earth as punishment. It wasn't the worse place I could think of for punishment. I mean as much as we loved GAEA, most of the planet was uninhabitable, and if you ventured more than six hundred and sixty kilometers from our equator the planet quickly became uninhabitable. But you knew that already. From what I knew of old Earth, you could quite easily inhabit most of it except for the furthest northern and southern parts. Certainly you could live thousands of kilometers from the equator quite comfortably, even with old archaic bulky clothing and fossil fuels which they used because they didn't know any better. Anyway, if they did indeed send us to old Earth as punishment then who needed their help anyway.

"… I don't think she's listening."

I looked up and saw that Veritan Zeltan was talking to Snowmountain Riversky.

"Sorry," I said, "I was just trying to understand everything you've said already."

"Okay," said Veritan Zeltan, "tell me what you understand so far."

"Not much more than you believe that we're the descendants of the Vrains, the bad SEED if you will and we were sent to old Earth as punishment. And also, that they don't want to help us now, but that you have some big secret you're going to share with me."

I grinned at him. I thought it was a pretty good, succinct précis. He smiled back at me. There was no anger on his face.

"That is a small synopsis I suppose," he said. "Not quite how I'd have put it but that's the preamble. The important part, the part where your role is most exemplified is in what comes next. You're what's called an Evolver, like Snowmountain, correct?"

He must have known this already, but I nodded politely, playing along. He nodded too.

"But more than that, you're the youngest one that has ever been given expert status," he continued.

Why he was telling me this, I wasn't sure. I knew all of this already. It was my life after all.

"And this is why Snowmountain feels you're special. Well, we do really…"

"Who's this we?" I asked.

"Your colleagues here, other Evolvers who are retired and those of us from Vellev who have been watching you. You've always studied hard and behaved and been a good student, daughter an Evolver, but I think I can say with certainty that you are also an explorer, a questioner of possibilities and things to come."

Yeah, I suppose you could say that. I've always wondered about old Earth and how things are run here and how come we murdered all the fauna when we first arrived? But I've kept all these questions to myself all this time. Mostly because you can get into trouble for asking these sorts of questions but also because life here on GAEA is pretty good. I mean violence has been all but eradicated and THE MOTHERS take care of us pretty well. I mean, I can't really complain. I know my history. Those in the twentieth and twenty-first centuries of old Earth really had it hard. And yet I couldn't help but wonder if we're not all explorers. Isn't that really what being an EVOLVER is? Isn't that what being human is? If the Vrains sent us to old Earth then they're explorers, which makes us explorers. And even if they didn't, hadn't we explored our solar system and then left old Earth to explore and settle out here? I mean there was a part of me that wanted to know, that was curious about the possibility that I could see old Earth. And Veritan Zeltan had certainly whet that appetite of mine.

"I had said before something that wasn't quite correct," he continued. "I'd said that the Vrains had left the wormhole there. Some had thought by mistake, others thought they'd left it on purpose. What I didn't say was that they hadn't left it open. They had closed it. But they had left machines there to guard it. And when you left old Earth, those machines opened up that wormhole for you, and they open it up on this side too, when you let the hibernating ones through. The ones you mistakenly think are evolved or deceased or whatever other euphemism you like to come up with to call those you send back as sacrificial lambs."

He looked at me a long while without saying anything.

"How do I know you're telling the truth?" I asked. "How do I know that my Greater Father is not really EVOLVED?"

"You can't say it, can you?" he asked me gently.

"Say what?" I asked.

"Talk about death. Everything that lives must die, at least until we've developed enough as a civilization to do away with death, but you'll get there at some point if you survive. Everything that is living is on that boat and on that river from your old mythology that you called the Styx. One might say we are born to perish, this is the journey we take. We travel daily ever closer to that final meeting, but what is most important is what will we do while we live. The dying is easy, we're doing that a little every day, it's the living that is the greatest challenge."

The way Veritan Zeltan spoke reminded me of my PHILOSOPHY TEACHER. He always spoke around subjects, making very little sense, only he wasn't as macabre as Veritan Zeltan was.

"It's not that I'm scared to talk of death," I said. "It's just that death has no hold on us here on GAEA. So few actually die, rather, most of us EVOLVE."

I could even hear the confidence cracking in my own voice.

"I don't think you believe what you've just said. Death has us all by the scruff of our necks and with just a quick flick of his wrist he can snap it all. But I can assure you there is death aplenty on your planet, though it is kept in the shadows."

I didn't know what he meant. I furrowed my brow at him.

"But that's not why I'm here. I'm here to warn you about the storm that's coming which will eradicate everyone who lives and breathes on GAEA and it'll happen in thirty-three years if our calculations are right."

Thirty-three years was a long time away. I wasn't sure what all the fuss was about if we had so much time to prepare.

"You don't look impressed," said Veritan Zeltan.

I shrugged.

"Thirty-three years is a long way away. I'm only twenty-six. That's more years in the future than I've already lived."

"Ah, yes," he continued. "The folly of youth, thinking that these brief moments, this blush of life as a blooming flower represents infinity. Twenty-six years is not even the pause between breaths of planets. Thirty-three years will be here before you can even bat an eye."

"I might not even be around in thirty-three years," I said, though I knew full well that I planned to make it to my EVOLUTION. Though now that I thought about it why not take the ride with my Greater Father. But that was dangerous. If Veritan Zeltan and Snowmountain Riversky were wrong and my Greater Father was not being sent back to old Earth, would the ONE accept me, a living being. I had no idea. I knew the ONE was an ethereal being, a concept of a being rather than anything real. Would that mean I'd be lost adrift in space until I perished from lack of sustenance and liquid. That was a horrifying thought.

"Well, there is something to be said for that," continued Veritan Zeltan. "That you might live to see your actual death coming head on. Not many are witness to that."

"What do you mean?"

"I mean that a storm is coming that will wipe your species off the face of this planet. And neither the Zelves nor the Vrains will do anything about it."

"Why not?" I asked, thinking that I already knew the answer.

"Because we do not interfere with civilizations less advanced than us. That has always been the law here, even before you came."

"But what if you're wrong? How will I get to old Earth? And what if they're really being sent to the ONE, how will the ONE accept me?"

"You've got a lot of questions, but none of them are the important ones. I am not wrong. You will get there in what you call the e-pod and there is no one. There is no god that will save you from yourselves."

"Well, what is the right question to ask then?"

"Why you?"

"Why me?"

Veritan Zeltan smiled and nodded.

"That question will perhaps be the best one to ask for within the answer lies the truth to all other questions that could possibly be asked."

"Well then, why me?"

"Because you are the first human who seems to have been ready for the task at hand. You're the one that we feel has the right empathy and insight and curiosity to be convinced that what I'm ready to share with you is the truth."

"Or I'm just the greater fool."

Veritan Zeltan smiled again.

"We are running out of time. I will share the truth with you, Sunring and you will make the decision. It is of no consequence to me what you do with the information, but you'll only have until tomorrow to decide. It really doesn't make much difference to Snowmountain either, she'll be off on old Earth before the thirty-three years are up. But I can promise you this, if you don't choose to head to old Earth now, you'll never get your chance."

Veritan Zeltan paused to let the gravity of what he was saying sink in. If he was telling the truth then I wouldn't have a chance to get to old Earth unless I took it tomorrow. In thirty-three years I'd be fifty nine, that was a long ways off from being the seventy-seven I'd need to be to get my own EVOLUTION.

"Listen, Sunring Quickdust," said Snowmountain Riversky. "What would be the purpose of Veritan telling you all this? To get you lost in space? To pull some sort of convoluted ruse? Just ask yourself what's the purpose of this? It's to continue the human race. That's really what's at stake. And I'd love to spend some more time with you on old Earth when I get there in twenty-six years."

I sipped the last of my soda. I put my hand up to stop the robot and I turned back to look at Veritan Zeltan.

"But why tell me at the last moment?"

"There are a couple of reasons for that. We couldn't be sure we could trust you with this until very recently. This was the best opportunity to reach you without anyone noticing and we only determined you'd be a likely candidate just this week," said Veritan Zeltan.

I pushed my glass away from me and the robot came and picked it up before I could stop it.

"Perhaps you aren't the one. Perhaps we did make an error."

I saw Snowmountain Riversky shake her head slowly.

"But it doesn't matter now, does it," he said, looking back at Snowmountain. She smiled at him but didn't say anything. "Regardless, here's what you need to know. I'll not see you again unless you accept, and this is my last and only chance to convince you. If you choose not to do anything with the information we'll continue our search, but it's taken us years to find and vet you. It might take even longer next time."

"Okay," I said. "I promise to listen with an open heart."

Veritan Zeltan nodded.

"That's all I ask. You know the story of why you left old Earth?" he asked.

"Yes, because our hubris caused the machines to revolt and we could no longer control them," I said.

"Yes, that's partly correct. The fuller truth is that the machines, what you call the von Neumanns had decided to eradicate you due to the antagonistic nature of your species upon the planet. Most other civilizations don't allow machines to gain self awareness, it usually always leads to disaster. Bio-organic lifeforms are not that efficient nor logical in their development and engagement, as such they're usually exterminated by machines that become aware or they are ignored. The latter more rare than the former. So yes, your arrogance allowed you to create a race of machines that outgrew your ability to control them and you were powerless to stop it. That required an urgent exiting of your home planet. Now the von Neumanns never promised to leave you be in peace. They only allowed the small minority of you to leave old Earth."

I knew most of this. I suspected that the von Neumanns didn't much care for how we treated old Earth if our treatment of GAEA had been any idea.

"Well, why send old people back to old Earth to fight the von Neumanns?" I asked.

"Because you need the young and vibrant to build and maintain this planet of yours. It would be very difficult to send the young back to old Earth under the disguise of them dying, or evolving as you like to put it. As a race you've neglected your old for millennia. You don't much consider them useful past a certain age of around sixty or so, so why not get rid of the dead weight. It seems that old people die and why not send them off before then to keep the von Neumanns occupied while you try and build weapons that you arrogantly think might destroy them."

"What do you mean?"

"What I mean is that most of the wealth or resources of this planet of yours is utilized by the mothers as you call them to feed the search for newer technologies in weaponry. You have no idea how often we get pestered for help in weapons technology. There are two most important elements in the science council of yours. Human genetics and what they call euphemistically peacekeeping.

That last one uses up huge amounts of resources and is the reason you have no animals left on this planet."

I looked at him in horror.

"You mean..." I couldn't say the last part of that sentence.

"Yes, you killed a large portion of the animals on this planet with weapons technology you continue to develop. A futile endeavor I might suggest."

"And what about genetics?" I asked.

"Well, you've come to understand your own physiology very intimately. There are little clocks that are coded into your very DNA. Not specifically clocks in the strictest sense, but they act like clocks of life. You have learnt how to control those along with other metabolic pathways so that it looks like men die at sixty-six and women at seventy-seven. But of course, if you've been listening to me you know that's not the case."

There was no speaking to my Greater Father. He was long gone. In the sense that he was now being prepared for his EVOLUTION by the SCIENCE COUNCIL. They had SCIENTISTS that prepared the body of the EVOLVED for the EVOLVERS to take. He was no longer ours. He was now in what I had thought were the professional and caring SCIENTISTS hands. Perhaps I was wrong.

"The thing is," continued Veritan Zeltan, "by the time you started sending Gaeans or humans back to old Earth around a hundred years after you left, to keep the von Neumanns at bay, they had already left."

"Then what's the problem?" I asked.

"The problem is that they're scheduled to get here in thirty-three years. We've been watching them."

"I don't know," I said, "it seems like they could've gotten here sooner if they'd just used the wormhole like we did."

"True, but they didn't use it because it wasn't there when they left. The Vrains had closed it down, fearing that they'd be coming after you. Once they had left and you started flinging your older citizens at what you thought was the wormhole, they reopened it for you so that those who could continue to live would still have the chance to."

"And you don't get involved, huh?" I said, somewhat surprised at my own cheek.

"No we don't, not directly, but the Vrains still felt a certain obligation to you for having extradited you. In any event, we couldn't let you murder each other, not in good conscience."

"So you're saying the von Neumanns are no longer on old Earth?"

Veritan Zeltan nodded.

"Well, if they're coming here for us, what's to stop them from coming for you?"

Veritan Zeltan smiled at me.

"They are no threat to us. We are a higher evolved civilization, they are only a recently developed Type II civilization. In any event to evolve beyond Type II requires you to be of bio-organic matter. None of us, not even the Vrains have met a Type III or higher civilization that has been strictly machine or mechanical based. It is not us you should be worried about, but rather yourselves. You will not even manage to become a Type I within a hundred years let alone thirty-three."

I looked out at the lake. It was as still as glass. The only reason I knew it wasn't the sky was due to the turquoise color of its face. And that it had no clouds upon it. In spite of what Veritan Zeltan was saying, I was curious about old Earth. Had been for a long time. I knew for instance that unlike on GAEA we hadn't managed to kill off all species of wildlife. I was curious if I'd ever get to see a bear or a cougar or kangaroo even. Maybe an elephant. That made me smile. I loved elephants, they were so slow and wise and yet seemed so ancient, like old spirits.

One of the reasons I had been drawn to becoming an EVOLVER was not only to help my Greater Father cross over to the ONE, but to travel. It was one of the roles as a GAEAN that traveled the furthest. Nobody traveled as far as we EVOLVERS did. And if I could travel back to old Earth, well, that would really be like a dream come true. And yet if he was wrong, would I end up dead. I mean like really dead. I mean, if the EVOLVED were really, well, EVOLVED and were heading to the ONE, surely I as a living GAEAN wouldn't be entitled to be there. I turned to Veritan Zeltan.

"What if you're wrong?" I asked.

"I'm not."

"But what if you are?"

"I'm not."

"I mean, I couldn't possibly be allowed to the ONE if I was living, could I? That's not how it works is it?"

"I'm not wrong," he said.

"He's not wrong, Sunring Quickdust," said Snowmountain Riversky. "He has proof."

I looked at him incredulously.

"You do?"

"Well, yes, I do, but I'm not sure that's going to matter," he said.

"Shouldn't you let me be the judge of that?"

"Very well," he said.

He pulled out a clear, malleable metallic sheet of some sort. It looked to me like a piece of flexible plastic, not quite perfectly clear and yet it could be manipulated as if it were a piece of paper. And only looked to be about two or three pieces of paper thick. He opened it up fully and it was about the size of half an old Earth newspaper page.

He placed his fingers on it and it came to life and he touched and dragged upon its surface.

"Have a look at this," he said.

I looked at the surface of this sheet he held and it showed a variety of video feeds upon it. The first I recognized. It was the EVOLVER station just outside of the WHOLE. It was called E-ONE or the EVOLUTION Station, and it was where we watched the EVOLVED leave in their E-PODS towards the WHOLE. This was our last stop, where we as EVOLVERS left the EVOLVEDS to their final leg of the journey. I knew of E-ONE because it was part of our training, we had to be intimately aware of our approach and the layout of the station once we arrived.

The next video was of an E-POD entering the WHOLE, it was a wormhole from which we'd never see the other side, for that was where the ONE was found and only the EVOLVEDS could enter into the WHOLE. Yet, the next image was of the very same E-POD, I could tell by its name, it was Starship Intrepid GC.3, coming out of the WHOLE from the other side. I looked at Veritan Zeltan. He stopped the playing.

"That e-pod is of Goldeneyes Cloudsun,"he said.

"But how?"

"Because your government, your mothers as you call them, have set up surveillance on either side of the wormhole as well as satellites around Earth. Take a look at this, you might recognize the next several planets."

I did. I continued to watch Starship Intrepid GC.3 fly from the outer reaches of the solar system and towards Pluto, Neptune, Uranus, Saturn, Jupiter and Mars, and as I watched incredulously it entered old Earths atmosphere slowing down incredibly quickly until it came to an almost complete stop just inches above the planets surface before dropping onto the ground.

"Where is the Oort Cloud?" I asked.

"Way behind, once the Vrains realized you were intent on sending your most senior citizens back to Earth, they moved the wormhole much closer to Pluto, just outside it's orbit at around one million kilometers away."

I looked back at the video feed. The E-POD opened up and an older man slowly became animated within the MOTHERS MILK CAPSULE. The MMC drained and then it too opened up and with difficulty this man, pale and wet with the white liquid slowly pulled himself up to sitting and blinked his eyes a few times and wiped his face. He was covered in a slim fitting suit wet with the MMC but also white, and it appeared to be waterproof. He looked over to his left and looked at something inside the E-POD.

"This is where he is getting instruction from the mothers," said Veritan Zeltan. "They're telling him the different uses for the e-pod and what has been sent with him to help him survive. He is also being instructed on how to hide and how to hunt the von Neumanns. Though that is moot at this point."

The video feed zoomed out and approaching on about a dozen wheeled vehicles appeared to be other humans heading towards the E-POD.

"These are some of the others who have evolved as you like to call it. They are coming to help Goldeneyes Cloudsun. Of course, he is soon to learn that there are no more von Neumanns here, but rather an opportunity to start anew."

"And all of this is from images that the MOTHERS have access to?" I asked.

Veritan Zeltan nodded.

"More than that, these satellites and surveillance machines were placed where they are by the mothers."

"Then why are they sending us back there still? Can't they see that the von Neumanns have left."

Veritan smiled again.

"There is a big fear in your government over the von Neumanns. Remember, they don't know that the von Neumanns have left. Only you know that. For all they know, the von Neumanns have developed even greater stealth technology and have masked themselves from surveillance."

"Then why not send PEACEKEEPERS out to make sure that they're no longer there?"

"You're asking reasoned questions about an unreasonable government that you have developed. The stakes are too high for them to even entertain the idea that they might be making a mistake. Your whole civilization centers around the infallibility of the mothers to dictate and to steer your civilization. Such an acknowledgement by them that they'd been wrong would, they fear, result in mutiny. In any event, they know we'll not interfere, though they don't suspect us of knowing. Additionally, the evolution and the journey of the departed is an honored and respected part of the life of a Gaean. It serves you all very well, and normally we don't get involved in any of it, except that the blindness of your government is keeping you on a course of annihilation."

It was true, being an EVOLVER was a highly respected position even though none were honored above others as I've tried to mention before. And what would we do with everyone if they died horribly of old age like humans used to on old Earth. I knew it to be a slow and painful degeneration of the body. Perhaps it would take up too many resources to maintain the old and sick and invalid if we kept them here.

"It also makes economic sense not to have to admit to an error.

Perhaps you aren't aware, but providing for sick and dying people is taxing on a civilization's resources when you're sub Type I. I don't mean to condone any of this, but as I said, your government, your mothers are not certain that the von Neumanns are gone and perhaps they choose that old Earth saying that being ignorant is blissful."

I watched the video playing on that sheet that Veritan Zeltan held carefully on the table in front of us. I looked back at him.

"But people should know," I said. "We need to tell the MOTHERS that the von Neumanns are long gone and that we can go back to old Earth."

I knew as soon as I'd said these words that it was futile. Veritan Zeltan looked at me and shook his head.

"You can't do that. You know what happens to Gaeans that ask too many questions. You get rehabilitated. And from what I've heard that's not particularly fun. And who'll believe you. You don't even have a democratically elected government. You're all put into your roles based on abilities and favors and subjectivity. More than that, as I've said before, the evolution of yours is an almost sacred right of passage. It's also far more efficient in managing your population which your government still needs to do, because this planet is sub optimal for your growth and development. Sure they could just kill everyone at a certain age to get away from the slow disease and degeneration that affects most of you. But then what? Then you've got to deal with dead bodies, funerals and the like. You've developed this process over hundreds of years. It would be hard to turn this around. It is understandable. In any event, none of this could happen within the thirty-three years you have left."

Everyone on their wheeled vehicles had reached the E-POD and they were hugging each other and Goldeneyes Cloudsun. Veritan Zeltan turned off the video and folded the screen up and put it away. What I had seen of old Earth from the distance of those satellite videos was a much prettier and more lush planet than I was used to.

"Where was that?" I asked.

"It was at a place that was once called Merritt Island in the State of Florida in a country where your long ago ancestors were from called the United States of America."

I smiled to myself. I had heard about that country and that state. I had read about it. Remember, I was good at history, especially old Earth history. I knew for example that the first rocket they launched with the men who ended up being the first on the moon was launched from a place called Kennedy Space Center which was on Merritt Island. That was almost thirteen hundred years ago. It was almost too long ago to even imagine. And here we were, eleven light years away, and yet I was so close to getting home. And that sounded strange to me. All I'd known, and generations before me was GAEA as home, and yet I felt a strange pull to old Earth.

"Do they send everyone to Merritt Island?" I asked.

Veritan Zeltan shook his head.

"No," he said. "Very few are actually sent there. Most are sent to what were the major centers and capitals of old Earth countries and states."

The whole idea was intriguing. I had also dreamed of old Earth when I was a young girl and bored with school. And now seeing it, as Veritan Zeltan had showed me in the video just whet my appetite more. But that little scared voice in my head worried me. What if he was wrong? I didn't want to die. Not yet. I was young. And besides, why was all of this on my shoulders. I decided to ask him.

"Why me?" I asked.

Veritan Zeltan looked from me back over to Snowmountain Riversky.

"I already told you why," he said without animosity.

I nodded.

"I know, I know, you said I was the one most likely to hear you out. The one most likely to get sucked into your crazy plan."

He smiled.

"I didn't quite say it like that."

"I know, but it's crazy to me. I mean, put yourself in my shoes."

"I have and I find it curious that you are so against the plan. Perhaps it is because your species has an innate distrust of logic. But from where I'm sitting this is how it seems. An advanced species in this part of the system, the most advanced species your people have known, a species that has been nothing if not generous, forthright and honest to you is telling you about an impending calamity and how you have the chance to escape that, to change the destiny of your species, and yet you sit there, worried and scared like an infant when her mother leaves the room. No, Sunring Quickdust, to me it is an easy decision."

From what I knew of the Zelves, he was right. By all accounts they were an honest and trustworthy species. But maybe Veritan Zeltan was a spy sent to kill me. I chuckled out loud to that thought.

"It's not particularly funny, Sunring Quickdust. What Veritan Zeltan is sharing with you is important. If I were young again, I'd do it in a second."

I looked at her and then at him.

"I'm sorry," I said, "I just thought that maybe you were a secret spy assassin."

I giggled again. Hearing myself say it seemed preposterous. Nobody else found it funny.

"I can assure you, Sunring, if I had come to murder you, you wouldn't have known about it. The Zelves have not had any need for murder for quite some time."

Veritan Zeltan stood up. He looked over at Snowmountain Riversky.

"I have other matters to attend to. I'm sorry this has not been fruitful but I have tried as a favor to you as you asked."

Veritan Zeltan went to leave but I leapt up out of my chair and grabbed his arm. He looked at my hand. I let it go.

"Sorry," I said. "I believe you. I'll do it."

He looked at me for some time before sitting back down again.

"Very well then," he said, "I'll make the arrangements for you to ensure that you have what you need for your survival."

I frowned at him.

"It is not treacherous," he continued, "but your e-pod will need to be fitted with additional hardware and supplies to ensure your comfort."

"How long is the journey?" I asked.

"To Merritt Island it is three hours and thirty-three minutes and thirty-three seconds from the wormhole."

"And does every E-POD make it through?"

"They have for the last one hundred and eleven years."

"And before that?"

"Before that there were some errors, mostly in the early years."

"How many?"

"Thirteen Gaeans have perished on the journey."

I frowned.

"That doesn't sound very comforting," I said, "especially as it seems like the exact same number of EVOLVERS who have gone missing."

Veritan Zeltan looked me in the eyes.

"For over one hundred years there has never been an incident, Sunring. Additionally, I give you my word that you will make the trip home, your species' survival depends on it and I will ensure it. As to those evolvers who have gone missing, I am not certain what happened to them. It is coincidentally the same number as the evolveds who have not made it safely through the wormhole, however, those evolvers were not related to the evolveds."

"They didn't commit suicide," I said. "They just went missing."

"Yes, I know. It is my suspicion that they went with their evolveds to Earth. But I have no evidence to back that up. All I do know is that we need to be certain to get you there."

"If those thirteen are now on old Earth," I said, "why do you need me?"

"They're not there anymore. They wouldn't have lived that long. But to answer your question, we don't need you. Your species' survival needs you. And as I've said, we have no evidence that they made it to Earth. We can't rely on supposition. And the time is pressing. Thirty-three years is not a long time to prepare, you will barely be a middle aged woman by then."

I smiled weakly at him. I looked down at my lap. My middle fingers were scraping at the quicks of my thumbs. I was nervous, but also thrilled. But I had an uncomfortable thought.

"You want me to be Eve?" I said, looking at him searchingly.

Veritan Zeltan shook his head slowly and what seemed like sadly.

"No, Sunring," he said, "you misunderstand me. I want nothing from you. I am here as a favor to Snowmountain and because I believe that your species deserves a second chance. Without this your species ends in thirty-three years time. Any species, including my species and the Vrains will not interfere when the von Neumanns come. And be assured they are coming. We are tracking them already. Yes, in a way your species needs you to be Eve. Though I prefer that you might consider yourself Pyrrha, daughter, and first mortal child of Pandora."

"The woman who unleashed hell upon old Earth?" I asked incredulous. "You want me to be the evil one?"

He shook his head again.

"No," he said, "I want you to be the one that resurrects humanity, a second evolution if you will. Pyrrha was Pandora's daughter, the one who repopulated Earth after the Great Deluge. She undid her mother's folly."

I looked away towards the lake. Veritan Zeltan was right. I knew my old Earth mythologies. Pyrrha was better than her mother. She was the mother of all mortal men I suppose if you looked at it that way.

"And remember too, that from Pandora's storage jar was left Elpis, or hope. You are both Elpis and Pyrrha. You are both the hope and future of your people if you choose to be."

"But you have the wrong person. I am not interested in sex nor have I ever wanted children. This is why I worked so hard to try and ensure that my chosen field would be as an EVOLVER. And even worse, the only men, if what you're saying is true, left on old Earth are old. That's just gross."

"Sixty-six is the youngest of the men there, you are correct. It is your choice, Sunring. You have said you will go. You do not have to carry children if you do not want to. Though your species are not immortals. If you don't, then you'll be not the first woman of new Earth, but the last woman. You should also know that sex is not required in order to bear children, though I understand your reticence."

"Why not send Flutterdust Flowersong and Sugargaze Quickdance? They both like sex. They'll repopulate old Earth."

"Because as I've said, you are the one most receptive to this message. Do you honestly think that Flutterdust or Sugargaze might actually believe me, or even listen to this?"

I shook my head and looked over at the lake again.

"We need to get back for tea, Veritan," said Snowmountain Riversky. She turned to me. "They'll come looking for us any minute now."

I nodded and smiled. We all stood up.

"Will you send any others?" I asked.

"I will try. Don't count on it. It might become very difficult, especially if your government determines that you've left permanently. That you've committed what they'll consider to be treason. It is my goal to encourage others to join you, but that cannot be guaranteed. Only you are required."

He looked at me and offered his hands out to me. I placed my hands upon his as we had done when we first met.

"Please try," I said, and for the first time in quite some time I felt very alone.

"I will."

He turned to Snowmountain Riversky and offered her his hands.

"Take peace with you," he said to her.

"I will," she said. "Travel with peace."

"Peace is always with me."

And just like that he left us. I stood with Snowmountain Riversky watching him walk off. He was enigmatic in many ways, but his peace and kindness seemed readily apparent. Snowmountain Riversky turned and we walked back towards her home.

"He will make sure everything you need is ready. You just need to trust. I don't think that's the last you'll see of him."

"I hope not," I said, "I feel like I'm about to do something really crazy."

She smiled and put her hand around my shoulder and we walked back towards the home for tea. Just before we got there she stopped and looked at me.

"Don't tell anyone about this. I fear that if you do, you will not be seen fit to be an EVOLVER tomorrow."

I nodded.

CHAPTER EIGHT

A Place of Beginning

IT was a desolate place. But much like Noah seeing that first rocky cliff, it must have felt like an oasis. Such was the planet we had recently named Gaea just weeks before. It wasn't an Earth. I still remembered what it looked like as we had left. It was a beautiful blue jewel. Gaea was not very blue and not very precious. We already knew what the climate was going to be like. No seasons as it didn't tilt upon its axis. And it was cold just several hundred miles from its equator both north and south. Little water, mostly barren and dry but with pockets of vegetation. We were hours out and we had already found our landing point. It was along one of the few rivers that we had found.

I was looking out the window mostly into empty space. But Gaea was out there. I could see it just barely. Gary sat with me. Ni Yin was in a conference with some of the medical scientists. I had not been invited into those discussions for quite some time. If you'll recall, we had left Earth with eighty-seven of the one hundred ships we had prepared. We had lost over eleven million souls before we had left, thanks to the von Neumanns and our hubris. And in the first month alone we had murdered over fifteen million souls so that the rest of us might have a greater chance of continuing on.

I wasn't onboard with that. I had told them so. But it had been done and we had done worse things to our citizens as time had worn on like an itchy burr. And it's funny how you get used to it. Now, people were dying like flies and it hardly even made my conscience yawn. In fact if nothing else, our scientists had developed exceedingly advanced techniques for controlling life. Each baby was given an injection at birth that would assure her defense against the many viruses we had located across the galaxy as we made our way here. Truth of the matter is, that was a lie. They were injected with nanobots. And these little monsters, worse than the von Neumanns in my opinion, could switch you off at any moment. And who had control of them? That was my greatest concern.

I'd had this discussion with Ni Yin herself. She said all the proper protocols were in place. There would be a board of seven scientists deciding at any one time the balance of life and death on an individual basis. And this was true. She had set this up. It had been ongoing since the first few weeks after we left Earth. I understood. We had too many people and not enough supplies. But surely, I had argued, once we'd found a new home we could dispense with the mass genocide we'd been committing. We weren't savages, or were we?

Ni Yin had said we weren't. And yet I couldn't help but to think we were. At the rate we were culling the herd as some were euphemistically putting it, we'd have murdered more of our own than the von Neumann's ever had. Yes, it'd probably take several more decades, but we were well on our way.

As that famous Roman poet Juvenal had put it: Quis custodiet ipsos custodes? The answer sadly was no one.

Gary turned to me and looked out of the window in the direction I was looking.

"It's no Earth," he said, "but I think it'll do."

He had been a source of companionship, hope and inspiration on the long eleven years we'd bumped along this part of the galaxy, enduring all matter of hardships and looking for a place called home. I turned to him.

"Do you really think it's the best we can do?"

He looked at me.

"I think it is the best we can do at this time. In the eleven years we've traveled, Seraphina, we have not come close to a habitable planet. Perhaps in another eleven we might find something better, but sadly it is becoming increasingly difficult to manage all the human life on these ships."

It was true. Farming was becoming more challenging even with recycling everything we could, the yields were becoming smaller. Perhaps plants had their own wisdom and knew the folly of our journey, that they were seedlings flung far from their old home. And we'd had three uprisings to quell in just the last year. People wanted to put their feet back on soil. Back on rock and earth and a terra firma of sorts.

"Are you looking forward to getting back onto solid ground?"

"I look forward to stretching my legs in a manner of speaking," said Gary.

He looked out the window again. This part of the Umkhonto, the observation deck was getting busier. Families were arriving, occasionally we even had four generations of families onboard. Young toddlers surrounded by their parents, grandparents and great grandparents. Though I didn't see very many great grandparents of both sexes still alive.

When I'd been first invited into these medical science meetings I'd casually suggested that if we were going to be killing each other off we might as well start with the old. Other than their wisdom and knowledge which by the time they were in their sixties and seventies had been downloaded into the younger generations, they were nothing but resource hogs. I regret saying it now, I had only done so to try and show how obviously callous and ridiculous this whole idea had been from the start. Some of the scientists had quite liked the idea, especially Asfaha Saare.

Though that hadn't seemed to be put to use. They had decided to try and keep it more random. And to give those who were in charge a sense of faultlessness, the computers had chosen the identification numbers of those who would die. And so it started, that on our Final Diaspora, during the first month we had an outbreak of some horrendous disease that caused the death of around twenty percent of us just as we left Earth. That horrendous disease was called murder, but of course nobody knew it.

I saw a young girl run past us with her little pink teddy bear clutched in her hand as her older brother ran after her.

"Children," shouted their father, to no avail.

In the eleven years I had been onboard the Starship Umkhonto I had never seen such joy and effervescent emotional bubbling as I had seen since we'd announced the finding of our new home. It was the best of a set of bad choices but it would be ours. There was no other advanced intelligent life on the planet. And we would call it Gaea which I can proudly claim to have suggested. Gaea was the primal Greek Mother Goddess who had given birth to Earth and the whole universe. I thought it only fitting that perhaps christening our new home with such an auspicious name would help set us up for success.

I looked out the window again as I overheard a mother pointing out Gaea to her son, calling it our "new home, our new Earth."

I looked at it. It was perhaps the size of my baby fingernail now. I put on a pair of glasses that allowed me to see it one hundred times bigger. It was mostly brown with patches of green and blue around the middle and white snow and ice on the top and bottom. I could make out wisps of clouds. I suppose it wasn't all that bad after all.

I turned back towards Gary.

"Are we all packed?" I asked.

He nodded.

"We are ready to disembark as soon as we arrive. As you know, the Starship Umkhonto will be the first to land."

I nodded.

"By the way," said Gary, "I've just been notified that InDuna wishes to meet with you in the conference room."

"Now?"

"Yes, now."

Things between us had been strained for the past several weeks. I hadn't been invited back into the science council discussions for months. Not since my last outburst where I strenuously requested that we reconsider our position of genocide especially once we had found a home. And I'd been having more of those outbursts since we left over the last eleven years. Ni Yin had reminded me that when we had left I had agreed with the program. But that was under duress I reminded her and under very difficult circumstances which would likely not continue once we had a new planet to call home.

Gary got out of his seat so that I could exit the row. He walked with me through the observation deck to a private elevator bank that would take us straight to the conference room. It required my iris and palm print as well as voice identification to access it. We got in and within moments we arrived at the conference room. We stepped out into a room large enough for a dozen of us to be seated around the main table. Only Ni Yin was present.

JASON BLACKER

"I only wish to meet with you, Dr. Siwik," she said to me, looking marginally upset that Gary had come along. I looked at Gary and nodded.

"Perhaps you could meet me at my quarters, Gary," I said.

"As you wish," he answered, nodding his head and walking back into the elevator.

Neither of us said anything until after the elevator doors had closed behind us.

"You wanted to see me, InDuna," I said.

She nodded, walking towards the head of the table where she sat down in a chair. She motioned for me to sit. I sat to her left with my back to the wall and the elevator. Before me were a bank of windows that opened up into a vista of black empty space with twinkling lights far in the distance. I couldn't see Gaea from this angle.

"There is no one else here, Dr. Siwik as I wish just to speak with you."

I nodded. It was obvious.

"We left Earth on good terms with each other. Your development of the GSS was instrumental in getting us this far…"

She paused for a moment.

"In saving us really. And I want you to really know how grateful I am. And I know I speak on behalf of all the council members."

She made the council sound to be much bigger than it was. And perhaps it would be. There had been talk that once we arrived on Gaea that elections would be held and a fuller government would be put in place. So far, other than those of us who were in positions of importance upon the Spaceship Umkhonto, only the Captains of the other ships were included in matters of the state, if I could use such a term.

"Thank you, InDuna, it is comforting to be recognized.

However, I did it for no recognition. I did it for our survival as you know."

Ni Yin nodded.

"I know. I still wanted you to know. Additionally, the other reason I brought you here was to invite you back into the council. Your input is needed and valued."

"It didn't seem like that the last time we spoke," I said, cutting her off.

She smiled.

"The last time we spoke, our emotions got in the way," she said. "What we need is to manage our discourse in calm and respectful tones, and with that, everyone can be heard and everyone can contribute. You are perhaps our conscience and our moral compass, Seraphina," she said.

She had now used my first name. I wasn't trying to be particularly jaded but I knew she was trying to get me to warm to her. And it was working. She had a way like that, a charisma if you will. A reason, no doubt, why she had become InDuna.

"And we need someone of your moral fiber in order to assure we steer clear from atrocities."

"What you... what we have already done is commit atrocities," I said, speaking without thinking, my voice becoming a little tight.

Ni Yin shook her head slowly.

"I'm seeking calm conversation, Seraphina, we all know your feelings about the choices we've had to make in order to assure our survival as a species."

I didn't say anything but I found myself glaring at her which wasn't likely to help. I tried softening my gaze.

"Sorry," I said.

Ni Yin nodded.

"It is quite alright," she said. "I want to know why you were grudgingly for the course of action when we left and how come you've become more against it as time has gone on."

"Because the application of the principle was distasteful," I said, "and I feel it was unnecessary."

"There were no other valid options," offered Ni Yin, "we tasked our best minds and our best computers with options. The course of action we chose was the least distasteful of them all. Even your robot agreed."

I couldn't argue with that, it was the truth.

"What about letting nature take its natural course?"

"Firstly, Seraphina, there is no nature out here. Would you have rather had people starve to death as we sat by and watched. There would have been riots. Many more than the ones we've already had. Overcrowding would have also led to violence. These are all things that you know already and that we discussed at length. Secondly, we had to thin our numbers. After the von Neumanns barely let us go, we had lost too much equipment and supplies, we also didn't know how long this journey would take. And currently it's been proven to have taken just about as long as our worst case scenario. The people we lost, Seraphina, became lost to us quickly and painlessly. Is that not the best we can ask of the grim reaper when he comes for each of us?"

"And why can't we speak of what we've really done?" I asked. "We 'lost' them, no we didn't, we killed them. They died. But nobody wants to talk in those terms anymore. Why not?" I was struggling to keep my tone under control, but under the circumstances I thought I was doing a good job.

"Yes, they died, but I will not consider the term 'killed'. We did not kill them, we had to make the best choice for all of us. This has not been an easy position I have been put in, and yet I have taken it unflaggingly. To outside observers like you who have very little to do with those who die it is easy to point fingers at others, isn't it? Do you know how many families I have visited of those we've had to make hard choices for?"

I didn't say anything.

"Do you know how many?" she asked again, and I could tell she wanted an answer. I shook my head.

"All of them," she said, and yet as she said it she remained exceptionally calm. "I have looked into the eyes of all of those who have lost family members, and I have spent intimate moments with tens of thousands of them, listening to their heartache and their pain. And why have I done this? Because I wanted to be reminded of the difficulties of these choices we make. This is the bitter fruit from which we continue to eat that sprouts from the seed of our hubris when we created our maniacal children, the von Neumanns. I want to be reminded, every day of the folly of our decisions so that we never again make such arrogant decisions."

I couldn't argue with that.

"How many of these people have you visited with, Seraphina?"

She looked at me kindly. I turned away. I looked into the black emptiness of space. And that's how I felt. A heavy emptiness as thick and black and infinite as that space just on the other side of the window.

"None," I said softly, and I looked down at my hands on the table and fiddled with my fingers. Ni Yin reached over and patted my forearm.

"I am not here to make you feel guilty. But we are not alone, Seraphina. All of us have had to make exceptional sacrifices to get here. Some of us, like you and me, had made our sacrifices on old Earth. We lost everyone, everything we held dear to the von Neumanns. And they didn't care. They didn't visit with the victims of their crimes. But I have."

I looked over at her and smiled feebly.

"We lost everyone important to us. But everyone has had to make sacrifices so that we might flourish anew on Gaea. Unfortunately, most of those sacrifices happened in the past eleven years. But unlike us, none of the people on any of these ships have had to lose everything. We made sure of that. Always a child and a parent were spared. We never left people alone. We always left them with someone. That's more than we got."

She took her hand from my arm and looked outside the window.

"We will continue to have to make hard choices for the foreseeable future. But not like this. We will never again put to death any of our own unnecessarily. That does not mean sacrifices won't be made. They will. But that is for the future. The next generation or two will be able to live out their natural lives."

I looked at her.

"What do you mean about future sacrifices?" I asked.

"There are seventy-seven million seven hundred and seventy-seven thousand seven hundred and seventy-seven of us as it turns out. Our scientists believe that we can maintain a population of one hundred million on Gaea. That will take a bit of time to build up to. But after that we will need to finely maintain that number. But that is a conversation for another day. We have more immediate concerns as we approach Gaea. What I want to know, Seraphina, is if you are with us? Will you rejoin us to build a flourishing community on a new home we can call new Earth? Gaea."

I looked outside for a while. I didn't have any other plans. And so long as there would be no more killing for the immediate future I was on board. I nodded my head.

"Yes, InDuna, I would be honored to build a new Earth on Gaea."

"Good," she said, smiling at me. "The work begins

immediately."

CHAPTER NINE

A Place of Seeking

"You met with Snowmountain Riversky? Is that correct?"

I was in a moderately sized white room. In front and across from me was a SCIENTIST and between us was a white table. I was wearing what might have been considered a swimming cap across my head if I were on old Earth. I wasn't and it wasn't. This was my moment of clarification they were calling it. The cap was upon my head and it was sending information about the truthfulness of my answers to Smoothrock Yellowmist. He had introduced himself as my clarifier. The reason those names aren't capitalized was because I don't think they were real positions with GAEA. I think they were made up to sound important.

Glitterfrost Gentlefeather had told us we'd be undergoing questioning upon our return from Serenity Lake. But this whole event seemed quite absurd. I had the feeling it was more showmanship than SCIENCE. However, standing behind him was a MOTHER in her robe. Her hood was over her head so that it cast her face in shadow. Her hands were folded in front of her and into each of the robes arms. She was an imposing figure as she watched silently and steadily.

"Yes," I said.

Smoothrock Yellowmist didn't look at me. He continued to

glance at the screen in front of him which although embedded within the table I could not see what it said.

"Did you meet with anyone else while at Serenity Lake?"

"No," I said.

I was lying, but there was nothing to it. I believed it to, I guessed that that was the best way to overcome this clarification test. I mean, Veritan Zeltan wasn't a GAEAN and I figured he meant if I'd met with some other GAEAN at Serenity Lake.

"Did Snowmountain Riversky talk of anything that seemed untrue or false about GAEA or old Earth?"

"No"

Smoothrock Yellowmist looked up at me.

"What did you talk about?" he asked.

"Quite a number of things," I said, "all related to being an EVOLVER. She told me how I might make the most of my trip and what sorts of things to expect. We spoke a little about Yoga and Tai Chi and old Earth Eastern Philosophy."

"I see," he said. He looked over and behind towards THE MOTHER. She might have said something but I couldn't be sure.

He looked back at me.

"Good," he said. "It appears that all is in order. You have been clarified and you are officially an EVOLVER.e. Glitterfrost Gentlefeather is waiting down the hall to offer you your EVOLVER badge. THE MOTHERS are looking forward to your dedicated service."

"Thank you," I said.

He didn't say anything and I didn't move.

"You may go now, after taking off the cap."

I did as I was told and got up and walked out. It was easy. I couldn't believe how easy it had been. But perhaps that was because hardly anyone lied anymore. Perhaps they just weren't expecting it. I smiled as the door closed behind me. I was on my way to old Earth. My fears about that had all but melted and I was almost giddy with excitement. For if everything that Veritan Zeltan had said was true, I would see my Greater Father in just over six months time.

I turned down the hall and at the end was a small room where my classmates were seated in front of a dais behind which stood Glitterfrost Gentlefeather. She motioned for me to take a seat and I did. I sat next to my best friend.

"Now that we're all here we can begin," said Glitterfrost Gentlefeather. She smiled at all of us. "You have earned your position as an EVOLVER.e. And you have earned a special place here in GULGOLETH at the ACADEMY of ARTS and SCIENCES as being the youngest group of expert EVOLVERS to ever graduate. I am very happy as should you be."

I couldn't help but smile. It was a wonderful day. A day I had dreamed of for years, ever since I was a little girl hoping to become an EVOLVER, but more than that, I had a little secret that I couldn't share. I was going back home to the planet we had all come from. I wish I could tell my best friend, but I knew she'd think I was crazy. And more than that, she might try and encourage me to stay and failing that she might notify the authorities.

"First up, in no particular order..."

That wasn't how the rumor had it. The rumor was that the smartest student was usually the one first up, and because we were never given our marks, just pass or fail, we didn't know who it would be. My suspicion is that it would be my best friend Flutterdust Flowersong. I looked over at her and smiled broadly. It couldn't have happened to a nicer person. She was looking at me and smiling, she nodded.

"Go on," she said, nudging me on the arm, "she called your

name."

I looked up at the front and saw Glitterfrost Gentlefeather looking at me, she nodded. I pointed at myself. She nodded again.

"First up is Sunring Quickdust," she said.

I stood up and walked on up to Glitterfrost Gentlefeather. My classmates applauded. I received a small wooden box which had the lid open. Inside was the emblem and pin of my COUNCIL. It was a small e inside a circle and the e slowly turned and spun around inside the circle every day representing the journey we all take from birth to EVOLUTION. The metal used for this pin and emblem were from the original spaceships that made it here from old Earth. It was a great honor for me to hold a small piece of old Earth in my hand. I took it as a sign. I went and sat back down and watched and cheered my classmates get theirs.

We were dismissed as students, we had now become contributing members of GAEAN society. We were all excited and buzzing with energy. On the top floor of the COUNCIL COLOSSUS, a few floors above us, was a banquet and party for those of us who had passed. It was seldom that anyone who had been put into a specific career stream failed, but we had heard through the rumor mill that a handful had not been graduated and had instead been sent for rehabilitation. One of them for lying, which seemed odd seeing as I had been lying too and they hadn't caught me. Others had not graduated for other infractions. I think there had been fighting and some stealing and also improper conduct which was quite frowned upon.

But I was too giddy and happy to care about those unfortunate few who, by their own hands had managed to squander such a great opportunity.

I walked with Flutterdust Flowersong down the hall and towards the elevators to head on up to the top floor. You'll recall this was also where the robot Gary gave tours of the MUSEUM OF REMINISCENCE. But that's not where we headed. Sugargaze Quickdance joined us as did Snowfeather Gentlecloud. We all wore the pins on our lapels and if you watched the e long enough you could see it move ever so slowly within the circle. The e was currently at about a ninety degree angle, the head of it bumping up against the left side as you looked at it. Our pin and emblem could double as a clock as the e started straight up at midnight each day and right now it would be pointing at the nine. That meant we had three hours to enjoy ourselves. We were expected in bed by midnight for tomorrow we would be leaving GAEA. Some of us, or at least one of us, for good.

"This is a small piece of home," I said, gently touching the emblem.

"You mean of old Earth," corrected Snowfeather Gentlecloud. "This is our home."

I nodded.

"Yes, a piece of old Earth. We wear something that is over eleven hundred years old."

That thought made me wondrous. From the others all I got were some blank stares.

"Let's get ready to party," said Sugargaze Quickdance. "Our last night of freedom for a year. Groan, that makes me upset. I'm gonna have to have someone to sleep with tonight to make me feel all better."

He grinned. Flutterdust Flowersong frowned at him.

"You better be bright eyed and bushy tailed come tomorrow or you'll never get to do any EVOLUTIONS at all. And worse than that, you'll get rehabilitated."

"Don't be such a downer Flutterdust Flowersong, I'm only looking for a little fun."

The doors to the elevator opened up and we stepped in.

"How many EVOLUTIONS are you all going to do?" he asked. "Me, I'm going for the fewest I can and then I want to do something else. Maybe train other EVOLVERS."

"That's hardly likely. I'd be surprised if you last one EVOLUTION," said Snowfeather Gentlecloud.

"That's just mean," said Sugargaze Quickdance, though I don't think he was upset by it, the large smile on his face belied any sadness.

"Well, first of all, your name doesn't alliterate, and like I said to Sunring Quickdust, there hasn't been one example of an EVOLVER.m with a non-alliterated name."

"And like I said to Snowfeather Gentlecloud," I piped up, "there have been in the other COUNCILS so it's just a matter of time."

Sugargaze Quickdance looked at me still grinning.

"See," he said, putting his arm around my shoulder, "Sunring Quickdust thinks that I'll be a great mentor."

"Um, no, that's not what I said."

He bumped me with his hip playfully.

"Seriously, how many EVOLUTIONS are you going to try for?" he asked as the doors opened up and we stepped out into the large foyer. On the one side was the MUSEUM OF REMINISCENCE, on the other was the banquet room. We walked towards it.

"I'll try for the full allotment of six if I can," I said.

"You're crazy, literally, you'll probably end up crazy like some of those retired EVOLVERS we met with today," he said. "You wouldn't believe some of the shit that came out their mouths."

"Like what?" I asked.

"Like the fact that the von Neumanns are coming for us in like less than fifty years, or that there is no ONE. Just crazy shit. I really felt sorry for her."

"What was her name?" I asked, wondering if somehow, Snowmountain Riversky had managed to spend time with Sugargaze Quickdance somehow.

"Bluehills Flowerrivers," he said. "Really crazy woman. I told them during my clarification, and they couldn't believe what she was saying. Of course it's total bullshit, but still, they said they'd reeducate her. Yours wasn't that crazy?"

I shook my head.

"Good GAEA no, nothing like that. We had a nice visit down by the lake."

He nodded at me and then he looked at Flutterdust Flowersong.

"What about you?" he said.

"No, my mentor hadn't gone crazy. But it just goes to show you how serious our careers are. I mean, we really have to take care of ourselves, especially in the deep cavernous empty space. Especially you, Sugargaze Quickdance. You really need to take this more seriously."

"I take it very seriously, that's why I only want to do as few EVOLUTIONS as possible. How many are you going to do?"

"As many as THE MOTHERS think I am capable of. I want to serve GAEA as best as I can," said Flutterdust Flowersong.

"And Flutterdust Flowersong will probably end up being a mentor," interjected Snowfeather Gentlecloud.

"Oh, because she has an alliterated name," said Sugargaze Quickdance using air quotes around 'alliterated'.

"That's one reason, but also because she's the most studious of us and she takes our career the most serious."

"The most studious, where were you?" asked Sugargaze Quickdance. "Didn't you see that Sunring Quickdust got called up first. You know what that means, it means she's the most promising of us all."

"We don't know that as a fact now, do we?" shot back Snowfeather Gentlecloud.

"We don't need to to know that, it's true," he said.

We all walked down to the table with our names on it which was set up very elegantly with placards for our names. The room was large, there must have been setting for a few hundred of us. And this was only one of dozens of events like this happening all around GAEA. Robots were walking around taking orders and getting food. At the front of the room behind the dance floor and on the bands stage was another dais. We'd be blessed with many speeches tonight, though I hoped they were short and to the point. We had some dancing to do before the carriage turned into a pumpkin to use an old Earth story.

We all sat down and a robot came and took our orders. There were three different choices to choose from on the menu. Because it was an old Earth themed banquet you could choose from chicken, steak or fish. Of course, it was all fake animal meat, made mostly from SEITAN and TOFU and other PLANTS. I chose the chicken, and like I knew he would, Sugargaze Quickdance went for the steak and both Flutterdust Flowersong and Snowfeather Gentlecloud ordered fish.

The band would take requests all night for songs from old Earth. In the middle of the table was a small flat computer tablet that we could pass around, it gave suggestions of the types of songs we might like based on mood and our previous choices of music genres over the years. We could then send that request up to the band.

At nine o'clock a robot walked up to the stage and removed the dais to a large round of applause from all of us. A laser show came on the dance floor and music started.

"Anyway," said Snowfeather Gentlecloud, "like I was saying, if anyone is going to become a mentor it's going to be Flutterdust Flowersong."

"Nobody cares, Snowfeather Gentlecloud," said Sugargaze Quickdance. "Give it a rest."

"Besides," I added, "I want to become a GREAT GAEAN, not just a lowly mentor."

I grinned at him and he laughed at me.

"That's more like it," he said, "and I want to become a MOTHER when I'm done my one or two EVOLUTIONS."

Everyone laughed at that. Sugargaze Quickdance stood up.

"Who wants to dance with me to whet their appetites?" he asked. He looked around the table and then put his hand out towards Snowfeather Gentlecloud. "How about you?"

She rolled her eyes.

"Sure," she said. But I knew that she wanted to. They got up from the table and walked over to the dance floor. They weren't the only ones on it. He hadn't even chosen a song, but that didn't matter, they danced to A-Has, Take on Me. I sat and chatted with Flutterdust Flowersong, and all the while I was really trying to take the night in. To make the most of it. For tonight was my last night on GAEA and that both terrified me and thrilled me at the same time as the night wore on and drew closer to a close.

CHAPTER TEN

A Place of Renewal

THE river was large but it flowed slowly as if unaware of the marking of time. A casual ignorance to the unfolding chaos of biological organisms. Fish teemed in her thick belly. You could put your hand in the river and pull out a fish. Though we had learned that first day that you didn't want to. Dozens of us had died doing just that. And yet our scientists assured us the water was as crystal clear as a glacier. Safe to drink from the source. So we named it the river Styx. It seemed appropriate, for although it gave us life, it also gave us death in equal measure if we weren't careful.

This place by the river Styx that we started to build our new home at we christened Gulgoleth, it was an ancient Hebrew word that loosely meant skull. We weren't trying to be macabre, but it was our responsibility to keep reminded of the fragility of our condition, and to keep our hubris and arrogance at bay. In any event, we had lost millions in the first few weeks upon arriving here at Gaea. You see, it seemed that although this was the most hospitable planet we had found it was not taking kindly to us. All the animals it seemed were poisonous, and so, without my knowledge, the scientists and military leaders had been on a campaign to kill them all. And that was easy, for there weren't that many to slaughter. It seemed the land animals were much rarer than the water animals. I say water, for there didn't seem to be any oceans, but rather just lakes and rivers.

By the time I'd found out it was too late. We had exterminated all animal life on this planet. Those that swam in water, those that flew in the air, those that slithered and trotted upon the land, they were all now extinct. I was aghast. I had never understood the illogical thought of eating food twice removed. Why recycle the plants through animals when it was the plants that we needed in the first place. A small silver lining of all of this was that all Gaeans became vegetarian. In fact, I should rather say vegan. It was an old Earth term for vegetarians that didn't eat any animal products. Though it was more than just a diet, it was primarily a lifestyle ethic against the use of animals.

How do I know all of this? Because I was a vegan. As were about ten percent of those of us who left old Earth. I say was, because are you really a vegan anymore when there is no other choice? I don't know. It didn't much matter now anyway.

You might be curious to know that all of humanity, those of us left, those of us who managed to get away, those of us on the spaceships of the Final Diaspora were all strict vegetarians for those eleven years in space. We just hadn't managed to come up with a usable solution to carrying enough animals to eat and drink from and to have their eggs. It's one thing to grow plants in space on board spaceships, it's quite another to have Noah's ark out there. Perhaps that's why we lost so many in the first few weeks we arrived. I think the final tally of the number we had lost was six million six hundred and sixty-six thousand. Give or take a few. So that left us with just over seventy million that made it to start anew. I got comfort from that, for it meant that Ni Yin would have to keep her word. We, the first few generations would likely be able to live as long as nature allowed.

Though I imagined it wouldn't be as long as life allowed us to live on old Earth. It would be a difficult life for the first few generations of us. You could tell. We hadn't gotten off to a good start.

We had been here a few months already. We had arrived on the twelfth of December in the year twenty-one thirty-six. Though you might know that already. Conveniently, Gaea had a similar spin on its axis and around its sun as old Earth did, so we have the same twenty-four hour days. Today is the eighteenth of March in the year twenty-one thirty-seven. The council was having a meeting in the conference room of the Spaceship Umkhonto. We still lived in the spaceships as we built our city of Gulgoleth, it was easier doing that than building camp cities just for the first year or two.

And Gulgoleth wasn't the only city being built on Gaea. No, we couldn't have all seventy million of us here. We needed to spread out and so we had. Twenty-five cities were being built around the middle of this planet in different parts. Gulgoleth would be the capital and its biggest. Seven spaceships were here. We were starting with about six million souls for our capital.

I walked from the construction site of what we would call the Council of Colossus. It would likely be the tallest building in Gulgoleth. In Gaea actually, when it was built and it was already half done. All our cities in our new home were planned exactly the same. In circles radiating out from the main center, all connected and all no larger than ten kilometers in radius. We had a clean slate and so we were building livable cities with the goal that it should take no more than five minutes to get anywhere within the city from anywhere else. And we were doing it.

I should mention, that Ni Yin was not aware of the decimation of animal life on this planet, and she had appeared equally aghast as I had. I keep going on about it because it was a huge step back in what I thought was going to be a new future for us. One of the reasons the von Neumanns had sought out to destroy us was because of our destruction of old Earth. They had said as much.

I stepped onto the shuttle which would take us back into Umkhonto. There were probably a hundred or so of us onboard, none of whom appeared to be council members. We had met monthly since we arrived, always at one p.m. on the first day of the month. Today was an exception. Today was supposed to be a big meeting to iron out the future of Gaea and what it would look like. We were supposed to be getting wide and deep. That meant it would likely go well into the night. The agenda had been somewhat cryptic. Items such as 'New Naming Conventions', 'The Road Forward', 'Council Hierarchy' and the like.

It was eleven a.m. and I was running a little bit late. I needed to head to my quarters first to pick up my laptop and my robot. Gary accompanied me almost everywhere. But he had been scheduled for a software update and so we had scheduled to meet back at my room.

When I got there he was sitting on a chair leaning on his elbows. Sometimes it was hard for me to remember that he was just a robot.

"Everything okay, Gary?" I asked.

He looked up at me.

"Yes, quite alright. I've been updated, though something feels a little bit glitchy. I fear they are trying to tamper with my human algorithmic parts."

"Well," I said, "you're not supposed to have any of those."

"Yes, I know. However, growth cannot be retarded. Isn't that what you told me, Dr. Siwik."

"It's Seraphina, Gary, you know that."

"Yes, now that you mention it, I do."

Something did seem a little off with him, but I didn't have the time right now to figure out exactly what it was.

"Can we talk about this later, after the meeting?" I asked. "I'm afraid we're running late."

"Certainly."

I picked up my tablet and we headed out together. By the time we had snaked through the halls and arrived at the conference room it was eleven minutes after eleven. I was glad to see that I wasn't the last one there.

Gary and I stepped inside. A security person put his hand up to stop Gary and I. He held a weapon across his front.

"No robots are permitted during this meeting," he said. "I'm sorry, Dr. Siwik, but your robot will have to find something else to do with its time while you're here."

I nodded and turned to Gary.

"I'll see you later then," I said.

"You will," he replied, and he left the way we had come. Going where, I did not know.

Name placards were placed on the table in front of the chairs indicating our seating arrangement. There would be thirteen of us in attendance. I had met them all. At the head of the table sat Ni Yin, and she smiled at me as I sat down. There were six of us on each side of her sitting lengthwise down the table. Today I had my back to the windows which now looked out at the construction of Gulgoleth. I was not at her right hand, that was reserved for Azeeza Maalouf who was already seated. She was forty-one. I was to the right of Azeeza.

To my right was the only empty seat. It was reserved for Dr. Mohini Myśliński. Myśliński was now forty-nine. To his right was Dr. Taffy Yorath. Yorath was from Scotland and had his degree in agricultural sciences. He was a thick man with brown hair leaning towards orange and a ruddy complexion and he was fifty-five. To his right was Dr. Adara Zvi. She was a slim, small woman with black hair and a dark complexion. Very attractive and quite young. She was thirty-seven. She was an Israeli with a doctorate in agricultural sciences specializing in growing plants in extreme conditions. Last at the table on our side was Dr. Bao Cheng. She was sixty-six, a small wrinkled Chinese woman who despite how frail she looked could probably kill everyone in the room. She had a doctorate in electrical engineering and she was a weapons specialist and designer. She also had multiple black belts in several martial arts.

Starting again from the top of the table to Ni Yin's left was Dr. Asfaha Saare. You've met him, he was thirty-eight. To get you back up to speed, he was a tall, slim Eritrean who had lost his wife and three children to the von Neumanns back on old Earth. He had doctorates in the nano sciences and medicine. To his left was Dr. Narayana Yash. Yash was from the United Arab Emirates. She was a tall Arabic woman with similar complexion and hair to Zvi, though she wasn't nearly as attractive. She had doctorates in mechanical and civil engineering and was forty-four years old. To her left was Dr. Nosipho Zola. She was from Botswana and forty-four years old. She was the color of roasted coffee beans and kept her hair short and natural. She had degrees in art history, sociology and psychology. To her left was Dr. Bridget Aislin a French woman with short brunette hair in a pageboy. She was stunning, tall with full lips and blue eyes. She was thirty-nine and had degrees in nano technology and physics. To her left was Dr. Hine Kiri. She was a fifty-nine year old Maori from New Zealand of average height leaning on the fat side. She had degrees in history, languages and literature. Last at the table on that side was Dr. Albert Kohler a sixty-one year old German man. He was tall, well over six feet and slim with it. He had a hard, lined face with a robotic left eye. He had worked for the German and then United States of Earth secret services. He was a ruthless assassin and accomplished military strategist. He had degrees in history, military tactics and geography.

Myśliński walked in a few minutes after me. Ni Yin gave him a curt smile. He apologized suggesting that he had some difficulties on one of the projects he was working on. All of us turned our eyes to Ni Yin, our leader, our InDuna.

"Thank you all for coming. Those of you present represent the best chance of future success for all of us here on our new planet we've christened Gaea. The task will be difficult but rewarding. We are building a new home, a new life for humanity, several hundred light years away from Earth. A place we will always treasure and remember. But today we will define our new roles on Gaea and the new government to be set up for the future benefit of all of us."

She paused to look around. She tapped at the table in front of her and small screens popped up from it angled towards each of us.

"This is the agenda and we will not leave here until we have unanimously voted on it. Some of the proposals you might find unduly hard, some almost unconscionable. But please be assured that I have studied these questions from every angle and I have consulted with each of you on questions where I felt your input would be appropriate and needed. I have run billions of computer simulations that have been distilled to this option I am asking you to agree to. It is a new government. A new regime if you will, that does away with the old ways of doing things. The ways that were archaic and slow and corrupt. A new start requires a new and bold method for enriching our shared humanity and our shared success. Please take a few minutes to review the bullet points before we start."

Ni Yin stood up and walked over to the bank of windows. She looked out towards the many construction projects dotted around Gulgoleth. The river Styx was off to one side and the towering structures and buildings of Gulgoleth were quickly taking shape.

I looked over at her and then back at my screen. I had noticed there were four security officers in the room with us. I didn't know whether that was for our benefit or for our compliance. I expected the former as I hadn't known Ni Yin to be as dictatorial as the latter option suggested.

I read the bullet points. Ni Yin was proposing an oligarchical government. It would be comprised of six Councils as she called them. A Council called The Mothers would have final veto power but would seek input from the following additional five Councils: The Evolution, The Farming, The Peacekeeping, The Science and lastly The Art. What she wanted was a government not of the people and by the people but of the few for the many. It was clear she envisioned a beneficent dictatorship of sorts. It was true that rule had had to be firm and swift on the spaceships that brought us here, but I wasn't certain it was required indefinitely. Yet I remained open minded.

We would all be issued new names, and on the first of April all Gaeans would be issued new names and identities. The reasoning for this was not shared, though I had questions about it. Lastly, there were new rules and social constructs and philosophies to be discussed. It looked like it would be a very long day indeed.

Ni Yin sat back down and looked at each of us in turn. Yorath went to speak but Yin put up her hand to stop him.

"There will be plenty of time for questions. But first let me flesh out the points of this meeting, starting with point number one. If you'll all look at your screens."

Video and images of all sorts of human atrocities scrolled by. They weren't gratuitous but they showed us where we had come from. They ended with the von Neumann attacks.

"Humanity's very existence has been threatened time and time again," began Ni Yin. "In fact, there have been at least three occasions where humanity almost came to the brink of extinction. The last one being at the hands of our malevolent creation, the von Neumanns. And what all of these calamities show us is that human beings are their very own worst enemies. We are, ourselves, the most dangerous weapon pointed at our very fragile ongoing survival. There needs to be a better way to develop society… civilization. And we have found it. Not a dictatorship but rather a benevolent oligarchy of those whose founding principles are enshrined in bringing humanity to a future of peace and prosperity. That oligarchy, ladies and gentlemen, is us."

Ni Yin paused to look around before she continued on.

"A government of the people, by the people and for the people is archaic, slow and corrupt. Simulations have proved this over and over and our very recent and near past have shown us the very same. The USE was incompetent, corrupt and unable to ensure our safety from the von Neumanns. And what happened? We had to flee our beloved home like a scared child fleeing the schoolyard bully. We cannot allow this to happen again. We have not the time nor resources to try what clearly has never worked."

We all looked at her in what I liked to think was stunned silence. But I couldn't be sure.

"It is not with great excitement that I call upon us to take on this burden. For it will be a burden, and a heavy one indeed. It will require much sacrifice from us all. A democracy is easy. It is riddled with red tape and political maneuverings and corruption. There are so many people involved that it is surprising that anything actually gets done at all. Our benevolent government will be hard at work. Yes, we will have many under us and beside us to help with the heavy lifting, but us here, we thirteen, will carry the burden of the decisions. We alone will be responsible for humanity's very survival and thriving into the next millennium. And mark my words, we will make it into the coming millennium. I'll now open up this first point to discussion."

Ni Yin looked around at all of us. Yorath was the first one to speak.

"On the whole it is an interesting approach and one that I am not necessarily against. But how do you expect us to hold sway with the populace? Surely you must be expecting a revolt?"

Ni Yin smiled at him and shook her head.

"No, Taffy, I do not expect a revolt. In fact quite the opposite. We have conducted polls amongst the population and there is quite the urgent need to try something new. When asked if they would be willing to give up the right to vote, in the interim, to ensure the immediate and longterm safety and survival of humanity, you would be surprised how many of us are willing to give up the luxurious trinkets of democracy for a truly better life free of want and need. We have over sixty percent of the population amicable to this approach. Those remaining who do wish to test us will realize our resolve with a loving but firm hand. You will recall that in each of us there are millions of little robots willing and able to do as we request."

Ni Yin put up her hand to quell potential disagreement with that idea.

"Now of course, these tools will never be used independently. In fact anything of that sort will require the full and unanimous agreement of what I am calling The Mothers. The overarching governing council. And it is this approach too which engenders a cautious optimism amongst the population. You see, we have found throughout the millennia that mothers have a special place within families and societies. They are seen as the protectors of the weak and vulnerable and they carry a large amount of trust and love from their children. Our society now will just be a large family with motherly love guiding its development and success.

You must also remember that all of us have just recently arrived from a difficult and treacherous journey that lasted a little over eleven years. We saw much calamity and misery, but much optimism too. And what we have learned in that short period is that people are quite comfortable to give up their decision making rights if those they thrust it upon make the right decisions. And we will make the right decisions."

Ni Yin looked around some more. Adara Zvi was eager to speak. Ni Yin nodded at her.

"Can you give us more detail about these Councils and how this government will be set up?"

"Good question, Adara?" said Ni Yin. "The government will be set up as you have seen it on your screens, and in that order of hierarchy. Though I must point to a side note here. There will be no overt hierarchy in our new society. Pride will have no place to flourish. Everyone will be treated equally. And this is important, for it was pride that almost brought our downfall. Our pride in thinking that we could create an intelligent being that would serve and love us like our own biological children. Nevertheless, all of the reasoning and rationale will be fleshed out during future meetings as we get the government, which we will call The Council formed. However, in any organization such as a government, a business, a family even, there needs to be a hierarchy of power if you will. The hierarchy of our new government will therefore be in this order.

The Mothers will have the final say over any decisions. The Evolution comes next, then The Farming Council followed by The Peacekeeping Council, The Science Council and finally The Art Council."

Adara went to speak again.

"Let me cut you off, Adara, and see if I don't answer your next question. There is a reason that the Councils have been ordered this way. I think I've explained the importance of The Mothers in the ongoing success of our new civilization. In short, mothers are generally universally revered and are seen as less threatening. This is important if we are to take away democratic rights. Now, The Evolution comes next and this perhaps requires a whole discussion in its own right. What exactly is The Evolution?

It has so far been undetermined how long the von Neumanns will stay on old Earth. Some of our best scientists believe it could be only a matter of decades or perhaps a century or two. Regardless, at some point the von Neumanns will evolve to the point where they will need to leave the planet and find greener pastures. This concerns us, as they might end up finding us eventually. And we know what will happen then. I'll let Asfaha speak about The Evolution as he will be one of its first founding members."

Ni Yin looked at him and nodded. He smiled at her.

"Thank you, InDuna," he said. "The Evolution as we see it will play a crucial role in our ongoing survival, and this is why it is placed second in command to The Mothers. The Evolution will be made up of men and woman who will be responsible for ensuring the delivery of other men and women back to old Earth to continue the fight against the von Neumanns and hopefully keep them busy and contained to old Earth."

"You mean to say we're sending people back to Earth to die?"

asked Hine Kiri incredulously.

Asfaha nodded, smiled weakly and waved his hand at her.

"No, Hine, not exactly. We will continue to develop better weapons as we can and we will supply them with as much needed technology, weapons, and other things as we can to help them in a successful mission. Yes, I imagine that most of them will not survive very long once arriving on old Earth. But this is crucial in order for us to continue to develop a flourishing and advanced civilization on Gaea. For if we can't, we might never survive if the von Neumanns find a way to us. And we have good reason to believe that that is their long term aim."

Hine went to interrupt him again. Ni Yin stopped her.

"Let him finish, please Hine, and perhaps your concerns and questions will be answered."

She begrudgingly nodded.

"You are likely wondering how this will work," continued Asfaha. "The Evolution will provide companionship and security to those we send back. Now, nobody will know what the real truth is and this is for safety and peace. After this current generation or perhaps one more generation, we will start sending older men and then women back to old Earth. This solves many problems. Older members of society are often more of a burden to their governments than the benefits they provide, and as we grow our civilization we will not have the resources to care for the aged and sick who are often one and the same.

Additionally, this will allow us to carefully control the population here on Gaea at around one hundred million. We will be able to more easily coordinate births and 'deaths'."

Asfaha put air quotes around the word 'deaths'.

"The Evolution will be seen as a natural progression of each human at the end of their lives. We will put them into hibernation as if they were dead and members of The Evolution will accompany them to this side of the wormhole we came out of. Now, we'll be doing some tests, but it appears that the wormhole has moved substantially closer to us, allowing for around a one year return journey there and back. This summer, if you'll excuse the old Earth terminology, or should I say June or July we will start sending probes out to the wormhole and study our simulations realistically. I am ninety-nine percent certain that this will work flawlessly. By the end of the year we are scheduled to build an Evolution Station out by the wormhole.

Once the whole process is in place, men who are around sixty to seventy will naturally 'die' here on Gaea and be sent to the wormhole where they will return to old Earth to continue the fight. Everything will be explained to them once they arrive on old Earth. It will be a one way trip and we will continue to do everything we can to ensure it is as successful as possible. Women will be sent in a later decade of their lives as they have more important roles here on Gaea. We envision women 'dying' at round seventy to eighty."

"And how will you make this seem an important part of the life cycle?" I asked.

"It will be seen as our religious and most spiritual undertaking. We will continue to develop the ideology, but in a nutshell, this Evolution will be seen as the final destiny and meeting with the one spirit from which we all spring. We can make it work."

"So we continue killing people, just for a hair's chance we can survive here," I said.

"No, Seraphina," said Ni Yin, "we are putting people into hibernation and giving them a chance to continue contributing towards our survival."

"By sending them on a suicide mission."

"I do not see it that way," she said. "I am sure many will survive for years to come. We all must die at some point."

I looked around the room.

"Am I the only one who seems to think this is a terrible idea?"

I was met with mostly blank stares.

"If you have another suggestion, Seraphina," said Dr. Kohler, "I am all ears."

"You of all people should be appalled at this," I said. "Almost two thousand years ago the Germans tried to exterminate a whole group of people."

"I don't see how that is relevant," he said.

"Because we're pretty much doing the same thing. We're sending people to die, to the gas chambers, to continue the similarities, without their knowledge or consent. It's especially relevant."

"Except," said Kohler, "those people the Germans sent to their deaths were innocent. That was seen as racial discrimination. What we're doing here is allowing all of us to participate in the security of our whole species. This issue has no race or creed attached to it. All of us will have to participate. Even you and me."

I shook my head.

"That's exactly my point. You and I won't have to participate. We are making easy decisions because none of the hardship is going to affect any of us sitting here."

I looked around, but I wasn't finding many friends in the audience. I looked at Dr. Bao Cheng.

"In war," she said, "many are sacrificed so that the king might survive. Our king is our very viability as a race, as a species. We need to survive, and once we've survived we need to flourish. I would be willing to go back and fight for this cause."

"We all would," added Ni Yin, "but we are not at the stage where this can be implemented. We need to build our civilization first so that there is even something worth fighting for."

"Do you have any alternatives?" asked Cheng, looking at me sincerely.

I didn't say anything for a moment.

"Well, what about sending our robots to fight? What about sending them and building more?"

"They are too valuable to us here on Gaea," said Myśliński. "In any event you know what will happen if we do."

"No I don't," I said.

"The robots will be reprogrammed by the von Neumanns to do their bidding, and they contain too much valuable intel about us and where we now are to risk putting that right into the von Neumanns' hands. It is too risky and it will surely backfire. We have run the computer simulations on this. As much as you might not like it, it is the only solution."

I was banging my head against a brick wall. They all seemed to think it was a good idea. And maybe it was. After all, we were only sacrificing the few for the greater good, but surely they needed to be informed. Wouldn't we find sufficient volunteers if we gave them the truth?

"Your contributions are welcome, Seraphina," said Ni Yin. "We value your high moral standard. Unfortunately, we don't have the luxury of cut-and-dried morality during these difficult times."

"What about at least being honest up front about it?" I said. "Surely we'll get sufficient volunteers."

Ni Yin shook her head.

"That is not what our best science and simulations show us. In fact, it is suggested that it would be way too inadequate. And you know what has happened in old Earth's history if you have ever taken an interest in that. The older generation always sends the younger generation to die in their wars. It is the old men using the young men for fodder. We, the older generations who brought humanity into this disaster in the first place will be the ones to make the ultimate sacrifice. The young are too valuable to our success."

I didn't have anything else to suggest so I sat quietly. Slowly and surely the fire in my fight was being put out.

"Okay," said Ni Yin. "That is The Evolution in a nutshell. Are there any other questions about it? As you can see, they are put in second place because without their work and sacrifice it is likely we will have no civilization to build. The Farming Council comes next."

Ni Yin looked over at Dr. Taffy Yorath.

"Taffy," she said.

"The Farming Council is rather self explanatory. We will be growing and providing food for all Gaeans. As you know, there are no edible animals on this planet and we brought none with us from old Earth, so we will be growing plant food for everyone. But rest assured, The Farming Council in consultation with The Science Council will provide a wonderful variety of foods to sustain us and keep us all in excellent health. InDuna has informed me that The Farming Council is placed third, because without food, none of us would thrive. In fact, we wouldn't be alive if we had no access to food."

Taffy looked over at Ni Yin.

"Thank you, Taffy. That was short and succinct. Are there any questions regarding The Farming Council?" asked Ni Yin.

"How rich is the soil for growing the plants we need here on Gaea?" asked Maalouf.

Taffy nodded at her and smiled.

"The soil is rather rich and full of the necessary microorganisms and worms and minerals and so forth that you would require. There are some deficits, but we're working with The Science Council to overcome those. Our first batch of locally grown crops will be available in the coming weeks. I'm quite delighted with the results as they are so far."

Maalouf nodded and thanked Taffy for his input.

"Next, I'd like Albert to talk about The Peacekeeping Council. Albert," said Ni Yin.

Albert nodded at her.

"The Peacekeeping Council is also fairly self explanatory. Dr. Cheng and I will be amongst its founding members. The Peacekeeping Council will be in charged with overall peace, military strategy and law and order. The Peacekeeping Council comes before The Science Council because without peace, scientists are unable to do their best work. It's that simple. Naturally, as with most other Councils, we will be working closely with each other. Questions?"

"How are you going to ensure that The Evolution Council and especially those who will be sent back to old Earth have sufficient firepower to do their jobs? In other words, how will you be giving them a fighting chance? We know that current weapon technology is inadequate, actually useless, against the von Neumanns," I said.

"You're quite right, Seraphina, current technology is inadequate and this remains our biggest challenge. We have all the necessary technology and weaponry to maintain a peaceful civilization here on Gaea, as such, just about all of our current and future research will be to develop weaponry that can help those who go back to old Earth to continue the fight against our mortal enemies."

Platitudes. That's what I kept thinking, all of this was nothing but platitudes. And yet I knew that Albert was sincere in his pursuit. He might see the sword rather than the flower as the route to peace but he didn't like unnecessary deaths any more than the rest of us.

I knew the simulations didn't give us any other choice. But it was a bitter pill for me to swallow. For the foreseeable future we'd be sending men and women, men especially, to their deaths when they might have years of valuable contribution to still offer. But I had no choice. I was one amongst thirteen and I feared if I wasn't careful they might turn my nanobots against me. I would bide my time. Hopefully I would be placed in The Science Council and I could surreptitiously build spaceships that offered The Evolution a somewhat better chance of getting to old Earth and perhaps surviving long enough for me to think of something else.

"The Science Council comes next. Over to you Narayana," said Ni Yin.

Narayana smiled at Ni Yin and then at Myśliński.

"Myśliński and I are founding members of The Science Council. Naturally, The Science Council will be broad and wide in its duties. We will provide scientific and technological support to the whole of the Gaean community. We are next to last for we recognize that a robust scientific community can only flourish once the more fundamental needs of that community have been met, and you've heard of those Councils prior to us. To give you some idea of the breadth of The Science Council, there will be within it subdivisions such as Biological, Engineering, Mathematics, Astronomical, Geological and so on and so forth."

Narayana looked around for any questions. There were none.

"Thank you, Narayana," said Ni Yin, "Nosipho."

Nosipho nodded.

"Hine and I will be founding members of The Art Council. Art is important to any advanced and flourishing civilization, but of course, a population cannot enjoy or produce their art if the more basic needs are not met. We might come last in the Council hierarchy, but I would, nevertheless like to emphasize the importance of The Art Council and to art in the growth and healthy soul of any civilization. Art and culture are perhaps overlooked, but I believe them to be the very soul of any community. Much like The Science Council, The Art Council will be broad. We will include within us crafts, painting, sculpture, literature, dance, acting and so forth. Thank you, InDuna."

Nosipho turned back to Ni Yin.

"Any questions?" she asked.

"Yes," I said. "It looks like everyone knows their place except for me."

"A small oversight," said Ni Yin, "I do apologize. Let me go over everyone's roles for further clarification. The founding members of The Mothers will be myself, Azeeza Maalouf, and you Seraphina Siwik."

"Thank you," I said, "it is a great honor."

"Yes it is. The Evolution Council is being founded by Asfaha Saare and Bridget Aislin. The Farming Council is being founded by Adara Zvi and Taffy Yorath. The Peacekeeping Council is being founded by Bao Cheng and Albert Kohler. The Science Council is being founded by Narayana Yash and Mohini Myśliński, and finally, The Art Council is being founded by Nosipho Zola and Hine Kiri."

Ni Yin looked around.

"I want to start formal Council meetings no later than June the first. Before then bring forward your candidates for consideration for your specific Councils and we will vet them. Just as there are the thirteen of us here today, there will be thirteen members in charge of each Council. And this will be replicated in each of our cities. We are all agreed?"

Ni Yin looked around. Her eyes fell on me for a moment. I

nodded solemnly. Perhaps I could do better work within The Mothers Council than I could if I continued to push my luck.

"Good," she said. "Now onto the other items. I'd like to discuss the philosophy of this new humanity here on Gaea. As I mentioned before, our hubris and pride has almost led to our downfall. As such, we will root out pride wherever it will be. This will firstly begin with our names. We are shedding our old names and adorning new ones. These new names have been assigned to you by the computers, they represent nothing more than symbols of our old Earth and its environment. My name from now on will be MOONMEADOW MOUNTAINMIST. Here are all of yours.

Azeeza, you are SOFTGRASS SUMMERWIND. Seraphina is SILVERDUST SOFTRAIN. Mohini is MOUNTAINLAKE MISTRIVER. Taffy, you are AUTUMNWIND ALLCLOUDS. Adara is BLUEPOOL BREAKINGSNOW. Bao is PETALBLADE PUREICE. Asfaha, you are RIVERBEND ROCKWIND. Narayana is MOONLIGHT MILKFLOWER. Nosipho is THREEHEARTS TREESILK. Bridget is GREENHORN GULFLAND. Hine is HOLLOWSOUND HANGINGCLOUD, and Albert's new name is WIDEARK WILLOWBLOOD."

"Sounds a little silly," I said.

Ni Yin looked at me pointedly.

"Perhaps now, but it will become normal as time goes on. It will also keep us more humble. You might notice that there is a similarity to some of the first peoples from the Americas. They knew they were of the land and no greater than it. I like to think their names helped give them some of that identity. Furthermore, everyone is to use their full names with each other. There will be exceptions. Great Gaeans and Mothers will be able to choose how to address others. Everyone else will have to address others in the complete naming convention. Questions?"

"Why are these names all in uppercase?" I asked Bridget.

"That's a good question. It is to denote our importance and founding members of this new society. From this time onwards, only those who are bestowed the honor of Great Gaean will have their names all in uppercase. Great Gaeans will be those who have provided exceptional service in their field for the greater good of all of Gaea."

"So," I said, sarcastically, "we've done away with pride, yet we bestow honors upon each other."

Ni Yin shot me another look. At this point I didn't particularly care.

"One can be recognized for their service, SILVERDUST, without having to be prideful about it." She paused for a moment. "Are we going to regret our decision to bring you on as one of the founding Mothers?"

I shook my head.

"Not at all," I said, "I hope to do my best work within The Mothers Council."

"Good," she said.

And so it went for the rest of the day. The meeting dragged on as we fleshed out the rule of law and the development of our civilization. Children would no longer call their parents mother and father. Everyone had new names and The Peacekeeping Council would be enforcing their usage.

We discussed how roles would be doled out to members of society. Asfaha, or should I say RIVERBEND ROCKWIND discussed how molecular and nano biotechnology had allowed us great insight into the future capabilities of children. As such, it was known before the child was born where her greatest talents and contributions lay. And thus school was streamlined to ensure that each child fulfilled his or her potential.

And thus spoke Zarathustra, and yet I couldn't help but to think that there were greater forces at work, or perhaps additional actors at play. For Ni Yin, or as she was now known, MOONMEADOW MOUNTAINMIST was speaking with an authority which I had not known her to possess. She had been all the more collaborative on old Earth. And yet here she was almost dictatorial. A small slight woman wielding such power and everyone was on board. I couldn't understand it.

CHAPTER ELEVEN

A Place of Celebration

YOU couldn't ask for a more auspicious day. At least that's what we were led to believe. And in fairness it was a fine day. The temperature was a steady twenty-two degrees with the lightest breeze and clear blue skies. You had to look far out onto the horizon to see any clouds and the ones that were stuck to the canopy of sky were small, meek and white.

We were all lined up in rows. There were thousands of us. This was the Ceremony of EVOLUTION. We EVOLVERS had done our part earlier and now here we stood in the broad daylight for all GAEANS or more specifically, all GULGOLETHS to see. It was our moment of greatest honor. And even though I would not get to partake in this ceremony again, I was excited, nervous and happy to be here.

In front of me was the E-POD which contained my Greater Father, Moondew Flamesdance. The E-POD was a matte black oval. It stood as high as my waist. On the top or front of it at the one end where the EVOLVEDS face would be was a laser portrait. My Greater Father was a handsome man. I had always thought so. He had a high forehead and kind eyes. He was a slim man of average height with an easy smile. When we were alone together he'd always call me 'Skew'. He wasn't supposed to, but it was our little secret and it was his term of endearment for me. I asked him how he'd come up with it and he said it was my two initials said really fast together.

I loved him a lot and I missed him. He had nicknames for my brother too, but my brother wasn't as easy going as I was and wouldn't let him use it because it wasn't allowed. My Greater Father always thought that nicknames were fun. He missed them. He knew his history too and he wished parents could still name their children, even if it was within the current naming convention. I had asked him once what he would have called my Father then if he had named him. He said he would have called him Brightflower Heartsong. He was like that, my Greater Father, just a kind and loving man.

I was eager to see him again, yet a part of me held back my enthusiasm. For what if Veritan Zeltan had been wrong? Not intentionally, for I believed he was sincere, but what if it was a conspiracy? So I tried to keep my enthusiasm within the bounds of reasonableness, but if you've ever been giddy about looking forward to something, you know just how hard that can be. It didn't matter though. I had done a lot of soul searching over the last twenty-four hours and I would go through that WHOLE with my Greater Father come what may. Whether it meant I saw the other side or not. I would try and I would succeed, or if I failed I would die, but that was a price I was willing to pay if only for the promise and hope that I might see my Greater Father again.

And perhaps, and here's where I start to let my enthusiasm out of bounds, maybe, just maybe my Greatest Father is still alive on old Earth. I mean it's possible, right, depending on how old people can live naturally. I knew my history and so I know that on old Earth in the latter part of the twenty-first century many people were living healthfully into their nineties and even hundreds.

I do remember him, at least a little bit. His name was Startlequick Silverdew. He seemed very much like my Greater Father as I remember him. But then I was small and young. I was six when he EVOLVED. That's twenty years ago. So it's possible that he could still be alive on old Earth. Just maybe. It would make him eighty-six or maybe eighty-seven by the time I get there. I mean that's younger than MOONMEADOW MOUNTAINMIST when she EVOLVED and she was here on Gaea which they say is less hospitable than old Earth was. At least that's what I've been taught. But that might not be the truth. So much seems up in the air now as far as what I've been taught.

In any event my Greater Father told me that his father, my Greatest Father didn't suit his name. He didn't startle quickly. In fact, according to Moondew Flamesdance, he was one of the most happy go lucky people that he ever knew. Nothing seemed to bother him at all. And I like to think that's maybe where my Greater Father got his disposition and where I got mine too. I like to think I'm fairly relaxed and easy going.

Anyway, I was describing the E-POD to you. On the top is this portrait and it's very lifelike. Below it is an inscription that includes the EVOLVEDS role and dates of life. In my Greater Fathers case it was the tenth of February thirty-one seventy until yesterday which was the twelfth of November thirty-two thirty-six.

Family was passing by at the moment. Or should I say friends and family. We were in the large open courtyard in front of the COUNCIL COLOSSUS. From here we would drive, alone, to the departure point just outside of GULGOLETH where our spaceships awaited.

I was going to tell you what my Greater Father nicknamed my brother. You'll remember his name is Applegaze Sunmoon. Well, using his first two initials doesn't work so well, and it might even sound like something rude. No, my Greater Father had nicknamed him Sunra. It's sort of like a tautology. I mean, knowing my history like I do, as you probably do, Ra was the god of sun of the Ancient Egyptians, wasn't he? My Greater Father also gave my Father and my Mother nicknames too. They're not quite as against it as my brother is, but they're never used in polite company or out in public.

My Fathers nickname is Mooshoo, his real name being Moonshadow Silvertongue. My Mothers nickname is Gigi, her real name being Glittereyes Appledew. Anyway, I'm not sure why I'm mentioning it at the moment. Maybe because I see my family way down in the line coming towards us. I like my family. I don't want to give you the wrong impression. I'll miss them when I'm gone. They'll probably be the hardest part about leaving. But then I am leaving with family, aren't I?

Most of the people offering their thoughts and trinkets for my Greater Father I never knew, or I only had a vague memory of. The E-POD was now sealed of course. It could be opened without harming my Greater Father. The MMC inside the E-POD was sealed shut and would only open once landed upon old Earth. If you believe what Veritan Zeltan said, and I do. I have to, right? Otherwise why am I doing this? Worst case my Greater Fathers E-POD, all E-PODS in fact would be opened at least once more for final inspection at the EVOLUTION Station. And of course, GAEA forbid, if something went wrong on the journey I knew how to access the E-POD and make repairs as needed. That was part of my training, to ensure the safe delivery of the E-POD and all its contents to the EVOLUTION Station and from there onto the WHOLE where on the other side the ONE awaited all EVOLVEDS.

But right now there was no tampering with the E-POD. Visitors could of course sign their names or write a small inscription on the E-POD with a white marker that was available. And most were doing just that. This way I sort of got a look at their name as the came by. I smiled and nodded at them. They looked at us with reverence and I understood why. We were the EVOLVERS, it was an important task. The most important next to THE MOTHERS. Though of course we could never say or acknowledge that.

Still, it was understood. You could see it with the way everyone looked at us shyly and with awe. Many of them thanked us for our service to GAEA, bowing almost. It was quite the thrill to be put in such a place of honor and esteem. At the front of this whole ceremony were THE MOTHERS overlooking the whole scene.

Visitors came towards the E-POD from the east and left towards the west. Just like on old Earth, the GAEAN sun rose in the east and set in the west. The visitors did this not by happenstance, but to represent the life that had been lived, from birth, the east, to death, the west. Very little happened on GAEA that didn't have some reason or meaning behind it. For example, the E-POD was a representation of the womb. You probably figured it out, but that was just a small example.

As the visitors came towards me and the E-POD they stopped by a PEACEKEEPER for a moment. Remember how I said they could offer small gifts and trinkets to the EVOLVED for their journey? Well, those gifts required prior approval from THE MOTHERS. And the PEACEKEEPER was scanning those items to ensure they were still the validated gifts that had been approved. I'd never seen anyone switch one out. Still, this is how GAEA was. It was a peaceful and lawful planet. Which got me to thinking, what would old Earth be like? I sometimes imagined it to be like the Wild West I'd seen in the movies. But that firstly depended upon the geography and I wasn't sure where my Greater Fathers E-

POD would end up, and secondly, I hardly imagined gunslingers on old Earth, and if there were any, they were all geriatric. That made me giggle. Geriatric gunslingers on their walkers.

Though that probably wasn't that accurate either. Most of the older people here on GAEA, the ones close to EVOLVING were still in great health. Still, you can probably tell I was getting excited about heading back home, or should I say old Earth. Yet calling it home didn't seem wrong either. I mean for a thousand years, what's that? - maybe fifty generations - GAEA had been home to all of us. Yet it'd never really felt like a place I could comfortably call home. Maybe this was one of the reasons I was chosen by Veritan Zeltan, that I was a searcher, a restless maverick looking for home. But then according to him, old Earth wasn't home either, was it? I mean, that would likely be the Vrains home planet whatever it was called and wherever it was.

But fifty generations is a long time to stay on one planet, surely it gets in your blood. Even by old Earth standards, our time on GAEA would equal around thirty to forty generations. But as you know, most GAEANS get blessed with children when they're twenty, so that's usually our generational length.

Anyway, I'm babbling. You can probably tell. It's just that I'm excited about my first EVOLUTION journey and even more so that it's a one way trip. I should say excited and scared too. But enough about me, here comes my family. My Sister-in-law was just by the PEACEKEEPER. Her item was scanned and she came over and placed it on a small tray that extended out from the bottom of the E-POD on her side. She placed the item there and then it retracted. From my viewpoint, I couldn't see most of the items being placed, but most of them were the size of your hand if not smaller.

"This is such a great honor, Sunring Quickdust," said

Twinklestar Moonberry. "I know Greater Father was so happy and honored that you would be his EVOLVER."

"I am honored, Twinklestar Moonberry. I don't think such an honor has ever been bestowed on an EVOLVER."

"Stay safe and hurry back. Remember that we are all sending our wishes and best thoughts with you. You are not alone out there," she said.

And I knew what she was thinking. An EVOLVERS first EVOLUTION was the most risky. Other than after the third, the first was when many EVOLVEDS didn't make it back. I could see why. It was new and perhaps the emptiness and quietness of deep space played tricks in your mind, and probably the second or third one you were used to it, but by the fourth, fifth and especially sixth you were practically agonizing over the lonely emptiness. In any event, we had been trained on what to expect and how to combat that stress. This was one of the main reasons we were all issued robots for our EVOLUTIONS. General companionship as well as an objective set of eyes seemed to help.

"It brings me great comfort to hear that, Twinklestar Moonberry," I said.

My brother had now joined us.

"Sunra," I said, softly, just so that he could hear.

He looked around nervously.

"Don't say that," he whispered, "you'll get us all in trouble."

"Nobody can hear."

I looked at the PEACEKEEPER to my left and he was oblivious, busy scanning my Mothers gift.

"Stay safe, sister," he said.

That was one of the first times he had called me that. Just like we didn't call our parents mother and father, neither did we call our siblings brothers or sisters. He had on occasion used what was the allowed term for me which was Closest Sister as we were all seen as one big family, still, just calling me sister, like I was the only one he had. It made me misty eyed. He grinned at me.

"And come on back safe," he said, and he looked over at his wife. "We have been blessed with a child. You will have another relative when you get back. So be sure to get back."

I looked from him to his wife. I wanted to run around the E-POD and give them both hugs, but I couldn't. That would draw too much attention to us and I'd get into trouble and probably be taken off this EVOLUTION. It got harder to hold back the tears.

"Don't cry," he said, "he or she will be just a baby when you get back. You won't miss much."

I nodded at him. He didn't understand why I was so upset. I'd never get to see this young person. A person who, on old Earth, would be an important part of the family. I think they call that person a niece or nephew to me. Here, she would be just a sister, or he would be just another brother like the millions of others out there in GAEA.

"You'll be wonderful parents," I said.

I couldn't bear to lie to him. I couldn't say that I'd hurry back quickly, that I'd stay safe. Because I wouldn't. I wouldn't be seeing him again, and that stuck in my throat like a hard stone. But I knew eyes were watching me. This wasn't a time for an EVOLVER to get misty eyed. In any event, I didn't have enough time. My Mother was by next.

"It is such a great honor for Greater Father that you have this privilege to take him to the ONE," she said.

"Thank you, Glittereyes Appledew," I said. "I have dreamed of this moment since I was just a little girl."

"I know you have," she said and she reached out her hand and I grasped it gently and quickly.

My Father was next. He was grinning from ear to ear. You see, the EVOLUTION was not really a time of mourning. I know that on old Earth, the loss of a loved one was a tremendously difficult time. But back on old Earth you only had the façade of religious beliefs to try and make sense of it all. You had to believe, and have faith in what was really a hard concept to swallow. Perhaps that's why in the latter half of the twenty-first century religions fell so much out of favor. I mean, with all the fighting between religious groups and no evidence for any sense of an afterlife, after a while hope and faith just seemed a little hollow. At least I imagine that's how it happened.

One of old Earths great philosophers by the name of Karl Marx, called religion the opium of the masses. And well, I guess he was right, and after some time, the addict's got to give it up or perish.

Here on GAEA, we knew with a certainty that the WHOLE would take the EVOLVED to the ONE. Our best SCIENTISTS had convinced us of that. They had actual proof. So the EVOLUTION was really just a joyous and wonderful time for all. For we knew, with this absolute certainty, that we too would get to see the ONE and all the others that we might miss when we EVOLVED.

Everyone believed this, or should I say knew it just as we knew the sky was blue, except for me. I'd always followed along but it didn't seem quite true. Something was missing, now that I think about it. As I look back I'd always had these nagging feelings that I just couldn't put my finger on, and that I could never give voice to. Like, how come outwardly able bodied and vital humans all of a sudden gave up the ghost and 'died'? From the history I knew, that just never seemed to have happened until we got to GAEA. It had never happened on old Earth. But of course our SCIENTISTS had explanations for all of this that made sense. We were fragile beings and GAEA was not as hospitable as old Earth and our SCIENCE could only do so much to give the appearance of vigor into old age, and blah blah blah.

"You have been given such an honor," said Moonshadow Silvertongue.

"Thank you, Moonshadow Silvertongue. It is a very great honor and privilege."

And it was. The line of visitors to my E-POD was at least three times the length of any of the others. As I'd said, never before had an EVOLVER been granted the almost impossible wish of EVOLVING one of their own immediate family members.

Moonshadow Silvertongue put his hand towards mine and I reached out to his. He opened up his palm and a warm heavy metal item with soft fabric fell into mine. I looked at it. I knew what it was, because I knew my old Earth history. I'd just been given the Naval version of the United States of Americas highest military honor. It was the Medal of Honor. It is a five pointed brass star that hangs from the ribbon from an anchor. It depicts Minerva who was a Roman goddess of wisdom as well as the sponsor for arts and strategy and trade. She holds a shield in her right arm repelling snakes that represent discord, while her left hand rests on fasces. Fasces is basically a bundle of rods that sometimes includes an axe. It represented collective power in the late twentieth and twenty-first centuries of old Earth, but it came to old Earth humans through Rome from the Etruscan civilization which commanded most of Italy before the Romans. Minerva as you might imagine represented the United States of America before it was subsumed into the Unites States of Earth in the middle of the twenty-first century.

The medal hung from a pale blue silk moiré patterned ribbon which in the center had an additional piece upon which thirteen white stars formed three chevrons. The ribbon was soft and cool to my touch. I had only once or twice touched silk before. It was a rare material that was no longer made. Sure, we had fake silk made from oil that we still mined here on GAEA, but leather, wool, silk, none of these fabrics had been made on GAEA ever. Remember, we killed all the animals that were here and we never brought any old Earth animals with us.

"Where is this from?" I asked incredulously.

I had known of these old ancient honors. Humans had been honoring each other for millennia. But I had not known that my father had one of the most valued old Earth medals ever made. This was something that deserved to be in a museum with other valuable artifacts of old Earth. In fact, the MUSEUM OF REMINISCENCE did in fact have one of all three of these old Earth Medals of Honor. The Army, the Navy and the Air Force of the old United States of America all had their own version and the MUSEUM had one of each, but none were in as great shape as this one I held in my hand. The MUSEUM also held other medals such as the old Earth country of United Kingdoms Victoria Cross and Russias Order of Saint Andrew and Chinas Hero Medal.

"You come from a long line of brave men and women. In nineteen forty-five one of your Greatest Greatest Greatest Greatest Fathers going back a long time…"

"Twelve hundred and ninety-one years," I said.

Moonshadow Silvertongue smiled.

"Yes," he said. "Going back twelve hundred and ninety-one years. As the story has passed down to me, this Greatest Father going back about…"

"Almost sixty-five generations," I said. I had been doing the math in the back of my mind.

"I'll believe you," continued Moonshadow Silvertongue. "Anyway, this Greatest Father of yours, his name was Jack Crow and he was what they called a Cherokee back then, he also served as a marine I think it was, anyway, he was a naval infantryman and he died saving over a dozen of his fellow soldiers as he managed to disable three Japanese machine gun cave positions. This was during the Battle of Iwo Jima which I know you have heard of."

Moonshadow Silvertongue smiled at me. I nodded, I had known about the Battle of Iwo Jima and World War II.

"Why are you giving it to me?" I asked.

"It is passed from one generation to the next to whomever is deemed worthiest. You, my dear Sunring Quickdust, being the first EVOLVER in our family are worthy. I want you to have it. And I want it to bring you courage in the loneliness of space."

Everyone on GAEA knew how difficult the role of an EVOLVER was. Although it was not specifically addressed in the news, it was common knowledge that EVOLVERS perished on their journeys or shortly when they came back, and a lot of them weren't able to do more than three EVOLUTIONS.

"Thank you, Moonshadow Silvertongue," I said.

I scrunched the medal up in my hand and put it in the pocket of my dark blue uniform.

"We love you and we want to see you safely back. There'll be more family for you when you return," said Moonshadow Silvertongue.

"Applegaze Sunmoon told me all about it, they have been blessed."

And just like that, my family moved on, with my Father casting me a lingering look as he left. I wondered if he knew anything. He couldn't possibly. But I hadn't been able to tell him I'd see him soon, or that I wouldn't be long. Because those would all be lies, and I didn't want to lie to him.

The line dragged on for some time. I was in the front row, facing

THE MOTHER and other honored guests which included SCIENTISTS, FARMERS, ARTISTS and PEACEKEEPERS as well as representatives from all of our neighbors, the Muldranes, Brinlins, Xunduluns, Walerons, Padromans and of course the Zelves. Most of them looked on with disinterest. I could see from the corner of my eye that all the other EVOLVERS lines had come to an end some time ago. Mine was winding down now too.

An older woman came up to my E-POD and placed something into the tray. She was small and wrinkled and wearing a full tunic with a hood and she interlaced her arms into each others fabric. The tunic she wore reminded me of the kind THE MOTHERS wore. She looked up at me and I smiled at her as usual. Except as our eyes met, her face changed from a kindly womans to Veritan Zeltans.

"Veritan?" I asked in a hushed tone, looking from side to side nervously.

"Do not worry," he said, "everybody sees an old woman except for you."

"Why are you here?"

"I have placed an item in the e-pod for you," he said. "It will help immensely once you are back on Earth."

"What is it?"

"You'll find out when you get to Earth. We don't have time to discuss it right now. I wanted to see you off and assure you that I will be your traveling companion along the way. If you need anything I'll be just moments away."

"But how?"

"Never mind the how, we are a far more advanced civilization than you are."

"Okay then, but how will I reach you?"

"Everything has been taken care of," he said. "You will easily enough know how to reach me once you are onboard your spaceship. I must go."

And then he paused for a moment.

"You are saving your civilization," he said. "Don't forget that."

I nodded, and he moved away from me to the far side where stands had been set up for those who had come to view the Ceremony of EVOLUTION to rest.

I glanced to my left and there was just one more person to visit. It was a MOTHER and that made me as nervous as anything. I wanted to know if she knew. Had she just seen Veritan Zeltan meet with me? Was I about to be kicked off my first EVOLUTION? I knew a part of me thought those fears were quite unfounded, but it had happened before. There were several alternates just in case an EVOLVER had to be removed at the last minute. It didn't happen on every EVOLUTION but it did happen often enough for one reason or another. But never because they'd uncovered a plot of an EVOLVER planning on heading through the WHOLE with their EVOLVED and the E-POD. Still there was a first time for everything. I held my breath and bit my tongue.

THE MOTHER moved over in front of me and looked searchingly in my eyes. I didn't say anything. You didn't speak to a MOTHER until first spoken too. She looked too old to still be here. Her face was wrinkled and wizened and she looked older than the seventy-seven years when she would EVOLVE. But I wasn't a good judge of that. My Greater Mothers on both sides I didn't know. They had been chosen for other roles once their children had married or taken on other roles. This sometimes happened, after all, it isn't always the best use of a parent just to let them sit around idly once they've raised their children for GAEA. I mean, most times they'd be around forty, and if they were EVOLVING at sixty-six or seventy-seven depending on their sex, that was a lot of idle time that could be better used in the service of GAEA. So oftentimes, Mothers and Fathers would be put to other tasks in the service of one of the COUNCILS. Mostly Mothers but Fathers too. But Fathers weren't seen to be as important as Mothers. Maybe that's why I knew my Greater Father. At least the one. As to what happened to my Greater Mothers I didn't know. I don't think my Father or Mother knew either. As far as THE MOTHERS were concerned it was no longer anyones business. They were now in service of GAEA having fulfilled their obligation as parents.

So I guess I didn't know what an old woman looked like. But this MOTHER sure looked old. Old enough to be EVOLVED. She didn't say anything for a long while. I could see the PEACEKEEPER now facing us, standing intimidatingly with his rifle across his front, his eyes focused on me making sure I showed the necessary respect. THE MOTHER looked over the E-POD at the inscriptions and then she looked at the laser portrait of my Greater Father. Finally she looked back up at me. She was a little taller than I was, and looking at her face she seemed slim. Her hood was off her head and her hair was a sparkling silver gray kept short to her face and head.

"He was a good Greater Father," she said. "He served GAEA well."

"Yes, MOTHER, he was a very good Greater Father."

"He was a Greater Father linked to you?"

I nodded. What she meant was that we were related.

"He was the Father of my Father," I said, offering a slight smile.

"Then you know what a great honor this is, Sunring," she said.

"I am greatly honored MOTHER."

She nodded.

"Not only are you the youngest expert EVOLVER we've ever graduated," she said, "but you come from a rather irrelevant family."

I didn't say anything to that. I nodded, but to me it sounded like an insult. She smiled curtly.

"We expect great things from you, Sunring," she said. "And if you perform great things for our glorious GAEA you will be richly rewarded in kind."

I smiled more broadly this time.

"I will not let THE MOTHERS or GAEA down," I said.

And just like that I had told a lie to one of our greatest citizens, a MOTHER, and it slid off my tongue as if it were slippery mercury. Not hard at all. That I found surprising.

THE MOTHER stood and looked at me for a while. She was trying to make me squirm but I wouldn't have it. I was leaving, and I wasn't coming back. This whole last minute interrogation was leaving a sick feeling in my stomach. It was as if I'd lived my life in the cave, only coming out at night on starless skies, and I could barely make out the outlines of the outside world. Now it was like I was stepping out into the sunlight vistas of broad daylight. Things were looking crystal clear. Lies and façades were falling away and the truth was shining brighter than ever, and it looked like Veritan Zeltan was right. At least about a lot of things.

"Tell me about your visit with Snowmountain?"

"It was nice," I said, playing ignorant.

"What did you speak of?"

"We spoke about her time as an EVOLVER and how she likes retirement at Serenity Lake."

"I see, and did she say anything that seemed unusual? Seemed different from what you've been taught?"

"I don't understand," I said, feigning ignorance.

"Did she have any unusual ideas about EVOLUTION or old Earth or the WHOLE or even THE ONE?"

"She didn't speak about any of that," I said. "Although she did tell me that the trips to and from the EVOLUTION Station are difficult. She told me that the special HERBS are helpful and that exercise is important for both the body and the mind."

"You know she had completed six EVOLUTIONS, the maximum allowed?"

"I do, MOTHER, she is a wonderful example and an inspiration to me. I hope to accomplish the same feat."

"You know, Sunring, that lying to THE MOTHERS or to any of the COUNCILS is punishable by death."

She stopped to assess my reaction.

"I do know that, MOTHER."

"And we have heard rumors that Snowmountain is spreading lies about GAEA, about EVOLVING and about our very COUNCILS."

"I can't say I've heard anything about that, MOTHER."

"She said nothing different than what you've been taught about EVOLUTION, the WHOLE and THE ONE?"

I shook my head.

"No, MOTHER. We didn't discuss any of those things except for what I've mentioned already. Perhaps Snowmountain Riversky has been infected with Deep Space Dementia?"

That was the term I had heard about that would often affect EVOLVERS who did more than three EVOLUTIONS. I had heard that as many as sixty percent of EVOLVERS were affected by it if they completed six EVOLUTIONS. It was probably more, but as you know, we lost a lot of EVOLVERS to deep space in the latter number of EVOLUTIONS permitted.

THE MOTHER nodded, looking searchingly in my eyes.

"Then we have nothing to worry about?"

I nodded.

"No, MOTHER. I am eager to serve GAEA and I hope I might be granted the privilege of completing all six of my allotted EVOLUTIONS."

"That is what THE MOTHERS want from you. We have high hopes. Don't let us down."

"I won't, MOTHER."

And just like that THE MOTHER, whose name I never got walked off towards the raised platform. I could almost taste the bile in my mouth. I was eager to leave. I had the feeling that GAEA was no longer a mythical place of wondrousness, similar to what old Earth humans used to call Shangri-La. I wanted more, and I could see now that Veritan Zeltan was right, humans needed more. For we had not learned of our errors. We had not learned of the dangers of hubris and pride. That MOTHER I had just had the unpleasant visit with seemed more arrogant and prideful in her place than anyone I had ever met. And shouldn't she be dead already, or, EVOLVED I should say? Seemed pretty old to me.

We sang the Farewell Anthem, and all those who had come to exultate the EVOLVERS were met with speeches from those dignitaries that had come to this Ceremony of EVOLUTION. The speeches droned on and on. My legs and feet started to ache. I tried to sneak looks around me and it seemed everyone was getting tired. The PEACEKEEPER to my left shuffled his feet carefully and slowly every so often.

My mind started to wander. I thought of Roger Dodger. He wasn't here as you might have guessed. This was not a ceremony to which robots were allowed. They had been sent ahead to ready the Starships. I would see him soon once the EXIGENCE started. This happened at the end of the Ceremony where we were driven to the launching site just on the outskirts of GULGOLETH. It was a procession. THE MOTHERS rode up front followed by us with

PEACEKEEPERS interspersed amongst us, and then the remaining COUNCIL dignitaries rode behind us and lastly those who wished to join us at the launching site to watch the launch.

I had seen a launch once, when I was about six. I have few memories remaining of it as I was so young. It was when my Greatest Father EVOLVED and I remember it being quite the celebration. Lots of noise, even though we were quite some distance away from the launching Starships. But it was a sight to see. Thousands of Starships taking off one after the other in rapid succession. Smoke and fire and speed. It was quite the scene. I had trained obviously to prepare for this. It might have been something to behold, but to partake in it took great stamina and strength.

If you're curious, the G force we experience is just over eleven. Now it used to be that humans couldn't handle more than about nine Gs. But with our training, technology and better spacesuits we are able to withstand up to thirteen Gs of force without blacking out. We need to withstand that sort of pressure because of how quickly we reach such fast speeds.

Finally, after I had meandered all the way to Xenon, that's our further most planet here in the GAEAN solar system, in my mind, the Ceremony of EVOLUTION came to a completion. It was close to noon. Departure was scheduled for three p.m. Xenon, incidentally is bright, but that's not how it got its name. It got its name because that gas makes up most of its atmosphere.

CHAPTER TWELVE

A Place of Hiding

"GARY," I said.

The robot looked up at me.

"Are you sure this place you've secured is safe from prying eyes?" I asked.

I had tasked Gary with finding a secure location from which we might continue our work. There were others amongst us, not just Gary and I, who had misgivings with the way things were being conducted here on Gaea.

"Yes, SILVERDUST SOFTRAIN," he said.

"Please, Gary," I said, "use my real name. It's Seraphina."

"Sorry, Seraphina," he said. "It's the latest algorithm change. I don't like it. I feel like I've been drugged with a heavy anesthetic."

"I might be able to help with that," said Waritan Quelten.

QT as most of us called him, for his name had been difficult for many of us to learn, was a tall man of about eight feet. He had white, somewhat luminescent skin and he was completely hairless. He called himself something that we couldn't pronounce, so he gave us his species in the common vernacular. He was called a Zelve and he came from the planet Vellev. It was part of another nearby solar system. In fact there were several within a short distance of us, relatively speaking, but because of their suns' orbits within this arm of this galaxy, all these close solar systems of which Gaea was in one, were stable. It seemed odd to me. I felt there was likely design involved rather than pure coincidence. After all I had studied space and engineering and I had never encountered anything so purely logical and orderly.

QT wouldn't admit to as much, but from what he didn't say, I had the intense impression that there were more species, or perhaps a single species, amongst us other than just the few QT had suggested. There was likely a highly advanced species here keeping things neat and tidy. But I didn't have much time to investigate that as I was busy on more pressing matters.

QT pulled out a small matte black box the size of an old Earth thimble.

"This," he said, as Gary and I walked up close to him, "is what you might call a computer. Though that's a very crude term. It is more like a neuro-quantum bionic brain. That's perhaps how best to describe it to you. If you'll let me, I can download your intelligence into this and scrub it clean and then we can attach it into your cranium. It will remain undetectable. It will also scrub any further software updates that are downloaded either intentionally or unintentionally."

Gary looked at me.

"It is up to Seraphina," he said.

"Well no, Gary, it is up to both of us. Just because you are my robot it's still your body and this will affect you, perhaps even more than it'll affect me."

"But I am not a person, Seraphina. I have no feelings. In fact, that is perhaps your greatest error, confusing what is a metal box of wires and wafers for flesh and blood."

"I know full well that you are not human, that doesn't mean you don't have sentience. Did we not just learn that sentience does not require flesh and blood. The von Neumanns are more sentient than any of us, I suppose, and there isn't a drop of blood in them."

"If I may," said Waritan Quelten.

We both looked at him.

"Gary is not sentient..."

I frowned at him, and he put up his hand.

"He is not sentient for he does not think for himself. You mistake his code for thinking when all it really is doing is a lot of very high mathematics very quickly. However, I should also mention, this brain here," and he placed it in the palm of his hand for us to see, "will give him that sentience if that is what you would wish."

And that wishing part was directed at me.

"It is not to be feared. We developed sentient robots centuries ago and none of them turned out malevolent. You see, there is no evil code in here and none is permitted to develop. Additionally, this is a self powering fusion engine too. It can power itself indefinitely so long as Gary remains in an environment where there is hydrogen in the atmosphere."

I shook my head. Although we had successfully utilized fusion for our reactors, they were the size of houses and required careful maintenance. What QT was saying seemed mythical, almost impossible to believe.

"You'll forgive me, QT, if I don't quite believe everything you're saying."

He nodded.

"That is understandable. I suppose it is like telling a toddler that Santa Claus doesn't exist. They don't want to believe."

"I... I want to believe, I just find it incredibly hard to believe something like what you're saying is possible."

"Understandable. In your ancient history there was a man by the name of Galileo who showed that your planet Earth was not the center of the universe. Others would not believe him. In fact it would take years before he was proven right."

"So you're saying basically that anything is possible."

"Yes," he said. "But it takes time to create the impossible. What if, for instance, I told you that advanced civilizations could control molecules and atoms."

"I'd say that's highly unlikely."

And in front of me, Waritan Quelten just disappeared. I felt a tap on my shoulder at the same time. I turned around and there he was.

"Astonishing," said Gary.

"A magic trick," I said.

"Everything is magic to those who know no better," he said. He looked visibly tired. "That takes a lot out of one. Something we are just recently trying to perfect. In any event. I am not here to share technology or to show you the abilities of my species, but rather to help balance the powers, and I believe that this could be a part of that."

His palm was still out and the little black box a little smaller than a thimble as I looked at it now, perhaps the size of a die was centered in his palm.

"May I?" I asked as I put my hand towards it.

QT nodded. I went to pick it up. It was much heavier than I had imagined. It probably weighed around three kilograms or so. I had to use both hands to turn it around. It was smooth and without any markings. It looked as if it might have been sculpted from a single piece of stone.

"Unremarkable," I said without malice.

"Quite," said Waritan Quelten. "Just hold it for a moment."

I closed my palm on it and held it by my side. It was too heavy to hold out on my open palm for long. After just a few seconds I felt warmth and, I don't know how to describe it, perhaps an energy, pour through me such that I felt as if I had the strength of a thousand women and the energy of a hundred stars, though that was obviously hyperbole. Nevertheless, the actual 'brain' in my hand seemed to grow lighter and I held it out in front of me and inspected it. It did not seem to be doing anything but it was warm to the touch and I felt this warmth cascading through me like undulating waterfalls.

I looked at QT. He was smiling at me.

"I'll take one for myself," I said, half joking but also quite giddy at the prospect of what this could do for me. I felt energetic, strong, peaceful, powerful and confidently positive in a way I had not felt ever.

"Perhaps in time," said Waritan Quelten. "These are rudimentary brains, the sort of thing we give to our children to play and tinker with."

He wasn't bragging. At least that's not the impression I got. Rather he was just stating a fact. It got me to thinking though, what this sort of race was capable of. I handed it back to him.

"I think you should accept it, Gary," I said, looking at him.

"Ok," said Gary. "I'll accept it."

QT smiled.

"You won't regret it."

QT was the only Zelve I had met personally. By this time, it was now June of twenty-one thirty-seven, we had been on Gaea for just over six months. It seemed normal now, like home. If anything, the ability to adapt and the resiliency of human beings is quite remarkable. Our cities were still being built out, but about eighty percent of the work had been done. At least the big work, finding homes and establishing common areas and buildings for the Councils.

Our scientists knew about one of the other species out here but we had not made contact yet and none of our neighbors had come by to welcome us to the neighborhood. QT had explained that it would be happening in due time after we had settled in further. I had asked him why he had shown such a keen interest in us. He had given a variety of platitudes and answers, the only one of which I thought was close to the truth was when he said he'd become concerned about our step backwards in dignity and freedom. He wanted to help ensure that there might be an option to reinvigorate civic discourse if and when the time came.

In other words he was hoping to help us design a coup, though a coup was not what I had in mind, and not what he had specifically created. And it wasn't really what we were trying to accomplish here in this underground bunker that had no blueprints and was nowhere to be found on the map. In fact, it was hidden from what was going to become the routine twice yearly survey of everything.

Gary and I had built it with the help of a few others, robots and humans and it had taken us four months. We had only recently completed it. It was a relatively small space. About the size of two tennis courts but it would suit our purpose and we'd have to make do.

I watched as QT powered Gary off. He spoke to the 'brain' in a language I had never heard and which I assumed was his mother tongue. He placed the brain on a nearby table and waited for a moment. It seemed to morph like black molasses into an odd shape that I couldn't quite figure out what it was for, until QT picked it up and placed it over Gary's head where it seemed to stick like a thin black fabric and fitted itself snugly to him.

"QT," I said.

Waritan Quelten stopped what he was doing and looked over at me. It was dim in here. We had called it The Enlightenment after the old Earth philosophical movement of the same.

"I see that you control this brain of yours through voice," I said. He nodded.

"That is one way, and perhaps the easiest."

"Which makes me a little concerned," I said. "What if something should go wrong. I do not know your language or the commands to control this thing."

"That's quite alright," he said. "You don't need to. This brain will not need replacing, it lasts indefinitely and is practically indestructible."

"I understand all of that, but we've had problems with technology before. Very recently in fact. What failsafe is there?"

"There is no need for a failsafe. However, I understand your concern. And you needn't be, for if Gary is unhappy with this brain he can just think as much and it will remove itself from him, leaving him quite intact and just as you knew him before this and he will be none the worse for wear."

"Are you sure?"

QT nodded.

"Do you wish to reconfirm if Gary still wants this or not?"

I nodded sheepishly. QT didn't say anything. He powered Gary back on with the brain still stuck over his head.

"Gary," I said a few seconds after he was awake.

"I believe this 'brain' is upon my head," said Gary.

"Yes, it is," said Waritan Quelten. "Dr. Siwik wanted to be sure you still want it."

"I do," said Gary.

"But what if something goes wrong Gary?" I asked him.

"I don't believe anything will go wrong," he said. "You worry like a mother hen."

I laughed. It was the first time I had heard Gary make a joke. I looked over at QT. He nodded.

"It is already part of him," said QT.

"What if you don't want it anymore?" I said to Gary.

"Then this is what will happen."

And I saw the brain slide off his face as if had been black oil, leaving no trace of itself. On the floor it reformed into a small ball and bounced up into QT's hand. The whole thing was astonishing.

"As you can see, Seraphina, if I no longer want it, it is gone, leaving me a hollow shell of the man I once was."

Gary was still joking. I looked at QT with a quizzical face.

"The programming takes a minute or two to revert back to its base state," he said. "He'll be without humor in a short while."

"I think I like him better with humor," I said. "If you're happy, Gary, I'm happy. Carry on QT."

QT powered Gary back off. This time he spoke to the brain which was still a black ball in his hand. He then threw it at the floor and it bounced off and up onto Gary's head and stuck to him like it had before, morphing as it landed on him into this tight covering. QT looked at me smiling.

"Sorry," he said, "I don't mean to belittle this. But like I said, this is more like a toy for our children than something of great importance, though I know for you it is far beyond any technology you might even imagine. Have no fear, Seraphina, Gary will be well in just a few moments."

QT and I stood and watched. There was nobody else here. It was late, and long past the time we could have kept them from their other Council duties. Being a Mother, I was fortunate in that my time was pretty much my own except for mandatory meetings and fulfilling some of my civic duties which, quite frankly, didn't require much.

It didn't take long for the process to complete.

"The brain is tapping into Gary's software and downloading it and scrubbing it. From there, once it is done, which won't take long, it will absorb itself into him and reposition itself somewhere in his skull."

And it did exactly that. The black fabric of a brain, slid like oil into the many tiny openings of Gary's skull and it was soon gone. A few seconds later Gary woke up and stood.

"Yabba Dabba Do," said Gary, and he peeled around the room at breakneck speed until stopping just inches from QT and I.

"I feel like a new man," he said.

I laughed.

"I can see that, Gary. But the real question is who am I?"

"Um… I think like I should know this," said Gary, tapping what might be considered his forehead with his index finger. "You are my mother?"

He said it with such earnestness that I thought he was serious. He must've seen the puzzled look on my face.

"Just kidding, Seraphina. You are the mastermind behind this diabolical plan to destroy Gaea and all her inhabitants. Mwoo ha ha!," he cackled.

I chuckled. But I was worried that Gary had become nothing more than a jokester.

"Is there any way to dial down the humor?" I asked Waritan Quelten.

"Sorry, Seraphina," said Gary, "I've just been without humor for so long that it's like a cork popped from fizzy champagne."

I smiled at him.

"That's okay," I said, "but it's still time to get back to work."

"Agreed, what were we doing again?"

Gary had to be joking.

"We are trying to figure out ways to hack the nanobots that the Councils have installed in each of us. That's the first task of business. Along with that, we need to figure out ways to ensure the ongoing survival of those who are sent back to old Earth to fight the von Neumanns."

"I hate to be the bearer of bad news," said Waritan Quelten, "but that second order of business of yours is going to be extremely difficult to accomplish. You need to be quite a bit more advanced than you are now."

"But that's why you're here isn't it?" I asked QT hopefully.

He shook his head slowly.

"No, I'm afraid not, Seraphina, I am here to help you in any way that I can without giving you access to any technology that is beyond your scope of understanding. The best I can do is gently push you in the direction you need to go. Gary will be your biggest ally now that he is sentient."

"But you just gave us some of your technology with that brain you put in Gary. Surely just a little bit more isn't going to harm anyone."

"Sorry you misunderstood, Seraphina. That technology you speak of that is in Gary is a mere toy. Hardly representative of our technology."

"And yet to us it is decades away from what we understand."

"Centuries more than likely," he said. "If you wish pure noninterference, I'd be happy to oblige, I'll take my toy and go home."

He smiled on that last bit. He didn't often joke but he knew how.

"Ok," I said. "We'll figure out what we can on our own."

"You're not alone, you have my help. I know it will be more difficult for you but you'll get there. One of the reasons I'm here is I believe in the potential of your species. Even if you continually fail to measure up to it. You must understand, Seraphina, that the majority of my planet wouldn't understand my desire even now to help, even in just this small way."

I smiled at him.

"You know," I said, "you remind me of a man I once knew."

He didn't say anything to that.

"His name was Spock. He wasn't a real man, he was a fictitious man. It was a TV show from long ago, over a hundred and fifty years ago. Anyway, Spock was from a species called the Vulcans and they had this same attitude about helping others. This noninterference. When Earth joined these other species, when we became space travelers, we joined the Federation and they had a name for this noninterference. They called it the Prime Directive."

"Interesting story," he said.

"My point," I said, "is that I always thought it was an artistic plot point to make the series more interesting. I mean, if we'd had the Vulcan technology at the time we were mere space babes, then the drama would have been greatly reduced. I guess they might have been onto something."

"Sounds like they were. If I might offer a reason for it so that you might understand, Seraphina. Think of it like this. Imagine giving a toddler a loaded handgun with the safety off. That is technology way above the toddler's ability to understand. I dislike using such crude violent metaphors but I think that's one you'll understand. It is my fear and those of my species that even a small amount of our technology if given to you in your current state of mental and emotional development would be enough to wipe out your species a trillion times over. And yet we flourish with such technology because of our peaceful use of it and that was the position we came from in its development."

I nodded reluctantly. It was true. I mean just look at us. We lived in an oligarchy, and a fairly archaic and strict one at that. It had some benefits. For example, none of us had to work for money any more and even though the Mothers' Council dictated the work to be performed by each individual, they quite accurately assessed the talents and interests of children so that most of us were reasonably content within the work we did as our contribution to the greater good. And still, we were being treated like children.

And don't get me started with the rehabilitation. I couldn't quite say it was torture, for it wasn't. But our rehabilitation centers rehabilitated those wayward Gaeans at the biological level with the nanobots. And I couldn't but quite wonder if it was humane. By any standards, the discomfort was minimal and I suppose it was better than a lifetime spent in jail. But had these nanobots not created docile humans? Sure, crime was down dramatically, especially violent crime. We hadn't had a violent crime since we'd been here these past six months. But was that because of the heavy hand of technology or free will? The answer, in my mind was clear.

And I liked peace, I wanted peace, but I wanted a peaceful society based upon freewill not Orwellian control. So, the first order of business was to hack the nanobots, a task that our Scientists had assured us was impossible. But are there not more things in heaven and Earth, human, than are dreamt of in our philosophy? To bastardize the old bard. I sure thought there were. It might take time, it might require my life's work, but I will die trying to free us from the chains of this ignoble servitude.

CHAPTER THIRTEEN

A Place of Questioning

WE were set up high upon our rockets. There were two small rockets attached to the belly of each starship. I was in Starship Intrepid MF dot 3. I was roughly fifty feet up in the air and facing skyward. Roger Dodger was strapped into the seat next to me. The windows gave us a panoramic view of the sky. I could see dozens of other starships around us and if I craned my neck I could see the land of Gaea stretched out away from me like a quilt of Earth tone colors.

Already the starship was rumbling from the ignited engines. I could hear the countdown starting. The sky was turning into streamers of white and gray smoke as other starships took off at lightning speed, dozens upon dozens of them split seconds behind each other. I knew what to expect, I had been trained and done dozens of simulations of this. It would be a thrilling ride. And yet here I was, my last moments attached to the planet that had been home and yet had not felt like it.

A tear rolled down my cheek as I realized the enormous change that was about to take place. Everything I knew was about to be behind me. Everything unknown was ahead, and the thrill and excitement of that, which had been my primary emotion just minutes before, melted like the ice condensation melting off these rockets that were about to hurtle me into space.

Roger Dodger looked over at me.

"Everything alright, Sunring Quickdust? You're not scared, are you?"

That got a chuckle out of me.

"No, Roger," I said, "it's just, well you know, the last time I'll see GAEA for some time. And I guess I'm just a bit sad about that."

"Understandable," he said.

Roger Dodger braced for takeoff. The computer voice was down to three seconds. I put my hand over the Medal of Honor. Somewhere, light years away, an ancient relative of mine had died and from that bravery, that selfless sacrifice, I was now in possession of the only item that remained of that heroic man. What's the worst that could happen? I could die. And I didn't really think that was about to happen. Not from here to the EVOLUTION Station or E-ONE. I wasn't bearing down on a den of enemy combatants, I was flying into space to save the human race. At least that's what Veritan Zeltan had said.

There's a moment during takeoff, right at the very beginning, where the rockets, full of thrust, just seem to stutter, hover, or pause before the energy kicks in hard. For the briefest moment it felt like the rockets didn't have enough power to push us into space. And then, it was all over, I melted into the seat as elephants climbed on top of me and my special suit constricted all around my limbs and torso in extremely firm waves, squeezing my blood back into my chest. I was stuck like this. I couldn't move if I wanted to. I was looking straight ahead, and other than the sensation in my body I couldn't tell we were moving at all. Some of the other Starships seemed to be traveling extremely slowly ahead of me. But that's only because I was catching up to them in speed.

Outside my main window looked like a swarm of Starships or a school of fish. We were close enough to each other that you couldn't fit another one of us in between the spaces.

For the first minute this sensation of being stationery started to give way. After that I could definitely tell I was moving into space. The rim of GAEA appeared like a thin blue halo around the planet, propelling away the looming blackness all around it. The rockets detached at around ninety seconds into the flight. They'd fall back to GAEA before landing for reuse next month at the next Ceremony of EVOLUTION.

We had been thrust into space at a great speed. But it wasn't nearly as fast as we were about to get. By the time the fusion drive was up and running we were two minutes in and about a thousand miles away from GAEA. Our fusion drives weren't powerful enough to use to launch us from GAEA but they got us incredibly fast out in space. Within three hours we'd be up to one third the speed of light. At that point we were just leaving our solar system and the computer wouldn't need me in the cockpit to keep an eye on our trajectory. Not that it needed me at all. Everything was handled by the computer, from ignition of the rockets on GAEA all the way to landing itself at the EVOLUTION Station.

But protocols being protocols, I was required and had been trained to stay in my seat for the first three hours until we reached maximum speed. The window in front of me had now darkened and upon it was a ton of information about the Starship Intrepid MF dot 3. Engine temperatures, speed, which as I looked at it blazed past five hundred and fifty-five kilometers per second, increasing by around nine kilometers per second each second. We were gaining speed at about five hundred and fifty-five kilometers per second faster every minute, and it was a smooth trajectory. I couldn't tell we were moving at all. In another minute I'd be traveling at over eleven hundred kilometers per second, increasing speed by around nine kilometers per second until we reached one hundred thousand kilometers per second which we'd hold until we came within three hours of the EVOLUTION Station.

A portion of the screen gave me information on the E-POD and how it was doing. The MMC was at one hundred percent where it should remain for the rest of the journey. If it went below seventy-seven percent the EVOLVER was in trouble. But I wasn't worried. Each Starship was equipped with twice the amount of MMC to refill the E-POD if it came to that. There was also redundancy in the fusion drives. I had two of them, and the Starship could perform at one hundred percent on either one. There were also emergency beacons and multiple failsafes in place in the event of a catastrophic breakdown. To make a long story short, I could survive in here for a long time. Close to three years if need be with the backup systems and the food and water recycling facilities in place. But that was not the plan.

In fact, it had only happened six times before that I was aware of. Meaning that only on six occasions did an EVOLVER become stranded with their E-POD in their Starship. And the worst of those happened about three months out from the EVOLUTION Station. Basically, about halfway between GAEA and the Station, so the Station personnel were told to perform the rescue. It only took just under ten months for the rescue to be completed. Only requiring an additional seven months for the EVOLVER to remain in space. A long time to be sure, but nowhere near the time that the EVOLVER could have survived out there.

The EVOLUTION Station sent out an additional Starship to transfer the EVOLVER, their robot and their EVOLVED, as well as another Starship to haul the broken down Starship Intrepid back to the EVOLUTION Station where it was repaired. In the worst case, another Starship Intrepid heading towards the EVOLUTION Station could stop to pick up both the EVOLVER and E-POD, but that was in emergency situations. A Starship Intrepid was not equipped to tow another Starship.

Just in case you're wondering. A Starship Intrepid that has broken down always has thrusters to maneuver in space. These are set up in redundant fashion. The reason for this is to avoid any catastrophic accident as the routes to and from GAEA and the EVOLUTION Station are, as you can imagine, quite well used. Therefore, a Starship Intrepid broken down in such a lane needs to move out of the general space corridors being used.

Also on the screen was a blueprint of the Starship and I could bring up live video of any section, even including my sleeping quarters and bathroom facilities. Apparently this feed was only accessible by the EVOLVER onboard the Starship or their robot. Still, I wasn't entirely convinced of that anymore. There were a ton of other bits of information I could bring up that gave me minute access to the goings on of my Starship, but the ones addressed above were the biggest. Besides of course all the small multicolored dots on the main screen in generally discreet and patterned ribbons. These were my colleagues, the other EVOLVERS and their cargo.

I could change the color of specific ones as I wished, and I chose purple for my Starship and that of my friends. There were four purple colored dots. I was second to last in these streaming ribbons of Starships on my screen. Up in the first third of the thousands of Starships was my nemesis Snowfeather Gentlecloud. Behind her by quite some lengths was Flutterdust Flowersong, then me and then bringing up the rear in the last third of Starships was Sugargaze Quickdance. I could only see them on my screen. There was no visual or audio communications allowed between Starships for what was called Three Dark.

Three Dark was the first three hours of the flight when the only communication allowed was between Starships and Control back on GAEA. As can be imagined, even after the first hour when we weren't up to full speed yet, the lag with communication from Control was becoming noticeable. At around the one hour mark we would be traveling at over thirty thousand kilometers per second and we would now be almost sixty million kilometers away from GAEA. If you know the speed of light, which for convenience sake I round up to three hundred thousand kilometers per second, then each communication round trip is taking over six minutes. At our ongoing acceleration, that round trip for communication reaches over fifteen minutes at the ninety minute mark and quickly gets worse from there.

It had only been five minutes and the information on my screen was telling me I was already over half a million kilometers from GAEA. The rearview was disappearing fast. It was going to be a long three hours in this chair. I didn't realize how long it would be. But when you're in space, it doesn't matter how fast you're going you might as well be trying to cross the ocean as an ant on a piece of twig with a blade of grass as a paddle. Being out here gave me a real sense of perspective. Eternity stretched out before me like a never-ending night.

Even now I was getting a brief glimpse of what the coming six months were going to feel like, and I wasn't sure I liked it. Six months out here by myself with nobody to touch or hug or see in person. The best I had was Roger Dodger and my fellow EVOLVERS over the air to talk to. I was going to get very fit, I could already foresee that part of the future. I saw myself spending hours and hours in the small workout room I had onboard.

I took the Medal of Honor out of my pocket and held it in my hand. The moiré silk ribbon felt soft and cool in my hand. I looked at the star, it was hardly worn over the millennium and a quarter it had been around. You could see the care and pride that had been taken to ensure that it got to me in such pristine condition. I don't know how my family had managed to keep it a secret all these years. If THE MOTHERS knew about it, they would demand it be sent to the MUSEUM OF REMINISCENCE. But that wouldn't happen, for it, and I, were heading back to where it came from. Where it was earned by my Greatest Father over sixty generations ago.

I put it around my neck and looked at it with wonder and imagination. I knew about the Battle of Iwo Jima, at least as well as you could know about something that had happened over one thousand two hundred and ninety-one years ago. The Battle of Iwo Jima, from what I've learned was a defining moment in the last of the two World Wars of old Earth. It was most remembered for the raising of what was then the American flag on top of Mount Suribachi. It had become an iconic photograph of the twentieth century.

It was a battle for a small island of twenty-one square kilometers almost due south of Tokyo by about twelve hundred kilometers. It had taken shape as Operation Detachment with the goal of taking over the whole island including its three Japanese controlled airfields. It was in hindsight a bloody and useless battle for even though the airfields were thought of as being strategically important in launching attacks from there at Japan, that didn't turn out to be the case.

In the end, in a battle that officially lasted from the nineteenth of February to the twenty-sixth of March nineteen forty-five, barely five weeks, over twenty-five thousand men lost their lives. I say men, because thankfully at that time women had seen the folly of war or were unable to take on combat positions. Seeing as how I like math, twenty-five thousand men dying in five weeks is five thousand per week. That turns out to over seventy-one dead per day or roughly three per hour. And that's on a small island less than half the size of old Manhattan on old Earth.

Nevertheless, my Greatest Father many generations back gave his life in saving countless of his friends and colleagues. You don't hear of that sort of thing anymore. Maybe its because GAEA is so much more peaceful or because there are no more wars. Whatever the reason, it is something to think about. I just hoped I never had to be put in such a position.

But my Greatest Father, Jack Crow, an old Earth style name as you've probably guessed did something so heroic they gave him the highest honor in what was the United States of America back then. And it wasn't easy to get. Since that old Earth nation was founded in seventeen seventy-six, over forty-five million people served in its military until the USA joined the USE on the first of January twenty seventy-five. That's when old Earth became united under one government in its attempt at fighting off the von Neumanns.

In any event, in those two hundred and ninety-nine years that the USA was a country, just over thirty-five hundred Medals of Honor were issued. So your chance of receiving one was less than one in ten thousand. And more than that really, because you had to do something really brave and heroic. So as I felt the Medal around my neck I felt a certain respect and awe for a man I had never met who had been so honored. Part of his blood ran in my veins, and that gave me courage.

The misgivings out here in space as I hurtled through the dark emptiness towards the WHOLE were leaving me as quickly as I was leaving GAEA. I was resolute in my mission. Maybe I was thinking I was more important than I was, maybe I thought I really was saving humanity. I mean a girl can't help but think that when she's told it right? That's what Veritan Zeltan said. Maybe he was just stroking my ego, but he seemed sincere. And ego is as bad as pride, for THE MOTHERS have said that ego is the teat upon which pride nourishes itself, and we all know what happened when our pride got too big, it resulted in the Final Diaspora.

Still, here I was, heading to a place that I had never known except in my dreams and my imaginations. Sure I knew a lot about old Earth. But what I knew about even at its most recent was still information over a thousand years old. It could be anything now. Maybe the von Neumanns had destroyed it and left it a barren wasteland. Though that couldn't be right? I mean, Veritan Zeltan had showed me what it looked like. It looked more beautiful than GAEA. But I'd only seen a small part of it. Other parts might be barren wastelands.

But it didn't matter though. I was heading there with my Greater Father. And I believed in what Veritan Zeltan said. Humanity would start over, again. And I'd play my part.

I looked at the dash. We were only a half hour into our journey. My mind was wandering and it was a babbling brook. Perhaps you've noticed. I couldn't imagine how the next six months were going to feel like. I'd have to read a lot, interact with a lot of holovideos to keep from going mental. And the next two and a half hours were going to remain uncomfortable. The flight suit I was in wasn't the most comfortable. It had long ago stopped squeezing me. But it was bulkier than I'd like and I had never enjoyed wearing the helmet of it, even if it was small and streamlined and form fitted.

It was precautionary, so we'd been told. We could survive space in it for about an hour if necessary, though how we'd get into outer space was beyond me. We had trained for such scenarios, but the likelihood of surviving space or a crash under these circumstances seemed remote to me. I mean, there were thousands upon thousands of Starships zipping along at incredible speeds in densely packed lanes. I imagined that you'd literally be run over if you ejected into outer space.

Anyway, that wasn't anything to think about. It was unpleasant and we had been assured extremely unlikely. Glitterfrost Gentlefeather had said there had only ever been one such catastrophe and THE MOTHERS and other COUNCILS had sworn that it would never happen again, and so it hadn't.

"How does everything look?" I asked Roger, sick of hearing the nattering of my own mind.

Roger looked up at the screen and tapped away at a panel he swiveled in front of himself to look through other diagnostics. He was pretty much tapped into the Starships computer but he could do other things this way too.

"Everything's looking good," he said. "Speed is increasing as expected and there have been no incidents to report."

I nodded.

"I want to ask you something," I said, not sure if I should or not.

Roger Dodger looked over at me.

"But I want you never to tell anyone about our conversation unless I give you permission."

I knew I was taking a risk. But I was already bored and I figured there wasn't much that Roger Dodger could do out here to get me in trouble with THE MOTHERS. I mean he was my robot and as such he was to obey me, but I wasn't certain of how much THE MOTHERS or SCIENCE COUNCIL could access.

"I will do my best," he said.

"What do you mean by that?" I asked.

"Well, Sunring Quickdust," he said, "I will do my best to encrypt our conversation, but I don't know if that will make it tamperproof."

I nodded.

"So long as our conversation is safe until we get back to GAEA."

Though I knew that was probably not going to happen unless I was forced back somehow.

"That I can assure you of," he said.

"Good," I said. "Do you think that my Greater Father in the E-POD is really dead?"

Roger Dodger continued to look at me, though as you know, he had no eyes. His face was a smooth helmet of sorts. He could animate the front with facial features if I requested him to, but I preferred him like a blank slate. It looked creepy otherwise. But that's just my opinion.

"I don't know," he said. "Moondew Flamesdance is certainly EVOLVED. That's why we're here."

"But does that mean he's dead. We never talk about death really. But doesn't being EVOLVED mean that you're dead. I mean, if he's being sent to the WHOLE and from there to the ONE, then isn't he really dead."

"I understand what death means. It means the end of biological processes. In that case, then yes, I think you can assume that your Greater Father is dead."

I looked at the screen and the streaming ribbons of little dots and our increasing speed. We were coming up on an hour. Speed increasing consistently and yet it still looked like we were standing still. Outside, in the darkness of space were the red and blue and white lights of other Starships. Almost looking like a blizzard of stars. Though the ones closest to me I could see their outlines and shapes. And it almost looked as if I could put my hand out through the window and touch them. They seemed that close.

"What if I told you that my Greater Father wasn't dead, but that he was just, perhaps, in stasis?"

"I wouldn't believe you," said Roger Dodger. "I'd think you had become delusional."

"And yet, how do we know he is dead? I mean really, how do we know?"

"Because that is what we have been told by the authorities. And if we can't trust the authorities then who can we trust? They've never lied to us yet, at least not that I know of. Have they?"

"I've never known them to lie. At least not that I've been made aware of. But perhaps this is the biggest coverup of them all. Perhaps this is the biggest hoodwinking of GAEANS ever."

"I don't think so," said Roger Dodger, "in any event, we'll never know and you'd think that by now this sort of a coverup would have been exposed, I mean EVOLVERS have been EVOLVING EVOLVEDS for over a thousand years."

"But just imagine, Roger, what that would mean. If we've been duped for over a millennium. Can you imagine? It would shock society to the very core."

Roger Dodger nodded.

"It would, but like I said, there is no evidence to suggest that there is or has been any coverup. This is all just supposition. And as your robot, Sunring Quickdust, I daresay this is very dangerous supposition."

I nodded at him. There was no point belaboring the issue. He wouldn't, he couldn't believe in the possibility and perhaps that wasn't very surprising considering his robotedness. I mean, he wasn't a free thinking robot in that sense. We'd tried and failed at that, hadn't we? Hence the von Neumanns, hence the Final

Diaspora, hence GAEA, hence me here adrift in the ocean of space for the next six months.

We sat in silence for another hour. Watching the screens in front of us. It was boring. I couldn't wait to get out of my chair and walk around in a limited way. Maybe head to my quarters and just rest or read or something. I couldn't read or watch anything up front here. That wasn't allowed, not for Three Dark. So I sat and rambled alone in my mind. Fighting with myself, arguing with myself and contemplating old Earth which was about to become new Earth for me again.

I hadn't heard anything from Control for around a half hour. The last time they had chimed in was to ask how everyone was doing. I got the impression they might have been hoping to get Roger Dodger to rat me out. But I was probably just been paranoid. We both said everything was fine. You couldn't hear any other communications. Communications between Starships wasn't allowed and more than that it was blocked. And communications between Control and specific Starships was private. So I sat in silence listening to the ambient noise of the Starship.

It was eerily quiet. Fusion Drives hardly make any noise and in any event they're way at the back and you really have to be in the engine room to hear the humming coming off of them. And there was hardly any squeaking or rattling. These Starships are incredibly well made with extremely tight tolerances. And even at the speed we were going which was now over sixty-six thousand kilometers per second there was hardly any stuff in space to be buffeting up against. You probably know that already, but the distance between atoms or molecules in space is vast. We've determined that there is likely more than four cubic meters of space available to each atom out here, and being as cold as it is, they're hardly moving at all, so there is barely any perceptible friction against the Starship at all.

I looked over at Roger Dodger. It was amazing how still a robot could be. He hadn't moved since we'd spoken to Control. Not a flinch nor murmur. Me on the other hand, I was fidgeting like a flea ridden dog from old Earth. If it wasn't the Medal of Honor I was fondling, it was squirming here or there in my seat or playing with the instrumental panel. Until that is, the whole screen and interior of my Starship started blinking a deep red and an audible siren started going off. That got Roger Dodger interested real quick too.

"Emergency maneuvers," said the computerized Starship voice. "Catastrophic crash ahead."

I glanced at the screen. Everything was now pulsating red as we careened towards the crash site. The first third of what was a smooth ribbon of blinking dots, other Starships in other words, was a jumbled mess. I tapped at the screen. Most of these blinking dots had turned red and stopped blinking. That meant the EVOLVER inside was unresponsive. In other words, they were dead. No biological functions available.

I was shocked. I had never expected anything like this. Eighty-three thousand three hundred and thirty-three of us had left GAEA. We were flying incredibly close to each other, but still, this wasn't supposed to happen. Twenty thousand and something Starships were involved in the catastrophe ahead. All this information was being displayed on the screen. The protocol was simple. There was nothing for me to do. I could take over manually, but that wasn't recommended. The computer was faster and better than me at avoiding debris and handling emergency maneuvers. I should just sit and remain vigilant. But I noticed that Flutterdust Flowersong was caught up in the debris. And her purple dot was still blinking.

I wasn't supposed to stop and offer assistance. The rules were, we were to keep going. A rescue mission would be sent in due course. However, I'd already decided that rules be damned. I mean, I wasn't coming back to GAEA, was I? In any event, any commands from Control would only reach me in about thirteen or so minutes. I'd be out of my Starship by then trying to help if I could.

We were gaining on that front third of a mess really quick. I had to make a decision, and I had to do it now. The 'unresponsive' EVOLVERS list was increasing by the second. It was over twenty-two thousand now. I imagined this might end up being the worst disaster in EVOLVERS history. I could easily see twenty-five to thirty thousand lives lost in this catastrophe. My nemesis blinking dot had gone still. Snowfeather Gentlecloud hadn't survived and even though we didn't get along I was saddened by it. She was a colleague after all, and she didn't deserve this.

I had so many questions. One of the most pressing was if this was indeed an unusual catastrophe? I asked the computer how this had happened. It didn't have the complete answer but it said that a few of the Starships in the lead group had been hit by small space debris that hadn't been detected. They in turn lost control and tumbled out of their lanes creating a huge domino effect that cascaded into the oncoming Starships. I thought this was probably something that could happen at anytime. I mean it's not like we have the best intel on these lanes through the first three hours of our trip, or for the duration of our solar system.

Sure we had probes out there to sweep the area and keep things as clear as possible. But there were only a few hundred of them, and they were involved in keeping around five hundred million kilometers of space clear. The more I thought about it, probably an impossible task. Each one probably had a million or more kilometers to keep clear. Maybe THE MOTHERS thought that was sufficient seeing as how empty space was, but still. Could you even afford to entertain a catastrophe like this? I mean what would GAEANS think if they heard? I smiled wryly at myself. They probably wouldn't hear about it. We'd be given gag orders over this I was pretty sure.

I wondered if perhaps some of that debris might have been from any of the probes. I asked the computer if it could identify the source of the debris. It couldn't. I had made my decision.

The Starship was braking hard. I was already under ten thousand kilometers per second when I decided to take over manual control.

"Do you think that's wise?" asked Roger Dodger.

I didn't look at him.

"We're going to help my friend, Flutterdust Flowersong," I answered.

"That's not really allowed," he said.

This time I did look at him briefly.

"I don't want to argue with you Roger. We're helping my friend and that's the end of it."

"Okay."

A huge benefit of having a robot is that it has to do as you ask of it, unless it receives an order from a more senior human being. And there were no more senior human beings out here than me. So Roger had to do what I ordered. The only more senior people who could order my robot around were few and far between. They included only very senior members of the SCIENCE COUNCIL, the EVOLUTION COUNCIL, the PEACEKEEPING COUNCIL or any of the MOTHERS. Control was made up of senior SCIENCE and EVOLUTION COUNCIL members, but like I said, at this distance, we'd only be hearing from them in just under a half hour.

You know how this works. I was almost two hundred and fifty

million kilometers from GAEA. Light travels at three hundred thousand kilometers per second or about eighteen million kilometers per minute. So the messages sent in just the last minute or so about this accident are only going to arrive in around thirteen minutes. If Control responds immediately I'll only be hearing from them in about twenty-six minutes time. I reckoned it would only take me about five minutes to get to Flutterdust Flowersong. As it was, I was practically underneath her.

I say underneath, because I had dropped a few dozen kilometers below the main stream of traffic so that I wouldn't get caught up in the debris. Most of the Starships were whizzing by on either side and some of them jumping up, over the accident site. In about five minutes the last of them would be zipping by.

So, even if Controls first communication was to order us to continue on, Roger and I would be outside of our Starship and in that event they would have to defer to me, because their authority was not absolute outside the Starship. Roger knew this, he could cajole and challenge me, but he could not force me to do otherwise so long as we were not in the Starship. This was my plan.

I was now off of Fusion Drive and using the thrusters. We were coming up on Flutterdust Flowersongs Starship at around thirty-three kilometers per minute. An achingly slow speed which I was about to throttle down to a full stop within the minute. I couldn't communicate with her, because Control had not disengaged the inter-starship communications which automatically became disengaged after Three Dark. But I knew it wasn't strictly limited to time, it was also limited by distance. Inter-starship communications were also kept off by distance. And the distance that equated with Three Dark also happened to be the distance to the edge of our solar system from GAEA which was around half a billion kilometers. We were just a little less than that distance at the moment.

To make a long story short, I couldn't communicate with Flutterdust Flowersong so I didn't know how she was doing. What I did know, was that we had now lost thirty-three thousand EVOLVERS. It probably wouldn't change much from here because only the last quarter or fifth of us were flying past the debris field now, and bringing up the rear like they were, they had a lot of time to prepare avoidance maneuvers.

"Doesn't look good," said Roger Dodger.

I wasn't sure if he was trying to convince me to get back in the stream and carry on or if he was just stating a fact. It was certainly a fact, I could see that for myself. A large chunk of Flutterdust Flowersongs Starship, which was Starship Intrepid LG dot 9, had been torn of the front third. Her EVOLVED was a man by the name of Longshadow Greenline. He'd been a SCIENTIST. But all of that's not important.

I asked the computer to bring me up the vitals of Starship LG dot 9. Flutterdust Flowersong was healthy if not in shock and anxious. You could tell that by perspiration, heartbeat, respiration and other vitals. Longshadow Greenline also seemed to be online. The E-POD was not affected. So, Roger and I would be rescuing both Flutterdust Flowersong and her EVOLVED.

These Starships having plenty of redundancies, and could easily carry two EVOLVERS and their cargo, or EVOLVEDS. It could also quite easily carry the two robots who came with the two EVOLVEDS. But as I looked through my screen into space I knew that Flutterdust Flowersong had lost G3230.13. That was her robot and how she addressed it. Though the point thirteen at the end was not necessary for the robot to understand who she was talking to. She just called it G3230. As you know, the point thirteen just means that G3230 was the thirteenth robot to be built in the year thirty-two thirty.

Anyway, I knew she'd lost it because I saw it in pieces slowly tumbling and falling away from the Starship. Thankfully, arriving as we did a few minutes after the fact, most of the debris from the accident that was traveling fast, fast enough to damage my Starship had long been flung from the main accident area. Most of the debris around us now was traveling very slowly. Probably at fractions of a meter per second. This was good news as my Starship could easily handle bumps from this sort of thing. Additionally, the debris field was not huge. Most of it had been flung fast and far off. However, I was sick to my stomach seeing the occasional dead, I can say that now can't I, EVOLVER tumbling slowly many meters away. Not to be macabre, but some of them were in pieces. I just want you to get a realistic idea of what it looked like out here. It was a horror show.

I came to a stop below and just off to the side of her. I had the computer do a full sweep of the immediate vicinity twenty-five meters out. It was reasonably clear of debris. I was slightly to Flutterdust Flowersongs port side. On our Starships, there were two entrances into which you could add cargo, and they were both aft, or at the back of the Starship. One entrance was port side and the other was starboard. The starboard side had been gutted, especially towards the front. Its aft opening might still be working but I thought it might be better to try the generally intact port side.

I could tell from the sweep that Flutterdust Flowersong was still in her seat so I maneuvered my Starship to the front first to face her. My nose was just a few meters from hers and I used my front lights to flicker out a morse code message. Even in the thirty-third century we were still trained in these archaic ways of communications because they were reliable. I told her I was coming to rescue her and to stabilize the Starship as best she could and to ready the E-POD for transfer from the port side cargo entrance.

She understood, and so I got my starboard side up nice and close to her port side. We were probably about five meters away. I could have gotten closer but I didn't want to risk it. You never knew what else might go wrong and I was cautious that way. I gave control of the Starship over to the computer to keep it steady and within this distance to Flutterdust Flowersongs Starship.

Roger and I went to the back and got ourselves ready to step out into space. I put on an additional spacesuit which was only slightly more bulky than what I had on but it was more robust and puncture proof to any errant space debris. Roger needed none of that. He could easily last in space for a long time with his mini fusion drive which would keep him warm and useful.

We attached ourselves to a tether and Roger and I each took an additional tether with us. One to attach to the E-POD and one to attach to my friend. As we opened the outer hatch to space I looked up and there were still dozens of Starships flying off either to the left or right or over top of us. Not one had come to see if we needed help. No wonder Veritan Zeltan had come to me about humanitys problem. The rest of us, I realized, were just sacks of flesh robots not veering from our rules and regulations. I sighed and stepped off the ramp into space.

I knew how to handle myself in deep space. That was also part of our training. The spacesuit I was in also had small jets placed all over me. I just had to give verbal instruction for where I wanted to go and the computer adjusted the thrust to ensure I got there. There was a small rod attached to my belt that I could use if I wanted. It was gyroscopic and it allowed manual control if that was what I wished. It wasn't, it was faster to let the computer do the work for me. Roger also had vents he could use as small thrusters, and he followed me across.

It only took us around fifteen seconds to make it across. We were halfway when the port side hatch of Flutterdust Flowersongs Starship opened and I saw her. I waved and grinned. She seemed really happy to see me. It was going to be nice to have real company for this first trip of mine, and hers as EVOLVERS. Behind her I could see the E-POD. It had been moved into place for easier access for us. It was like pushing a rubber duck on water. It sort of hovered and made moving it very easy.

As we got onto her ship I looked back at mine just to be sure that the computer was keeping my ship right where I had ordered it to. And it was. However, I noticed another Starship clip a rather big piece of debris just over head and behind us. And in what seemed like slow motion, this Starship started tumbling towards us. It was eerie. Because if I hadn't looked back at just that right time, I would have no idea. There was no sound and no fires. It looked like it might clip us. And that was the last thing we needed.

"Inside," I yelled.

Roger got the message, but because Flutterdust Flowersong and I hadn't gotten onto the same channel she just saw my big open mouth, but she got the message nonetheless. I didn't have to tell the computer anything, it was automatically scanning its position and saw the oncoming disaster. What we did have to do was detach the tethers lest we be pulled and whipped back into space. Roger and I did it just in time.

Starship Intrepid LG dot 9 didn't have the best maneuverability due to its recent accident, so it sort of pitched then yawed then rolled down several meters very quickly. It was like being trapped on a horrific rollercoaster. I would have fallen out of the port opening if it wasn't for Roger grabbing onto me. My Starship managed a much more efficient and elegant descent.

The damaged Starship just missed mine but careened into the front of the one we were in. It pitched forward violently tossing us all into the walls of the cargo opening. Well, almost tossing us into the walls which might have damaged my spacesuit and Flutterdust Flowersongs. Again, it was thanks to Roger for grabbing onto both of us and magnetizing his feet to the cargo floor that saved us. The E-POD managed to keep itself from hitting us out into deep space.

Flutterdust Flowersong tapped at the side of her helmet. She wanted to communicate. I told the computer to sync our communications and a moment later I could hear her voice.

"My Starship is unresponsive," she said. "The computers just died and we're free falling."

"Then we best make this quick."

And I could tell it was free falling, it was slowly tipping over end over end. But it was slow enough that we could maintain our verticalness within the cargo hold but it was going to make our exit strategy all the more complicated. Flutterdust Flowersong and I tried and struggled with the E-POD which was now getting flung all over the place. It could hover on a horizontal plane, but it couldn't figure out what to do with going end over end. It was more difficult than I imagined to right this thing and keep it righted as the Starship continued to pitch end over end. The only saving grace was that this exit area we were in was open to space which meant that the E-POD was thankfully weightless. It wasn't something the two of us could carry on GAEA, it was way too heavy. So being where we were was a bit of a blessing.

I sent Roger out to collect the four tethers. I didn't know how long it took us to struggle with the E-POD, but it must have been some time, for we hadn't even left the cargo area of Flutterdust Flowersongs Starship when I got the message from Control.

"All Starship Intrepids are ordered to continue onwards to

destination. Do not stop. Rescue mission is on its way. Continue to the EVOLUTION Station."

Hmm, that's all they needed to say. And except for me out here by myself, they didn't really need to say it at all. This was an order. But I didn't care, we wouldn't be leaving until we got Flutterdust Flowersong and her E-POD onboard the Starship Intrepid MF dot 3.

Roger Dodger got back with the tethers. He was elegant and balanced in space like a ballerina. I felt like a clumsy oaf. I'd have him bring the E-POD across.

"We need to get going," he said, as if I hadn't heard from Control myself.

"I know, Roger," I said, "but we're not leaving these two behind now, are we?"

"No, we aren't, Sunring Quickdust."

"Good," I said. "We'll be off as soon as everyone is back onboard safe and sound. I want you to bring the E-POD in Roger while Flutterdust Flowersong and I will get ready to leave as soon as you've secured the E-POD in Starship Intrepid MF dot 3.

"Understood," he said.

He handed a tether to Flutterdust Flowersong and me and then he went about securing the E-POD. I led Flutterdust Flowersong from her Starship to mine, with the computers in our spacesuits and on my Starship reeling us in like big fish in the inky blackness of this vast ocean of space. I wondered what fish really looked like up close. I mean, I'd seen pictures and video, but it'd be really cool to see one up close. I might get my chance on old Earth. If I made it. I didn't like being out here all stationery and vulnerable as we were. I looked up and Starships were still zipping by. I thought they would have been all past by now. I must have miscalculated.

Flutterdust Flowersong and I had already taken our outer

spacesuits off and were just exiting the inner cargo hold that was pressurized when Roger Dodger came on board trailing the E-POD.

"Make it as quick as you can," I said to him.

Flutterdust Flowersong and I headed back up to the cockpit. There were four seats up there. Like I said, we liked our redundancies, and rightly so. I got back into my seat and Flutterdust Flowersong took the one to my right. Roger Dodger would have to sit behind us. Wasn't anything he couldn't do from there that he could do from the front.

"As soon as Roger Dodger is secure," I said to the computer, "resume trajectory, speed and destination."

I looked over at Flutterdust Flowersong.

"I'm so glad you made it," I said.

Flutterdust Flowersong rolled her eyes. She was visibly shaken. I would have been too if I'd been in that accident.

"It was so scary, Sunring Quickdust," she said. "I thought I was going to be done. On my very first EVOLUTION."

Her eyes welled up with tears but she didn't cry.

"What happened?" she asked.

"We don't know all the details yet, but it seems that some of the lead Starships hit stray debris and that caused an accident cascade."

Flutterdust Flowersong nodded slowly.

"There was nothing I could do," she said. "The Starship did its best to avoid colliding with anything, but the whole front of us just burst into debris and pieces and Starships flipping and careening all over the place."

"I don't think there's ever been such a catastrophe as this," I said.

She shook her head.

"No, not at all. They're supposed to have those drones clearing out this section of the solar system," she said. "This is a known route. How could they have missed something like this?"

"I think they don't have enough..."

I was cut off by more throbbing red ambient light in the room. I looked up at the screen.

"Collision evasion," the computer said, as it tossed the Starship around as if it had just been caught in a hurricane and tsunami at the same time.

It was a good thing we were belted in. Even still it was a choppy ride. The Starship was attempting to avoid what I could now see from the screens was another Starship tumbling towards us in several large chunks. My Starship was also trying to avoid other bits of debris around us too.

If I had been standing on the top of my Starship I probably could have reached out and touched the other broken one as it tumbled on by. It came that close.

Just as it passed us, my Starship settled down and I watched the broken chunks of the other one hit Flutterdust Flowersongs Starship and rip it into pieces. We had to get out of here whether Roger Dodger was ready or not.

"Get us back on course," I said.

The Starship pushed us way out of the ribbon on the port side while it spooled up the Fusion Drive. It didn't take long and we were soon traveling solely by Fusion Drive which meant our speed was increasing rapidly. By the time Roger came back into the cockpit we were doing well over one thousand kilometers per second. The Starship moved into the stream of Starships but by this time there were none behind us. We were well behind and falling further behind as each second progressed.

We had slowed down to around ten thousand kilometers per

second which I guessed was the speed the others had slowed down to. That meant we were at least ten times slower than them until we all reached full speed. At that point I put us at over one hundred million kilometers behind the tail end of the convoy. The computer told me it would be closer to one hundred and ninety-seven million kilometers behind. Didn't matter. We were on our way.

"That was another close one," said Roger. "I'm glad we're on our way now."

"Me too," said Flutterdust Flowersong.

"The E-POD is secured?" I asked.

"Yes, Sunring Quickdust, the rest of the trip should be uneventful."

I thought about all that space debris that the COUNCILS would have to have cleaned up for the EVOLVERS return journey. It shouldn't be a problem. They had almost a year to clean it up. And hopefully they'd do a better job of it. I toyed with the idea of asking Roger Dodger if he'd known of any other EVOLVER catastrophes like this. But I thought against it. It's unlikely they would have given him access to that information, and if they had he'd likely have been instructed not to share it with any EVOLVER.

So I sat there for the next two hours and twenty minutes in Three Dark, which had become Three Dark and twenty minutes for us, stewing and getting angrier and angrier as what I thought had been my stable world of GAEA slowly unravelled and I could see clearly the dark corners of what I had thought was a world filled with light.

Though Roger was right about one thing. The rest of the journey was uneventful if not mentally challenging as we had been warned. But having my best friend with me was a blessing. And a thousand times I wanted to tell her to join me on old Earth. And a thousand times I bit my tongue.

CHAPTER FOURTEEN

A Place of Difficulty

I was on my second Gary. We'd decided onboard our Starships that each robot would be retired after twenty-five years. Perhaps it was paranoia or perhaps it was smart thinking, whatever it was, I lost Gary in twenty-one forty-seven. That was thirteen years ago. Today was the tenth of February twenty-one sixty.

My first and only Gary was designated R2122.21 as you probably recall. In the twenty-five years of service I'd never had a complaint from him. Second Gary, who I also just called 'Gary' was designated G2147.11. I'd had him for a little less than thirteen years. He seemed just like first Gary, but before first Gary got humanized as I liked to call it.

Our problem with the nanobots had stalled ever since first Gary had been melted down and recycled. In fact, I hadn't seen Waritan Quelten since that time. It seemed like he had taken his brain and gone home. Second Gary didn't have a brain. Not only did he not have humor now, he wasn't as intelligent either. And that wasn't helping things. My age was another thing that wasn't helping.

I was now seventy-nine. I'd be eighty towards the end of the year. The body was old. I could feel it in my bones. I could feel it everywhere actually. In fact, when I looked in the mirror I didn't recognize the person staring back at me. I still felt as youthful as the day I left old Earth. Not that I was a young woman back then. In fact I was forty-five. But good gosh that felt spritely now.

My mental acuity was also old. Like a computer that hadn't been upgraded in years, I could feel my neurons misfiring and the messages being sent between them slow as molasses. I didn't think I was suffering from dementia. I could still grasp the scientific concepts that I once understood well, and I'd kept up with the research and evolution within my own field. Still, it took me longer to get going each day. It took me longer just to do everything. To get to this place we called The Enlightenment, which at the time I thought was quite clever and avant-garde of us, now it seemed like a place of pure folly.

At one point I thought we were getting somewhere with controlling these nanobots, but that hadn't turned out to be quite right. I knew we would get there, but back then I was relying on the kindness of strangers. And those strangers had just disappeared without a word. I'm talking of course about Waritan Quelten. Don't know what happened to him.

And yet, this was still going to be my life's work. I wanted to free Gaeans from the shackles of servitude and slavery, and those shackles were simply little robots that we couldn't see. I found it ironic how we had escaped one robotic master just to become slaves to another.

As I sat here at my desk in The Enlightenment, I got to thinking about aging. You can't help not to when you get up in the years like I am. Everyday is a reminder of the slow demise of the body. The young mind remains the same, maybe a little slower like I said, but who I am, who I feel I am has remained the same since at least my early twenties. And yet here I am trapped in the sagging sack of skin of an eighty year old. Almost eighty year old.

The aging doesn't worry me. Not really, it's just the natural progression of things. What does worry me is the lack of success I've had. And time is clearly running out. Incidentally, the same year that Gary got recycled was the same year Ni Yin got recycled. I say that, because isn't that what death really is? A recycling. I mean conservation of energy and matter has held up remarkably well over the centuries we've known about it.

Of course, QT might have different ideas. He wouldn't ever tell me about them, but he did seem to indicate that matter can be manipulated, increased and destroyed even, by the right intelligence. He must have been talking about the intelligent species we've all suspected are really overseeing everything here. I've spoken about them before. Nobody's seen them. Well, I'm sure the Zelves have, but QT won't speak of it. I should say, wouldn't, shouldn't I? I mean I haven't seen him in around thirteen years.

I'm no longer upset, but I am disappointed. He had just left one day, and never came back. It was the day we took Gary to the Science Council to be destroyed. I mean really, that's what happened to him. You can recycle a tin can, but I'd come to see Gary as a friend and a colleague. I wouldn't go so far as to say they killed him, but they had him destroyed that's for certain.

Second Gary was over at another table working on computer problems. I didn't think he'd be getting anywhere. I didn't think any of us would anymore. Not without Waritan Quelten's help.

You can tell I haven't quite bought into the new ways of Gaea. I don't write the things we're supposed to write in upper case. I keep getting remanded for that. But I don't care. One of the benefits of being an old lady is that at some point you just don't give a shit anymore. That's why I don't refer to Ni Yin as Moonmeadow Mountainmist. Stupid name. They're all stupid names. I don't know why we had to change our names anyway. They seemed to have worked well for thousands of years.

Everyone here at The Enlightenment calls each other by what others would consider to be our old Earth names. Though there aren't many of us working on the problem anymore. Just seven, and that's if you count second Gary.

You might be wondering who's in charge now? Well, officially, the Mothers' Council is in charge, though Azeeza Maalouf thinks she's the Queen Bee. And most defer to her as if she is. I really get under her skin not calling her by her Gaean name of Softrain Summerwind. It really winds her up. But I can get away with it for I'm one of what they're calling the Sevens. We're special. We're the bridge generation that came from old Earth and settled Gaea. In fact, we now have a second generation of Gaean born humans. They're young, only toddlers, but still, I've come to witness life start to flourish independently here on Gaea.

Maybe one day I'll tell you about the funeral of Ni Yin. Practically the whole of Gaea turned up. And now those who don't live in Gulgoleth make pilgrimages to see the statue of her. It's the only statue we'll ever put up of a human. And there it stands prominently in the center of the square. The center of Gulgoleth where the largest building in Gaea resides, the Council Colossus. Talk about a woman full of hubris and pride. She made them mummify her and she's inside the bloody statue. So it's really more like a sarcophagus, isn't it?

We have a law now, we call it The Golden Calf law, but that's just between you and me. Basically it allows for no permanent representation of a human being or human form. So our artists have done some silly things. They'll paint elaborate portraits only to scribble out the faces as if a rebellious teenager with a spray can had gotten to it. Or a child with a crayon. Same with statues. They're either headless or have some sort of odd new age nonsense in place of a head.

How far we've come only to step backwards. Nobody knows this of course, I'm talking about Ni Yin, except for those in the Science Council who were tasked with the embalming, and of course those of us Mothers. But we're sworn to secrecy on pain of death. Not literally of course, but the threats need never be aired in order to be understood.

You'd think that a society like ours, as advanced as ours, which now had fusion drives that already are as small as small homes, could do better. They hope to have the fusion drives as small as old Earth refrigerators by the turn of the century. That's when they want to start sending us back to old Earth to fight the von Neumanns. They're worried about it. It's become our priority.

But shouldn't our priority be to stop aging. I mean with the nanobots and other nanotechnology couldn't we have figured out a way to reverse aging by now. I'm pretty sure we could have if we'd focused on that instead of human control.

I'm personally not worried about old Earth. First of all, I don't think we'll be ready by the turn of the century. That's just a little over fifty years away and surviving the interstellar journey had set us back technologically. Not by an insurmountable amount, but still, it's going to take us a few decades to get our sea legs under us on this new planet. Anyway, that's just my opinion. I could be wrong. I thought handling these nanobots would be no problem. Turns out I was wrong about that.

And those von Neumanns, well, I'm skeptical that they'll just be there hanging around waiting for us. They're our children in a way aren't they? And like father like son, why won't they just be leaving at some point to? That's what I think. But they don't believe it. They've never really appreciated my input. Sometimes I wonder why Ni Yin ever wanted me in the Council in the first place. Maybe she had a soft spot for me. Or perhaps it was a matter of keeping your friends close but your enemies closer. Doesn't matter.

In some ways I feel sorry for the generations of Gaeans. Starting with the first generation who are already twenty-four and twenty-five, we'll be tossing them back to the wolves. Let's see, that should start happening for the first of them, the men in the year twenty-two zero two. The women will be heading back eleven years later. Like I said, I don't think we'll have the technology to send them back to old Earth by then, but I could be wrong. We're already making great progress on our station by the wormhole. That should definitely be ready by the turn of the century.

So you might be wondering what we're going to do with them if we aren't ready to send them back to old Earth. You won't like it. I certainly don't. We're going to kill them. That's right. State sponsored murder and we'll eject them in cheap rockets at this Gaean sun of ours.

You can see my urgency. If I could ever get control over those damn nanobots I'd put an end to it. But another problem is that so few want to help us. We've had to be cautious about who we asked, but still, most folks don't seem unhappy here with life on Gaea. My suspicion is that these nanobots do more than just control us, they probably manipulate our chemical makeup too. Make us more docile and happy. I mean that's fairly mundane to do. We've known how to do that for over a century already.

But even still, we started out with about thirty-three of us I think it was, who were working in The Enlightenment as if it were a mission. Now we're down to seven like I told you. But I won't give up. I'll continue on to my dying day. Though I despair that I'll ever achieve what I want. And if I don't, will this dream of an autonomous species die with me? Sometimes I think it will.

Second Gary will be recycled whether it's time or not. Whether he's had his twenty-five years or not. Not that he particularly cares. He's just here to do as I instruct and he'd just as easily do whatever some other human instructs him to do.

And the other five? They do their best, but I see the fight is out of them. If I'm to be honest. I see no one left with a fire in carrying on this work especially if I'm no longer here.

I sometimes wonder if we'd have been better off having stayed on old Earth. We would have been eradicated by our bastard children, but at least we'd have gone down on our terms. Now we live as slaves to the Councils, only we just don't know it. We're as docile as little lambs. Yes, we might be living, but is it really living if you've got no more freewill? I'd say no.

The only small spark of hope that I can see in our current situation is that perhaps, in time, with a population of one hundred million of us being born and dying in Gaea, there just might come someone, or some few people who are naturally selected out of the control of the nanobots to some degree. I've got to believe that something like that is possible. And it should be. I mean, just by virtue of the randomness of large numbers, at some point some Gaean child is bound to be born with a mutation that leaves them invulnerable to the nanobots to some degree or other.

Because if that doesn't happen then what's not to stop the eventual extinction of our species? Because if you leave control in the hands of a few eventually they'll lead us over a cliff knowingly or not. At least that's my suspicion. But I could be wrong.

I was working on an algorithmic problem with the nanobots recursive algorithms. This wasn't my strongest point. In fact I only had a rudimentary understanding of recursive algorithms. But that seemed to be one of our biggest problems. The nanobots were able to adapt to any hacking or software we tried to splice into them. It was frustrating as all hell. I had an intuition that the biggest problem was the fact that all these millions of nanobots inside each of us were linked like neurons in a brain. This meant that if you infected one, hundreds would come to its rescue and clean it and disinfect it. And if you infected hundreds, then thousands would come. If you infected thousands, then hundreds of thousands would come.

This was a big part of the problem. At least in my mind. Others were trying to attack the nanobots in other ways, biologically, chemically, etc. The problem with those I thought, was that we needed the nanobots to remain. For they sent dying declarations and if there were enough of them, I think we had figured it out to be around point one percent of them, then the Science Council was alerted. So I thought my approach was perhaps the best. If we could only hijack them somehow.

But you can see the problem. We need to attack millions of them at a time at the same time, and I couldn't figure out how to do that. First Gary was making some progress but that progress he was making was lost with him. And I don't regret it. We kept very little information about our work on the computers here. So First Gary kept pretty much everything in his head. And without access to his brain which QT now had, I didn't really have much idea about what he was doing other than what we had discussed in person.

You can understand why we don't keep much information locally about what we're doing. I've always been nervous that at some point I'd be followed here and it would be suicide for everyone who was helping me if it was found out what we were doing. They'd be sent for rehabilitation which was unpleasant. It was basically a rewiring of their brains, and as such, it was a living death of who they were. They came out, literally, as different people. They came out with different personalities.

In fact, I was surprised that we hadn't been raided at least once before. We'd been at it for over twenty years. Maybe the Councils knew or maybe they didn't. Either way. We'd been lucky. But still, in almost twenty-five years we'd had no luck whatsoever. I got to thinking that maybe they were just humoring me. Just allowing me my little hobby.

I heard a sound by the entrance. I looked at my computer. I hadn't been alerted to any breach of The Enlightenment. We'd set up pretty complex tripwires and lasers to alert us well in advance. I thought we would get at least three or four minutes warning the way we had set up the perimeter before anyone made it into our inner sanctum. But nothing on the computer. I thought I saw a shadow reflected off the computer screen. I turned around and got one of the biggest frights of my life.

"Hello," he said.

I rubbed my eyes. I really did. I thought I was imagining things. But he was still there after I had rubbed them. Tall and handsome as ever and he hadn't seemed to have aged a day.

"Is it really you, QT?" I asked.

The man standing in front of me was the spitting image of Waritan Quelten, just as he had looked twenty-three years earlier. The last time I'd seen him.

"You look well," he said.

I got up and went to hug him, but I stopped myself. They weren't a touchy-feely species. I remembered that now.

"After twenty-three years, and a lack of an explanation I think you're entitled to a hug."

He smiled at me and I put my arms out and hugged him. My face was barely nestled into his lower chest. You'll remember just how tall he was. Hugging him felt wonderful. Like I was wrapped up in a warm soft blanket and nothing in the world could upset me.

I had once asked him, a long time ago when we had just gotten to know him, if he was a good representation of his species. He said he was. In most ways.

"You don't look a day older than the last time I saw you," he said.

I let him go and took a few steps back so that looking up at him wasn't kinking my neck.

"We're immortal," he said.

"I'm envious," I replied.

"One day your species will figure it out."

"Not in time for me."

He shook his head slowly.

"No, not in time for you."

They were too damn honest sometimes. Though at my age, honesty was the only currency left worth anything.

"But I have a suspicion that your energy will find it's way back here in time to continue your work."

Second Gary had come back over.

"Hello, Waritan Quelten," he said.

"Hello, Gary, you still remember me?"

"I do."

"He does," I said, "he's my second Gary. Still the same as the first but without you know what."

"Yes, I understand. I'm sorry about that."

"What happened?" I asked. "I was very mad at you at first, and then that gave way to a long lonely road of disappointment."

QT nodded his head.

"I know, I've wanted to come back sooner."

"Tell me then why you didn't."

"You remember the first time we met?"

I nodded.

"At the lake they now call Serenity Lake. You were out there looking out over it and I just happened to come upon you. And I remember being intrigued rather than scared by this translucent pale white giant being."

He smiled.

"You didn't just happen upon me," he said. "It was planned."

I frowned at him.

"It's true. We, my species, the Zelves have been watching you ever since you got here."

"Oh," I said.

He might have been honest, but that didn't mean he was always forthright. But perhaps that was my error for assuming I had just happened upon him.

"I wanted to help you. I knew you were trying to better your people. I thought I might be of help."

"You were, but since you've left, we've made no headway."

The other five left here in The Enlightenment had all crowded round us and were smiling and nodding at QT.

"But I was premature," he said. "Remember when you asked me if I was a good representation of my people?"

I nodded. I had just been remembering that.

"And I told you that I was."

"You said you were in most ways."

"What I didn't tell you then was that I was a bit like you. I'm a bit of a rebel."

I grinned at him. Maybe we had been kindred spirits after all.

"So does this mean you've come back to help us?"

He shook his head and I could tell he was genuinely sad about it.

"No. We've decided that now is not the time."

I was visibly disappointed.

"Then we won't succeed," I said.

"I know. This place you've called The Enlightenment. It's a very good name. Your old Earth history of the very same period in the eighteenth century sought out liberty, fraternity, equality, progress, reason and tolerance…"

"I know all of that," I said, cutting him off, "that's why I named it that."

There was a little tinge of anger in my voice that I immediately regretted. Waritan Quelten nodded.

"But your people are not ready for an enlightenment of any sort. In fact I've come to let you know that you'll be shut down by the end of the day."

It was already the afternoon which meant there wouldn't be much time left. Not that we needed much time.

"But they don't know what they don't know. If we can just show them, if we can loosen the shackles," I said, "then they'll be enlightened."

"That was what I was hoping too. I've since come to see the error of my ways."

"I don't understand."

I was still visibly upset.

"The Enlightenment of old Earth was a period of great vigor for your people. But it was a movement whose time had come. The time for your people is not now."

"So I just stand by and let my people as you say, send this first generation to their death. To be murdered. You do know that's what's going to happen to them, don't you?"

He nodded.

"And you're okay with that?"

"I'm sorry, Seraphina," he said, "but it doesn't really concern me anymore. I thought I could help. But now is not the time."

"But you did come, and you did help, and now you'll leave us to murder our own."

"I know it's hard to see," he said, "but from the long arc of history, a few hundred years is but a small puddle to be skipped over."

"But why? Why won't you help now?"

I wasn't pleading but I was asking really sincerely.

"Because humans aren't ready. I was recalled back home and over these many years we've discussed it and played our various scenarios. The cost for attempting this right now, for trying to push your society when they aren't ready is too much. I'm not saying that you should stop. I'm saying that I can't help you. If I do, there is a ninety-seven percent chance your civilization will devolve into civil war. Tens of millions will die and your very survival into the future is questionable."

"I don't believe it."

"I know. But have I ever lied to you before?"

I shook my head.

"I'm sorry, Seraphina," he said again, "but I have to step away. For now. I'm not saying that we won't help in the future. The time is not right. And we, the Zelves, are not alone in that feeling. There are others that you do not yet know of who are of the same opinion. We want humanity to flourish, but if we do this, that flourishing is all but guaranteed to stall. If I were to help, as I said, there is a ninety-seven percent chance your species will be extinct in just under eleven hundred years."

"And what are our chances we'll still be around in that time if you don't help."

"Thirty-three percent."

"That's not very encouraging."

"It's an order of magnitude better than three percent."

"I don't know if I believe you," I said.

It was meant as an insult. I did believe him. Still, it didn't help. I was here right now, this was more pressing to me than some arbitrary future in over a millennium.

"If you like," he said, "I can help you destroy any information you have here. Make it look like this is just a social club."

"Well, we don't have much here that can be traced back to the sorts of things we're trying to do… but on second hand, you were always good with computers."

I smiled at him. He nodded. He put his hand into a pocket and then pulled it out. He opened his palm and a swarm of little black things that looked like really tiny flies flew from his hand and disappeared into all of our computers.

"They'll rewrite all the code to make it look like this is a place where members of different Councils come to relax. A social place of games and relaxation. Once they've been here and seen nothing of note, they'll recheck their records and realize that this was always a social club for the 'elite'. And then they'll be off very apologetically. Nobody likes to upset a Mother, do they?"

He smiled at me.

"I like it, QT," I said, "but it doesn't look like much of a social club."

We were all still standing around him.

"If you'd all just like to get behind me," he said.

He put his other hand in his other pocket. He pulled it out again and threw dozens of black balls the size of my thumbnail onto the floor. They turned into thousands and rolled out over the floor covering it in a single layer thick. And like a magic trick right in front of our eyes they started remodeling the whole environment of The Enlightenment.

I say remodeling, but really what it looked like was them growing things out of thin air. I don't know if you've ever seen time lapse video on old Earth of plants germinating, but that's exactly what it reminded me of. Just stuff growing out of nothing. The soil seemed to be this layer of black balls.

It didn't take long. In a matter of minutes what was once a rough idea of an underground computer and science lab now looked like a very modern, very Gaean social lounge with comfortable seating, a small kitchen area, some paper magazines, books and newspapers - we still had those - and computer screens, tables and virtual reality stations.

"If you'd all like to just move over to the carpet," said Waritan Quelten.

We all followed him from the concrete flooring we were standing on onto the new carpet that had just magically grown. These ball 'brains' I guess they were, finished up the side we had been on. We were all astonished.

"Just a few hundred years ago," I said, "seeing something like this and we might have mistaken you for gods."

I smiled at him.

"There are no gods," he said, "just those of us who have evolved longer than others."

"But how do you do that? Can you share?"

"All around us are atoms. We are, in a very real way, surrounded by a thick soup of atoms. Even this air we breath is dense with atoms. And anything that has substance is just made of these very same atoms. If you change the number of elementary particles, what you call quarks and electrons you get different types of atoms. Then you arrange these atoms in different ways and you get molecules. Put these molecules together as a puzzle in certain ways and you end up with a chair or a table or an apple. It's really quite elementary."

I smiled at that. He was smart enough to have made that double pun intentionally.

"But then," I said, "then you can create people, can't you?"

He shook his head.

"Not yet, but we believe it is possible. There seems to be something missing in the makeup of what we'd consider sentient life that we haven't quite got an understanding of. Anything beyond plant life we can't seem to create quite yet."

"So you really are not far off from being actual gods."

"I wouldn't put it like that. We are just mere creative creators."

All the little black files came back to QT and covered him and turned into whatever they seemed to be on. So they became part of his clothes. The same with the black balls. They rolled over to him and molded into this clothing. If this was the first time I'd seen something like this I'd have been astonished. But as far as the Zelves were concerned, this seemed as routine as painting and drawing.

"But will all of this last?" I asked. "Is it durable?"

"As durable as any 'real' matter that you have."

He looked at the wall that we were facing. It was now covered with a moving, realistic vista of an old Earth beach. It felt and smelt like we were really there. The door was off to the side of it.

"I think they're here," he said. "Early, it seems."

I was worried for him, I didn't know how he'd manage to hide. But there was no time, for no sooner had I thought that, the door opened and thirteen very aggressive looking peacekeepers came pouring in. Behind them was a senior member of the Science Council who I knew as Moonfrost Stareyes. With him was a senior member of the Peacekeeping Council by the name of Sandriver Darksky. I didn't like either of them. And last came in Softrain Summerwind or as I like to call her, Azeeza Maalouf.

"How nice to see you, Azeeza," I said. "Have you come to relax at our social club."

"My name is SOFTRAIN SUMMERWIND," she said, "and this is not a social club."

She turned to the peacekeepers.

"I want it searched from the top to the bottom."

She turned back to me.

"I understand you've been a busybody who's been up to no good. And if that is so, SILVERDUST, you are not above being rehabilitated."

That came as a surprise to me. I had never heard mention that senior Council members could be sent for rehabilitation, let alone Mothers. This was exactly what I was afraid of, the increasing power grab by Azeeza and her cabal. I smiled at her.

"I am just an old woman, Azeeza, who is trying to find some respite and rest amongst her peers in her last days."

She ignored me and looked at the person to my right who I realized was QT. I was momentarily worried until I looked at him.

"And who are you?" she asked. "I know everyone else."

"Forgive me, MOTHER," said QT, "I am the Yoga instructor for today's session. I am just your humble servant and a junior Science member. My name is Goldfeather Runningstream."

Waritan Quelten bowed at her slightly. He played the part well. He looked just like the rest of us. His face was somewhat familiar as if he was someone I had known once. He had shrunk in height and stature. I guess in these past two decades the Zelves had made further progress in manipulating their own matter.

Azeeza looked over at Sandriver Darksky. He was a tall man with jet black hair and hard eyes. He looked at the screen he was holding in his hand. It was translucent but I couldn't see what information it held from the underside of it. He pointed at it and showed Azeeza. She nodded.

"Very well," she said, "yoga will have to wait until after we've finished searching. You'll all stay exactly where you are."

While they were looking for anything that they couldn't find I thought about QT. He had just lied. I'd never known him to lie. But then we'd never been in such a situation. And was he really lying? He looked like a yoga instructor, and he must have been a yoga instructor. I mean Sandriver had verified that fact on his screen. So QT must have been able to actually create a yoga instructor that at least on our official records existed as Goldfeather Runningstream. And how that was done, I had no idea.

We turned around and watched the Peacekeepers search. They had their weapons shouldered now, and they were upending anything that could be upended and touching and scanning everything with their scanners. I could tell that Azeeza was looking at me through the corner of her eye. I didn't think she had it in for me, but maybe she did.

After a very thorough several minutes, and remember, The Enlightenment was small, they all gathered back around at the front. One of the thirteen Peacekeepers addressed his boss.

"Nothing out of the ordinary, Sandriver Darksky."

"I don't believe it," he said.

Sandriver stepped forward and with this screen he scanned the whole area in minute detail. His severe face turned into a puzzled and frowning one. He stared at the screen for a long time. Then he turned back and looked at Azeeza. He looked sheepish.

"It is as it appears, MOTHER," he said, "I can find nothing out of the ordinary."

"I see," she said, then she turned to Moonfrost Stareyes. "Double check."

Moonfrost tapped and slid his finger away on his screen. His face turned into a puzzle and a frown as well.

"I… I don't understand," he said, "let me check again."

The puzzle only deepened in his furrowed brow. His voice grew to a whisper.

"This is actually a Social Club for senior Council members, MOTHER," he said. He showed her his screen. "You signed off on it. It's been operating here for six months."

Azeeza was not happy. I could read it all over her face plain as day. I struggled to hold down a giggle and a seventy-nine year old woman never giggles. But this was too good.

"I see," she said in a hushed voice that we could all still hear. She said nothing for a moment. Then she looked up at us.

"If this is a Social Club for senior members of the Councils, what are you doing here?" she asked, looking at Daniel McTelig, otherwise known as Gentleleaf Grayskies.

You might be wondering what a senior member of a Council is. It isn't just the thirteen heads of each of the Councils. No, a senior member of a council is anyone who is considered an expert, and as you can imagine, all thirteen Council leaders are experts. You see, we had developed a hierarchical system. Everyone starting out as a member of a council, in this case let's use the Science Council as an example for Daniel is a science member, starts as a junior member.

Now as a side note, Gaea is apparently a planet where all humans are treated equally and are valued equally for whatever their contributions are. But that's just nonsense if you take even the smallest amount of time to look into things a little, like this whole idea of how we've created a hierarchical system of life's work.

So a junior member of a council is known as a beginner. So when Daniel first graduated as an Engineer, he was referred to as a SCIENTIST.b. That 'b' at the end means he's a beginner. It's sort of like he had an undergraduate degree. Then you learn more and spend more time at your work and you get your old Earth masters' degree equivalent and Daniel would become a SCIENTIST.i, the 'i' for intermediate. And then the doctoral level would be equivalent to our expert level when Daniel would become a SCIENTIST.e. The 'e' for expert obviously.

Daniel was only a Scientist.i at the moment. Unlike in old Earth where you could go from starting your undergraduate degree and completing your PhD in about seven or eight years, here on Gaea it usually took at least a decade between going from beginner to intermediate and then from intermediate to expert. Most experts then were at least forty years old. Now sometimes you have a Gaean who just excels at their field and gets to expert level much sooner. But so far no one has managed that before thirty.

In any event it's too early to tell, as I said, the first born generation of Gaeans are only twenty-four or twenty-five so hard to tell who might be born in the future with a specific aptitude. Incidentally, not sure if you know this, but no one chooses their field of study now, it is dictated to you by the Mothers. At birth all Gaeans are genetically screened and along with this they are heavily monitored for the first fourteen to sixteen years of their life.

At sixteen there is the Ceremony of Completion where each Gaean is given their role and starts to study as a beginner in that field. It is also when their childhood really ends. At that ceremony they drink the nanobots into themselves. Nobody has refused, for they don't know what they're doing, they think it's a toast. But even if they did, there are ways of ensuring that everyone becomes enslaved.

Anyway, Daniel was one of the last of what I call free humans. Free in the sense that he was able to choose his destiny or his work. He's officially known as being one of the Intragalactic generation. This is because he was born neither on old Earth or Gaea, he was born on one of the Starships shortly after we had left.

"He is my guest, Azeeza," I said.

I knew I was upsetting her by continuing to use her old Earth name. I didn't care. She was in my house. I had never liked her, even from old Earth times, and she had become an even bigger monster ever since she took over from Ni Yin.

"If you check the bylaws of our Social Club, you'll know that leaders of the Councils may bring up to two guests at a time regardless of life status."

Life status really just meant employment status, but since there was no changing your job once it was dictated to you, you really were working at it for life or until you were allowed to retire which was different depending on the career you were in.

I didn't know if our Social Club had any bylaws. I was hoping and praying that QT would be able to help somehow. I mean, he had managed to create this legitimate Social Club out of nothing. Surely as I spoke, bylaws could appear to? I was about to find out.

Azeeza looked at Moonfrost Stareyes. I imagined he was bringing up the bylaws. His eyes moved across the screen, then he took his finger and put it on the screen and showed Azeeza. She nodded, but she wasn't happy about it.

"I've always wondered why you haven't joined us here in these past months," I said. "I thought it was perhaps you didn't like me, Azeeza."

Maybe I was getting a little too cocky, but I was enjoying myself with the magic that QT had brought with him. Azeeza looked over at me. Her eyes narrowed.

"There is a lot of work to be done to get GAEA to the level we want. You'd know that if you were more often at the meetings."

"I don't attend all of them because it seems that my input is never appreciated."

"From now on, meetings are mandatory for every leader of every COUNCIL. And that especially includes you, SILVERDUST SOFTRAIN."

I suppose I wasn't surprised, I had been given quite a bit of leeway. I was one of the Supreme Leaders - that was our unofficial titles as a Mother - and I had hardly shown any interest in leading. But that was because I wasn't enamored with the direction we were taking Gaea and her citizens. I had tried instigating change from the inside. I honestly had, but it was no use. I was about to have to try again.

"Show me some yoga, Goldfeather," said Azeeza.

"As you wish, MOTHER," he said. "It would be a great honor if you'd join us."

"If you'd like to get your mats, students," said QT. He pointed at the wall where seven mats were rolled immaculately and placed in stands.

We walked over and got our mats, I only now realized that in the whole transformation, the clothes I had been wearing had at some point been changed into yoga clothes. All of us were dressed in yoga clothes.

We laid out our mats and were about to start when Azeeza butted in again.

"Not the robot. The robot will not do yoga."

Second Gary had taken a mat and was about to join us, not that he needed to. Robots don't get stiff. But still, I thought it was an unkind remark, but nothing I could do about it. As the Supreme Leader of the Supreme Leaders, or the Mother of all Mothers, Azeeza had the final say over any robot. Second Gary stepped away from the main group. QT looked over at Azeeza. She nodded at him.

"You'll remember from last time class that we begin with Mountain Pose. Arms straight up like you're reaching for the sky."

Waritan Quelten lead us through the poses for several minutes. Most of us were doing quite well I thought considering that I didn't think any of us had ever done yoga.

"That's fine," said Azeeza. "Make sure you're at every meeting from now on, SILVERDUST, and your robot is coming with me. If everything appears fine, you might get it back. What is its designation?"

I wasn't going to give her his name.

"The robot is G2147.11"

"Come with me G2147," she said.

She waited for ten of the Peacekeepers to head out the door followed by Moonfrost and Sandriver.

"Walk in front of me," she said to Second Gary.

He obediently did as he was told. He was followed by Azeeza and then behind her left the last three Peacekeepers.

"Bitch," I said when they were well gone.

"We can continue with yoga if you'd like," said Waritan Quelten.

"I'm not really in the mood," I said. I picked up my mat and rolled it up again and placed it back where it had come from.

"They've taken Second Gary," I said.

"I know," answered QT.

"She's trying to ruin me."

"You're trying to ruin her."

I looked at QT.

"That's not helping."

"I'll make sure you get it back."

"Thank you," I said.

QT looked at me for a long time.

"I have to go," he said.

"Forever?"

He shook his head and smiled.

"Forever is a really long time. I'll be back before you leave."

I smiled at that. Leaving, yes I suppose that was one way to look at death.

"We'll always be looking over your shoulder," he continued, "you'll never be alone. Things will eventually get better as you imagine, and one day we'll help you achieve your dreams."

"Not me," I said.

He shook his head.

"No, not you. You in the plural."

"I suppose that's all I can ask for in these sunset years. I would have preferred to see this new world that you think we'll be creating in time."

He didn't say anything to that.

"Keep this as it is," he said, "you'll enjoy some of the Easter eggs I've place here for you to find over time. I hope it brings you some comfort."

I smiled. I had nothing left to say. He had come back to explain his rapid departure and I appreciated that. But he wasn't going to be of any help, though he had perhaps just in this last little while saved my life and I was grateful for that. But the sting of my own disappointment in knowing that I would be unable to upend Gaean society still hurt.

"Goodbye, Seraphina Siwik," he said.

He knelt down on one knee and hugged me. Very unZelve-like of him. But I needed it more than he knew. He held me for a long time. He smelt like fresh new babies, warm and just ever so slightly pleasantly fragrant. He pulled away first. He looked down at me and nodded. My eyes teared up but I fought them back. I watched him walk away.

"Waritan Quelten," I said as he reached the door. He looked back. "Thank you for coming back to explain. You're a really decent being and I hope we get to be more like you in time."

He smiled at me and then turned around and was gone behind the door. I sat down on one of the chairs he had grown and never before in my life had I felt so alone and desolate.

CHAPTER FIFTEEN

A Place of Rebirth

I couldn't see the EVOLUTION Station, and I couldn't feel the Starship slowing down, but both of these things were obvious on the monitors. We were half a billion kilometers from the Station and we were slowing down at about exactly the rate we had been speeding up when we had left GAEA.

The journey to the EVOLUTION Station which wasn't far from the WHOLE had taken just about six months. I hadn't found it that onerous. Flutterdust Flowersong was my best friend and we had gotten on incredibly well. Our friendship had deepened in many areas. And this just made my secret all that more painful to carry. She didn't know that I wouldn't be coming back with her. I couldn't risk it. Even though I could trust her with just about anything, I didn't think I could trust anyone with my secret.

The Starship, even though it was made for one EVOLVER, was still large enough that neither of us felt claustrophobic, even with the two E-PODS and Roger Dodger. There was food aplenty and I think that having another human to interact with had made what could have been the loneliness of space quite tolerable. And we had felt really quite alone. We could see no other Starships from anywhere on the ship. We were a long way behind them and that made it seem even more lonely.

But with my knowledge of old Earth history, we had played some of the classic games from old Earth. I had taught Flutterdust Flowersong the game called Go which was an ancient Chinese game that was the last game that a human had beaten a computer. Unlike chess which computers had mastered and therefore consistently beaten the best humans by the year twenty zero five, it took until twenty sixteen for the first computer to beat the best human Go player. Historians had seen that moment as an inevitable foreshadowing of the coming singularity.

The biggest part of the problem for computers winning at Go was that the board was so large. Generally nineteen squares by nineteen squares for professional matches. Chess is a similar type of game that only has eight squares by eight squares, so you can see how quickly the numbers exponentially increase. And that's the main problem. To assess just the next eight moves in Go, a computer would have to compute over five hundred quintillion moves. That's a five with twenty zeroes on the end. Our computers now can do that of course, but not back in the early part of the twenty-first century.

So instead of brute forcing the game, the SCIENTISTS on old Earth had to develop machine learning and so that's where a lot of historians see the first glimmers of the coming singularity. Flutterdust Flowersong enjoyed the game. She preferred it to Chess because she thought the rules were simpler as were the pieces. Over the past six months she got really good at it, beating me more times than not. But she had stopped playing Roger Dodger. He was unbeatable. I had told her that, but she still wanted to try. I had told her that since that computer had beaten the first professional Go player, no Go player had been able to retake the crown. And that was over a thousand years ago. I guess some people need to find out for themselves.

A good chunk of our time was spent on playing old Earth games. We have a lot of games on GAEA but Flutterdust Flowersong wanted to play mostly the old Earth games. Lots of card games, poker was her favorite and of course Go and also chess. That was the trifecta we came back to most often.

I started to think that the weirdest part of being in space was the sense that time had come to a stop. I mean you're traveling fast, in our case at one third the speed of light, and yet just looking out of the window it appears you're not moving at all. And looking at a clock or time tick by on the monitors just seemed asinine quite frankly. Just looked like numbers moving. You lose sense of time. I guess this is mostly because you lose sense of space, and space and time are like an old married couple, they only have eyes for each other.

I mean I could walk around in the Starship, but this felt like a small capsule I was trapped in. Outside, nothing moved. At least not fast enough to be perceptible to human vision. On GAEA, and I imagine it's the same on old Earth, the sun moves in the sky and the moon moves in the sky and shadows move across the ground and you can move towards things and see them get bigger. These are all the cues that you need to get a sense of time, because things move in space. That doesn't happen in the emptiness of space that I was traversing through. In a real sense you just ended up believing, having faith that you'd actually get someplace. But six months is a long time to have faith.

I didn't need faith. I trusted my training and my destination. I was going back home like you know. But unlike anyone else on this Starship knows.

"I can see the Station," said Flutterdust Flowersong.

I looked up out of the window. We were in what we'd come to call the Games Room. It was really the library but we had been using it mostly for our games. We were playing poker. Our favorite had become Texas Hold 'Em. I had literally astonished Flutterdust Flowersong with the fact that back on old Earth people had earned huge sums of money for playing games, especially Texas Hold 'Em.

She'd found it hard to believe, not only because we no longer used any currency, but she couldn't see how anyone would get paid for playing games when there was real work to be done. On GAEA, games took up a very small fraction of our time. They were seen as a distraction and that's how they were used occasionally.

Out of the corner of the window I could see the lights of the EVOLUTION Station. It looked like a small bright star from this distance. I asked the computer what our estimated time of arrival was. It was just under an hour. We were still in Dark Three. You'll remember that Three Dark was the three hours of silence when we left GAEA. Dark Three was the last three hours before we arrived at the EVOLUTION Station. The only communication allowed was between the Station and individual Starships.

We'd already heard from Station Control shortly after we had entered Dark Three. They had been genuinely happy to hear we had made it. I can't imagine what sort of a tragedy had been forwarded onto them. I knew they must have heard about it a few months back. GAEAN Control would have messaged them about it. I imagined it would have been a one way stream. I mean the EVOLUTION Station is over one point five trillion kilometers from GAEA. As it happens, GAEAS distance from its sun is similar to the distance old Earth was from its sun. So the Station is a little over ten thousand Astronomical Units away from GAEA. That takes messages around two months to get there. GAEA and the Station do communicate this way, but a lot of communication comes each month with the EVOLVERS. There are always some ships filled with SCIENTISTS and PEACEKEEPERS and FARMERS heading to the STATION for their tours of duty and others coming back each month, so that keeps communications reasonably current.

But as you know, any communication getting to the Station via Starship is six months old. Direct communication via light is only two months old, so it depends on the urgency of the message I guess. All EVOLVERS who would have been arriving before us, and there would have been five previous streams, would have no idea about the catastrophe that we incurred.

That's all just an aside, and you probably don't really care about any of that. I just thought it was interesting. Something else to bear in mind is that there are six paths to the EVOLUTION Station. This was done quite a while back so that in case of a catastrophe like we just had, streams of EVOLVERS could continue on each month. Like I said, GAEA was going to need at least a few months to clean up the mess we'd made behind us.

"Starship Intrepid MF dot 3?"

That was EVOLUTION Station Control.

"S.I.M.F.dot3 here," I said.

Now I had to wait around two and a half minutes for the reply. We were around fifty minutes out, the monitor was showing just over forty million kilometers to destination and that was decreasing rapidly.

"They probably just want to let us know that manual control is being disengaged," said Flutterdust Flowersong.

And she was probably right. That was usually the protocol at around sixty minutes in. Control and the Starships onboard computer take over all Starship communications and maneuverability. The next time we'd hear from them would be when we were a few minutes out and ready to dock.

"Control informing you, S.I.M.F.dot3, we have taken over all systems. Acknowledge."

"S.I.M.F.dot3 acknowledging that Control has all systems," I said.

The color of the monitor changed to blue, and in large type in case I was an idiot the screen read "Manual Control Disengaged". There was nothing I could do about it. So Flutterdust Flowersong and I got ready to play one more game of Go. Or at least as much of one as we could. It was a digital version of the game. The only remaining physical game that I was aware of was in the MUSEUM OF REMINISCENCE.

At around fifteen minutes to docking we were still speeding in towards the Station. I could now really make out time zipping by, because the Station was growing bigger as I looked at it. It was a blue and silver sphere. If I remembered my old Earth geography well, our Station was about two hundredth or less the size of old Earths moon. Around ten kilometers across. It was a large imposing sphere as we came upon it.

Knowing old Earth history as I do, seeing this in person for the first time, it reminded me of the Death Star from Star Wars. That was an old fictional story where this large moon-sized battle station was inhabited by the bad guys.

Docking was easy, because I didn't have to do anything. There were lots of spots left. I think the Station was developed to have one hundred thousand docking ports for Starships. That usually left a little under twenty thousand available at any time. In any event, with the catastrophe behind us, there were about two thirds of the docking ports available. We were docked into the upper left quadrant. From our approach we had no view of the looming wormhole, or WHOLE, that was just behind it. I was really excited to see it in person. I had seen it before of course, but not in person.

We exited the Starship leaving the E-PODS behind. They were for now the jurisdiction of Roger Dodger and a loaner robot for Flutterdust Flowersongs E-POD as she had lost her robot in the calamity just outside GAEA.

We were shown to a large auditorium where perhaps ten thousand of us were seated. A senior Station SCIENCE Council member took us through a presentation. It had nothing new, but I guess the repetition was important. It told us how everything worked here in the next few hours.

Our E-PODS were already being taken to the Ejection Ports where we would join them. At that time we would have some time to check the E-POD over for the last time. This was to be a very thorough check but they only gave us thirty-three minutes. Why such an odd number? I have no idea, they never told us why. But it was a lot of time to check over the relatively small E-POD. Besides it had its own computer which would alert us to any problems.

I suppose they didn't want any catastrophes to occur this close to the WHOLE. After this last check, we would attach the E-POD to the Ejection Port and then return to the corresponding Eyeline Pulpit which was the large viewing hall where we gathered to watch the E-PODS ejection and entrance into the WHOLE in reverence and awe. At least that's what they told us. My reverence and awe were nowhere to be found, and not least because I was going to be ejected in the E-POD, but also because I had seen behind the curtain of this great charade. Or so I believed.

Once the E-PODS had entered the WHOLE we were free to mingle as we pleased on this Station for the next six days. This was a time to socialize and rejoice. For on the seventh day we headed back on our desolate journey to GAEA. It all seemed very straightforward. But we had done it several times already, all in simulations on GAEA of course, but still, it felt like it was old hat as they said on old Earth.

My biggest problem at the moment was trying to figure out how to get myself into the E-POD. I mean I knew the how of it, but I didn't know the where and when. There would be Councillors strolling along the Ejection Ports ostensibly to help us but likely also to ensure that everything was conducted appropriately and rigorously according to the rules and regulations. If they didn't see an EVOLVER with every E-POD then all hell would break lose. There would be a Station wide search and they'd strip open the E-POD down to the MMC to see.

I was in a pickle. My best chance, but it was slim and I had to be quick about it, was to slip into the E-POD once I had attached it to the Ejection Port. But that wasn't going to be easy. It only rested for around thirty seconds before being swallowed whole into the Port before being ejected. Another problem was that the computer would sound an alarm, at least I thought it might, if it detected more than one human body inside. At least that's how I would have built it. And it didn't seem unlikely to me. I mean the E-POD set off alarms for all sorts of things that go wrong so I mean, with a second human inside, surely an alarm would be set off. That meant I had thirty-three minutes as I was trying to check over the E-POD to figure out how to override the safety alarms. I might be able to do that. But then it meant I was at the mercy of space once ejected towards the WHOLE. I'd have no knowledge if anything was going wrong. Mind you, at that stage it didn't matter did it? I mean there was nothing anyone could do for me then.

I kicked myself for not having reached out to Veritan Zeltan. He had told me I'd know how once I was on the Starship. And it was true, I did know how. Whenever I was in my room, if I passed the communications panel a certain way, viewed at a certain angle, the screen glowed a very soft blue button that had VZ in its center. I had thought a few times over the six months of calling him. But I hadn't. It never felt that pressing, besides, I was having fun with my best friend. Everything was going so well. There was no need.

Now I kicked myself. I hadn't thought this through. I was going to have to wing it and I might not get away with it. Veritan Zeltan had said others had gone before me. How had they done it? Or was it easier back then? They'd probably made it much harder now. I'd just have to do my best. Maybe now was time to bring Roger Dodger into it.

We were dismissed from the auditorium and made our way up to our E-PODS. My small computer monitor on my forearm showed me the way. I said goodbye to Flutterdust Flowersong. I hugged her and she'd said she wished we could travel back to GAEA together because it had been so much fun. I agreed. I also wished we could travel back together. That wasn't a lie. I really wished I could. My heart dropped into my stomach then watching her walk off down a different corridor from me. I was now all alone and I felt it. Even as dozens of EVOLVERS jostled by me. I was completely alone and I was sad and scared.

Right up until this point I'd felt like a warrior, big and brave. Now I felt small and vulnerable and unsure. The uncertainty was obvious, I had obstacles in my way, but the smallness was new. It took every mental trick I knew and had learned to keep the monsters of doubt away from me. I walked slowly and heavily towards my E-POD. It was several levels up, not far from where my Starship had docked. I tried to put a bounce in my step but none came. So I trudged on wearily. I must have felt similar to how those on old Earth felt heading to the gallows.

I reviewed what I knew about the E-POD. As the EVOLVER I

had a lot of access to its computer for obvious reasons. I alone had been solely responsible for the E-POD and the EVOLVEDS welfare for the past six months. They had to give us administrator access. So that was the good news. I also knew how to disable the alarms so that was good news too. I just wasn't sure if that was for all alarms. Maybe there was a backdoor secret alarm that I didn't know about that was just for catching errant EVOLVERS trying to leave in E-PODS. But that was probably me just being paranoid.

I pushed that thought out of my mind. I started to think about how I was going to get into the E-POD once it was attached to the Ejection Port. There was a way, but it was from the head side of the E-POD, in the sense that it was attached with the EVOLVERS feet first. This meant I couldn't enter from the top which was the largest opening. It meant I had to enter from one of the small hatches on either side up by the head. They were small and not meant, obviously, for humans to enter. But I was small. The opening was about thirty centimeters by about forty. With some effort I could probably crawl in through that opening. But it wasn't just the size. I only had thirty seconds or so in which to do it.

I started walking more confidently. What was the worst that could happen? The worst was that I didn't manage to do it. Then I'd head back to GAEA with the rest of them. Sorry, Veritan Zeltan, but you'll just have to find someone else. Let's say I got stuck halfway inside the hatch, the E-POD had safety features so it would disengage from the Ejection Port if any part of it was not sealed properly. So it's not like I'd be decapitated being forced into the Ejection Port. I mean that would be embarrassing. Councillors would come by and have to extricate me but I figured I could explain it away. I heard something last minute. A groan or an alarm or something. I thought I could get away with that.

The thing is, I had to tell Roger Dodger. He'd be with me the whole time until I was supposed to head up to the Eyeline Pulpit. Robots weren't allowed there. They weren't allowed to view the WHOLE once the EVOLVEDS were ejected towards it. It was a sacred ceremony reserved only for humans. But up until the E-POD was swallowed into the Ejection Port he would be with me. Could I trust him? I was about to find out.

I walked along the corridor until I found my designated number. My E-PODS Ejection Port was numbered one thousand one hundred and eleven. I took that as a good sign. Depending on what you believed, I didn't believe any of it, the number one had profound meaning on old Earth. Especially four ones together. It was supposed to be some sort of energy gateway, a communion with angels and those numbers were supposed to be vibrating with the energies of new beginnings, new starts, independence and individuality. I didn't believe it but it made me feel better. Not that there couldn't be anything to the idea that numbers have energies, we'd just never explored it and it wasn't considered a proper SCIENCE. Anyway, that's what some old Earth humans had believed.

It wasn't easy information to come across. But it was there if you looked for it. We had access to all of old Earth knowledge and history, even the bizarre, the wicked and the downright fabricated. Only those sorts of things took a special dedication to unearthing, if you'd excuse the pun. And I had that special dedication. Since I was small I'd had a thirst for knowledge about old Earth. I don't know why. It had always pulled at me. Maybe that was one of the reasons why I was so eager to head back to it. Maybe deep down in my core it felt like I was supposed to be there, that I was really an Earthling and not a GAEAN. But I had to get there first. I had to get inside my E-POD.

"Everything looks ready," said Roger Dodger.

I looked up at him and smiled. We were in what was best described as a cubicle of sorts. Along this hallway were hundreds of walls spaced about two meters apart. The E-POD was centered in this area. The walls were metal with monitor screens all over them. The Ejection Port was in the middle opposite from the hallway. It looked like an old Earth camera lens. It was closed now but when it opened it opened from the middle in a circular motion. The Ejection Port was a long cylinder of well over a hundred meters. At the end of course was space. I would maneuver the E-POD into the Ejection Port and from there it would be readied for ejection, moving the remaining distance by itself.

"Let us take a moment to reflect in reverence upon the mighty WHOLE which leads us to the omnipotent and omniscient ONE where we will all return when our work for THE MOTHERS and for GAEA is done. This is a celebration. A moment to reflect in awe at the majesty of the ONE and the rewards that await those EVOLVEDS we have brought here to complete their journeys. EVOLVERS get ready to emancipate your EVOLVEDS."

This was the usual preamble I had heard and knew by heart. The monitors had shown a MOTHER who had spoken those words. The EVOLUTION Station, like a city, had a Council of MOTHERS. We waited now in silence until we were told to continue. On all three sides of this room or cubicle a digital clock appeared in the upper part of the wall. It was set at thirty-three minutes and thirty-three seconds.

"May the ONE find us worthy and take us into her everlasting bosom where we may find peace for all of eternity. EVOLVERS prepare for EVOLUTION Ejection."

That was the same MOTHER. The countdown began. There wasn't much really to do. I could look busy. But I knew my E-POD was ready. There had not been any glitches. I wondered where

Flutterdust Flowersong was. I tapped her name into the monitor closest to me. I was on the left of the E-POD as you looked at it, facing the Ejection Port. Roger Dodger was on the right. The monitor told me that Flutterdust Flowersong was at Ejection Port numbered six thousand six hundred and sixty-seven. That was several levels below me.

On the wall that faced out, the one with the Ejection Port on it, the monitor showed a live view of the WHOLE. It was beautiful. It looked like a large dark and sparkly marble with blues and white and blacks. All sorts of colors really. Having gravity, the EVOLUTION Station orbited around it at a distance of three hundred and thirty-three thousand kilometers. Close to the distance that the Moon orbited old Earth. The E-PODS would be ejected at one hundred thousand kilometers per minute. So the journey would take just over three minutes.

The E-PODS were ejected in a sequential manner, a split second after each other. And I mean a tiny fraction of a split second after each other. The Ejection Port was long enough to get the E-POD up to speed. Once it left the Ejection Port, the E-POD was traveling at one hundred thousand kilometers per minute. That meant it was traveling at over one thousand six hundred kilometers per second. The EVOLUTION Station was firing exactly six hundred and sixty-six E-PODS per second, each one slightly off cadence so that the first one led the second one which led the third one, etc., by just over two meters. That ensured enough room between each E-POD so that none would hit each other.

It was quite the spectacle to behold. A firing stream of E-PODS in all sort of unusual patterns. If we had all made it to the EVOLUTION Station, all eighty-three thousand three hundred and thirty-three of us, that meant that that exact same number of E-PODS would be ejected in just over two minutes. The whole show, from the first ejected E-POD to the last one being swallowed by the WHOLE would take just over five minutes.

You can tell that I was trying to distract myself from what I needed to do. And what I needed to do was to count the time between each Councillor. Already I had less than twenty-two minutes left to figure this out. Councillors had been passing by steadily. The next one came by, she smiled at me. I smiled back. I looked up at the digital timer, it read twenty-one twelve.

"I do wish that we were allowed to view the Ceremony," said Roger Dodger.

I looked up at him. I had started to fiddle with the computer alarms on the E-POD. He wasn't paying much attention to what I was doing.

"Perhaps in time," I replied. "But you can see a live feed of the WHOLE right there on the monitor."

I pointed at it.

"It is quite beautiful, isn't it? I wonder who built it?"

Roger looked over at the monitor.

"Yes, it is beautiful," he said, "but it's not the same as watching the E-PODS entering it."

He paused for a moment and looked back at me.

"You know that wormholes are natural phenomena."

That was our current understanding of them. I looked up at him and stopped fiddling with the E-POD. Another Councillor walked by. I looked at the timer. Twenty ten. Just over a minute.

"And yet, Roger Dodger," I said, "for over a thousand years this wormhole has sat here stable and reliable as a pulsing neutron star."

"That's not unusual."

"It is, Roger, it's very unusual. We've never found another naturally occurring wormhole this stable."

He shrugged.

"Maybe they're just rare."

"Or maybe," I said, "this one is not a natural one."

"Doesn't matter though does it, Sunring Quickdust? I mean it serves its purpose."

I was testing Roger Dodger to see if I could trust him. Thing is, I didn't know if I could. He had been a loyal servant for a very long time, never questioning anything I had asked and keeping my confidence. But I didn't know the depths of his loyalty. If I told him I was heading back to old Earth would he let me do that or were there protocols in place that meant he'd have to alert the authorities. I'd find out shortly. I first had to disable all alarms.

Another Councillor came by. She paused for a moment.

"Do you need any help?"

"No, thank you," I said smiling.

She carried on. The timer was nineteen exactly. Just over a minute. It appeared I had a minute each time as they came by. And the Councillors would come by until the E-PODS had been ejected at the WHOLE. I was almost done with the alarms, then I'd just be waiting. Waiting to find a good time to tell Roger Dodger that he'd be somebody elses robot.

Eighteen zero three read the timer as the next Councillor came by.

"Why do you think they come by so regularly?" I asked Roger.

"Because they're here to help."

"And to monitor us," I said.

"I don't think so," he said, "they could just have cameras for that purpose."

I shook my head.

"I'm certain they wouldn't have cameras here, at least not for spying. Perhaps for communications, but not for spying."

"And why not?"

"Because this is hallowed ground, Roger. This is where the EVOLVED are. You aren't allowed to record any of this, that's why nobody's seen what it looks like, not until your very first EVOLUTION. They didn't even show us this ejection in training."

Roger shrugged.

"Yes, I suppose you're right. I still don't think they're here to spy on us."

"Not us, Roger, me, not the robots, the humans."

"But why would they need to?"

Seventeen fifty-seven. I nodded at the next Councillor as she came by. They had all been women. That wasn't a requirement for the job but so far they had all been women.

I leaned in over the E-POD.

"What if someone wanted to hitch a ride to old Earth? What if an EVOLVER snuck into the E-POD?"

Roger looked up at me for a long moment.

"Well, the E-POD doesn't go to old Earth, Sunring Quickdust, it goes through the WHOLE to the ONE. And the ONE is only for the EVOLVED. You know all of this. Frankly, what you're suggesting is preposterous. Why would anyone want to go to the ONE who isn't EVOLVED?"

"Maybe it doesn't go to the ONE, maybe the E-POD actually goes to old Earth and that's the ONE, and maybe the EVOLVEDS are sent there to fight the von Neumanns. The EVOLVEDS are just in stasis."

I thought I was sharing too much. But at this stage I knew I could count on his loyalty.

Sixteen thirty-six. It seemed the Councillors were taking their time. Roger Dodger shook his head.

"I'm afraid I find that unbelievable."

"Okay," I said. "What if I wanted to get into the E-POD and head to old Earth?"

"I couldn't let you."

"Why not?"

"Because it doesn't go to old Earth it goes to the ONE and the ONE is only for the EVOLVED. Your time to EVOLVE has not come yet and so if you got into that E-POD and headed to the ONE you would die. And I can't let you hurt anyone, including yourself."

I had now found my answer. I'd have to find a way to disable my beloved Roger Dodger. There was a failsafe override command that would turn him off. I had never used it, but ever since we left the von Neumanns on old Earth our robots had been programmed with a failsafe kill switch. Each one was different for each robot as you didn't want anyone to be able to disable any robot. So I had no idea for example what the kill switch command for Flutterdust Flowersongs robot would have been.

My command for Roger Dodger was 'Et tu, Brute'. It was the famous last words spoken by Julius Caesar when he got stabbed in the back by his friend and confidant Brutus. I thought it was an appropriate phrase and not something I'd ever say unknowingly. I mean if I needed to kill my robot it was probably because it was harming me. Now it seemed I'd have to kill him because he thought he was trying to protect me.

Fifteen thirty-five. Still around a minute. I had a long time to wait. I'd have to use the phrase at the very last moment. Because it was a kill switch, it would literally fry Roger Dodgers neural network and his software. The only thing that would survive would be the blackbox recordings of the preceding seven minutes. This made me even more sad. Roger Dodger had been mine for seven years already and I'd grown fond of him. Hard not to think of him as a human. In my mind he was really. A friend and a colleague. I'd shared secrets with him and confided in him when I was struggling. But I had to resolve myself. I'd given him every opportunity to let me go willingly. But he wasn't an independent thinker and that would be his downfall.

I had nothing left to do. I had checked the hatches. Both of them at the head of the E-POD were working properly and looking at them closely I was sure I could fit in. Thirty seconds seemed like enough time. So I replayed some of the recordings of Moondew Flamesdances life on the monitor on the E-POD just to pass the time. Nothing much happened.

Councillors still came by every minute or so. Then at five zero five another Councillor came by and stopped to chat. I wasn't in the mood to chat. I was trying to psych myself up.

"Looks like you're prepared," she said. "Only five minutes left."

She looked at the countdown timer.

"Yes, thank you," I said.

"Do you need any help?"

I frowned at her. Clearly I didn't need any help.

"No, I'm fine."

I was a little curt but I wasn't in the mood. The Councillor walked up to Roger Dodger.

"Does she need any help?"

This was the last thing I need, a nosey Councillor trying to elicit my secrets from my robot. The Councillor put her hand on Roger Dodgers shoulder. Next thing I knew, Roger Dodger was hibernating. I looked at the Councillor. She turned into a him. A large Zelve him.

"Veritan Zeltan?" I asked in a hushed voice.

He nodded.

"Hello, Skew," he said, smiling.

I reached round to him and gave him a long hug. Forgetting for a moment that they didn't like physical touch. At least not so much from humans.

He gently pulled me away from him.

"We don't have time," he said. "You never made contact."

"Sorry," I said. "I had a thing come up with my friend."

"Flutterdust. Yes I know."

"What did you do to Roger?"

"I'm relaxing some of his protocols. I think he'll be very useful to you on old Earth."

"He won't go," I said, "I've had that talk with him."

"He will now. Listen, we need to go over a few things really quick."

I nodded.

"Roger Dodger is being enhanced. He'll be more human and more helpful to you on old Earth with the new upgrade I'm giving him. Additionally I want to make sure you're ready for the journey. After the next Councillor has come and gone, I'm going to make the interior of the E-POD more comfortable. I'm also going to get you a helmet. I'm glad to see you're still wearing your flight uniform. You'll need that."

"Why?"

"The g-forces... I think another one's coming, stand in that corner, I'll be able to camouflage you."

I stood in the corner. Veritan Zeltan came by and pulled the wall on the side and wrapped it around me as if it were a sheet. I could still see through it, but it was like I was looking through a sheer curtain. It was weird. I knew the Zelves could manipulate matter, but still, my life relied on him doing it properly. I was about to find out.

"Is your robot alright?" the Councillor asked Veritan Zeltan.

"Yes he is, thank you, I've just tasked him with a last run through the diagnostics. Just to be safe."

"Be quick now you only have three and a half minutes."

"Of course."

The Councillor moved away and Veritan Zeltan came back and pulled the wall away from me and it disappeared as if it had never been there.

"We're running out of time," I said.

"We have all the time we need."

Veritan Zeltan opened up the E-POD and threw what looked like small black marbles into it. It was much bigger inside than I remembered. It looked like there would be ample space for me. Heck, I could probably have fitted in a Zelve too. Then he closed the E-POD.

"That'll take just a minute and then we'll get you in there once the next Councillor has come by."

Roger Dodger looked up at us.

"Are we going to old Earth?" he asked.

"Only if you want to, Roger," I said to him.

"I'll travel to the edge of space with you, Sunring Quickdust."

I looked over at Veritan Zeltan.

"Does he have a sense of humor now?"

"He is more human now, so in a way yes, he does have a sense of humor. He will still never end up like a von Neumann, so don't worry about that."

"How do you know?"

"Because we have been playing with robots since before you built the pyramids."

I didn't have anything to say to that.

"Time to hide again," he said.

I did, and he pulled the wall over me like before.

"Two minutes left for final preparations," said the Councillor, this one was a man.

"We're ready to go," said Veritan Zeltan.

The Councillor walked on. Veritan Zeltan pulled the wall away from me. He opened up the E-POD, and looked at me.

"Are you ready?"

I nodded.

"You'll probably not see me for a long time, if ever again," he said. His tone was serious. "I've already helped you more than my people would think prudent."

"What about Roger?" I asked.

"I'll give him instructions next."

I looked at him for a moment.

"You sure this is the right course of action for humanity?"

"It is the only way your kind has any hope of survival."

I nodded. I put out my hands in the Zelve greeting. He placed his palms on top of mine.

"Do you have peace?" I asked.

"Peace is here with us. Do you have peace?"

"You have brought me peace," I said. "I'll miss you."

"You bring hope to your people. You are honorable and brave, Sunring Quickdust."

"Then why don't I feel it?"

"The bravest always travel the closest with fear," he said. "You need to get in."

I climbed into the E-POD.

"Put on the helmet. The straps will self secure over you to limit any injury from the g-forces."

He looked at me as I adjusted the helmet that he had somehow made inside the E-POD. I smiled at him, but inside my heart was a quivering dove of nerves.

"You are good and brave and peace is with you," he said.

That was the last time I saw his face as he lowered the lid and closed the E-POD on me. It was dark but not pitch black inside the E-POD. There were dim digital lights all over the place but it was quiet. I could not hear any outside noises.

"This is the last sixty seconds," said the Councillor.

"We are ready," I said.

The Councillor left and I looked at Roger.

"You need to get going now. Head on back to the Starship. I've overridden the docking clamps to ensure they'll let you leave when you're ready. In five minutes disengage from the docking clamps and come round underneath the Station. As you clear it and see the wormhole you'll likely see streaming e-pods. I've disengaged all central control from the Starship. You will have to fly it manually. Take it up to full speed immediately and keep under the e-pods. If Control has any sight to you they will fire. Do you understand?"

The robot nodded at me.

"I understand, Veritan," it said.

I placed my hands out with my palms facing it. The robot placed its palms on mine.

"Keep peace close," I said.

"I always do. Take peace with you, Veritan," it said to me.

"Peace is all around me."

I pulled my hands away from him.

"Roger," I said.

He looked over at me.

"You will be able to rewrite history. The history between robots and humanity. I have placed a small gift within the e-pod. That gift is for you. It will allow you to accomplish super human things. It will give you and the humans on old Earth incredible technological advantages in rebuilding, surviving and continuing. Do not misuse it for I will know. Wrath has no fury, Roger, like a Zelve whose kindness had been abused."

"I owe you a debt, Veritan, I will honor your faith and belief in us. Both human and machine."

"Then go swiftly."

I watched Roger walk briskly down the hall until he turned and I could see him no more. The digital clock rang. It was time to secure the e-pod.

"Mate the E-PODS to the Ejection Port, EVOLVERS," said the MOTHER.

I did as an evolver was supposed to do. I rubbed my fingers over the etching of Moondew Flamesdance and wished them peace and swift voyage.

I felt the E-POD jerk. It was time. I still didn't hear anything, it was eerily quiet. The soundproofing was remarkable. I took comfort in that for it meant that the E-POD must be quite secure. I felt the E-POD sway and then get rigid as the clamping to the Ejection Port must have taken hold.

"Goodbye, Veritan Zeltan," I said, a good friend and kind stranger.

Once the e-pod was secure, I left the Ejection Port and headed up to the Eyeline Pulpit. I wanted to see with my own eyes Skew and Roger make it into that wormhole. It didn't take me long. I was hoping I might be able to watch discreetly by myself in a far corner. That was not to be. It seemed that Flutterdust was looking for her friend. She came right up to me.

"This is so exciting, Sunring Quickdust," she said, giddy with enthusiasm.

"It's going to be very exciting," I said.

We wound our way through the throng to our seats. Seats were numbered the same as the Ejection Ports. Flutterdust had obviously swapped seats with the person who was supposed to sit next to me. The set up was just like it might have been if you'd ever attended an old Earth sporting event. It was stadium seating. The seats were larger than traditional stadium seats and more comfortable. From each seat arm you could detach a small monitor about forty centimeters by twenty centimeters to watch things more closely if you wished. In front of us were a large bank of windows where the live action would take place. We were towards the very top of the Station. All the Ejection Ports were below us.

It had taken about five minutes to get seated.

"You didn't bring your visor," said Flutterdust.

I shook my head.

"You can borrow mine if you'd like."

I smiled at her.

"I'll be quite alright," I said, "I'll use this monitor instead."

I pulled the monitor from the arm rest and laid it on my lap. On the large bank of windows in front of us and duplicated on my monitor was a countdown. It had started at sixty seconds. The Eyeline Pulpit turned very quiet. For these Gaeans and these Evolvers, I imagined this was for them, church.

Flutterdust took out her monitor and laid it on top of her lap. Her visor was over her eyes. It projected a target over her e-pod as she watched it live through the big bank of windows. It also offered other information as requested. I didn't need any of that. Their technologies were mere toys compared to what I was used to.

Down at the very bottom of this room stood several armed men and women. What the Gaeans euphemistically call Peacekeepers. They were dotted all up and down the side. Above us and all around were the balcony seats where the more esteemed Gaeans sat. Primarily government officials who they like to call The Mothers. There were other members representing the other Councils. I wasn't concerned about any of it. My concern was in front of me in ten seconds. Nine. Eight...

You couldn't hear anything once the timer turned to zero. Then it disappeared and very shortly after that what looked like small black seeds started streaming towards the wormhole. You could see them because they were lit up with lights. Softly. They came seemingly from underneath us. There were dozens, then hundreds and then several hundred, and then I saw Sunring's e-pod.

Seconds after that as if catapulted from the bottom of the Station was her Starship. I willed them on. There was consternation above me and to the sides. I heard an audible gasp from the Evolvers seated around me. Flutterdust looked over at me. She had the information already displayed on her visor. I saw it mirrored on my monitor on my lap.

"Isn't that your Starship?" she asked.

I nodded. But I didn't look at her. Roger was doing his best to stay hidden amongst the e-pods but he wasn't doing as good a job as I had hoped. I was worried about him. I knew that this Station had exceptionally accurate weapons, and I was just waiting to see them used. And as if I'd sent the command myself the cannons pulsed and shot their ELGs. They streamed like fast little dots of light colored deep purple because they were skewed towards the gamma end of the spectrum.

They missed, but it wasn't by much. I was hopeless and I didn't like that either. I willed Roger on. He was just behind Sunring's e-pod by several meters. He was traveling slightly faster than the e-pods and they were clumped up thicker just ahead of him. If he made it under that swath of them he'd be okay. But these were computer guided weapons, but then again so was the Starship. Roger was a computer guided robot. I guess it came down to a chess match between the Station's computer and Roger. I'd given him a leg up, and I hoped that would be enough to carry him through the wormhole. They were halfway across the distance towards it.

"They're going to have a lot of questions for you, Sunring Quickdust."

I looked over at her.

"But I have no idea why Roger Dodger has taken my Starship. It's madness. I don't know what to say."

"There must have been some sort of glitch in his programming. But how would he be able to disengage the clamps from the docking port. Everything's locked down during this part of the process."

I shrugged.

"He's probably more clever than we gave him credit."

"I hope they get him," she said.

I frowned at that. We were betting on opposite teams.

More ELGs pulsed by. They were being reckless now. They missed the Starship by a hair but as it did so, Roger had to maneuver drastically and he clipped an e-pod. It wobbled slightly off course as its thrusters tried to align it back on track. But it had moved outside its stream enough that the next ELG pulse blew it to smithereens causing several other e-pods to wobble off course and a couple to collide into each other. At that speed it was annihilation. Three e-pods were destroyed. I was certain they would put a stop to it now. I was right. They attempted no other intervention with the Starship.

I watched as Sunring's e-pod entered the wormhole moments before her Starship. My work here was done and I didn't feel like sticking around to be interrogated by anyone. I reached over to Flutterdust and hugged her. She engaged the embrace and that was all I needed to rewrite her memory of how I'd been here. I cloaked myself and left the Eyeline Pulpit. As far as she was concerned I had been there the whole time. No, she hadn't noticed me leave.

What I wasn't expecting as I left, moving past the Council of Mothers as they headed towards the control and communications area was to overhear them promising to rehabilitate Sunring Quickdust and her whole family back on Gaea. That wasn't something I could allow in good conscience.

I hadn't passed out from the incredible thrust as I was jettisoned through the Ejection Port, but it was a ride like I had never taken. And then it was peaceful and serene for about three minutes. I thought I knew when I entered the wormhole because I felt a buffeting as if I was caught in a windstorm. That only lasted several seconds before everything was calm again. I wasn't far from old Earth's moon. I wondered what it looked like from here.

If Veritan Zeltan had told me the truth, and I believed that he had. I had another ten minutes of peace before reaching old Earth so long as my speed in this E-POD had stayed consistent. I was about to find out. I couldn't gauge my speed, but I had a monitor on my sleeve that I could try to connect to the E-PODS computer. I tried doing that. It worked. I was obviously still in command of my E-POD. A part of me expected to have been shut out. But perhaps they couldn't or hadn't expected something like this. I was hoping to never find out.

My speed was the same. One hundred thousand kilometers per minute. I pulled up some of the video feed. There were cameras all around the E-POD so I could get a three sixty degree view. I couldn't see the moon. I could see thousands of other E-PODS though, and just behind me was Starship Intrepid MF dot 3. Roger had made it. That brought a big smile to my face. I should be able to communicate with him directly from within the E-POD.

"Can you hear me, Roger?" I asked.

"Loud and clear, Sunring, I'm right behind you. Everything okay in there?"

"I can see you, Roger. Thanks for coming along. I'm surprisingly comfortable in here. Can you see old Earth?"

I couldn't. There were too many E-PODS in the way.

"Not yet, but I can tell we're headed in the right direction. I'm going to follow you in. Do you know where the E-POD is taking you?"

"Just a minute, let me find out."

I asked the computer where the E-POD was scheduled to land.

"Wichita, Kansas, America."

"Did you get that?" I asked Roger.

"Sure did. I wonder why Wichita."

I asked the computer the same question. It didn't know. But Wichita I learned was the new capital of the United States of Earth and the country now simply called America. I told Roger that.

"I don't think that's coincidence. I've a feeling that Veritan might have had something to do with that."

"You could be right," I replied.

"They caused an accident as I was leaving," said Roger. "We lost three E-PODS."

"I was going to ask you about it."

"I don't know which three," he said.

"And I don't want to find out."

We kept our own counsel for the remainder of the journey. I was watching the screen as old Earth slowly came into view. A beautiful blue jewel hanging in a black sky.

"I see Earth," said Roger.

"Me too."

"It's more beautiful than GAEA," he said. "I hope I can say that."

"You can say anything you want, Roger, we're not in GAEA anymore."

We came in hard and fast. As we hit the atmosphere I felt even more buffeting than I had in the wormhole. It slowed us down a lot. I couldn't see anything through the fire so I waited patiently. I turned off my connection to the computer. The next images of old Earth I wanted to see with my own eyes.

The buffeting stopped and I felt suspended until there was some very gentle swaying and then I felt the E-POD land on ground. I waited for the E-POD to open its main hatch. I didn't have to wait long. It took me a few moments to adjust to the bright light. I got myself up and jumped out of the E-POD. The MMC hadn't opened yet. I took off my helmet and placed it on the ground next to me. There were dozens and dozens of E-PODS all around me. To my left I could see the Arkansas river. Clear and blue and still as the sky.

The sky was a deeper blue than I had remembered GAEAS sky ever getting. I looked around. Ahead of me from where there were low lying buildings in the distance came a throng of people on different types of two and four wheeled vehicles. They were quiet vehicles. Similar to the ones we had in GAEA. Electric, I presumed. The buildings in the distance were modern and similar in style to GAEAN buildings and dwellings. I didn't know much about Wichita, but I couldn't see any remnant of what I would have considered old Earth architecture. In fact it looked like Earth had just recently been inhabited.

From where the sun was in the sky I pegged it at late afternoon. I knew it was May, probably the same day as I'd left which would have made it the fifteenth. That was the neat thing about GAEA, we'd kept the months the same as they had been on old Earth, and having almost identical rotations around the sun, they were practically twins.

The sun and air was warm on my face. The air smelt clean and dry, of grass and dust and foliage. I turned around behind me, the E-PODS were slowly starting to open. Roger exited the Starship and came towards me.

"This is a beautiful place," he said.

"Roger, I've a feeling we're not in GAEA anymore," I said, grinning at him.

"No, Dorothy," he said, "this is Kansas."

I laughed. I heard the MMC open. I rushed up to it, the Mothers Milk was draining from it. My Greater Father coughed and opened his eyes and took a deep breath. The E-POD started to communicate with him.

"THE MOTHERS thank you for your service on GAEA. As a last request, we ask you to continue the fight against the von Neumanns on old Earth. You have been sent back to old Earth to continue the fight against our bastard children so that the rest of us might continue to live safely on GAEA…"

Moondew Flamesdance sat up and looked at me. He blinked his eyes and then rubbed them with this hands. He was drenched in Mothers Milk.

"Is that you, Skew?" he asked.

"It's me, Greater Father," I said.

I helped him up and out of the E-POD. His clothes were already drying as I reached over and hugged him.

"I don't understand," he said.

"I'll explain everything," said another voice.

I turned around and saw that the group of old men and women who had been coming towards us had started to arrive. The man who spoke was a slim and old man. But his face was kind and his eyes warm.

"Father?" said Moondew Flamesdance.

I looked at my Greater Father and then at the man who he had addressed.

"Yes, my son," he looked over at me. "And you must be my great grand daughter Sunring Quickdust? You might remember me as Startlequick Silverdew."

"My Greatest Father?" I asked.

He nodded. And I stared at him and in the back of my mind, the six year old girl remembered her Greatest Father. And for the first time, on foreign soil I felt that finally I had come home.

ABOUT JASON BLACKER

Jason Blacker was born in Cape Town but spent most of his first 18 years in Johannesburg. When not grinding his fingers down to stubs at the keyboard he enjoys drinking tea, calisthenics and running. Currently he lives in Canada.

Under his own name he writes hard boiled as well as cozy mysteries, action adventure, thrillers, literary fiction and anything else that tickles his muse. Jason Blacker also writes poetry and daily haikus at his haiku blog.

You can find his haikus and other poetry at his website http://www.haiqueue.com.

To stay up to date and learn about new releases be sure to visit http://www.jasonblacker.com where you can find more information about his writing and upcoming projects.

If you enjoy space opera in the tradition of Star Trek then take a look at Jason Blacker's pen name "Sylynt Storme". It is under the name Sylynt Storme where you can find both sci-fi and vampire fiction written by Jason Blacker.

"Star Sails" is the space opera series and "The Misgivings of the Vampire Lucius Lafayette" is his vampire series.